RAGTOWN

USA TODAY BESTSELLING AUTHOR
KELLY STONE GAMBLE

Ragtown
Red Adept Publishing, LLC
104 Bugenfield Court
Garner, NC 27529
https://RedAdeptPublishing.com/

Copyright © 2023 by Kelly Stone Gamble. All rights reserved.

Cover Art by Streetlight Graphics[1]

No part of this book may be reproduced, scanned, or distributed in any printed or electronic form without permission. Please do not participate in or encourage piracy of copyrighted materials in violation of the author's rights. Thank you for respecting the hard work of this author.

This is a work of fiction. Names, characters, places, and incidents either are the product of the author's imagination or are used fictitiously, and any resemblance to locales, events, business establishments, or actual persons—living or dead—is entirely coincidental.

---

1. http://StreetlightGraphics.com

For Thea

PROLOGUE

Queho, the Renegade Indian, Part I

THE BRUTAL MURDER OF J.M. Woodworth in October 1910 was the beginning of a manhunt unlike any in the history of the new state of Nevada. Woodworth was a woodcutter in Searchlight, Nevada, working in the McCullough Mountain Range. The murderer, known to be a half-breed Indian named Queho, had been hired by Woodworth to clear trees on Timber Mountain. When a dispute arose between the two, Queho took a piece of timber, bashed Woodworth's skull, and left his broken body for the other woodcutters to find. This sparked a manhunt that went on for almost thirty years. But Woodworth's death was not the first time Queho had killed and certainly not the last.

Queho was born on Cottonwood Island, a sliver of land on the Colorado River, in the 1880s to a native woman from the Cocopa tribe. He was born with a clubfoot and was larger than most of the babies the women had seen before. His father's lineage was either unknown or not talked about, but he wasn't Cocopa. Rumor had it that his father was from another tribe or possibly a Mexican miner or white soldier who had forced himself on his mother. Shortly after his birth, his mother flung herself off a cliff into the raging Colorado River, leaving Queho and two older boys to be raised by his mother's relatives on the Las Vegas Paiute Reservation. The half-breed, clubfooted outcast would grow to be much taller than the others on the reservation. Some called him a giant, which furthered their ridicule and rejection. As he grew, he became sullen and at times violent.

His first kill was his half brother Avote. For reasons unknown, Avote had slaughtered a group of white settlers, and when this was discovered, his brother Queho, based on tribal tradition, was sent to execute him—better for the tribe to handle the affair than leave it to white men, who would take their revenge on the entire tribe. Queho lay in wait for his brother on Cottonwood Island then shot him in the back. In the eyes of the tribe and the white community who had sought justice, Queho was a hero. He was seventeen at the time.

He continued to live on the reservation, working at several of the local mining camps as a laborer. He was known for his quick temper and his moodiness, and one night while drinking with a Pauite named Bismark, he became enraged at the accusation that he had killed a medicine man. He murdered Bismark and two other Pauite who tried to stop him from stealing a horse to flee the reservation. From there, he headed to Las Vegas, where he attacked a shopkeeper, breaking both his arms and fracturing his skull with the handle of a pickaxe, and took the supplies he needed. By then a wanted man, by the Pauite for murder and by white men for attacking the shopkeeper, he headed to Eldorado Canyon, a place of endless mountains and crevices to hide in. That was where he met J.M. Woodworth.

When the deputy sheriff arrived at the scene of Woodworth's murder, the distinct footprints of a man with a clubfoot led them to the Goldbug Mine. There, the body of "Doc" Gilbert, a night watchman, was found with a shot in the head. Among Gilbert's missing possessions was his special deputy badge, number 896. Again, footprints were the key to attributing the crime to

Queho, and the posse that had formed then followed those footprints to the Colorado River.

Although many thought it would be simple to catch an "ignorant savage" with a clubfoot, Queho managed to elude the posse for several months. With no further murders reported and no clue to his whereabouts, the official hunt for Queho was called off in February 1911.

Over the years that followed, several thefts and murders occurring along the Colorado were attributed to the renegade Indian hiding in the canyon. Canyon Charlie, a well-known 100-year-old blind Indian who had little to steal, was found dead with a pickaxe wound to his head. Two Jenny Springs miners were found shot in the back. Two prospectors had also been shot in the back, while one had also had his head smashed in with what appeared to be an axe handle that was found upriver. The body of an Indian woman who had been gathering firewood, also shot, had been found near the river by her family. Maud Davis, the wife of a miner at the Techatticup Mine, was also murdered by a shotgun wound to the chest. Among the items that Queho was accused of stealing were basic provisions like food and clothing, guns, cookware, trinkets, silver pieces, and from the miners and prospectors, gold nuggets.

Although not all that was attributed to him held any evidence that it was indeed Queho who had committed the crimes, his ability to elude authorities had made him a legend. And in 1919, when the body of Maud Davis was found, his original bounty of $1000 was tripled.

"A good Indian is a dead Indian," the papers announced. Posses were again formed, but individuals bent on collecting the $3000 reward also traversed the mountains, intent on finding the renegade.

But Queho wasn't to be found. It was as if he'd become part of the mountainous desert terrain from which he had come. A decade passed before Queho was seen again.

In 1930, with Las Vegas bustling with the men, women, and children who'd set off across the country to find work at the Boulder Dam project set to begin in Black Canyon, Queho was seen walking down Fremont Street. The sheriff was alerted, but by the time he arrived, Queho had again disappeared, assumedly back to the canyon. But interest in his story began again, and hunting the elusive outlaw became a favorite pastime of the men working on the dam. The $3000 bounty still stood for Queho, dead or alive.

AUTHOR NOTE: Ragtown *is set in the 1930s during the first phase of the building of the Hoover Dam: the diversion of the Colorado River. Many of the characters in this book are not wholly invented but come from actual dam workers and their families. Their circumstances and actual events were gleaned, in part, from interviews and recorded oral histories. I portrayed these people with as much accuracy as possible and developed fictional characters to honor the people who were there, men and women who put their backs and their lives into this monumental piece of history. But ultimately, this is a novel, a work of fiction. It is a recreation of a time and a place and the stopping of a mighty river.*

In order to remain true to the vernacular of the 1930s, some of the language, particularly in reference to minorities, may be sensitive to some. Forgive me. It was a different time.

Chapter 1: Bighorns and Babies

Black Canyon, Nevada
Summer 1931
Helen

CREOSOTE LINGERED IN the dusty desert air. I closed my eyes and took a slow breath, pulling it deep into my lungs and into my body. I knew it was the same I'd been breathing for the past year, but there was something different about the air in the mountains. In camp, sadness was so thick I could almost touch it, and I could definitely smell it. In the mountains, it was just me and the plants and animals that lived high above the canyon. Everything was fresh and natural. It smelled like freedom.

"Helen."

I opened my eyes when Pepper called my name. Usually, it was my friend Grace who joined me on my morning walks. But as the days grew hotter and Grace drew closer to her due date, she stayed in camp and waited for me to bring her a desert flower or an unusual rock. My dad wasn't keen on me hiking on my own, yet at sixteen, none of the other girls in camp were much interested in my outdoor adventures. They focused more on learning to sew and cook and anything else they could do to land a husband. I had no desire to be away from camp with any of the teenage boys, who wanted to explore other things. So when twelve-year-old Pepper Allen begged me to show him the bighorn sheep, I had obliged.

"Hush! You'll scare them away." I spoke softly as I crouched behind a large boulder, pulled Pepper with me, and watched the trail that led high out of the canyon.

"I'm just sayin'," Pepper whispered, "that sure sounded like a rattler to me."

"Of course it was a rattler," I said. "And listen... there goes another over there. Those rattlers are everywhere, but they aren't going to hurt you if you stay out of their way. I keep telling you that." I looked at Pepper sitting next to me on his haunches. Although he was twelve, he looked and often acted like he was eight. He didn't have many friends in camp, as the other kids his age often picked on him because of his size and naivety. Pepper being four years younger than me, I tried to take up for him as much as possible, and Grace and I tried to include him in our adventures sometimes. I knew what it felt like to be alone, and Ragtown was a sad enough place without adding loneliness to the mix.

"How do you know? How do you know so much about rattlesnakes?"

I rolled my eyes. Pepper also liked to talk. A lot. "Can you be quiet, please? You would know about rattlesnakes, too, if you would read some of those books that Miss Smi—shh." I turned back to the trail. "Here they come."

"Look how big their horns are!"

I focused on the mountain sheep coming down into the canyon, as they did each morning in search of food.

There were thirty-two in the herd. They varied in size from the big rams with their curled horns, ready to lock with any other male who wanted to contend for his female, to the smaller juveniles that reminded me of the calves on my grandfather's farm. As always, they were led by the oldest ewe, who watched and protected her herd. They were majestic creatures, born of the mountain, of which we were simply guests.

"Helen!"

"Hush. Look, I told you their eyes were yellow—and not devil yellow like the other kids said. Yellow like sunflowers. Like they have been up on that mountain so long that the sun jumped right in their eyes."

I turned to Pepper and caught my breath. In his hand was a baby rattler, no longer than a crowbar, held at the base of its head, struggling to free itself from his grasp.

"Boy, are you daft? That thing is poisonous! The babies are the worst." I got a little closer, examining the snake in detail. "It's a Mohave, too, the most poisonous kind."

"What do I do with it?"

I stood and placed my hands on my hips. "Well, I guess you're gonna have to throw it and hope it don't bite you when you do."

His eyes grew as wide as the patch on his knee. He stood motionless, looking at me, frozen.

I sighed, dropped my arms to my sides, and walked slowly toward him. "Oh, all right, don't move now. I'm gonna grab it from behind."

I snatched the snake from him with ease, careful to avoid its pointed fangs. I hesitated for a moment to examine its sleek, scaly body then tossed it a good fifteen feet in one smooth motion. "Now, don't pick anything else up, you hear?"

He sat back down next to me and watched the herd continue their descent down the mountain. "What if one of them rattlers gets to the sheep?" he asked.

"If you were a little-bitty snake, would you try to curl up next to those big hooves?"

He shook his head, but I could tell by his scrunched-up face that he wasn't satisfied with my words.

"The sheep and the snakes, all the critters in the mountain, have been here for a long time, living together. It's like they all know this is home, and instead of fighting, they try to get along."

Pepper seemed to think about that for a minute and nodded.

I grabbed his hand and pulled him up. "Come on. We've been up here all morning, and we can't be too greedy with the sun. Besides, we both have chores, and I need to check on Grace."

"My daddy said this is our home now. So probably the sheep and the snakes won't bother us neither?"

I looked down into Hemenway Wash at the array of tents and varied scrap shanties. "No, we're just visitors. Our home is up the road, where they're building that town." The town, Boulder City, was being built for all the dam workers and their families, which meant one day soon, my dad and I and Pepper and his family would have real homes to call our own. It was all those of us in camp ever talked about, at least those who had someone working at the dam. It was our little bit of hope in a place that at times seemed hopeless. Pepper squeezed my hand.

One of the boys from camp was coming up the trail as we were descending, waving to us. Pepper tucked himself into my side as we got closer. "Helen!" the boy yelled. "Pepper's momma said to tell you to come quick. That friend of yours is having a baby."

"What?" Grace wasn't due for two more months, and although I knew babies sometimes came early, we had hoped to be in town, in our homes, when she gave birth. I hurried down the mountain with Pepper in tow, running through camp to Grace's tent.

"Is she all right?" I asked.

Betsy, Pepper's mother, followed, her usual light and carefree air replaced with a sense of urgency. "Pepper, go see if Mr. Emery has some ice."

As Pepper ran off toward the ferryman's makeshift store, she turned to me. "She's burning up. It's not good, Helen," she said.

I pushed past her and entered the small tent where Grace lived with her brother, Ezra. They had come from New Hampshire, a long journey for a pregnant woman, but Grace's husband, Billy, had come for a job, and when she discovered she was pregnant, Ezra brought her to find him. They'd been there for three months, and so far, no Billy. But Ezra had gotten a job at the dam site and was taking care of Grace until they found Billy.

Grace lay on a sleeping pallet in a white sleeper that had faded to a dull brown. Her black hair was slick with sweat and plastered to the side of her face. Her eyes were red, and she rested her hands on her stomach.

I sat beside her. "Grace?"

She turned to me and gave me a weak smile. Then suddenly, her body clenched, and she screamed. I'd seen women have babies before, so I knew what labor pains were, and I grabbed one of her hands so she'd have mine to squeeze.

Betsy came back in and tried to talk her through the contraction, and when it was over, she looked between her legs. She placed a hand on Grace's stomach. Grace wasn't talking and closed her eyes as the pain subsided. "Let her sleep," Betsy said.

When Pepper returned with only a soap-bar-sized block of ice, Betsy sent him to wet sheets at the river and then to find Ranger Williams. The nearest hospital was an hour away, and even if we could have gotten her there, the chances of her being seen before the baby came were slim. Betsy had been a midwife in South Dakota, and we were lucky to have her in Ragtown. But when she looked at me, her face was full of hurt. She shook her head, and I knew something was terribly wrong. I looked down, below the belly bump that Grace had tried so hard to protect, and saw a trail of blood.

I swallowed hard and tried to keep tears from rolling down my cheeks. I took the ice bar that Pepper had brought and slid it across her forehead, down her arms, and over her neck and chest. Her body was so hot that the ice seemed to sizzle when I touched her with it. Grace woke up with the next contraction and the next, and each time Betsy told her to push, but each time, Grace's efforts were weaker, and each time, there was more blood. "It's going to be all right," I whispered to her without much conviction. After about an hour, Grace didn't wake up.

"Grace?" I tried shaking her, gently at first then with more force. The bottom of her nightshirt was covered in blood, and Betsy was doing her best to coax the baby out. I started to panic and screamed Grace's name.

"Helen," Betsy said in a calm voice, a motherly voice. "Why don't you wait outside?"

I shook my head. I would not leave my friend.

"She's gone, Helen. But I need to get this baby out," she said.

Gone? Her eyes were shut, her cracked lips slightly open. I put my hand on her chest, but there was no movement. The metallic smell of blood clung to the air. My stomach and my head swirled, and I thought I would pass out, but I took a deep breath and nodded to Betsy.

Pepper had been told not to come back into the tent, so it was just Betsy, my dead friend, and me.

"If you're going to stay, I need your help," Betsy said.

I swallowed hard and nodded again.

She placed her hand on the top of Grace's belly, above the lump that held her baby. "I need you to help the baby down. She can't push, so I need you to do it for her. You push. I'll pull," she said.

I did as I was told, trying not to think of anything except the baby. I lightly kissed Grace's forehead and moved down her body, getting into a position to help Betsy. She had one of her hands inside of Grace, and it reminded me of my grandfather trying to help one of his cows give birth on the farm.

I shut my eyes and pushed. Betsy pulled. And then I felt the release.

I looked down as the baby came with a rush of red blood and no sound, not even a whimper.

Betsy quickly wrapped the baby in one of the wet sheets and held it up to me. "Get him to the river. Maybe we can at least cool him down before we send him on his way."

"Him," I said. A boy. I felt ill and needed out of the tent, but I knew the least I could do for Grace was hold her baby until he succumbed to his own heat. I cradled the infant in my arms and headed to the river.

AUTHOR NOTE: IN 2006, I volunteered at the Hoover Dam Museum for their oral history project about the Hoover Dam. I transcribed over fifty of the interviews that were conducted with people who had worked on the dam project in the 1930s and had the honor of interviewing a few myself. Their stories and experiences hit me right in the heart, and I soon had to learn everything I could about the building of the dam and, most importantly, the people who made it happen. I started writing about the dam and the people in 2010 and, at the same time, began working on other projects. But over the years, Helen and the other "31-ers" (those who worked on the dam project in 1931 and beyond) kept calling me back. Helen wanted her story told, and she's a tough young lady to deny. Thank you for joining me on her journey. I hope you enjoy it as much as I enjoy telling it.

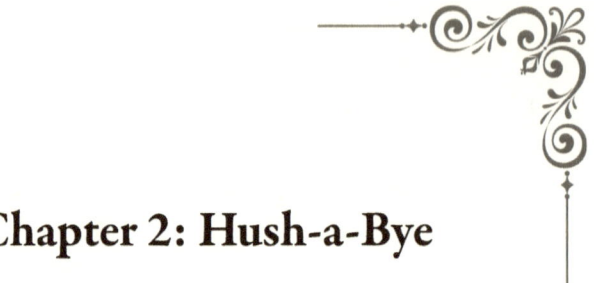

Chapter 2: Hush-a-Bye

Helen

WHEN I WAS YOUNG, MY grandmother used to sing me a lullaby at night, and I tried to remember the words as I held the baby in my arms and rocked him to sleep for the first and last time. His already closed eyes fluttered sporadically, most likely from the fever that wouldn't leave his small body. I'd been in the desert long enough to know what that heat could do to someone, especially an infant. But Grace was my friend, and I would hold her baby until she came for him.

There had been so much blood and so many of Grace's screams and cries before they turned to nothing but whimpers and prayers. And then silence. I tried to push it from my mind, the weight too much to bear. I shifted the baby in my arms, trying to keep his head above the tepid water of the Colorado, although I wondered if it would be merciful to submerge him. I didn't know. I would have liked to say that at sixteen, I didn't know much about death at all, but that wouldn't have been true. I was too young to remember my mother, but I remembered the pain and emptiness I felt when Grandma June and then Grandpa Jack passed. And in the year that Dad and I had been in Nevada, I'd seen a lot of death. I'd also seen a lot of things that were much worse.

"Did she name him?" My dad's voice startled me from the bank, and I quickly looked at the sun, high in the western sky, before turning to him. I hadn't realized it was so late in the day.

"No," I said, my voice barely above a whisper. If Dad was home, that meant Ezra, Grace's brother, was too. We tried to send word to the dam that she was in labor, but word rarely seemed to get there in time. This was no exception.

He sloshed into the Colorado's red water and sat next to me in the river's pool. He put one arm around me and touched the baby's forehead with the other, leaving a trail of water like a clay-colored tear.

"Where's Ezra?" I asked as I leaned against him and rested my head on his shoulder. His shirt was covered in soot from working in the tunnels at the dam all day, but I didn't care. I took a deep breath of his familiar and comforting scent, dirt mixed with sweat.

"Ranger was waiting for us when we got off the ferry. He took Ezra straight to Grace. I told him I'd get you and the little one." He patted the baby's forehead again. His eyelids had ceased to flutter.

"She just kept bleeding and bleeding. And then the baby—"

"I'm sure you did everything you could," he said. He pulled me even closer and kissed me on the forehead.

I was one of the few people in Ragtown who wasn't bothered by the heat and could usually see the pure beauty of the desert and the mountains. But that day, even I couldn't find any beauty in the canyon. I wanted to scream or at least cry, but the tears wouldn't come. Instead, I started singing again, rocking the silent infant in my arms while my dad rocked me in his.

I put a finger in the baby's tiny palm and hoped he would wrap his fingers around it, but his hand was still. I studied his face, eyes shut, heart-shaped lips slightly open, and hoped that his dreams were pleasant. I figured if God took babies, He surely didn't make them suffer. I wished it were the same for their parents.

"Ben?" Ezra stood on the rocky beach, wearing only his jeans and work boots. He sat down and started to untie his boots but instead settled his head in his hands, gripping his hair. Dad helped me up, steadying me in the slow current. My thin dress was plastered to my body, stained by the red clay of the water and the blood of my friend. We walked to shore, and I gently lowered the baby into Ezra's arms. Ezra's red-rimmed eyes closed as he held the infant close to his chest, the baby's head nestled under his chin.

"We'll leave you alone," my dad said to Ezra as he gently placed his hand on my back and guided me away. We passed the ragged makeshift homes littering the canyon of Hemenway Wash: tents, tattered sheets, cardboard boxes. Thousands of men and their families scattered about, having made their way to the Nevada desert in hopes of getting one of the few jobs available on the massive dam project while also trying to survive the desert and its heat. A teenage boy in a dirty nightshirt, not much younger than me, passed us, holding his stomach, another victim of the dysentery that ran rampant through the camp. An older woman, most likely his mother, shuffled beside him. Her face was twisted in agony, as if she knew the fate of her son. I tried to avoid the faces etched with desolation, the hollow eyes devoid of hope.

Four women died that day. And one baby.

ONCE I HAD CLEANED up after dinner, I grabbed my latest book and headed to my reading spot outside our camp, feeling I should be doing something for Ezra but not knowing what I could possibly offer him at that time. He was my friend, too, and yet I couldn't comfort him for fear that my own emotions would burst through. I was hurt and angry and felt as if my body had been drained of something I couldn't define.

As I reached the pile of cardboard that the Allens called home, I stopped to check on Pepper. I hadn't seen him since he'd brought the ice for Grace, his mother having sent him on tasks to keep him busy then telling him to stay away.

Pepper was alone under a cardboard awning. He sat cross-legged, staring off toward the mountain, his small frame swaying back and forth, and I recognized the lullaby he sang softly, almost under his breath. I sat next to him, and he stopped singing and glanced at me once with moist red eyes before returning his gaze to the mountain.

Pepper's father, Clive, worked in the same tunnel as my dad and Ezra. He was a small, kind man who seemed to share Pepper's curiosity and talked just as much. "I'm sorry to hear about Grace," he said as he approached from the river. I was sure his wife had told him the entire story, and I hoped they'd left out a lot of the details around Pepper. I started to get up, but Pepper leaned closer to me, and I hated to leave him.

Mr. Allen held a hand down to him. "Come on, son. Let's go find your mother."

Pepper looked at me. I forced a smile, and he took his father's hand.

I sat under the lone Joshua tree fifteen feet from the river's edge. I'd discovered the tree when we first arrived the previous year, and it was different than anything I had ever seen in Kansas. The branches, splayed open like fat fingers, were thick with sword-like evergreen leaves at their tips. Most pointed at the heavens. A few, however, refused to follow suit and instead reached toward the water.

One of the pleasant surprises about living in Ragtown was the availability of books, and I loved to read. Some of the older women had set up a makeshift school for the kids, and every two weeks, one of them rode the bumpy dirt road to Las Vegas with Murl Emery to trade books. I helped some days with the younger kids, and in return, I had access to any of the treasures brought back from the trip. Most of the books were informational, but I didn't mind. I would read anything, even though I preferred novels that would transport me to places I'd probably never see. The ladies knew that and made sure I had at least one new one with every trip.

Sitting on the rocky ground, my back against the bumpy lower trunk of the tree, I stretched my legs out, crossed them at the ankle and opened my book. I tried to imagine the English walled garden described by Francis Hodgson Burnett, the beautiful roses that bloomed despite lack of attention, and the wetness of the dew-soaked grass. For the next few days, I wanted to be Mary Lennox, living in an English manor and discovering her uncle Craven's secrets, but it was hard to concentrate. My mind kept going to Ezra and Grace.

I'd met Ezra first, about three months ago when he crossed the Colorado and landed in Ragtown. He walked into Murl Emery's ramshackle general store and asked how to get a job at the dam. I was immediately taken with him. He didn't have the distant look in his eyes that so many of the men had, and he was tall and muscular, not lanky and malnourished as was the norm around there. He talked fast with an Eastern accent that forced me to hang on every word. When he noticed me standing by the ice counter that day, he smiled, and my breath caught. My heart had crashed when I saw him with Grace then swelled again when he introduced her as his sister.

I soon fell for her too. She shared my love of books, animals, and the desert, and like Ezra, she had a positive outlook about the future. She was pregnant, barely showing, and had accompanied Ezra to Nevada, where her husband, Billy, had come to find work. It had been three months since they got there, and still no Billy, but I never pushed it. Grace would talk of a grand future—not as a possibility but with surety—and she had no doubts about a wonderful life after the dam was built that would include Billy, a nice house on a hill, and children filling the rooms.

I closed my book, still unable to focus, and instead watched three women cleaning their dishes in the river from dinner. Those of us who had something to eat ate straight from the can. Rarely did we have anything that required cooking, and we had too much heat without starting a fire, but occasionally, we all tried to find some semblance of normality, and eating out of bowls was one way to do that. The women talked, usually parroting what their husbands had said about the work site, and they didn't laugh much. I tried to tune them out by closing my eyes and focusing on the sounds of the river flowing by.

Soon, I heard boots crushing against the rocks coming toward me and turned. It was Cotton Vaughn, one of the men who worked on tunnel number three with Daddy and Ezra. "I've been looking all over for Ben," he said. He stood over me, his frame blocking the sun and casting me in a shadow.

"He went with Ezra to get a coffin for Grace. And the baby." I swallowed hard. The words were difficult to say. The thought of my friend and her baby in a dark box made me feel numb.

He sat next to me, close enough for me to feel the heat off his leathery skin. He was ten years my senior but acted closer to my father's age than mine, and I was never quite sure whether I should call him Cotton or Mr. Vaughn. For the past few weeks, after dinner, some of the men had been getting together to discuss the work conditions at the dam. That night, Ezra and Dad would not be making the meeting.

"I'm sorry to hear about that. Nice girl," he said.

I didn't know what to say, so I didn't respond at all. We'd never been alone, having a conversation, and although his words were meant to be kind, I was a little uncomfortable by his closeness.

He picked up a rock and skimmed it on the water. Two skips. My record was eight.

"Don't beat yourself up about it. That fever is a killer without having a baby thrown in the mix. Not saying a doctor would have helped much."

I looked sideways at him in profile as he scratched the stubble on his sunken chin. I didn't want to talk about it, especially with Cotton Vaughn. I wasn't sure why he was trying to comfort me, since we didn't talk much. We sat in silence for a full minute before he reached out with one large, rough hand and patted my knee. "Well, tell Ben I was looking for him. And if you need anything, let me know."

He left, and I sat alone under the Joshua tree with *The Secret Garden* open next to me. The sun was starting to dip behind the mountain, but I didn't go back to camp yet. I pulled my knees up close to my chest, hugged them, then rubbed the spot where his hand had been, trying to relieve the coldness that his touch had sent through my body.

AUTHOR NOTE: ALTHOUGH there is no official documentation to back this up, there are oral history records that state the temperature was so high it topped out the 120-degree mark on the outdoor thermometers and rendered them useless on many occasions. Inside the diversion tunnels of the dam, temperatures were said to exceed 140 degrees. Needless to say, it was hot.

On July 26, 1931, four women in Ragtown died of "the fever," which was most likely dysentery-related, compliments of the Colorado River, where they drank, bathed, laundered, and well, you know the rest. But it was water and most likely what kept most of them alive. I chose this day, July 26, 1931, to begin Helen's story.

In this chapter, I mention a familiar lullaby. While I know all readers will have their own lullaby that comes to mind when they read this, the one that I was singing (or trying not to sing) while writing was All the Pretty Little Horses, *which is also sometimes called simply* Hush-A-Bye. *I remember my grandmother singing it to me when I was little, and to be honest, it was creepy to me then and still is. But that creepiness seemed to work for these scenes. If you haven't ever heard it, you can find it on the internet. The lyrics are beautiful, but the melody is eerie; or is that just me?*

Chapter 3: Nowhere Else to Go

Helen

OUR CAMP WAS A LITTLE more extensive than some of the others in Ragtown. My "room," as I liked to call it, was the backseat of our Model T sedan. I kept my clothes and a few items I'd collected on the front seat, which was my closet. Old newspaper, yellowed and cracking, had been taped to the windows on the driver's side and the front then covered with a piece of canvas my dad got from the work site.

Random pieces of scrap were attached to the passenger side of the car. We had covered the scrap first with blankets and sheets, adding plywood as it became available. The area was small but large enough for Daddy's sleeping platform, the food pit we had dug into the hard, rocky ground, and a small sitting area at the entrance.

Basically, everyone in Ragtown had little and came with less. Some thought to bring a tent, but most made shelter out of whatever they could find. Lured with the promise of jobs on the dam project, I guess they figured finding a place to live would be easy with a paycheck. But there were twenty-five men for every job, the housing and dormitories for the workers were just being built, and the pay for workers was barely enough to feed their families, much less find a place to live outside of Boulder City.

Although our place was still just another ramshackle structure, we made it our home, and I didn't mind. It served its purpose, which for me was sleeping and avoiding some of the others in the Wash. I waited inside for Dad to return until after the sun set, but the walls were starting to close in on me, and I would much rather have been outside.

The desert at night was a different animal than by day. The sky was so clear you could almost touch the stars, and when they reflected off the flowing river, it looked like a path of diamonds moving swiftly between the darkened mountains. Rabbits darted here and there at the base of the mountain, food for the coyotes that didn't wander into camp. Between the occasional baby's cry, the rustling of critters by the mountains' edge, and the occasional telltale rattle of the Western diamondback, the sounds were eerie yet peaceful in a way. Definitely different from the hubbub of voices and general clatter during the day.

I knew Dad and Ezra had walked to the highway to catch a ride to the dam, but if they couldn't get a ride back, they'd have to walk. They'd been gone for hours, so I assumed that was exactly what they were doing. I crept along the rocky ground toward the path at the head of the Wash and stopped briefly in front of Ezra and Grace's small camp. I knew she was inside, holding her baby, waiting for their coffin. The scent of early decay brought on by the heat invaded my nose, and I left quickly before I began to taste it.

I found a large boulder at the path's entrance to the Wash and climbed on top to wait, away from the black widows, scorpions, and centipedes that tended to hide in the rocks. I turned away from camp, toward the darkness of the mountains, and took in a deep breath of dusty air. It was a lot better than being stuck in a tent.

I wished I had said more to Ezra, but I had no words to offer. I wondered if he would go back to New Hampshire now that Grace was gone… I didn't want to lose both of my friends.

I was lost in the stars, trying to identify two new ones, when I heard a strange scraping sound on the path. I couldn't see anything in the near darkness, so I listened as it grew louder. As the sound rounded the last bend and escaped the mountain path, I saw Dad and Ezra, dragging a large wooden box. Six Companies was stenciled in large white letters on the side, unmistakable even in the dark. I climbed off my perch and had my arms around my dad's neck before he had a chance to put down his load.

"Whoa, there, girlie. You about knocked me down." He had one arm around me and pulled me close while releasing his grip on his end of the box. "What are you doing out here so late?"

"I was worried about you," I said, avoiding looking at the box at his feet. Instead, I focused on Ezra, who had put his side down, too, and sat on it. He lowered his head, ran his hands through his hair, and let out a long breath. My entire body hurt for him, and I wanted desperately to hug him too.

"You don't need to be worrying about me. Ezra and I still have a little more to do, so why don't you try to get some sleep?" He coughed and gave me a weak smile, and I could tell he was tired. Regardless of what had happened today, he would still need to report for his shift in the morning. The work site was only closed on Christmas and the Fourth of July. Other than that, the men who worked the tunnels were there seven days a week, no matter what. There were no excuses for missing work at the dam, not even the death of your sister and her child. There were thousands of men just waiting for someone to miss a day so they could take their place.

"I want to help," I said with little conviction. I didn't really want to help. The idea of seeing Grace's body lifted into the box was not an image I wanted to keep in my mind. Not to mention the baby, the one that I had held and sung to until he succumbed to death. But I didn't want to be alone either.

"You could do something for me." Ezra's voice was low and gravelly. He stood and moved toward me. I swear he had lines on his face that weren't there the day before.

"Anything," I said.

"The mortuary in Vegas is picking her up in the morning. Her and the baby." He stopped and looked up then blew out a breath and shook his head before continuing. "I need someone to be there to pay them and get the receipt for me."

"Of course. I know you..." *Can't miss a day of work. Regardless of the reason.* "You're sending them back east, then," I said, more a statement than a question.

"No, they'll be buried in Vegas. No family to send them home to." He rubbed his eyes, and I could tell he was exhausted. He stretched and gave me a half smile devoid of joy. He bent over and grabbed the box and my dad followed suit. They both picked up their ends of the makeshift coffin and started moving toward camp.

"So you're staying?" I asked.

He shrugged. "I don't have anywhere else to go."

AUTHOR NOTE: WILLIAMSVILLE was the official name of the squatters' camp in Hemenway Wash, but it was called Ragtown by the inhabitants. It was but one of the many shantytowns, or "Hoovervilles," that arose in the area, along with Little Oklahoma, Texas Acres, McKeeversville, and Dee's Camp, all of which you'll find mentioned along the way.

Over a four-year span of building the dam, 21,000 men and a handful of women were employed as workers, contractors, and support staff. They came from every state, traveling across the country with their families, trying to survive the economic hardships of the Great Depression. Most truly had nowhere else to go. I tried to represent that diversity of origin when developing my characters; everyone hails from a different state.

Chapter 4: Watch Out for Black Widows

Helen

MY DAD SNORED SO LOUDLY that I sometimes wondered if people could hear him on the Arizona side of the river. I was so used to it that I usually slept right through it, but that night, I'd done nothing but toss and turn, and his added nasal sounds didn't help much.

After helping Ezra with Grace, he fell straight to sleep, barely remembering to take off his boots. He'd only get a few hours before he must report to the work site, so I didn't want to wake him. I crawled from my spot in our camp and quietly escaped through the canvas flap of our entrance.

Mr. Emery was opening his store at the dock, so I knew Dad had another hour before he had to get up. The camp was quiet, probably the quietest part of the day, and I crept down to the river to sit under my tree. The crunching of rocks under my footsteps echoed in my ears.

"Watch out for black widows." Ezra's voice startled me. I didn't see him sitting in the shadow of my Joshua tree. He was still wearing the clothes he'd worn yesterday, and a faint scent of death emanated from him.

"You should be sleeping," I said. I should have been, too, I knew, but I didn't have to work at the dam later. I heard the stories and saw the men as they returned from work each day, their shoulders down, covered in dust. I imagined working with no sleep was hard and even more dangerous than it already was.

"My room is kind of occupied right now," he said.

I sat next to him and didn't say anything. I figured at some point, he would ask what happened, and I didn't really know. Betsy said there wasn't anything we could do. God had made his choice, and all we could do was pray. And I had prayed. I squeezed my eyes tight, trying to get the vision of my dying friend out of my mind.

Ezra let out a deep breath. "You know she wasn't really married."

"Oh." I knew something was odd about her absent husband, but she never offered, and I never asked.

"She dated Billy Green for a few months last year. Then he said he was coming here to work on the dam, and it was done. When she turned up pregnant, our dad told her he wasn't raising another man's baby and told her to leave. I was already planning to head this way, so I brought her with me. She was convinced that Billy would make things right, if she ever found him." He picked up a handful of rocks and threw them, one by one, into the river.

"But she never found him," I said. I was a little hurt that she didn't trust me enough to tell me the truth, but I guessed if I had been in her situation, I would probably lie about it too. Ezra had gone along with the story, and I wasn't sure why he was telling me the truth that night.

He threw another stone at the water, this time with more force. "Oh, I found him, all right. He had no interest in taking responsibility. In fact, he said it probably wasn't his, as if Grace was sleeping around. It was all I could do not to beat him into the ground right there. But I never told Grace. I couldn't. She was so happy, even in this place, and I thought maybe Billy would change his mind. So I didn't tell her."

"Oh," I said again. I was always a little jealous of Grace having a good man that she was eager to start a life with, but as my dad always said, what you see on the outside is only what people want you to see. But Grace's dream, her fantasy, was so real, at least to her, and my head started to hurt from what he was telling me. "Does he work at the dam site?"

"He did. I went back to find him a week later, after I'd cooled down some, but he was gone. Showed up drunk and lost his job."

"You said you didn't have any family left in New Hampshire. But your dad—"

"Is an ass who doesn't deserve to know that his only daughter is gone," he said.

I knew Grace and Ezra's mother had passed a few years back, and she had mentioned her father but never gone into any details of their relationship.

He took a deep breath and stretched his legs out on the rocks. "So when I told you earlier that I have nowhere else to go, I meant it. This is it for me."

"Why are you telling me this?" My eyes started to water, and although I appreciated the truth, a part of me wished he'd kept the façade.

He put a hand on my knee, the same place where Cotton had done so earlier. But his hand was warm, and I hated myself for not wanting him to take it away. "Because I just needed to get it off my chest. And now that Grace's gone, you're the only friend I've got."

AUTHOR NOTE: MURL EMERY ran the ferry at Ragtown and also had a small "store" of sorts for the residents. He was known as a kind man by many, extending credit at his store to the unemployed

and selling goods virtually at cost, and I tried to portray him in that light.

 Fun fact! Black widow spiders don't "drink" water. They get their water requirements from what they suck out of their prey. They do like to hang out in damp places, because that's where all the good food is. They aren't typically aggressive toward humans but will bite if you get too close. According to National Geographic, their venom is up to fifteen times more potent than a rattlesnake, so watch out for the black widows.

Chapter 5: Nothing Comes without a Price

Ezra

I HADN'T SLEPT IN OVER twenty-four hours, and my mind and body were numb. I guess burying your sister and newborn nephew had a way of taking the fight out of you. I still couldn't quite wrap my head around what happened yesterday. When I had left for work, Grace had a little bit of a fever, but it was hard to tell in the desert whether it was a fever from sickness or just from the scorching heat. Either way, she was dead when I got home, and my nephew, the one I couldn't name, died in my arms. I knew he was dead before Helen handed him to me, but for some reason, I felt better remembering him taking at least one breath while I held him, so that was the memory I intended to keep.

I probably shouldn't have told Helen Grace's story, but I needed to get it off my chest, and I wasn't lying when I said she was the only friend I had. Sure, I had some of the guys at work, but I couldn't really spill all my secrets to them. I didn't know why I felt I could with Helen. She was a woman—or almost one—and one of the smartest girls I knew. Maybe I just thought she'd understand. Grace so wanted to believe her fairy tale. She'd been through so much with our father, and she was actually starting to shine in the middle of the desert. I didn't want to see that smile fade. I loved her, and I tried to protect her, and the fact that I couldn't weighed heavy. I just wanted to work—something I had some control over.

Ben and I walked slowly across the swinging footbridge that led to the Arizona side of the work site. Even holding on to the hemp ropes that supported the planks, the unpredictable sway made the crossing difficult. I looked down at the Colorado flowing below, and the fierce white whorls of foam reminded me of a rabid dog.

Several members of the night crew waited for the day shift to cross. With a good thirty feet left, Clive Allen yelled to them, "What's the call?"

Tired and covered in soot and dirt, one of the workers yelled back, "Sixteen and a half feet."

"Whadya do, forget to use the dynamite?"

The night crew took their banter in stride. "Yeah, well, the Jumbo broke down, but we got it working for ya. Have fun."

One of the guys looked at me and nudged the man next to him, and they all went somber. As my feet hit solid ground, I was met with a round of condolences. I just wanted to get my hands on my drill and not think about the empty tent that waited for me in Ragtown.

An experienced driver and one of the older men on the crew at thirty-five, Ben drove the Jumbo, an old gas-powered International flatbed that had been rigged with two wooden platforms and a moving scaffold over thirty feet high that held a few dozen drillers at once. After crossing the bridge, he slapped me on the back and went straight for his driver's seat.

I hated that he had been up most of the night, helping me, but he was a good man, and honestly, I had needed someone to push me through the night. Ben had lost his wife fifteen years before, and I was glad for his words. "We do all we can for those we love," he had said, "but sometimes, we have to accept that God has other plans." It wasn't that his advice was any more than others would say, but his tone was how I would imagine a man would talk to an adult son: frank, yet compassionate and reassuring. Not at all what I imagined my own father would have said.

In the equipment shed, several men lingered, speaking in hushed tones about the need for a workers' union. I was glad they weren't talking about me.

Cotton Vaughn came alongside me and lifted his chin toward the group. "What you think about this talk?"

Gavin Sweet stood in the middle of the group of men, talking as usual. He didn't work at the site, just hung around and tried to look busy when the supervisors came around. He talked about the benefits of the union, particularly his own, the Industrial Workers of the World.

I shrugged and continued with my safety check. "It sounds good, but nothing comes without a price. I'm just happy to be working."

Cotton lowered his eyes and said, "Sorry about your sister."

I reached for a water bag, took a long swig, then wiped my mouth with the back of my hand. "I just need to be working."

Cotton must have noticed my unease and changed the subject. "New guy on the rig today. Took Riley's spot."

Riley had come down with pneumonia a few days before. I'd heard on the ferry that he died during the night and was replaced on the rig before his body had a chance to cool. "Transfer or somebody I gotta train?" A trainee slowed us all down, but a transfer always thought he knew everything. I wasn't sure which was worse.

"He's been working the bottom in tunnel four. I guess he's moved up," Cotton said. Tunnel four lay right above us, so I'd probably seen the guy, not that I would recognize him. Those on the bottom caught all the muck from a blast and by noon looked like nothing but gray ghosts walking.

I grabbed my hard-boiled hat off the rack and took one more swig of water before turning toward the tunnel. "Well, let's go see why they didn't want to keep him in tunnel four."

AUTHOR NOTE: THE JUMBO was one of the most interesting creations at the Hoover Dam. During this phase, the men were creating four tunnels, each approximately three-fourths of a mile long, fifty-six feet in diameter, through the hard rock of the canyon. In order to do that, they had to drill holes at specific intervals, pack them with dynamite, blow it, clear it, and do it again. It took about a ton of dynamite for every fourteen feet of tunnel. A lot of dynamite! It was difficult work and slow, since some of the upper holes had to be drilled using makeshift scaffolding, followed by the lower holes, etc. Then one man, Bernard "Woody" Williams, came up with the idea of taking one of the flatbed trucks and equipping it with a scaffolding system that would hold up to thirty drillers at one time. And the Jumbo was born. If you google "The Jumbo Rig at Hoover Dam," you'll find the complete story with pictures, and it's well worth the look!

Chapter 6: The New Guy

Ezra

RILEY HAD BEEN A GOOD partner to work with. He kept to himself and focused on his job. I had fallen into a routine that involved little chatter, interrupted only by the yells and hoots of the others who could be heard over the sound of the drills and dynamite.

However, the new guy, Pete McGee, never shut up. He drilled and talked, blew the hole with water and talked, and talked while the powdermen packed dynamite. I glanced at him after the last charge blew and could swear that his lips were moving as the deafening sound of the dynamite exploded.

Pete was also a lot faster at the job than Riley had been. While I had always been able to finish drilling my twelve feet into the solid rock wall before Riley, I'd had to almost double my pace to keep up with Pete.

At the sound of the noon whistle, Pete laid down his equipment and jumped off the Jumbo with as much gusto as he had when we started the day. First from the truck to the line for the prepacked lunches provided by Anderson's Mess Hall, he ate most of his straight from the little square box while he walked to the shaded patch used for breaks.

I waited for Ben. When we got to the barren spot we called the picnic area, Pete was in a lively exchange with several other workers.

"Don't you ever quit talkin'?" Clive Allen asked. Clive sat with his short legs tucked under him as though praying. His left ear looked like a lump of oatmeal, having been mutilated in a farming accident when he was a kid. He had it cocked toward Pete so he wouldn't miss a word.

"No, I do not, little man," Pete said. "Why, the other night, one of the dolls at the Railroad Pass told me I even talk in my sleep. Have any of you been out there yet? That's a fine place they opened, and the ladies... Well, you have to see them."

Pete lived at Little Oklahoma, one of the tent communities along the highway between Las Vegas and the work site. It was a long road to Vegas from the canyon, so someone built a casino right in the middle of the tent cities. They said it was so all the dam workers would have some entertainment, but I thought it was just a way to take what little money we got on the job.

"You oughta stay out of that place," Clive said. "They'll take this money you're out here working so hard for."

"Aw, what's the use in keeping it? Besides, those gals have to make a living too. And it keeps me out of Vegas. Remind me to tell you sometime about my last trip up there." He shuddered.

"I have a feeling we won't have to," Cotton Vaughn said under his breath.

I don't know why, but that made me smile, and I hadn't done that in at least a day. Cotton was usually the one talking, but he was no match for Pete.

"Boston, right?" Pete asked, drawing out the *O* in an attempt to mimic my accent.

"Ezra Deal, New Hampshire," I said between bites of my sandwich.

"Well, that's a mouthful. Hey, sorry to hear about—"

I held up my hand to cut him off. I was tired of the condolences. I just wanted to eat my lunch and get back to work.

Ben introduced himself, and Pete tipped his hard-boiled hat. "Double ugly, right? You always been a truck driver?"

"Used to haul ore out of the mines in Treese, Kansas. Had a nice little place out there, then the bank went under and called my note. Didn't have nothin' then except a car and a daughter to feed."

"You from Oklahoma, Pete?" Clive asked.

Pete stretched his long legs in front of him and lay back on his elbows. "No, I just live out there with the Okies. I made it out here from Iowa. Worked in one of those banks that's been closing all over."

"You worked in a bank?" Cotton asked, the surprise in his voice not lost on me. "What did you do in a bank?"

Pete smiled. "I dressed up in a fancy suit every day and played like I had something that those Iowa farmers didn't have. When the bank closed, they weren't too happy to see my smiling face joining their soup line, so I hitched out here."

"Hey, men. Looks like you've had a hard morning." Gavin Sweet walked right into our circle and started talking. Ben got up without a word and headed back to his driver's seat.

"Aren't you one of them IWW guys?" Pete asked.

"Yes, I am, and you should be too. They got you men living like animals out here, not paying you hardly anything, working you to the bone. It isn't right."

"Right now, they're building the town up the highway there for us," Clive said. "They got it all laid out, gonna start on the houses any day now. Shoot, the dormitories are already taking in men. A room and a real shower. Nothing wrong with waiting for something good."

"Working to the bone is at least working," I said. Gavin's clothes were barely smudged by the dust.

"You're right, Easy," Pete said. He stood and brushed his pants legs. "Working is working, and I'm getting back to it."

I got up too. I had enough on my mind without getting mixed up with someone like Sweet. As Pete and I walked away, he stopped and turned back to Gavin. "What does IWW stand for, anyway?"

"Industrial Workers of the World. We are a brotherhood. We work together and take care of each other."

Pete rubbed his chin and looked off into the distance. "Industrial Workers of the World. Huh. I thought it stood for I Won't Work."

I laughed outright, and it sounded a little foreign to me.

Pete slapped me on the back as we turned to walk back to the rig. "How the hell you think they let a Yankee and a banker on the top row of the Jumbo?"

I decided right then I was going to like Pete, even if he did call me Easy. He may have been a blowhard, but he was a welcome relief from the dryness of the desert.

AUTHOR NOTE: NOTWITHSTANDING the harsh climate, work conditions at the dam were less than desirable. The International Workers of the World (IWW) was considered a radical labor organization that eventually gained enough support for the dam workers to strike. Members of the organization were known as "Wobblies."

Chapter 7: The Hell Hole

Ezra

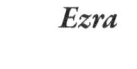

I WALKED SLOWLY THROUGH the dark tunnel, careful to avoid the rocks and loose debris that had yet to be mucked from the most recent blast. It was difficult to see through the dusty fog, but the green haze that surrounded the lamps was hard to miss. The familiar smell of gasoline fumes from the trucks mixed with the acrid stench of one hundred sweating men filled my nostrils. Just breathing would almost kill you. I walked out into the daylight, removed my hard-boiled hat, and wiped the sweat from my brow with a dampened sleeve. I blinked several times and deeply inhaled the hot desert air, getting a brief feeling of being born again.

A new guy was vomiting next to the entrance of the tunnel. He would learn not to eat a big lunch before going into the hole.

"How you doin', son?" Ben asked as he and Pete came alongside me. We slowly descended the winding trail that led to a safe spot next to the water to wash off some of the sweat, dirt, and dust of the day. It never all washed off. I was sure some of it would be with me forever.

"Tired," I said. I knew he was referring to Grace's death, but I still couldn't wrap myself around that. I felt a little guilty for not completely breaking down and losing my mind over it. She was my sister, my best friend, and I felt like I had failed at protecting her, as I had most of our life.

It was never my intention to leave New Hampshire in the way we did. I'd always thought I would join the army one day, and looking back, I should have done that the day I turned eighteen. But Grace was just sixteen, and I knew if I left, there would be no one to get between her and our father. He was a cruel man, and when he was drunk, which was often, he was even worse.

As a child, I watched him treat my mother like his servant then use her for his punching bag when he needed some kind of release. By the time I was twelve and old enough to stand between them, I was his favorite target. I was sixteen when my mother came down with polio, and six months later, it had crept up her spine and stopped her lungs from working. Those six months, most of which we spent quarantined in the house, taking care of Mother, he was a different man. He didn't drink and hadn't hit any of us. But after she died, it was as if all the anger and rage had been building inside of him, and he unleashed on Grace and me both. I tried to take all of it for both of us, but sometimes, I wasn't there, and she, two years younger than me, had black eyes and a split lip more than once. I couldn't protect her all the time, though I tried.

When I turned eighteen, I couldn't leave her there. I'd started looking at Grace in a way no man should look at his daughter, and I feared leaving her alone with him. I was trying to find a job, something that would give me enough money to get a place where I could take Grace with me.

When Grace turned up pregnant, an entire scene occurred at our house. It escalated into a fistfight with my father when I pushed him back after he struck her with a closed fist, and I beat him until he could barely stand. He told us both to leave, calling her a whore and saying he wouldn't be responsible for raising another man's baby. He said if he ever saw me again, he'd kill me.

So my plans changed real quick, and that was okay. I figured there was always a chance Billy would do Grace right, and besides, there were jobs out here, so maybe we could both start over. I would miss Grace—she was smart and funny and would have been a good momma to that boy. The way his little mouth hung open, his lips forming an O, would haunt my dreams forever. I pushed it back down into my heart and continued to walk in silence with Ben and Pete toward the river.

Over the previous months, the muckers had used some of the larger pieces of blasted debris to form a small makeshift dam in the river at the end of the path. The result was a slowly swirling pool area large enough for half a dozen men to stand waist deep in the water, while the river raged a few feet away. I laid my hat at the river's edge, walked straight in as far as I could go, then dropped to my knees, completely submerging myself for a moment. When I couldn't hold my breath any longer, I stood and watched the bubbles where Pete had gone under the water as well.

Ben sat on the edge of the shore, removed his boots, and put his feet into the murky water. Using his shirt for a makeshift bowl, he poured the tepid liquid over his head. The water ran down his body, leaving dark-red streaks like dried blood on his rawboned chest.

From that point at the base of the work site, we had a full view of the entire operation: men going in and out of the two tunnels on the Nevada side of the river, others dangling from harnesses high above the canyon, and still more traveling back and forth and up and down on the elaborate web of pulleys and cables, wooden skips, and transport cars.

"I'm sure glad they didn't put me up there," Pete said. He motioned toward the high-scalers seated on wooden bosun's chairs and dangling by inch-thick hemp ropes from the rim of the canyon, seven hundred feet above the river. One of the high-scalers slung his drill over his back, packed a hole with dynamite, lit it, and swung himself clear. The blast echoed off the canyon walls, the gray debris falling to the water below.

"They gotta be crazy," I said.

"Nah, just hungry," Ben said. He looked around at the hundreds of men that covered the canyon.

"It's pretty amazing." It was like nothing I'd ever seen, but I tried not to get caught up in the immensity of it all. I had my one small piece and a sister to feed... *Damn.* "Seems like an awful lot of work to tame one river."

"It's more than that," Pete said. "No one would put this much money in a project just to slow down some water."

Ben stood and slid into his wet shirt. "That's right. There's lots of places they could've put this kind of money. But Hoover decided to throw it in this hole. Now, why you think he would do that?"

"He's got something to prove," Pete said as he made his way out of the water. "Nothing like proving it in a big way."

Ben reached for his hat. "You got somethin' there. And shoot, he knew finding men like us to work here would be the easy part."

"Yeah," I said. "A man's gotta eat."

Ben looked around the canyon again. "We all got somethin' to prove too. It's kinda like goin' off to war. Every man wants to win, even if they ain't sure what they're fighting for."

When we got back to the top of the trail after cooling off in the river, Ben needed to stop and catch his breath. Cotton was gulping water from a water bag when we got to the Nevada side of the bridge. "Fumes were really bad today. Those big fans don't seem to blow it out like they should." The four tunnels were set to be a mile long each. The fumes were getting worse the deeper we got into the mountain.

"Wait an hour for the ferry or catch a ride to the Wash?" Ben asked.

"I need to get back and make sure everything went okay today," I said. And besides, I hated the ferry.

Ben nodded.

Cotton waved a hand over his shoulder. "I'll wait for the water ride. See ya at the hole."

"Well, I got a train to catch," Pete said, "and a few ladies at the Railroad Pass that need my money. Heaven awaits. And I'll meet you all back in hell tomorrow."

AUTHOR NOTE: PEOPLE came from all over to watch the construction at the dam, and the high-scalers were the stars of the show. Their job was to remove the rock from the canyon walls using basically the same method as the tunnel drillers—drilling a hole, packing it with dynamite, and blowing the rock. The big difference was the high-scalers did it dangling from the top of the canyon on thin bosun chairs supported by hemp rope. Using jackhammers that weighed over forty pounds, they would drill a hole, pack it with dynamite, light it, swing themselves free while the blast went off, then return to their hole and clear it. It was difficult and dangerous work, but even though they were dangling hundreds of feet in the air, they tried to have a little fun. When the supervisors weren't looking, they had contests to see who could swing out the farthest or do the best "tricks," which delighted the onlookers. It took a special kind of man to do that work!

Chapter 8: A Fine Line between Brave and Crazy

Ezra

HELEN WAS WAITING FOR us at the mouth of the Wash. She wrung her hands and kept glancing back toward camp. When she was excited, the freckles across her nose went dark, and her pale lips turned the color of a pink rose. It made her look older and not so much like a starved pup.

Ben saw her and quickened his pace. "What's wrong?" he said.

"There's a man down there that's lost his mind. Stripped his kids naked and staked them out in the sun. Mr. Emery went to get Ranger Williams, but those two boys are going to die if they lie there much longer," Helen said.

Ragtown was a place like I'd never seen and could never have imagined. The people were starving and desperate. Add to that heat so intense that the rattlesnakes even hid during the middle of the day, and sometimes, people just lost their minds. I figured that was one of the reasons that the ranger patrolling this area had a strict rule about weapons. If he found you with one, you were out of there. While it would have been nice to have a gun for protection from all the riffraff, a crazy man didn't need access to one.

Ben and I ran down the rocky trail to camp. Helen passed me, her worn hat tucked in the bib of her overalls, one long red braid swinging back and forth behind her as she ran. She was small and quick, and I struggled to keep up.

When we reached the camp, a circle of ten or so men surrounded another man, who quickly shifted from one man to the next, cussing and threatening them with a hayfork. In the center of the circle, two small figures lay naked on the ground. Their hands and legs were spread wide apart and appeared to be tied to tent stakes. They weren't moving.

Ben was coughing uncontrollably when he reached us. "Dear Lord," he said in between coughs. "What the hell happened?"

"One of the boys gave a can of beans to Johnny-behind-the-rock without asking his daddy first.

They've been out there for over an hour now," Helen said.

"Where did he get a hay fork?"

"He used it for a tent pole. Tore down the whole thing to get to it."

I alternated my stare between the man jabbing at the spectators and the two small bodies on the ground. I didn't want to get stabbed, but somehow, we had to get to those boys, and none of the other men seemed too keen on making a move.

Ben whispered something to Helen, and I heard her say under her breath, "If Ranger finds out we have a gun—"

"No." I reached for Ben's arm. "You'll get fired. You can't do that."

Ben shook his arm loose. "Those boys are gonna die before Ranger gets here. I can't let that happen."

I could see the boys clearly now. They couldn't be more than six or seven. Their skin was as red as a cock's comb. I walked toward the circle, trying to focus on the man with the hay fork while others in the crowd tried to reason with him to no avail.

Too much going on and not enough sleep, or maybe I wasn't thinking clearly, but as he turned his back to me to jab his weapon at someone else, I broke the circle and tackled him from behind. We hit the rocky ground together, me landing on top, the hay fork a few feet away.

The man struggled against me, and I hit him square in the temple with a closed fist. Then another. And another. I felt all the anger inside of me boiling up—anger at my father, at Billy, and even at Grace for dying on me, and I hit him again. He bucked and threw me off him, swearing as he rolled over. He tried to get to his feet, but I kicked him hard in the abdomen with my booted foot, throwing him back to the ground. I grabbed the hay fork and raised it high over my head, directly above him. His face tensed, and his dark eyes filled with anger.

As I lowered the fork, a strong hold around my midsection pulled me away, and I missed my mark by inches. "That's enough, son," Ben said from behind me. Four men held the offender down and, after untying the boys, hog-tied him with the same rope to keep him until Ranger arrived.

The boys' skin had started to blister, and they were covered with red ants. I turned away, unable to look at them, and focused on Helen. "Are they alive?"

"Barely."

I INHALED DEEPLY, THE smoke from a Camel filling my lungs, then leaned back and exhaled, watching the smoke drift into the blackness of the night sky.

"All that man had to do was move at the right time, and you'd have been a pig on a spit," Ben said.

"Well, he didn't. Besides, somebody had to do something." I took another long drag then snubbed the cigarette and put the small butt back in the pack for later. "It's this damned hellhole. The desert makes people crazy." If it doesn't kill them.

The two boys were severely burned, not to mention the bites they had received from the ants that had attacked them while they lay on the ground. They were wrapped in wet sheets and laid in the river until Murl Emery arrived. He took them by ferry to River Camp, where an ambulance was called.

The man didn't fare much better. By the time Ranger got to him, he looked like every man in Ragtown had taken at least one shot at him. He lay in the sun, cattle-tied, covered in blood, his eyes swollen shut, until the Las Vegas sheriff's deputies arrived to take him away.

"I ain't saying you didn't do good," Ben said, "but there is a fine line between brave and crazy."

"Well, I'm neither."

"I know," Ben said. "But that anger you're holding can sure make you go one way or another."

"I'm not angry. I'm too tired to be angry," I said without conviction.

I stood up and stretched. I knew I needed to sleep, but the thought of crawling into the tent that Grace died in didn't appeal to me much. It reeked of death, and I figured I'd burn it and find another one. Helen came out of their camp, holding a thin sheet. I'd wondered if she would treat me differently after what I told her last night, but she hadn't. Maybe she realized that I did the best I could do. "All of your sheets were... used," she said.

I tried to smile and took the sheet from her. "Thank you for taking care of things for me today. I hated to ask."

She reached into the front pocket of her overalls then handed me a small piece of paper. "The undertaker said her burial will be Friday."

I wanted to thank her again for everything—not just for handling my business today but for understanding.

"Well, good night. I'm going to curl up next to the river, so thanks for the sheet," I said. I walked away from their camp, ready to take my boots off and soak my feet in the water before I lay on the rocks and shut my eyes. The water was calling to me, and instead of just soaking my feet, I stripped down and walked into a wading pool, taking the sheet with me. It would dry by morning, but it would keep me cool through the night.

Ben was right. I was angry. Angry at my father and the way he'd treated my mother before she died and how he had disowned Grace, but that was anger I'd learned to keep hidden for so long. Angry at Grace, for dying on me, but I knew that would pass. Then there was Billy Green. I knew he was still out here, and God help him if I found him again.

Lying on the rocks, wrapped in the dampened sheet, I watched the stars light up the desert sky. It had been a long day. And tomorrow, I'd do it all again.

AUTHOR NOTE: JOHNNY-behind-the-rock was mentioned in one of the many oral histories related to Ragtown. Too old to be employed on the dam project, he lived alone behind a large boulder with nothing to his name but the clothes he wore. He rarely came from behind his rock, moving throughout the day to stay in a shady spot. He rarely spoke and survived on what others gave him. He was known only as Johnny-behind-the-rock. I don't know his story, I'm not sure anyone does, but I'm sure it was tragic to live as he did. I wanted to remember him in some way, even if it is only a mention in a work of fiction.

The ant scene is a fictionalized account gleaned from a true event that took place in Ragtown. I included it to show the cruelty that desperation can breed.

In 1931, the average cost of a pack of 20 cigarettes was 15 cents, which is just under $3 in 2022 dollars. Cigarette manufacturers had interesting advertising campaigns to convince smokers that certain cigarettes were healthier than others, some even claiming to cure asthma, hay fever, and a "cold in the head." One advertisement I found for Camels stated, "More doctors smoke Camels than any other cigarettes." Yet according to another ad, Luckies were less irritating because they were toasted, and dentists preferred Viceroys because they were filtered.

Chapter 9: Wild and Unchecked

Helen

I STAYED CLOSE TO THE trail that the bighorn sheep used to walk down the mountain in search of food and water, leaving their heart-shaped tracks in the dust. Daddy didn't like me wandering in the mountains alone—he tended to believe the stories about a renegade Indian living in the hills and figured he was just waiting to grab some girl like me. But after watching Grace being hauled to Vegas in a wooden box marked with the Six Companies name and a few more days hanging around camp, staring at a sagging canvas ceiling, I needed to find some beauty. And I needed to be alone, so I snuck away while Pepper was helping his mother with afternoon chores.

It was different without my friends, but I didn't mind my own company. The sounds of my footsteps—and no one else's—were pleasing. Once out of sight of the camp, I stopped, shut my eyes, and inhaled the sweet, rock-dry aroma of the desert. It was the same scent I first noticed when I arrived in Ragtown a year before, an ancient smell, something completely unfamiliar, begging me to explore.

Normally, I brought my camera with me when I came up the mountain. It was a small Brownie that Daddy had given me for my birthday three years before, and I loved to find something beautiful, wait for that perfect shot, and know that I would have the image forever. I was very careful with how much film I used. I knew it was expensive to buy, and getting the pictures developed was too. Although Daddy didn't seem to mind, I always felt a little guilty when I asked him to get me more. That day, however, I just wanted to explore and experience the freedom of the desert.

I took off my hat and tucked it into the pocket of my overalls. I raised my face to the afternoon sun and felt it press against my skin, a benevolent hand from the heavens. Different from the Midwestern sun, its presence couldn't be ignored, not for a second. The heat wrapped around me, hugged me. Most people in Ragtown acted as if the sun was burning them into the ground, but it seemed to open my body.

The rays could be dangerous if I was too greedy, so I tucked my hair back under my hat, save for a few stray red wisps that were determined not to be tamed, and continued up the trail, remaining alert to the ground for any snakes that could have been warming themselves in my path. I could always detect a light cucumber-ish smell whenever a snake was close by. I thought they could smell me, too, but they never seemed to bother much. Maybe they knew I belonged here too.

I'd never been especially comfortable inside a house or a tent. There, where others seemed more relaxed, I felt walled in. Everything was dingy and small with the smells piled on top of one another. Outside, I could breathe and move. Everything my eye touched was crisp. In Kansas, since it was just Daddy and me, I started doing women's work at a young age, but I always rushed through it, wanting to run to the field of wildflowers behind our house. I'd sit beside sunflowers as big as dinner plates and as bright as the sun itself, watching the mass of flowers wave gently in the wind, enveloping me with a perfume of lemon mint and wild ginger.

The desert was different. Better. Stronger. While I adored the wildflower fields of Kansas, I felt like an observer, a visitor there. In the desert, I felt inseparable. It welcomed me, responding to my touch, my scent.

I stopped at a familiar point, a large boulder that overlooked the canyon. After checking to make sure none of the local wildlife had chosen it for a shady spot, I sat cross-legged and looked out across the canyon. I reached for a yucca plant, avoiding the stiff, saw-like edges of its leaves, and brushed my fingertips gently across the bell-shaped white flowers growing from its center. They felt silky-smooth and clean, almost cool to the touch. I held my hand to my nose and took a deep breath, taking in the faint scent of dill.

A scampering sound from behind made me turn just in time to see the long dusty-orange and grayish-black body of a chuckwalla as it ducked underneath a nearby rock. "Good afternoon," I said.

I looked across the river to the mountains on the other side, the black, orange, gold, and red that changed colors throughout the day as the sun moved across them. An ever-changing rainbow but not like one you would see after a storm. This rainbow was solid, always there, one I could touch, climb, be a part of. I looked back at the rock behind me, seeing only a glimpse of the chuckwalla's tail, and wondered if he had grown from the black and orange rocks.

A large creosote bush grew not far from my rock, and after checking for the rattlesnakes I knew used the bush for shelter, I took the time to gather some of the leaves and small branches to grind into my special salve that Daddy used on his feet and his chest. He wasn't too fond of the unique scent that the pungent creosote mixed with the perfume-like brittlebush stems produced, but it helped heal his feet and even relieved his cough, so he didn't say much about it.

Leaving the mountains once I was amongst them was difficult, but I knew I shouldn't be gone too long. There were a lot of new people in the Wash, more arriving each day, and not all could be trusted. Just a little longer. I made my way down another path on the east side, toward the river, taking time to stop in front of a familiar beavertail cactus. In the early part of June, the cactus's prickly pads had been covered with pink flowers. One flower, brilliant as the brightest prairie phlox, still remained. It had held on throughout the summer.

I knelt next to it, careful to avoid the spines that protected it. "If an old wildflower disappeared, no one would notice. But you are special. Even got your own bodyguard." The people in Ragtown called this place ugly, but I didn't care what they thought. They were faces moving past whose hearts were so filled with sorrow that they couldn't see the beauty right in front of them.

Grace understood, and I think Ezra, in his own way, did too. At night, he often sat by the river, lost in his own thoughts, calmed by the sound of the rushing water.

I sat next to the cactus and watched the pink blossom move gently in the hot wind. "I know what you're thinking," I said to the flower. "But Ezra is different than the others. He's like your cactus, rough and a little dangerous but dead set on protecting what he loves most." But it didn't always work out that way, and just as the flower would eventually fall victim to the environment regardless of her thorny guard, Ezra could only do so much. I cursed out loud, something I never did when others were around, and slapped my thighs hard with my palms. "I know, I shouldn't be thinking about him." But I couldn't stop.

My eyes shifted to the broken ground. I hadn't noticed before, but the cracks and fissures were similar to the lines on my hand. Darker and more pronounced, but the mountain was a much bigger creature than me. I held my hand to its skin, trying to feel it breathe. I lay down with my ear against the red dirt to listen, but all I could hear was the sound of the river nearby. I closed my eyes and saw Ezra, sitting by the water. I had to stop thinking about him.

I stood, brushed my worn overalls, and took a drink from my canteen. The sound of the river was enticing, and I watched it rush by, wild and unchecked.

But not for long.

I knew the government's reasons for the dam project were sound. They wanted to harness the power of the water and, at the same time, give starving men an opportunity to eat. Since the mines closed in Kansas, it was Daddy's and my only chance at survival. But in the process, they were destroying a part of the mountains in an attempt to tame a beast that had gone unchecked for longer than I could imagine. My mountains, the place where I felt I belonged.

"We'll be fine. It's going to be all right," I said to the earth around me as I made my way back toward the trail. Dad, me, the desert, even Ezra... different but fine. My stomach was heavy as I remembered the last words I had said to Grace: "It's going to be all right." I wished I could believe that.

AS I GOT CLOSER TO camp, I noticed a lot of activity, which was unusual for that time of day. The workers from the night shift should still have been asleep, and the day shift was on the job site. Those still in camp were women, children, and the men who weren't working at all. I looked up at the sun, barely past the midpoint in the sky. Something was wrong. As I got to the end of the trail, Cotton Vaughn was waiting for me.

"Murl Emery said you was probably up there," he said, pointing toward the top of the mountain.

"What's wrong?" The peace that the mountain had filled me with was replaced by fear, and I could hear it in my own voice.

"Why does something always have to be wrong?" he asked.

I put one hand on my hip and looked at him. I was not in the mood for games. "For one thing, Mr. Vaughn, you are standing here, and it's barely midday. Aren't you supposed to be at work?"

"First of all, my name is Cotton, so quit calling me Mr. Vaughn like I'm some old man. As for being here instead of in the hole, they cut our hours back today, said they was tired of people overheating and passing out, so get used to us all being here in the afternoon." He reached into the pocket of his worn jeans and pulled out a small bottle of vanilla. "And happy birthday. Your daddy told me, and I like the way this smells on ya."

I stared at the bottle in his extended hand for several seconds. "I... I don't know what to say." The only interaction I'd had with Cotton Vaughn, other than the night by the river, was listening to him and Daddy talk about work. To be honest, the way he got a little too close and stared a little too long made me uncomfortable, but then I felt bad about that because there he was, giving me a birthday present.

"Well, with all those big words you usually use, it's a surprise that you can't find any." He moved a little closer and held the gift out to me.

I took it and turned it over in my hand. "Thank you. I'm just surprised is all."

I opened the bottle, dabbed some on my wrist, and held it up to take in the scent. I only had a small amount left in the bottle Daddy had given me for Christmas, and I'd been careful to wear it only on certain days. But Cotton noticed?

He reached for my hand and roughly pulled my wrist up to his nose. "Yeah, you should wear that all the time," he said. "Makes you smell like a woman, even when you're dressed like a boy."

I jerked my hand back and started walking toward camp. He was by my side, and I tried to move ahead of him, but he matched my stride. I didn't want to be rude—after all, he had just given me a birthday present—but I wasn't comfortable with the way he grabbed my hand as if he had some right. He didn't even bat an eye when I pulled my hand back, and I considered that he didn't even realize that his action made me uneasy.

"You ought to go out to that Railroad Pass with me some night. They'll let you in if you're with me. You like dancin'?"

I stumbled on a small boulder in my way and lost my footing. Cotton grabbed my arm to keep me from falling and held on a little too long.

No one had ever flirted with me before, and I wasn't sure what to do. When I was little, there was that one boy, Skip, who used to pull my hair all the time, but that was different. I was seventeen, and Cotton was a man. Flirting with me. I looked over at him, trying to avoid eye contact. He wasn't much taller than me, and his dark hair was both too long and cut too short in other places, like he did his own barber work with a pocketknife. His skin was dark and cracking from the sun, like the floor of the mountain. When he smiled, I could see his teeth were starting to yellow from the tobacco that he often had pushing out his bottom lip, which only made his chin disappear even more.

I saw Daddy and Ezra sitting outside our camp and took off at a jog, waving another thank-you to Cotton but needing to get away from him. He yelled from behind me, "Don't forget about the dancin'," and I cringed. Daddy seemed to be okay with Cotton, so I doubted that he was a bad man, but he was just not the way I envisioned a man flirting with me to be. It was Cotton Vaughn, not Ezra.

"There's my birthday girl," Daddy said with a smile as I got to camp. I slipped the small bottle of vanilla into my pocket and sat on the ground next to him. He reached over for a quick hug and kissed my forehead. "Not much of a girl anymore, though."

"I heard they cut your hours. That can't be good," I said.

"Not at all," Ezra said under his breath.

Daddy handed me a package, larger than what Cotton had given me and wrapped in brown paper. "Can we birthday a little bit? There's going to be enough talk about that goin' around."

I unwrapped the package, careful to take my time. I already felt guilty because I knew he had spent money on whatever he got me, and I didn't need anything. I think giving me a gift made him feel better than me. In the package was a short-sleeved swing skirt dress the color of sunflowers. I stood and held it up to me. It looked like a perfect fit, and I couldn't wait to try it on. "It's beautiful," I said. "But I don't—"

He held up a hand to stop me. "We're going to be moving to town as soon as those houses are finished. And when we do, they are going to be having dances and parties and all the other things that they can dream up. The prettiest girl in town needs a pretty dress."

I leaned down and kissed the top of his head. I did love the dress, but when he said the word "dances," all I could think about was Cotton Vaughn holding me in his arms, putting his dirty hands on my pretty yellow dress. "Thank you. It's perfect." I tried to envision dancing with Ezra instead and found myself blushing. I pushed the thoughts away.

Daddy slapped his thighs with both hands. "Good. I'm glad you like it. Now, I know there are going to be a bunch of men hanging around here tonight talking about work, so what should we do until then? Wanna hitch a ride into town and see how that's coming along?"

"Really? Oh, yes. I'd love to." I folded the dress quickly and rewrapped it in the brown paper.

Ezra stood and brushed his jeans. "Have a good time. I'm going to wash up and wait for Emery to get back. He's supposed to be picking me up a new tent."

Ezra had given his old tent to a family that had been living under a piece of cardboard. They didn't mind the smell, and after scrubbing the canvas with lye and soaking it in the river, you could barely tell that it was once full of death. Ezra had been hanging around our camp a lot more in the past few days. I guessed without Grace around, we were his only family. I put the dress in the front seat of Daddy's Model T, opening the packaging one last time to run my hand over the soft yellow fabric. Then I closed my eyes and tried to picture Ezra doing the same.

AUTHOR NOTE: ONE OF my favorite things about Helen is her ability to find beauty in nature, regardless of her circumstances. I spent a lot of time in the desert writing this, looking for those bits of beauty that Helen could see. In doing so, the desert grew on me. There is a certain peace to be found in nature, and I've realized that different landscapes provide a different kind of comfort.

Gambling and alcohol were not allowed in Boulder City. The Railroad Pass opened its doors on August 1, 1931, which is about the same time the events of this manuscript take place, so I did take some creative liberty by including the casino. It stood just outside the city limits and gave the workers a place to have some fun. It's still there today, and gambling is still not legal in Boulder City.

Chapter 10: Men Are... Hard

Helen

I RARELY LEFT RAGTOWN. In fact, it had been months since I'd wandered close to the highway, my only view of the comings and goings from town being from my perch high in the mountains. As we got closer, I realized a lot had changed in the short time since I'd made it that far out of the Wash.

Trucks and cars lined the highway, heading in both directions. Dust and fumes whirled around us as we stood by the road, Daddy with his thumb out, waiting for someone to stop and give us a ride to Boulder City, the town being constructed by Six Companies for the workers. It was a short walk, and I didn't mind, but Daddy said it was too dangerous. "Not only do we have the traffic to deal with, but I don't want to have to pass McKeeversville on foot."

I would have thought seeing a man with a girl would get us a ride faster, but Daddy told me to keep my braid tucked under my hat and to keep my head down. A man in a pickup truck stopped, and Daddy and I jumped in back. He didn't even turn around to look at us. I guess it was assumed we were heading to town.

I knew McKeeversville was another tent city, similar to Ragtown, but I hadn't seen it up close. As we rode by, it looked like piles of debris littering the desert floor, and I wondered if Ragtown looked the same to those that didn't live there. After a quick turn and a short trip up a winding road, the truck pulled over and dropped us off at the top of the hill, where we could easily see the town being laid out before us. Orderly. Boundaries drawn in the dirt. Construction going on in every direction.

I smiled. A real town in the making. One day soon, our home. "This is going to be wonderful," I said.

My dad put his arm over my shoulder and pulled me close. "Yes, it is, Helen. Just a little more time in the desert. I promise. It will be worth the wait."

Boulder City was laid out in the shape of a triangle. We stood at the apex near a large brick structure with a sign that read Bureau of Reclamation Administration Building. It was on the tip of the summit between Hemenway Wash and Eldorado Valley and had a frontal view of the entire city, with a backside view of the future lake site. I could see everything from there, and I wanted to explore. Daddy pointed at the western leg of the triangle, where homes were already built, some of brick, most of wood. "That's where the bosses live," he said, "and the government types."

We cut a zigzag across a large, cleared lot of sand and dirt, swarming with gardeners that were preparing the ground for grass, trees, and flowers. "This is where the park is going to be, and they say they're building tennis courts and a rec center. Maybe I should get you a tennis racquet for Christmas?"

I laughed and waved a hand in a wide circle around me. "This is like Christmas!"

We walked along the streets, past buildings in progress, with signs designating their future function: a church, a barbershop, a bank, a candy store. "A movie theater!" I stopped and shut my eyes, envisioning the town complete, with people walking the streets, stopping to say hello to others that passed them by. It was like a dream, one that I would soon be living. I opened my eyes and grabbed my dad's hand, pulling him deeper into the town.

As we got to the middle of the sand flats of the giant triangle, we stopped and watched two men building a house. Several were already built, but none were occupied. They were working fast, like ants on a hill, and Daddy and I tried to imagine which of the houses would be ours. One of the men stopped and moved toward a water bag, saw us, and smiled.

"How long's it take you to do one of them?" Daddy asked.

The man wiped his brow with his arm and stared too long at me before looking back at my dad. "Not much to it. Wooden posts for a foundation, flooring, framing, put up siding, put on a roof, and tar paper it. Two shifts for one of these bigger ones." He pointed at a smaller, one-room house across the dirt street from where we stood. "The dingbat houses take about twelve hours."

"With all these men, they'll be done in no time," I said. I didn't care if it took them thirty minutes to build one. It was a house, and we would make it a home.

"Come on," my dad said. We didn't want to be there when it started getting dark, but I didn't want to leave. We walked up the east side of the triangle, back toward the top of the hill, and passed three large buildings, each two stories high and shaped like an H.

"Dormitories for the single guys."

Like Ezra. "You'd think they would have built the houses first," I said. There were a lot of single men in Ragtown, and I assumed the other tent cities as well, but for the most part, there were families.

"Well, I'm not so sure they thought we'd bring our families to the desert. I don't know where they think we'd have left them, though," Daddy said. We walked past a large mess hall, and the smell of food made my stomach pang. It had to be close to dinner time, but I didn't really want to leave just yet.

Across from the dormitory complex, the large company store was open for business.

I pulled on Daddy's arm. "Oh, can we please go in? Just to look? I promise I won't take long."

He laughed and dug in his pocket and pulled out a nickel. "I think you gotta be a buyer, not a looker."

"No, I don't want to—"

He held up a hand and cut me off. "I can afford a few nickels for your birthday."

We walked in and wandered the aisles, eyeing everything, taking it all in, everything from food to clothing to a complete bedroom set with a dresser and drawers. I picked up a bag of flour and a can of lard, but my dad made me put them back. "No, you spend that nickel on woman stuff. Just for you. We ain't starvin' yet."

I picked up a new hairbrush, one with wide bristles that wouldn't pull my thick hair, but I couldn't decide on the large selection of hair clips. I chose three and held them out for my dad, who immediately selected one with a butterfly made of clear and yellow stones. "Well, of course, the butterfly. That's you."

"A butterfly?" I turned the clip over in my hand and imagined it against my red hair with my new yellow dress on.

"You have definitely turned into a beautiful woman. A butterfly for sure," he said.

I rolled my eyes. "You're my daddy. Of course you think I'm beautiful."

He shook his head. "I see the way men are starting to eye you, and I know what those looks mean."

I waved a hand at him and made my way to the front of the store. After paying for my goods, I tucked the bag into my overalls, careful not to damage the delicate clip.

As we left the store, a small cyclone of dust whirled in front of the open door, wavering slowly left to right, and then suddenly leapt out of sight, beckoning me to follow.

"Let's go there," Daddy said, pointing at a small building with a sign that read Eat at Browder's and another sign below it that simply said Cafe.

I looked down at my worn overalls and back up to him. "I look—"

"Like the prettiest date I've had in a long time." He offered his arm to me like a gentleman. I giggled and slid my arm into his elbow.

When we walked in, I took off my ballcap and let my long braid fall down my back. The café was full of men, most still wearing their work clothes from the dam. I took a deep breath: coffee and bacon. We made our way to an empty booth toward the back of the café, and I could feel the stares from the other patrons.

A big woman with long brown hair, a toothy smile, and a name badge that read Karen handed us two menus. "I haven't seen you two around."

"We live down by the river," my dad said. "But not for long."

I looked over the menu, and my mouth watered as I read the items available: burgers, chicken sandwiches, eggs and bacon, and all the french fries you could eat. I didn't want to spend my dad's money, especially since I knew his hours had been cut back, but it all looked so good, a welcome change from the beans that awaited us in Ragtown.

"Well, I hope to see more of ya, then," Karen said.

I looked up just in time to see Daddy smile and wink at her then buried my face back in the menu. He'd had a woman friend or two come by the camp since we'd lived in Ragtown, but he hadn't been on a real date in a long time. I hoped to see him meet someone someday.

We decided to split a cheeseburger, and when we told Karen it was my birthday, she promised a surprise after our meal. When she walked off, my dad's gaze followed her.

"I think she's got eyes for you," I teased.

He gave me a broad smile. "Well, I'm quite a catch. But I'm more concerned with all the eyes on you these days."

I felt my face get warm. It had been just my dad and me since I was five years old. I barely remembered anything before that except small flashes of my grandparents and nothing of my mother. He taught me how to cook, which was why I wasn't very good at it, how to clean, which I did quickly and sometimes haphazardly, and how to drive a tractor, which I liked much better than cooking and cleaning. We'd been best friends forever, and nothing had been sacred between us. But talking to him about boys—about men—felt a little awkward. I thought of Cotton and wondered if he'd said anything to my dad about asking me to go dancing. I hoped not.

I tilted my head toward the café. "They are just looking. I don't pay them any mind."

"Well, you will. And when you do, I want you to be careful. You need a good man that will take care of you. But some men tend to try to break a woman's spirit, and I don't want you to fall for some pair of bones just because he's pretty. I'd hate to have to kill some guy because he isn't treating you right." He took a long drink of his coffee and looked at me over the cup.

I thought about telling him about Cotton, but if I said the words out loud, they would become real. And I was afraid he'd approve of Cotton Vaughn, and I wasn't sure I did. "I'll be careful. And if any of them give me any grief, you'll be the first to know."

He looked around at the café full of men and shook his head. "It ain't easy for me to talk to you about this stuff, girlie. Men are... hard. Some are weak for women or alcohol. Some are just downright mean. Most of these guys out here are good, hardworking men that I'd be proud to call 'son,' but there are others—"

"Like who?" I figured as much as Cotton hung around, if Daddy didn't approve, he'd say so.

He looked up toward the ceiling for a minute as if he was thinking. "How about this. When I see one that I think is worthless, I'll warn ya."

I smiled wanly, even though I felt a bit deflated. I wanted names or something more concrete. I considered pushing him but realized it might not have been a comfortable conversation for him, talking about men with his teenage daughter, so I decided I'd talk to some of the women in camp instead.

He took a big drink of his water and licked his lips like it was the best-tasting water he'd ever had. "You excited about starting school?" The past year, school for me had consisted of reading books that Smitty Goon and the other former teachers who lived in Ragtown had recommended. Once we were in Boulder City, I'd take a test to see where I stood, and then I'd be riding the bus to Las Vegas every day to go to school.

I shrugged. "A little. I'll miss reading what I want and spending time in the mountains. And that long bus ride—I like to be home when you get there."

He pointed a finger at me and raised one eyebrow. "Let me tell ya somethin'. That mountain will always be there, but getting an education, especially for a girl, is a gift you can't turn down. You promise me you will work hard and graduate from high school. Who knows? You might go off to college someday."

I doubted that would ever happen, but dreams were free. "I promise. But I think it would take a miracle for me to be able to go to college."

"Miracles happen every day, girlie. Sometimes you gotta look for them, though."

A man in a uniform walked down the aisle as if looking for someone in the booths. He had a toothpick hanging from his mouth and stopped briefly at our table, looked at me, and tipped his hat. His uniform was crisp, and his name badge said Bodell. I smiled. Once he was out of earshot, my dad said, "And stay away from that one."

Once we'd eaten, Karen brought me a small bowl of vanilla ice cream while she and my dad sang "Happy Birthday" to me. I wanted to cry, not only because I wasn't used to the attention but because I hadn't had any ice cream in over a year. I shared it with my dad, and we ate it slowly, savoring every spoonful.

After dessert, we started walking back toward Ragtown. Daddy stopped when we were almost to the top of the hill and sat on a large boulder for a minute to catch his breath. He'd been coughing a lot more lately, but said he was taking the medicine the doctor gave him, and it would be much better once they broke through the mountain. "I just need some of that nasty-smelling rub you make for me," he said. "It's not that bad."

Once he was breathing normally again, we stayed on the boulder for a minute and took everything in. He put a hand on my shoulder. "Helen, you need to remember a name for me."

"A name?" I said.

"Ida Browder. Remember that name. If you're ever in trouble and I'm not around, you go find Ida Browder. She lives right over there on Utah Street. All you got to do is ask, and someone will point you in her direction."

I furrowed my brow. Our day had been light and happy, but Daddy's voice was suddenly serious. "I don't understand. Is everything okay?"

He stood and reached a hand down to me. "Everything is just fine. But you never know what could happen. Maybe I'll go out with some pretty woman like Karen some night and not show up home for a few days."

I frowned. I knew exactly what he was talking about, and it wasn't the off chance that he'd take off with Karen for a few days. I didn't want to think about anything bad happening, but accidents happened at the dam all the time. He was a truck driver, I reminded myself, and it was one of the safest jobs out there. But still...

He started walking, and I was next to him. "Now, let's get back to the Wash before it gets dark out here."

We made our way back to the top of the triangle, and as we crawled in the back of another truck willing to drop us at Ragtown, I looked back at Boulder City, washed in the red and orange of the setting sun. I sat in the bed next to my dad and leaned my head on his shoulder. "Thank you for today. It was the best day ever."

He wrapped an arm around me and kissed my forehead. "Better days are coming, girlie. Pretty soon, every day is going to be the best."

AUTHOR NOTE: BOULDER City was a town specifically built by the government to house workers on the dam project and their families. The government planned it with an emphasis on clean living, and once it was built, Boulder City was a little oasis compared to the tent cities that surrounded it. There was a recreation center, a beautiful city park, several stores, an ice cream/candy shoppe, and a movie theatre that operated around the clock. The movie theatre was air-conditioned, so of course it was a very popular spot. It was the ideal of a small town, in the middle of the Great Depression.

Chapter 11: A Dam Accident

Ezra

AS A BOY, I SPENT EVERY Sunday morning at the Whitefield Methodist church, listening to Reverend Lucas talk about the wondrous rewards of heaven and the punishment of an unforgiving hell. The Reverend's descriptions were always vivid, meant to evoke a desire for one and a fear of the other.

By sixteen, when my mother died, the images I had of heaven and hell were not as awe-inspiring. Maybe, by that time, I had begun to question the existence of such beauty and such ugliness, the good versus the bad, the righteous versus the sinner. Or maybe I had heard about them so much that they didn't seem so scary anymore.

Grace, however, had been very interested in these extraordinary places. She could imagine the glorious whiteness and purity of heaven as clearly as she could visualize the unbearable heat, the darkness, the nothingness of hell, the beauty of one less her goal than the avoidance of an eternity in the other.

I hadn't thought much about those images of the worlds of the afterlife in years, but with the death of Grace and the baby, I'd been hoping that the heaven part was real and that they were in it. It was almost two hours to shift's end, and standing outside the tunnel on my last break of the day, I looked back into the darkness of the tunnel and thought of the hell of my childhood.

The massive mountain shook from a blast in the distance, fire shot from the solid wall, and the crumbs of the interior fell in every direction, covering the men nearby with soot, dust, and smoke. I had to look away, blinding myself temporarily in the scorching sun. I took a deep breath, trying to clear the toxic fumes from my lungs. I wouldn't let that be my eternity. There had to have been a better place.

Our supervisor, Frenchie, stood outside the tunnel and motioned to me. "Okay, time's up. Replace Digger on the bottom row."

Rotating break times in the afternoon was one of the new rules that accompanied the decrease in workday hours. Instead of shutting down the entire operation for a fifteen-minute recess, the men rotated out and back in, which landed us on a different spot on the Jumbo each time. I usually started my day on the top platform and ended it on the bottom row.

Pete had pointed out that the efficiency of this new policy was questionable. Moving the crew around every fifteen minutes caused a loss of orientation and risked mistakes. And with mistakes came accidents. But Six Companies, the company contracted by the government to do the job, seemed to be more concerned about getting it done quickly than doing it safely.

"Sure thing, Frenchie," I said.

Over Frenchie's shoulder, a Stetson hat peaked the trail, and I knew it could only be attached to one person: Frank Crowe, the man Six Companies had entrusted the entire project to, the one the men called "Hurry Up."

Crowe was on the site day and night, and I wondered when or if he ever slept. As he got closer, I saw another familiar face: Bud Bodell, Six Companies' chief of security and also one of the policemen in Boulder City. The word around the site was that Crowe was okay, but Bodell could be a real jackass. I'd had little contact with either one and didn't care to.

As I walked back into the fifty-six-foot-wide tunnel, I stayed close to the side to avoid the passing trucks. I was careful to avoid jutting rocks while my eyesight adjusted to the darkness. The air was filled with smoke and fumes, and the ground shuddered from the simultaneous operation of thirty drills on the solid rock. Through the glare of the floodlights, I saw the Jumbo in the distance and heard the loud drills slowly decreasing. A dump truck full of dynamite backed up to the wall, while three others passed going the other direction, filled with muck from the previous blast. Pete's voice was loud over the voices of the others.

"Come on, Molly. It looks like we're waiting for you."

"Shut your damn mouth, Banker. I'm clear. Clear!"

The drillers left their positions on the truck and walked toward the entrance, allowing the powder crew access to the Jumbo scaffolds. The lights flickered out to avoid the chance of stray sparks. The powder men, their arms filled with dynamite thrown from the back of the dump truck, climbed onto the big rig and began pounding the explosives into the twelve-foot holes left by the drillers with twenty-foot wooden sticks. The trailing primer wires were braided together and connected to the cable that led to the blow man, Beau Dandy.

"Move this thing, Ben!"

We were too deep to pull the Jumbo all the way out before a blast, so Ben stopped the truck one hundred fifty feet from the wall. The powder men jumped off the rig and, along with the muckers who had been working the right side of the tunnel, joined the drillers at the front of the Jumbo to wait out the blast.

"Let's go, Dandy! I'm moving into the dormitories today if we ever get done here!" one of the men yelled.

With a final "all clear," Beau Dandy pushed the T-handle on the detonator box, which began a series of sequenced blasts, each causing an earsplitting explosion. Gold and red light flared in the dark, and the blasts were muffled by the sound of flying debris crashing on the tunnel's floor. The ground shook violently, and I reached for the hood of the Jumbo to steady myself.

Before the dust could clear, Clive Allen headed for the wall, grabbing a banjo shovel on the way. "Let's get this mucked out!"

"Slow up, Allen. Wait for the damn dust to clear..."

But Clive had already begun attacking the pile of rock with his shovel.

A late charge caused me to lose my footing, and I fell to my knees on the rough floor of the tunnel's bed. I jumped up, leaving my hat behind, and ran to the back of the truck in time to see two other men scrambling toward the rubble.

The dust was thick in the air, so I pulled my shirt up to cover my face and moved quickly through the large chunks of rock and debris. Fighting to stay afoot, I stumbled and reached for a nearby shovel, but its neck had been severed in the blast.

Clive was buried under a mass of smoking rock, and we attacked the pile blindly, fingers scrabbling through rubble and dust. Moose Martin, whose size and strength had earned him the nickname, slung the largest pieces to the side, while the rest of us dug with bare hands into the hot rock.

I touched something soft and wet and pulled back quickly. Taking a deep breath, I carefully moved the rocks and saw the front of Clive's head, the place where his face had once been. "I got him!" I yelled. The others continued to dig, uncovering his torso, mostly still intact but looking more like a badly dressed deer than a man.

Pete was standing between the truck and the rubble, turning back and forth between us and Frenchie, who was running through the tunnel toward us. "Get him across the bridge," Pete said. "If he dies in Arizona, he'll lie here 'til a coroner arrives."

Understanding the urgency, Moose was the first to respond. He jumped off the pile, grabbed Clive's body, slung it over his shoulder, and started running for the entrance, passing Frenchie, Crowe, and Bodell on the way.

When the rest of us got out of the tunnel, Moose was on the bridge, steadying himself with one hand, holding Clive's body with the other, being careful not to lose his footing as the bridge swung capriciously back and forth over the river. When Moose reached the Nevada side of the river, he carefully laid Clive's body on the ground and yelled for help from the men in diversion tunnel number two.

Crowe, Bodell, and Frenchie stood away from the rest of us, watching the calamity unfold. Bodell and Frenchie were in a heated discussion. Crowe silently removed his Stetson and lowered his head.

Ben kicked his truck tire and cursed, something I rarely heard him do. "Dammit. He's got a wife and kid."

Pepper. He used to help Grace carry sheets to the river, and his mother was with her when she died. He'd just lost a friend, and now the poor kid was going to lose his daddy.

Cotton Vaughn pushed through the rest of us, his face redder than a lit match, and walked straight toward the three bosses. He threw something at their feet and pointed a finger in the face of Frank Crowe. "Here's what happens when everything is a 'hurry up!'"

We were standing there, covered in the dirt and our friend's blood, and Crowe didn't say a word. He looked across the river then back at us. He lowered his tall frame to the ground, pulled out a handkerchief, and wrapped the piece of bloody flesh that looked like a charred oatmeal cookie in it. After handing it to Frenchie, he slowly walked back toward the bridge. Frenchie didn't unwrap it but instead held the parcel out toward Cotton. Cotton closed his fist over Frenchie's. "No, you keep it. Clive won't be needing that ear no more, and maybe next time we tell ya something, you'll listen."

AUTHOR NOTE: ACTUAL records of dam accidents were not kept, but there were at least 96 construction-related deaths and who knows how many injuries and illness that didn't result in death. Carbon monoxide poisoning was the most common cause of dam-related deaths, and most of those were not recognized as such. They were usually written off as consumption or pneumonia.

Fun fact! You've probably heard the rumor that there are bodies in the cement of the dam. There aren't. There is no one buried in the dam. Yes, they worked quickly when they were pouring the cement, and there were accidents, but no one's body was left in the cement. There is, however, a dog buried in a concrete crypt near the dam, but I'll tell you more about him later.

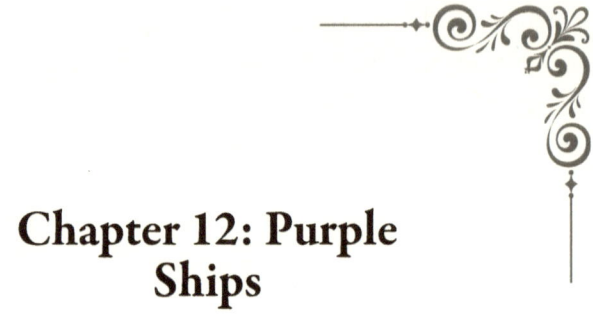

Chapter 12: Purple Ships

Ezra

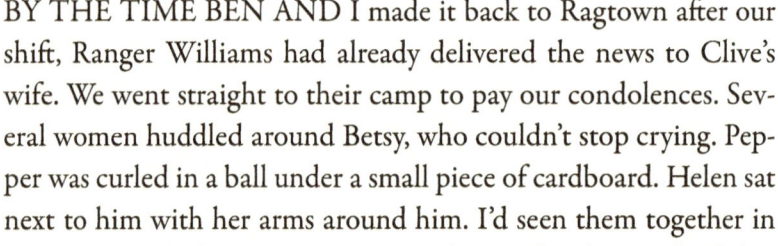

BY THE TIME BEN AND I made it back to Ragtown after our shift, Ranger Williams had already delivered the news to Clive's wife. We went straight to their camp to pay our condolences. Several women huddled around Betsy, who couldn't stop crying. Pepper was curled in a ball under a small piece of cardboard. Helen sat next to him with her arms around him. I'd seen them together in that position before. It was getting to be too familiar, and I didn't like it.

Ben went to the women, and I sat on the other side of Pepper. He didn't look up, and I could barely hear a whimper. I looked at his small frame, made even smaller by his position, and tried to guess his age—eight, maybe nine. I remembered Grace telling me he was a lot older than he looked and that he had been born wrong, which made him act younger too. I didn't understand all that, but he looked so frail. I didn't really know what to say to him, but I felt I needed to say something. "Your daddy was a good man."

He turned to look at me. His face was dirt-streaked with wet tears. "Was you there?"

I swallowed hard. "Yeah," I whispered.

"Are you sure he's dead? Maybe he was just not moving, and they thought he was dead. Maybe he'll wake up later?"

I put an arm on his back and had to squeeze my eyes shut for a second before answering him. "No, he won't be waking up."

He lowered his head then curled back up. Helen pulled him in closer and gave me a sympathetic smile. I didn't say anything else.

Ranger Williams came to collect Clive's wife and Pepper to take them into town for paperwork. At least Clive had died working in the tunnel, so she'd get a small amount of money. After they left, everyone seemed to go back to their usual routines, as if death was just another occurrence of the day. I wandered back to my tent and crawled inside. My hands hurt, my head was throbbing, and I just wanted to lie down for a while. There was already a rumble on the ferry about the hazardous conditions at the site, and I was just not ready to talk about it. I woke up a few hours later, hot, sweating, and feeling the burn in my hands.

Along the banks of the Colorado, large boulders extended into the water at various points, forming natural pools on the south side of the massive stones. Some of the larger areas, like the one directly north of Murl Emery's ferry office, were for the women and children, leaving the smaller, more randomly placed sites for us men. Walking south along the bank, I found an empty pool about fifty yards from the ferry platform. I had already washed my clothes at the jobsite. They'd dried to me on the trip home, and I just wanted to try to scrub the whole scene with Clive out of my mind. The water was calm, and although I knew it wouldn't save Clive, I figured maybe it would soothe my mind for a few moments. My hands were burned from digging in the hot rock without gloves, and I slowly stripped to my underwear and walked in waist deep. Across the river, the canyon wall seemed to change colors—orange, red, brown—as the sun hit it.

The other men were already gathering to talk about work. Their concerns for our safety, especially after the accident, were growing, and many of them, including Ben, held the new position that they would stand with the union if it came to a strike. I wasn't so sure about that.

My experience with strikes was they usually went one way: everyone was fired on the job, and a new group was brought in. There were men standing on the edge of the mountain, just waiting to take our jobs, risks be damned. I couldn't see any reason why Six Companies would handle it any other way. I had gone there to work, and I didn't want to give up a job, even if it was one that was dangerous in a lot of ways, trying to make a point. I needed to eat, and there weren't a lot of other ways to do that but work. All the men had come because it was pretty much their only way to survive, but they seemed to have forgotten that. I hadn't.

I knew the job was temporary, a few years at the most, and I had been saving a lot of my wages so Grace and I could move on once the dam was complete. But I had spent a lot of my savings getting her body taken care of, and now, I needed to work harder so I could eventually get out of there and do something different. Maybe I'd join the army after all, since I didn't have family to take care of anymore. Travel the world, far away from the desert. Striking was the last thing I needed. A vision of Clive Allen's mangled body filled my head, and my entire body tingled uncomfortably. Death in that place seemed so easy.

I dropped to my knees, surrounding myself with the dark soundlessness of the water, and tried to wash away my thoughts. I held my breath as long as I could and stood, panting, again engulfed by the desert heat.

Helen's voice startled me, and I turned quickly. She sat with her back against a large boulder, her legs outstretched.

"I don't have any clothes on!"

Helen reached for my worn blue jeans at her feet, rolled them into a ball, then threw them with amazing accuracy. "I wasn't looking, anyway," she said.

I struggled to put on my pants in the water, almost losing my balance several times before managing to get both legs in while standing in the muck. I walked out, pants soaked and dripping, water running through the fine sand and silt on the bank, back into the river. I sat on the rocky shore and reached for my socks and boots. "How's Pepper?"

She sucked in a sharp breath. "They aren't back yet. I feel sorry for him." She shook her head and offered me a weak smile, as if she was holding in a lot. She was strong. I knew that.

Helen had been a lot different in the weeks since Grace died. She seemed to talk to me more—maybe it was because before, she had Grace to talk to, and I was the only one left. Or maybe she wanted to talk to me anyway, but Grace was in the picture. Either way, I liked her company. She didn't talk about work all the time like the men did, and she was a lot easier to look at.

In fact, I'd been thinking a lot about her in the past few days. I used to tease her and call her a kid, even though she was just a few years younger than me, but she wasn't a child. She was a beautiful woman, even if she was a little skinny, and if her daddy hadn't been within strangling distance, I might have tried to bed her. I shouldn't have been thinking about that at that moment, but I was. I figured I should take Pete's advice and visit the ladies at the Railroad Pass if I wanted to relieve some tension.

"The men are talking about nothing but work, and I got tired of listening to them," she said.

"Yeah, I don't want to hear it either. It was a bad day—the worst—but I'm not interested in walking off a job I came three thousand miles to get."

Helen stood, straightened her skirt, and walked the few feet to sit down next to me. "What are you looking at out here?"

Her dress was thin as mountain air, her hair brushed straight and held in place with a shiny yellow barrette in the shape of a butterfly. She smelled of vanilla. I felt a tingle in the pit of my stomach. Railroad Pass. Two dollars. Gotta keep my head straight. I turned back toward the water. "Nothing, really. Not much to look at."

Helen laughed. "Not much to look at? This is the most beautiful time of day!" Her green eyes sparkled like the tail of a firefly.

"Beautiful? Big black mountains in a big brown desert with a dirty river running through it. Girl, you've been in the sun too long."

Helen waved my comments off. "Look how the sun makes golden flecks in the mountain. It's like there's something out there waiting to be found. And this big brown desert, as you say, reminds me of cinnamon."

I laughed. "Keep reading those books, and nobody is going to know what you're talking about."

Helen pointed across the river at the mountains looming over the Colorado River. "And when the sun sets, there can't be anything more beautiful anywhere in the world. The clouds look like purple ships. And the sky is an orange-and-red sea." She sounded so serious, her words spoken with an intensity that I hadn't noticed before.

"You sound like you like this place."

"It's a part of me now," she said. She looked at me, her brow furrowed as if thinking of something else to say. She began searching the ground, picking up and discarding different stones until she settled on a small, rounded river cobble the size of her thumbnail. She touched it to her lips, closed her eyes, and smiled.

"Open your mouth," she said. She brushed my lips with the rock. It was smooth as a grape.

I pulled back quickly. "What?"

"Open your mouth. You can taste the river in it. In Kansas, I used to chew on a piece of hay at my grandfather's farm. I knew I belonged there. It was part of me then." She rubbed the stone against her cheek and again held it out to me. "I belong here now."

I shook my head and laughed. "That's okay. I'm not much of a rock eater."

She looked at the small stone in her hand. "It's horrible what happened today."

Everyone in camp had heard by then. I hoped they spared the women the details that I couldn't seem to shake from my mind. I stood, grabbed my shirt, then reached down for Helen but flinched when she touched my burned hand. "Well, there ain't nothin' beautiful at work. That's for sure," I said through gritted teeth.

She reached gently for my hands and turned them both palms up, toward the sun. "Ezra, these look bad. Come with me, and I'll put some of my salve on them. You'll be surprised how quickly they heal."

"You mean that stuff that smells like burnt manure?" I liked that she was trying to take care of me, but it was still fun to tease her, even if I knew she was right.

"It's honey and creosote and a few other things. And it works." She turned to walk away, but I stayed with her.

"Honey? So that's what makes it smell like the horse you got it from was eating a lot of corn."

She shook her head, but I could see a hint of a smile at the corner of her mouth.

"Okay, I'll let you put the salve on my hands, even eat a rock while you do it, if you'll do one thing for me."

"What's that?" she said.

"Don't talk about work," I said. Or Grace. Or Clive.

AUTHOR NOTE: WORKERS were concerned about their safety, not only because of accidents but because of the lack of drinking water in the heat and the condition of the air in the tunnels. Hourly wages were between fifty cents and $1.25 depending on the job, with an average of all workers of about sixty-three cents an hour. In today's money, sixty-three cents equals about $11.25 an hour.

Helen finds beauty in the desert where others don't, and she feels that she is part of it. She wants Ezra to feel the same way, but she doesn't know how to make him find any comfort in it, especially when he sees nothing but the ugliness of his situation. When I was a kid, I would pick and chew on the wild onions that grew around my home in Kansas. Others chew on hay from their fields, or simply walk in their grass barefooted. It's a way that grounds us to a place; it's home. Helen doesn't know how to explain it, but that is what she is trying to convey to Ezra when she asks him to put a rock in his mouth. However, if I took you to Kansas and said, "Chew on this thing I just pulled out of the ground," you would probably react the same way Ezra does. It has to be an almost instinctive action. Then it is home.

Two dollars at the Railroad Pass is from a worker's journal entry. He wrote that he paid one of the women two dollars to "blow it," so we know what that cost.

Chapter 13: Queho and The Great Gatsby

Helen

SINCE WE'D ARRIVED in the desert, I'd had a routine. In the morning, I got up with my dad, made sure he had something to eat before work, then cleaned up anything he'd used for his breakfast. Even an empty can of beans couldn't be left out for a few hours because the ants would attack it, and that opened up an entirely new problem. So I would bury it to dig up later and take to the makeshift dumpster that the government had placed at the head of the Wash.

After he left for work, while it was still under one hundred degrees, I would go up in the mountain, sit by the water and read, or help the ladies with the kids at the tent they used for a school. I didn't stray too far from camp and only went into the mountains when one of the ladies nearby said she'd keep an eye on camp for me. There were a lot of unemployed drifters in Ragtown, and they had been known to grow desperate. Mornings were what I called "my time," when the day shifters were at work and the night shift was still sleeping. It was the quietest time of the day and definitely my favorite.

In the afternoon, I did my chores. Dust got on everything, and if I didn't wipe down what little we had every day, it was sometimes hard to breathe. The canvas walls of our camp were the biggest part, and I beat them every day with a stick, not only to clear the dust but to ensure no black widows, scorpions, or other venomous insects had decided to make a nest. Once a week, I took the sides down, one by one, washed them properly in the river, then rehung them to dry.

I would then take Daddy's and my clothes from the day before to the river and scrub them clean with lye soap and desert rocks. I owned two pair of overalls and two thin dresses, other than the new one my dad had bought me for my birthday. The dresses were a lot cooler to wear, but they weren't very practical. Our clothes dried quickly, laid out on the shore, except the socks. Socks were the hardest part of my laundry routine. I checked all of Daddy's for holes because he said if he got any, his boots would rub sores on his feet, and if I found any, I darned them with the small sewing kit I got at Emery's store. He still got sores, but my salve helped a lot with those.

By the time I finished all that, the men from the day shift were coming home, so I had dinner and cleanup and a few hours left in the day to talk with my dad or look at one of my books before soaking our sheets in the river to keep us cool at night and crawling in the backseat of the Model T to dream about faraway places.

I liked routines. I could usually tell the time of day by the task I was on, and when I was at the river, I would get some of the camp gossip. I knew the men had a tough job at the dam site, but the women in camp didn't exactly have it easy. On top of their chores, many of them had kids to take care of too. I didn't envy them and tried to help with some of the younger ones when I had a chance. They sure seemed a lot happier when they were gossiping at the river, though, so I figured it had a purpose and listened without trying to be part of it.

But with the new hours at the dam site, my routine had been upset, and I didn't like it. The men were all there in the afternoon, and trying to get things done between weaving around them and fighting for space at the river was difficult. I'd had to switch my chore time to the morning, which meant my time was saved for the afternoon. I had to find a quiet spot to read, or limit my time in the mountains because of the heat, or sit and listen to the men talk about the strike, which I didn't like to do.

Pepper had become my shadow since his father died. He didn't talk as much as he used to, and his sparkle had dulled, so I allowed him to tag along when he wanted. His mother, Betsy, was still waiting for the hundred-dollar settlement from Six Companies for the loss of her husband, and according to Pepper, she had put an ad in the newspaper, trying to find another husband. Going back to their home in South Dakota, where Pepper said the sky was so blue you could almost see to heaven, was not an option for her. She and Pepper would have to find a way.

Mr. Emery had just gotten back from his weekly supply trip to Las Vegas, and Daddy had given me two dollars to load up on food for the week before all the good items were depleted. Pepper and I passed a group of men on our way. Among them was Cotton Vaughn, talking as usual.

"Hey, Helen," he said.

I let out a slow breath.

"You're up in those mountains a lot. You don't know where that Injun's hiding, do you?"

The other men laughed openly, and although Cotton was smiling, he at least wasn't laughing at me.

There was a legend that a renegade Indian, Queho, lived in the mountains surrounding the camps. They said that he snuck into the camps and stole and that he wasn't opposed to violence when the need arose. There was a big reward for his capture, and a lot of the men spent their extra time hunting him or at least talking about it.

I was a bit leery about the story. There were reports all over, from Ragtown to the Railroad Pass, of people seeing him, and I found it hard to believe one man, Injun or not, could possibly trek that distance every day. They said he had a clubfoot, too, which would have made it even harder for him to do all he was accused of. They also said he raped and killed a woman outside the city limits not too long ago, which made him more than just a common thief and murderer. But I was up in the desert a lot, and I would probably have been an easy target, and I'd never seen him. I thought he was a ghost, an excuse for the men to use anytime something went wrong.

I put one hand on my hip and gave him my best sarcastic look. "Sure. We have morning tea on Tuesday and talk about the stock market. He usually makes some fancy little dessert to go with it and serves it on a china tea set."

The men all laughed, and I turned to continue on my way to Emery's, but Cotton decided to join me. "If he has a china tea set, it's stolen," he said.

I let out a deep breath. Men gossip was so much different from women gossip. The women talked about kids, men, and what kind of curtains they were going to hang in their new houses in Boulder City. The men talked about work and outlaw Indians.

"You shouldn't be going up there alone. He's dangerous. Maybe now that we're off in the afternoons, I should go with you. Just in case he decides to make an appearance."

With Grace gone, Daddy was a little reluctant to approve my mountain adventures. I convinced him that if Queho was up there, I could outrun him and scream louder than a banshee. Besides, I didn't have anything to steal, and I wasn't looking to bother him. Daddy still didn't like it, but he knew how hardheaded I could be at times. I liked my time alone, and the thought of having Cotton go with me made my head hurt.

"I'm fine. I've got Pepper to go with me, and besides, I've got too much work to do right here," I said.

He glanced at Pepper beside me like he was a bug. "Pepper?"

"I ain't afraid of him," Pepper said.

Cotton bent over and got in Pepper's face and said in a menacing tone, "Not until he scalps ya."

Pepper cowered behind me, and I grabbed his hand. "Leave him alone, Cotton." Then I grabbed Pepper's hand and kept walking, hoping to leave Cotton behind. "Don't listen to him, Pepper. If he saw that Indian, he'd run like a spooked rabbit."

"I bet if Ezra Deal volunteered to join ya, you wouldn't turn him down, now would you?"

I stopped walking and looked at him. His face was twisted in an angry frown. "What's that supposed to mean? And what business is it of yours? How dare you—"

He held a hand up and smiled. "I was just teasing."

I opened the door to Emery's store, glad that Cotton had decided to go back to the men he was talking to. How dare he say those things to me. Who did he think I was? I picked up cans and read labels and slammed them back down a little harder than I should have. Pepper stood next to a box of licorice whips, and Mr. Emery handed him one.

"Hey, where's that smile? The best part of my week is seeing you bounce in here with that big smile of yours."

"Sorry, Mr. Emery. It's just—"

"Men," he said.

I gave him a warm smile. "Yeah. Exactly. There's too many of them hanging around lately."

"Well, that's something I don't normally hear women complain about," he said.

I started to reply then turned at the sound of the door to the store opening. It was Ezra. My heart skipped a beat, and I wasn't sure if it was because I was glad it was him or because I was glad it wasn't Cotton. Maybe a little of both.

Mr. Emery snapped his fingers and started digging in a box of his new supplies. "I got what you wanted, Ezra. I don't know much about books, but one of the ladies who went with me said it's a new one, and... here it is." He handed Ezra a wrapped package.

"A book?" I said. In all the time we'd been in Ragtown, I'd never seen Ezra read a book. But what did I know—he may have needed his private time just like I did. But Mr. Emery said it was a new one, and I was curious if not a little jealous.

Ezra took the package from Mr. Emery and handed it to me.

"What... You want me to open it?"

He smiled. "Well, it is your birthday present, so yeah, you probably should be the one to open it. Sorry it's late."

I know my mouth was hanging open wide enough for flies to come in, and I just stared at Ezra. I glanced at Mr. Emery, who raised his eyebrow and gestured toward the package. I looked at Pepper, who shrugged as he gnawed on his licorice whip.

The brown paper it was wrapped in made a crinkling sound as I turned it over and over in my hands. I had read so many books, always borrowing them from the library or school when I was in Kansas and trading them with the ladies since being in Ragtown. But I'd never owned one. A book. My very own. And Ezra was giving it to me.

"It's going to be hard to read if you don't unwrap it," Ezra said. He reached into the cold soda cooler and grabbed three Nehi orange sodas. I carefully removed the brown packaging from the book and stared at the cover. A woman's noseless face hovered over an amusement park. Her yellow irises were actually nude women, and she was shedding a green tear. "*The Great Gatsby*," I said, my voice barely above a whisper.

"Sounds like a magician," Mr. Emery said.

I didn't care what it was about. I knew it was going to be my favorite. I hugged the book close to my chest and closed my eyes. "Thank you."

"You're welcome." Ezra popped the tops off of the three Nehi sodas then handed me one, handed Pepper another, then nodded to Emery and left without a word.

I stood there, holding a cold soda in one hand and a new book in the other, and couldn't move. My feet felt cemented to the dirt floor, and my stomach was turning. I knew I needed to finish my shopping, but all I really wanted to do was run after Ezra and give him a big hug. And then start reading the book. My book. One of those was not going to happen, though, and the other would have to wait.

Pepper snickered beside me, and I turned to see a faint smile. "Helen's got a boyfriend."

I gently pushed his shoulder at the teasing and felt my face flush.

"Men," Mr. Emery said as he began to place items on the makeshift shelves in his store. "There's just too many of 'em hanging around these days."

I took a sip of my soda and almost moaned as the cold, sweet liquid filled my stomach. "Maybe it isn't all bad," I said.

AUTHOR NOTE: DURING this phase of the dam project, a lot of men spent their off time searching the mountains for Queho because there was a big reward for his capture. It became one of their pastimes. I began this story with an account of his life up until the time Helen's

story begins. But Queho's story continues long after his death, which I'll share with you later.

The Great Gatsby, released in 1925, was not a popular book until long after the author died in 1940. Therefore, in 1931 when Helen receives her copy, it would have been an older, little-known book. However, the theme of the illusion of the American Dream seemed a perfect complement to Helen's situation, so I thought it was a fitting first book for her.

Chapter 14: Anybody's Girl

Ezra

IT WAS AS IF THE WALKING dead filled the ferry. After leaving the dark toxic pit, we silently made our way upriver to the scorching hellhole that was our home. Skeletons, gray ghosts, wandering the shore for ten, one hundred, one thousand years. I leaned on the railing, facing the Arizona shore. I hated riding the ferry.

I preferred walking back to Ragtown, but Frenchie had sent Ben down to the Six Companies clinic to get some medicine for his cough. It had been getting worse, and today, he couldn't seem to stop. He wasn't back to the tunnel by the time the shift was over, so I figured he'd catch a ride back to Ragtown on one of the supply trucks.

As the tunnel got deeper, more and more men were getting sick. In the early stages, the Jumbo was pulled out completely for the blast, giving everyone on the truck a little bit of fresh air. Now, with the hole almost a quarter of a mile long, the Jumbo was simply pulled a safe distance away. Many men took their break time without leaving the tunnel, making lunch the only time they were out of the noxious haze.

I was watching the water flow under the ferry, my eyes barely open, when Cotton slapped me on the back, nearly causing me to upchuck in the river. I turned my head slowly toward him but continued to lean on the railing. "What?" I said. Even speaking made my head hurt more, so I took some deep breaths to try to clear some of the fumes out of my system.

"Striking is looking like a much better idea," he said. "Hell, if we live long enough to walk."

After the accident with Clive, Cotton had become very vocal about the things that Six Companies was not doing to keep us safe. He had an entire list. He wasn't wrong—it was a deathtrap from the fumes to the inadequate equipment and such—but again, I was just there to work. I knew once we broke through to the other side of the mountain, the fumes wouldn't be as much of an issue, and I thought Frank Crowe was starting to see some of the things going on. Ideally, he'd make some changes, and the talk of striking would just go away.

I rubbed the bridge of my nose with my thumb and forefinger and didn't say anything. I just wanted some peace on the ride back to Ragtown. Cotton must have realized I was tired of talking about it and changed the subject.

"So, what's going on with you and Helen?" he asked.

Helen? I had to say that caught me off guard. I had been feeling a little differently toward Helen in the past month, but I didn't realize it was noticeable to anyone else. She'd been very kind and helpful to me, but there was something more, and I didn't want to go any further with it. But yesterday, after I gave her that book in Emery's store, her face lit up like Christmas, and her eyes twinkled like gold underwater. It was the best use of seven nickels ever spent. My body responded in a way that would have been obvious had I stuck around. Instead, I grabbed a Nehi soda and hurried out of there to try to cool myself down. "Nothing. We're friends."

Cotton let out a sigh of relief. "Good, because she said she'd go dancin' with me, and I don't want to mess with her if she's someone's girl."

If my head didn't already hurt, I knew it would then. She'd never said anything about Cotton—in fact, she acted like she didn't like him much at all. But women played some silly games sometimes, and even if Helen was a little smarter than most, she was still a woman. "As far as I know, she isn't anybody's girl." Even as I said it, I doubted whether I really felt that way or not.

But Cotton was at least ten years older than Helen, and he'd said some things in passing that made me think there was more to his story than he'd let on. Not that it was any of my business, but I knew he'd been married before, and I also knew, from listening to him talk at lunch break, that he tended to twist the truth sometimes, always in his favor. I shook my head, but just that slight motion made me want to lie down. Maybe I should say something to Helen, or at least Ben, I thought. Or maybe I should just mind my own business.

As the ferry finally docked, I stopped in Emery's store for a cold soda pop and a brick of ice then made my way through Ragtown. It was the middle of the day, but I was too tired to care. I crawled in my small tent, cracked the brick of ice in two, and put a chunk under each armpit. As the ice melted, it would keep my body cool while I slept, and I needed that right then more than anything.

"EZRA."

I felt someone kick my boot and woke from a dead man's sleep. I was soaking wet from the ice and somehow still hot. I leaned up on my elbows, and Helen was at the entrance to my tent.

"What's wrong?" I rubbed my face several times.

"Daddy's not back yet. I'm afraid something is wrong." She was on her hands and knees, peering into my tent, her long hair falling over her shoulders and almost touching the ground.

"Cotton said he was going to tell you that he went to the doctor instead of riding with us today." I was a little irritated that Cotton hadn't done as Ben had asked. After all, he thought Helen was his girl.

"He did," she said, "but it's almost dinner time, and he isn't back yet. It shouldn't take this long, should it?" Her forehead squeezed together, and she wasn't smiling.

Dinner time. I'd been asleep for almost four hours. I took a deep breath and sat up the rest of the way. A trip to the clinic, even if they were full, shouldn't have taken all afternoon. "Okay," I said, "let me get up, and we'll see if we can find out what's going on."

She scooted back away from the entrance to my tent and gave me room to move around enough to get out.

She was standing, looking toward the entrance of Hemenway Wash with her hands on her hips. I stood up too fast and almost fell back down and caught myself by putting a hand on her shoulder.

She turned quickly. "What's wrong?"

"Nothing," I said. Other than a pounding headache and the overwhelming desire to throw up.

She started to respond but was interrupted by a familiar voice.

"Mr. Emery said I might find you here," Ranger said. He was wearing his full uniform, as always, and was looking at Helen. "I'm supposed to deliver a message to you about your father."

Helen put a hand on her chest and paled.

"They took him to the hospital in Vegas. He's got pneumonia," he said. "He said to tell you not to worry about him and get someone to stay with you until he gets back." He glanced at me when he said that then back to Helen.

"Pneumonia? But he just had a little cough. How long is he going to be there?"

I could tell she was trying to control her voice, but the fear in it was easy to read.

"If it isn't too bad, usually about a week. They'll have him on the medicine, and we hope he'll be back to work in no time," he said. Again, he looked at me, holding my gaze for a little longer. He knew as well as I did that a lot of those guys who got pneumonia didn't ever return. In fact, he knew it wasn't pneumonia at all—it was poisoning from the fumes in the tunnel—but Six Companies would never admit to that, so they called it consumption or pneumonia, depending on the severity.

"I don't understand. He didn't seem that sick..."

"The thing is, if they send him home on medication, he still has to go to work. If he gets too sick to go, they replace him. The only way your job is held is if you're in the hospital, so it's better that they're just getting him well there," I said. It was the truth, but I still had a bad feeling about it and didn't want to let on just yet.

"Can I see him?" Helen said.

Ranger smiled. "I'll see what I can do." He nodded to both of us then left to attend to his next problem.

Shoulders down, Helen slowly walked toward her own camp. I followed her, not really knowing what to say or what to do but knowing a young woman out there alone could easily be taken advantage of. "Do you have food?" I asked.

"Yes," she whispered. I didn't think eating was on her mind, but she couldn't starve herself waiting for something to happen.

"Someone will sleep at your camp until he gets back," I said. "Cotton and I can alternate."

She stopped abruptly. "Cotton?"

"Yeah. He won't mind, and between the two of us, we can make sure nobody gets any ideas."

"I can take care of myself," she said. When we got to her camp, she motioned me inside. It was small, but the way they had it set up, there was standing room, at least if you bent down some, and there was enough room on the outside of the car for a sleeping platform and still some sitting area. "You have to promise you won't tell anyone," she said as she went to the front seat of the Model T and dug around for something. When she came back to me, she was holding a brown leather holster stamped with a large US.

"Helen—"

"Shhh," she said. "I know they aren't allowed here, but Daddy has one anyway. As long as nobody finds out." She pulled a black revolver from the holster, careful not to touch the trigger, and laid it in my palm. "It's loaded. Don't touch the trigger."

The cold steel lay in my hand, and although it looked old, it had been well taken care of. On one side of the barrel, .38 Smith and Wesson was clearly engraved. I turned it over carefully in my hand, and on the other side of the barrel, just as clear, were the words Government Issue. On the side, just above the dark-brown grip, in gold lettering, was D. J. Carter, United States Army.

"It was my Uncle Dwayne's," she said. "When he was killed, my daddy got it. We keep it hidden, just in case."

I slid it back into the holster and handed it to her. "You know he'll get fired if Ranger finds that."

She put it back in her hiding place in the car. "He's not going to find it. And before you ask, yes, I know how to use it—I'm a better shot than my dad. I can take care of myself, if I need to."

I shook my head. The thought of Helen brandishing a handgun to fight off a hungry man came to mind, and no matter how independent she was, in my head, it didn't turn out well for her no matter what. "Just keep it where it is. I hope you won't ever have to use it."

When we walked out of her tent, Cotton was standing not twenty feet away, his eyes on the entrance. He didn't look very happy to see us walking out of her camp, but I motioned him over. Helen whispered beside me, "Don't tell him about the gun."

I hadn't intended to. "They sent Ben into Vegas," I said. "Pneumonia."

"Oh, damn, that ain't good," Cotton said. I shot him a look that made him backtrack on his words. "I mean for you, anyway," he said to Helen. "Don't worry. I'll make sure nobody gets any ideas." He looked her up and down, and I wondered if I needed to keep her from him.

"We'll alternate," I said as if I had any say in Helen's life. He squinted at me but then agreed.

AUTHOR NOTE: The first paragraph of this chapter is a reference to Dante's Inferno. *There was something about the men riding the ferry from hellhole to hellhole that made me think of Dante's classic, one of my all-time favorites.*

A 20-bed hospital, built by Six Companies, in Boulder City was not available to the dam workers until November 1931. Prior to that, if someone was sick or injured, they were treated at the on-site clinic or sent to the hospital in Las Vegas.

Chapter 15: Poison and Marriage

Helen

THE ONLY THING THAT kept me from crying about my daddy was the fact that I was mad enough to spit. I could take care of myself, and I didn't need a couple of hairy legs thinking I was a weak female who needed a man around to protect her. Sure, I understood how desperate some of the men in Ragtown were, and I'd seen some crazy things happen in the year I'd been there, but if I needed help, I could scream louder than a barn owl protecting her babies. What I didn't like was Ezra and especially Cotton sleeping in my dad's spot in our camp, guarding the entrance like they had any right.

After they decided that Cotton would stay with me the first night, I broke off a chunk of lye and threw it his way. Then I headed to Smitty Goon's camp to find out more about pneumonia.

Miss Goon was one of the ladies that ran the school for the children in Ragtown. She was a schoolteacher in Ohio before coming to Nevada with her brother George, who was one of the high-scalers at the dam. She and I walked to the dam site one time to watch him do his work, where he looked a lot like an acrobat high above the canyon, but she couldn't take it, and we didn't stay long. I thought it was fascinating, and I knew why people came all the way from Vegas to watch them work.

Miss Goon was about the smartest person I knew. She read more than I did, and when I needed to know something, like which plants were poisonous, how to mend a shirt, or what pneumonia was all about, I turned to her. George was sitting outside their camp with four other men, and they were talking about the conditions at work. It was getting to be an every-night discussion: the dangers at the dam.

It wasn't that I wasn't concerned. I knew it was dangerous from the stories I heard every day. But I just got tired of hearing nothing but ugly. And my dad being gone made it the ugliest place in the world to me.

George stood and reached out like he wanted to hug me. I took a step back. "Sorry to hear about your dad," he said.

"Thanks, George. Ranger said he'll be back in about a week, though."

One of the other men said under his breath to another, "Who's her dad?"

And the second man responded, "Ben Carter."

"Oh," the first man said then shook his head and looked at the ground.

I felt like I was going to throw up.

George's eyebrows scrunched together, and he slowly lowered his head. "Oh, well, that's good, then. If you need anything, let me know, okay?" Maybe George wanted to get in on the sleep-in-Helen's-tent rotation.

"Thank you. I was looking for your sister."

Miss Goon came out of their camp with a bowl of dishes and silverware and smiled at me. "I thought I heard your voice." She held the bowl in one hand and slipped her other arm through mine then started walking toward the river. "Let's let the men talk," she said.

As we walked through the camp, several people turned toward us then quickly looked away. I tried to stay focused ahead, toward the river, but I could feel their stares. When we got to a private pool near the edge of the water, Miss Goon waded in and began washing her dishes. "How are you holding up?" she asked.

I sat on the bank, crossed my legs, and rested my chin in my palms. I knew Miss Goon would tell me straight, and although I may not have liked what I heard, I needed to know. "I see how everyone is acting about my dad. It's like he's got a death sentence with pneumonia, but no one is willing to tell me that. Maybe I'm just imagining it, or maybe I'm just scared. He's all I have." I felt my chin start to tremble and stopped talking. I couldn't imagine being without him. We'd taken care of each other for so long.

Miss Goon laid her wares on the rocky shore to dry and sat beside me. A long period of silence hung between us as the sun across the water began to set behind the mountain. Finally, she said softly, "What plans have the two of you made in case of an emergency?"

She meant in case he died. I knew that, and like everyone else in that desert, yes, Daddy and I had had that discussion. It wasn't pleasant, and at the time, I hadn't wanted to hear it. And I didn't want to now. "He told me if something happened to him at work, Six Companies would give me enough money to get back to Kansas." I didn't tell her about the woman in town he had mentioned on my birthday. In fact, I wasn't sure who she was to him, but if something happened, I guessed I'd find out.

Miss Goon took in a deep breath and let it out slowly. "If he dies in an accident, yes."

The realization of her words hit me. "But not from pneumonia? I don't understand. He got pneumonia from working in the tunnels, right? So isn't that their responsibility too?"

She folded her hands in her lap and turned to me. Her eyes filled with pity, and I didn't need that, not yet.

I needed answers. I needed to know what the hell was going to happen if... "Please talk to me, Miss Goon. No one is saying anything, and I have to know."

She took in a deep breath and let it out slowly. "Every man that has died at the dam, so far, has died from pneumonia or consumption. With the exception of those that were obviously killed in an accident. And yes, the dust they breathe in all day could cause both, but they could be breathing that dust right here where they live."

"So Six Companies conveniently doesn't have to pay," I said.

"Right. The biggest problem is, it may not be pneumonia at all. That's what they will treat him for, and he could come out of it fine. But if it really isn't pneumonia, all that medicine they give him will have no effect."

I thought back to Daddy's symptoms over the past few months: coughing, headaches, feeling tired more than usual, and maybe other things going on that I hadn't noticed. I wanted to curse for not paying closer attention. "He's had all the signs of it for the past couple of months. I just didn't think it was that bad. What else could it be?"

"How much have you listened to the men talk about work? They work in a tunnel that's now about half a mile long, with not only dust but toxins from the gasoline they burn. Some say it's so thick that there's a green mist that hovers over the lights."

"Poison? Are you saying Daddy was poisoned at work? How can they let that happen, and how can they not be responsible for it?"

"They call everything pneumonia—that's how they don't take responsibility for it. And that's one of the reasons the men are talking about striking. It's not even safe for them to breathe at work."

My eyes filled with tears, and I covered my face with my hands. It couldn't be happening to us. "I need to see him. I can't just wait and see what happens." I almost choked on my words.

"Mr. Emery makes his trip into Vegas on Thursday. That's the day after tomorrow. I'm sure he won't mind you riding along."

Yes, Mr. Emery. I would speak with him first thing in the morning.

"Helen"—I felt Miss Goon's hand on my knee—"if something happens, we'll all pitch in and get you back to Kansas. I promise. George and I have some money saved, and I'm sure—"

"I don't have anyone in Kansas. I don't have anywhere to go." My mind flashed to Daddy's mention of Ida Browder, and although I was sure she told Daddy she'd help me if anything happened to him, I couldn't imagine that would mean taking me in like family. I didn't even know the woman or what her relationship with my dad had been.

Miss Goon put an arm around me and pulled me close. I rested my head on her shoulder. Just a few days before, Daddy and I had been dreaming of our life in Boulder City, and now, it was nothing but a nightmare. "Miss Goon? What do women do if they have nothing? I can get a job, but what can I do?"

"The best thing to do is get married," she said matter-of-factly.

A chill ran up my back. I always thought you married someone you loved, not someone who was going to feed you. I thought of Betsy doing whatever she could to find a husband so she and Pepper didn't starve. It was all wrong. "What else?" I asked. Maybe I could work in a library somewhere, or at a restaurant like Karen at Browder's Café.

"Real jobs for women are hard to find. A lot turn to... other things." She shook her head. "You're pretty and young, and there are a lot of men right here who can't keep their eyes off you. And you have a car. Don't say no to an offer of someone taking care of you. The alternative is not pretty at all."

"Neither is marrying someone I don't love," I said.

She pulled me closer. "No. But we are women. Our choices are limited. We have to be smart. The idea of falling in love is best saved for the books you read. This is real life. Survival is our first priority."

I began to cry openly. I couldn't hold back the tears any longer, and I needed to get it all out. The hurt, the anger, the resentment, the idea that Daddy might suffer, and for what? So he could die and I could starve? I cried at the idea of having to marry a man and take care of him in a lot of different ways just so I could have a can of beans once a day. Starving to death seemed like a better fate.

Miss Goon wept with me. I didn't know if it was because she felt sorry for me or because she felt sorry for us. That was our lot, simply because we were born women.

AUTHOR NOTE: PENICILLIN did not come into widespread use until the 1940s. In the 1930s, pneumonia became so prevalent it was at one time listed as the third leading cause of death. So pneumonia became a catchall for anyone exhibiting the symptoms. Poisoning from the toxic fumes in the tunnels was either not recognized or ignored. It is unknown how many people whose death certificates listed pneumonia as the cause were actually victims of poisoning from breathing the toxic fumes in the tunnels.

Chapter 16: I'd Be a Good Wife

Helen

WITH THE WINDOWS ROLLED up, I locked myself in the Model T and waited until I heard Cotton snoring. It was so hot the windows had steamed up, but it was better than sharing open air with a man I did not want in my tent. Quietly, I snuck out and past Cotton. He stank like an old racehorse, obviously not taking my lye soap request seriously. It was going to take forever for me to get that stench out of my tent.

I walked quietly through the camp, conscious of my feet crunching the rocks, hoping not to wake anyone. I slipped down to the river and sat under my Joshua tree, watching the twinkle of stars reflecting on the water.

Get married. The thought of it made me ill, not because I didn't want to someday, to a man I loved. But even Daddy had told me that I should not say no to a man who wanted to take care of me. I thought about my other options, and other than being one of the ladies I heard about on the hill behind the Railroad Pass, I couldn't think of any.

I did have the car, and at least if something happened to my dad, that would be my dowry, what I could offer someone. Maybe I could use it as a bargaining chip to get a proposal from someone who didn't make me want to throw a boulder at his head. I tried to picture myself with Cotton, George Goon, or one of the other single men I knew, but my mind settled on Ezra. He was the only one I could say I could care about, and if I tried not to lie to myself, I could care about him a lot.

I picked up a handful of pebbles and threw them violently toward the water. I didn't get to pick a husband, though—I had to let someone choose me.

But I was getting ahead of myself. First, I needed to talk to my dad and see for myself how sick he was. Then I could make some decisions. I was seventeen. I was a woman, not a child, and I needed to start acting like one. I fell asleep with my head against my tree and woke to the sounds of the day shifters getting ready for work. I heard Cotton yelling my name and got to him to shush him before he woke up all the children in camp.

He scowled and pointed a dirty finger at me. "I can't protect you if you sneak off in the middle of the night. Don't do that again."

I knew he meant well, but how dare he feel that he had the right to get mad at me. I could do as I pleased. I didn't say a word but went back to my camp and opened the entrance wide to start airing it out before the sun came up. I gathered Cotton's sheet and put it outside, sprinkling vanilla on Daddy's pallet, where Cotton had slept, before taking the sheet to the water's edge for a good scrubbing with lye.

Cotton was sitting outside my tent when I got back from the water, eating a can of beans. When he was done, he handed it to me and headed to the ferry. George Goon stopped by to see how I was feeling that morning on his way to the ferry, and I wondered again if he was trying to get on the sentinel rotation. He couldn't have snored any louder than Cotton. I waited to see if Ezra would check on me before work, but he didn't, and my heart fell. I held my head up and straightened my shoulders. That was okay. Tonight, Ezra would stay in my tent, and I'd do whatever I had to do to make sure he knew I'd be a good wife.

In case I needed to be one real soon.

AUTHOR NOTE: THE MODEL T Ford, available in various styles, was produced from 1908 to 1927. You may have heard a Model T referred to as a "Tin Lizzie," and the story behind that nickname is kind of interesting. In 1922, a man named Noel Bullock entered his unpainted, hoodless, beat-up Model T, which he had named Old Liz, in a race in Pike's Peak, Colorado. The crowd jokingly called Old Liz "Tin Lizzie," because in her condition, she reminded them of a tin can. But Old Liz unexpectedly won the race, and it was reported in newspapers across the country, leading to the new nickname "Tin Lizzie," which was given to all Model Ts.

Chapter 17: All Dolled Up

Ezra

I DIDN'T KNOW THE GUY they got to fill in for Ben to be a Jumbo driver, and after a few hours, I decided he'd never driven a truck like that before. He was slow, had to back it up at least three times to get us straight against the wall for us to drill, and smiled too much. He seemed happy to be in that pit, but I guessed if he was starving yesterday, the place might have looked like heaven. I gave him a week, if he lasted that long, and he'd see that it was far from paradise.

Yesterday, after Ben had started coughing uncontrollably and Frenchie sent him down to the infirmary, I figured that they would give him some kind of medication, cool him off, and send him back to work or at least home for the day. I was as surprised as Helen when Ranger came by to tell us he had been taken to Vegas. Something must have happened, or Doc must have seen something else that would have warranted sending him to the hospital.

During my morning break, I cornered Frenchie for information. Ben was my friend, and Helen deserved to know the truth. The pain in her eyes last night was so intense that just thinking about it made my stomach hurt. Frenchie saw me coming and let out a long sigh. He looked just as tired as the rest of us, although he didn't do the same kind of labor we did. He did have to deal with the guys in suits as well as those of us covered in muck, so I figured his labor came in a different form. "What's wrong, Deal?" he asked.

"What happened with Ben Carter yesterday? Ranger Williams said he was sent to Vegas." I pulled a snubbed Camel from my pocket and searched for a match. Frenchie held a small box out to me.

"Doc said when he got to the shack, he was coughing up blood. A lot of it, I guess, and they couldn't get it to stop. I sent him out of here just in time."

Just in time. Sounded to me like he should have been sent weeks ago. "He's got a daughter, you know. It's just the two of them out in the desert."

Frenchie looked down and slowly shook his head. "I guess Ranger can get ahold of the state to take her in or get her back to family."

I took a deep drag off my cigarette. "No family. And she's not a kid. She's seventeen."

"Damn," he said. Damn was right. If she had been a boy, she might have been able to lie about her age and get a job—if not at the dam, somewhere. If she were a kid, the state would at least take her in and feed her and give her a place to live. But she was a seventeen-year-old girl, and that meant she would be on her own. And there weren't many things she could do, at least not many that were good enough for Helen. "She might want to find a husband fast."

I threw my butt on the rocks and ground it with my boot. That was probably going to be her only option, if Ben didn't make it, and from what I'd seen out there, when they started spitting up blood, it wasn't good. Every woman was looking for a husband, though. I heard they hung out in town in front of the single men's dormitories, even though only a few men were living there, and at the new casino at the Pass. Some even put ads in the paper, which, rumor had it, was what Clive Allen's widow had done. I'd always known Helen as a carefree woman, childlike in her love of the outdoors that everyone else seemed to hate, smart, and independent. I couldn't imagine her mixing in with those others that seemed so desperate.

"Damn," I muttered to myself as I went back to the tunnel. It had been barely a month since I buried my sister, and as much as I hated to admit it, I was starting to get used to being on my own. Not much I could do now, but when I got to town, I could do what I wanted, go where I wanted to go, without having anything to tie me down. But I could step up for Helen—after all, I did like her, and I couldn't deny I'd been having some feelings for her. But did I want to take her on as my responsibility?

At lunchtime, while most of the men were occupied with talk of the union, I took inventory of the single guys I worked with. Moose Martin was a good guy, but he liked to party in his off time. Sam Cox liked to fight and could be downright mean, so I couldn't imagine how he'd react to a woman that spoke her mind. Tex Mahoney gambled all his paycheck away, Molly Woodward was dumber than a rock, and I was pretty sure Beau Dandy liked boys. And of course, there was Cotton. I couldn't quite picture Helen with him. Or maybe I didn't want to.

Pete and I sat away from the others, trying not to get involved in the IWW talk. I finished my sandwich and took a big gulp from my water bag. "Pete, what do you think about getting married?"

He smiled and patted my shoulder. "I don't think you're my type, Easy."

"You know what I mean." I was trying to be serious, even though I knew with Pete, that was sometimes difficult.

"Well, I've never been with a woman I can't live without, and as long as there are those willing to give it up for free—or a few quarters, as the case may be—I can't say the idea makes much sense to me." He opened his second sandwich and took a big bite, talking with his mouth full. "You're only, what, twenty? You in love already?"

I wasn't even sure what being in love felt like, but I did like Helen. I shrugged, not knowing what to say.

"I guess there are some advantages. Assuming the woman—and you are talking about a woman, right?—isn't too ugly or boring or she can't cook. And it helps if she hasn't got eight sisters and a mean old daddy or a mom that wants to make your life miserable."

I shook my head. "She hasn't got any family, and she's definitely not ugly or boring."

"Oh, so you do already have one picked out!" he said.

"No, I don't." Or did I? Damn. Damn. Damn.

Pete stood up and bent to either side, stretching his back. "It's your money, Easy. If that's what you want, then do it. Right now, this tunnel is my woman, and I'm ready to drill another hole in her."

I glanced at Cotton as I stood to join Pete, and he was ears open to Gavin Sweet, talking about the union. He was a follower, no doubt, but I figured that wasn't all bad. He was a good worker, and I knew he liked Helen. And who knew, Ben might live through it. Maybe it was best if I waited to see what happened before I made any decisions that would affect me for the rest of my life.

THE SUN WAS A HAIR past straight-up noon when I walked back in to Ragtown. Although the loss of our twelve-hour shifts had put a dent in my ability to replenish my savings, I sure didn't mind having the extra time to sleep, even if it was in the one-hundred-ten-degree heat. I'd gotten into a routine of sleeping for a few hours in the afternoon, getting up and getting dinner, then going back to sleep before the sun went down, ready for my four a.m. start time in the tunnels. I guessed the loss of hours hurt the family men more than someone like me.

After grabbing my chunk of ice and a soda from Emery's, I walked through camp toward my tent and saw Helen coming toward me. She was wearing the yellow dress she got for her birthday, with her red hair hanging loosely around her shoulders, pulled to one side with a butterfly clip of colored stones. I stopped walking and almost dropped my ice. She was a vision amidst the dust of the camp, and when she saw me and smiled, I felt a tug in my groin. It took me a minute to notice the brown sack she was carrying, and I made myself move to take it from her.

"Where have you been, all dolled up?" I said. She seemed to be acting like herself again, not as angry or sad as she had been the day before. I hoped she'd been to see Ben and that things were looking good for him. That would have been a big relief in a lot of ways.

"I've been to town," she said. "I'm going to make stew for dinner. I hope you like stew," she said.

She knew I liked stew—and especially her stew. That was what she made every Sunday, and she always made extra. It was a special treat from eating out of cans all week. But it wasn't Sunday.

"You went to town by yourself?" It was a decent walk into Boulder City, and the highway was full of trucks and cars going back and forth to the work site, so it wasn't safe. And thinking about Helen in her pretty yellow dress catching a ride with someone she didn't know made me cringe.

"Miss Goon and Pepper went with me. I applied for some jobs at the café, the new candy house, and the movie theatre. They just started building the hospital, but I filled out a paper there, too, just in case. There are more things going up every day, and surely, someone will hire me." She seemed determined to take care of herself, and she also seemed hopeful and in good spirits, and I didn't want to dampen her mood.

"Have you heard anything about your dad?"

She swallowed hard and shook her head, forcing another smile. "No, but Mr. Emery is letting me ride into Vegas with him tomorrow, and I'm confident he's just fine. Probably flirting with the nurses and telling them silly jokes."

Several people were watching us—well, watching her. No one walked around in a dress made for parties in the middle of the day. And if they did, they sure wouldn't look as good in it as she did right then. When we got to her camp, she took the sack from me and shooed me away. "Go get your nap. I have my chores to do, and then I'll have dinner waiting for you when you get up. And if you have anything that needs washed, bring it to me so I can—"

"Helen, you don't have to do all this."

She scrunched her brow together briefly then smiled again. That was a lot of smiling that I didn't think was all real. "It's just my way of saying thank you for watching out for me while my dad is away. I'm sure he'll thank you himself when he gets back. And it's no trouble at all," she said. "Now, go to sleep. I've got work to do."

AUTHOR NOTE: Putting ads in the local newspapers to find a husband was done by quite a few women during the Great Depression, many with small children. While researching for Ragtown, *I viewed a lot of those ads and was saddened by the idea that they felt it was their only means of survival.*

At this point, Helen is really starting to understand that she is going to have to be proactive in order to survive. She still has hopes that her dad will recover, but if the worst happens, she has to be prepared to get married or take care of herself in any way she can. The reality was, a seventeen-year-old girl living alone in a car wasn't likely to get a job, but she was determined to try.

Chapter 18: A Better Man

Ezra

SLEEPING IN HELEN AND Ben's camp was a bit different from sleeping in mine, and I had to say, I did like it better. In my tent, the sun was always present, the cheap canvas not enough to keep the rays out completely. Ben and Helen used bits of plyboard and tarp under their canvas, which made their tent dark on the inside. That was probably why I slept more than my usual couple of hours. The evening shift was long gone for the work site by the time I got up.

I grabbed the bar of lye that Helen had left next to my sleep roll and headed for the water. I found her sitting under a Joshua tree, reading the book I gave her. She was wearing her overalls again, and her hair was tucked under her cap. "Sorry I slept so long," I said. I wanted to strip down and take a long wash, but I wasn't too keen on doing so with her sitting there. Instead, I walked into the water with my clothes on and cleaned myself and my clothes at the same time.

She closed her book and set it beside her. "I'm glad you got some sleep. A few hours here and there can't be good for you. And I've got the stew ready." She looked up at the sun and laughed. "I'm sure it's still warm."

She didn't seem to mind that I was bathing right in front of her. I took my shirt off and scrubbed it with soap, rinsed it, wrung it, threw it on the rocks on shore, then washed my upper body. I did the same with my jeans, but instead of throwing them, I put them back on after washing my lower parts. They'd dry just the same, whether I was wearing them or not.

Helen waited for me to finish, then we walked back to her camp together, me dripping wet and her leading the way. We passed a large group of men, day shifters, sitting in a circle, talking about the possibility of a strike. Cotton was among them, and when he saw us, he jumped up and joined us.

"I hear you're goin' to see your daddy tomorrow." He was looking at Helen as if I weren't even there.

I walked behind them and watched, trying to imagine them together. Helen was almost as tall as he was, and he was almost as skinny as she. I guess size didn't matter, but the way she leaned away from him and kept turning back to look at me made me think she wasn't too keen on the idea either.

"Yes," she said. "He's going to be fine. I know it."

Cotton dug in his pocket and pulled out two quarters and handed them to her. "Here, you'll be gone most of the day if you're going to Vegas, so make sure you get something to eat. They won't take that company scrip up there."

Helen stopped walking and looked at the coins in her hand. "Oh, I can't take that, Cotton. Thank you, but I just can't—"

He stuck his hands in his pockets and refused to take the money back. "Sure you can. Ben can pay me back when he gets out, but in the meantime, I said I was going to take care of you, and that's what I'm going to do."

She looked back at me, and I shrugged. Damn, I should have thought of that.

"Thank you," she said. "If there's something I can do..."

"Well, now that you say that, there is something..."

Helen crossed her arms over her chest and lowered her head.

"You can smell that stew all over camp, and if you happen to have an extra bowl..."

She let out a long sigh. "Sure, Cotton. There's plenty. And thank you again," she said.

As the three of us walked back to Helen's camp, I looked at Cotton again. Maybe he was a better man than I gave him credit for.

AUTHOR NOTE: BECAUSE it was so hot in the desert, the residents in Ragtown didn't cook on an open fire every day. Sunday stew on a day other than Sunday would have been a rare treat and saved for a special occasion. But Helen was pulling out all the stops to attract Ezra and pulling Cotton closer instead.

Chapter 19: Wobblies and the Blue Room

Ezra

AFTER A GOOD, LONG sleep, a good scrubbing at the river, and two bowls of the best stew in town, I felt revitalized. I didn't go back to sleep before my shift last night. Instead, I stayed up and talked to Helen until the three a.m. ferry was ready to haul us back to work. Maybe it was the company that had me feeling so good.

We'd talked about our childhoods, hers growing up in Kansas without a momma, and mine, mostly the good stuff before my mother died. I skipped any mention of my father, his cruelty not something I wanted to bring out. I told her I had wanted to join the army but didn't because Grace was more important to me, and I wanted to take care of her.

Her eyes were full of life. "My uncle Dwayne was a soldier. Daddy wanted to go, but he had me, so he really couldn't."

"Yeah, that's all I ever wanted to be when I grew up." I threw my arms wide. "And yet, here I am."

She was quiet for a minute, and when she did speak, it came out in a whisper. "Well, there's nothing holding you back now."

"Things have changed. It's like my life was going one way then suddenly took a turn. And now, I don't know if I can move it back. It's not easy to change."

She laughed and rolled her eyes at me in that carefree way of hers. "You are working in a hell zone to change the course of a river that has been flowing one way for a thousand years. How hard can it be for one man to change his own course?"

I had to smile. She'd made it sound so easy, and yet, I couldn't deny that it was still a possibility. Maybe a dream, but with Helen, it seemed as if dreaming was okay to do.

It didn't take but a few hours of being on the Jumbo for that good feeling to be lost to a memory. Washed in the tunnel's blue-green haze, I wasn't sure what time it was or if the sun had even come up yet. The work had started to slow, and everyone was getting tired and restless from breathing the fumes and gasses trapped in the cave. The air was thicker than usual, and everyone seemed to feel the extra weight.

Hurry Up Crowe had been walking the work site since before our shift began, talking to the supervisors, pointing, and asking questions. After witnessing the death of Clive Allen, we all assumed he recognized the dangers that lurked inside the tunnels. His presence was all the talk in between the morning blasts.

"Maybe he is ready to make some changes."

"He's got to see how dangerous it is in here."

"Hell, we can barely breathe."

I made it to the mouth of the tunnel for my break and looked at the sky. It must have been about eight a.m. Frank Crowe was standing right outside the tunnel, and for a brief second, our eyes met. I tipped my hard-boiled hat to him, but he didn't seem to notice. With one last look down number three, Frank Crowe nodded once to Frenchie then walked back to the bridge that provided passage to the Nevada side of the site. Hands clasped behind his back and walking with a good stride, he looked at the entrances of the other three tunnels. Each time, he gave a single nod.

Frenchie called for an all-man break. The Jumbo drove the drilling crew out, leaving the muckers to finish the debris removal from the previous blast. As the men unloaded from the truck, Frenchie motioned for the driver to go back and get the muckers, which meant whatever he had to tell us was big news.

"Vaughn, Dandridge, Baker." Frenchie gestured for the three men to follow him to an area outside of earshot of the rest of us. Cotton shrugged and followed.

"What the hell?" Pete stood next to me, looking in the direction of Frenchie and the three men. He glanced back occasionally to see the progress of the Jumbo hauling the muckers.

"This don't look good," Tex Mahoney said.

I was looking at Frenchie's back but tried to focus on the faces of the men he was talking to. Frenchie used his hands while he spoke. Something he said caused Jimmy Baker to kick dirt at Frenchie and Beau Dandy to throw his hard-boiled hat to the ground. Cotton stood motionless, his face devoid of emotion.

Frenchie walked back to the rest of us, Beau Dandy yelling at him from behind the entire way. "You gotta be kidding. I can barely feed myself now."

"They cut us back a nickel an hour. Said they gotta save some money since we's movin' so slow!" Jimmy Baker yelled to the other men as they approached the group.

"Just the nippers?"

"And the blowmen," Beau Dandy said.

"For now. First the nippers and blowers, then everyone. You know how that works!"

Cotton said nothing. He walked straight toward Pete and me, and we waited for the Jumbo to arrive. We knew there was more.

Once everyone was gathered, Frenchie raised his hand to quiet everyone. Once he had our attention, he scratched the back of his neck and tried not to look into anyone's eyes. "The problem, they say, is that it takes the muckers too long to get that stuff out after a blast. The drilling crew is spending too much time waiting."

"We get it out before the second blast."

"Yeah, you try it, Frenchie," someone shouted.

Frenchie waited for the chatter to die down. "So in order to speed things up a little, the drill team is gonna be mucking, too, until this hole is through to the other side."

"What?"

"I ain't no mucker!"

"You can't throw us down in that scum!"

Mucking was without a doubt the hardest and dirtiest job, usually given to the guys that didn't speak English well enough to complain much. For the drillers and powdermen to be asked to muck in addition to our own jobs meant fewer breaks and a reduction in status. My heart began to beat faster as I realized Crowe and Six Companies were unconcerned about our safety, sure, but they also wanted us to put ourselves in further peril to get the work done as quickly as possible. I was numbed by the realization, my hopes of some relief quickly dashed and replaced with a mixture of anger and hopelessness. Crowe was obviously banking on the idea that most of us were desperate enough to do whatever it took to keep the job, and although I wanted to yell, and I would have loved to hit something, in the end, I was just that desperate.

I looked around the work site, squinting in the sun. Groups of workers stood at the entrances to the other three tunnels, and they didn't look any happier than our group. "They're telling everyone," I said.

One of the guys, covered in soot, walked to the front of our group. Under the dirt, I could tell it was Gavin Sweet, the IWW man who'd been hanging around lately. He spoke loudly enough to be heard over the bicker. "Men, they can't do nothing on this project without you. They aren't trying to make it better. They are cutting your wages! And that's just the beginning. I've seen it before."

Tex Mahoney walked from the crowd and stood beside Gavin. "They're gonna kill us if we let them. I'm not gonna let them!"

Frenchie removed himself from the crowd and reached for his two-way radio as others slowly laid down their equipment and joined Gavin and Tex. Cotton sighed, gave me a brief twitch of his lips, and joined the group. Pete and I stayed back and were joined by a handful of others who had no intention of walking off the job.

The noise from the crowds at all four tunnels increased in volume as the number of strikers grew. Up on the canyon wall, the high-scalers reeled their lines to the top of the rocks, standing down to support the workers below. The ever-present sounds of machinery at work in the canyon had been replaced with the growls of a thousand angry men. My small group backed up, separating ourselves from the strikers.

"This can't be good," Pete said, pointing at the bridge. Four men were coming across, two in uniform, carrying weapons. I didn't recognize any of them, but Pete's groans were noticeable.

"Oh no," he said as he sank closer to the canyon wall, trying to remain out of sight.

The lead man in uniform threw Frenchie a shotgun and said, "Consider yourself officially deputized." He walked to the front of the gathered workers. The other union busters surrounded the group, weapons at the ready.

The lead man smiled and looked around, listening as the crowd continued to protest. Then he pulled a side pistol from his holster and shot in the air, calling for quiet. "Good morning. Most of you don't know me."

Pete had gone pale.

"You know him?" I asked.

Pete steadied himself against the canyon wall with his left hand, holding his right on his stomach, fighting off an invisible pang.

Gavin stepped forward. "I know who you are. The Las Vegas chief of police has no jurisdiction here. We're in Arizona."

The chief smiled again and stepped closer to Gavin. "Well, let's see. You are right there. But as a federal deputy, I can come across that bridge, right?" He reached in his pocket and pulled out a familiar badge, breathed on it, wiped it on his shirt, then flashed it for everyone to see. "Pretty thing, ain't it? Got it this morning."

Gavin continued, "These men are on strike. They haven't broken any laws."

"That's a good thing. We're here to make sure that don't happen." He stepped closer to Gavin and, after studying him briefly, motioned to his feet. "Those sure are some fancy boots. I'd bet money you aren't here to just dig holes in this mountain. What's your name?"

Gavin raised his chin. "Gavin Sweet. And I am a member of the Industrial Workers of the World, and these men are—"

The chief cut him off with a laugh. "I figured you were one of them Wobblies." He pulled a piece of paper from his pocket and scanned it quickly. He smiled about halfway down the page and looked back at Gavin. "Been hanging out up around Texas Acres, Sweet?"

"May have."

The chief waved the worn paper in the air. "This here is a list of people that we are supposed to treat real special. And guess what? Your name is on the list, Gavin Sweet." He waved to one of the men with him, who came forward and held Gavin by the arm.

"Hey. You can't do this!"

I shook my head when Gavin tried to challenge the chief again. I didn't have much experience with the law, but I knew if I was surrounded by a pack of men carrying badges and guns, I was better off saying as little as possible.

"Do what? My men and I are here to escort all the strikers off the site, peaceful-like." He waved the paper at Gavin again. "But you head Wobblies get a personal escort. Ain't that nice? I'm even going to put you and some of your friends up in my fine Vegas hotel for a few days. It's called the Blue Room. Maybe you've heard of it?"

Pete vomited at the chief's mention of the Blue Room, the nickname for the infamous Las Vegas jail. I moved a little closer to the rocky wall behind me, careful to stay out of the spray. The sound caught the chief's attention. He waited for Pete to finish.

"Hey, Red. Whatcha doin' over there?"

Pete spoke softly, "I'm not striking, sir."

"Something tells me you been to my hotel."

Pete swallowed hard. "Yes, sir."

The chief smiled. "Good. Be sure and tell your buddies here how nice it is, will you? That's where we are going to be keeping the troublemakers."

He gave his list to Frenchie. "Check them off. If they're on that list, they're coming with Gavin and me. Otherwise, if they aren't working, they're leaving."

AUTHOR NOTE: "HURRY Up" Crowe was the nickname given to Frank Crowe, the general construction superintendent of the dam project. He was on a deadline to complete the project and wanted everything done quickly. In other words, everything was a "hurry up" to Mr. Crowe. According to the contract with the US government signed in 1931, Six Companies had seven years to finish the project, or they would be subject to penalties that would come out of their final pay-

ment. Under Frank "Hurry Up" Crowe, the project was completed two years early.

Chapter 20: Fremont Street

Helen

MR. EMERY LIKED TO get things done early, and I was sure glad for that. I hadn't slept all night, not since Ezra went to work, thinking about my trip to Vegas that morning. I was in my yellow dress again—I wanted to look pretty for my dad. I was waiting at Emery's Store at six a.m., and by seven, we left the Wash in his pickup truck, beginning our two-hour drive to Las Vegas.

Though Ezra, Cotton, and even Miss Smitty and George, seemed all doom and gloom about my situation, Mr. Emery wasn't, and I appreciated his optimism. He was a religious man and told me he'd been praying for us, and I appreciated that too. I had certainly done my share in the past few days, but a little outside prayer never hurt.

"There sure is a lot of traffic out here this morning. More than usual," Mr. Emery said as we passed the road into Boulder City and then McKeeversville. "It's a good thing we got an early start."

But I wasn't watching the traffic. I stared out the window. I hadn't been that far from Ragtown since I first got to the desert. I'd been into Boulder City a handful of times, and I'd seen the tents set up among the construction there. I also knew McKeeversville was another Hooverville—not as big as Ragtown but people living in a makeshift community to work on the dam. What I wasn't prepared for was the number of people that populated the open area along the highway.

A seemingly endless number of tents, cardboard boxes, and stray mattresses lined the road and continued back into the empty desert. For miles in any direction, the makeshift living quarters of hundreds—thousands—looked like a junkyard full of rats. I tried to avoid the hungry eyes of the dirty children as we drove past.

"You okay?" Mr. Emery asked.

I faced forward, trying to concentrate on the road. "I had no idea there were so many."

"More coming every day," he said.

As we topped the hill at Railroad Pass, I saw the new casino below, a white stucco building with flashing lights. It looked foreign against the desert landscape. There were several small shacks behind the casino, no bigger than outhouses.

"What are those?" I asked Mr. Emery.

He said nothing as a thin woman in a simple cotton dress came out of one of the shacks with one man, only to reenter with another.

"Oh," I said.

Mr. Emery cleared his throat. "It's sad, one of the many side effects of a bad economy. Society begins to loosen morals, and I hate to think what comes next if we don't get this country turned around real soon."

I felt the heat rise in my face. I wasn't naive enough that I didn't know about prostitution. There was a time when I, too, would have blamed the loose morals of the women involved, but after the past year, I was starting to understand it differently. Those women were victims of a society that chose to push them aside and offered them no other options for survival. I didn't say that to Mr. Emery. I doubted he would agree.

We passed more tents and shanties on the open desert floor. Mr. Emery started pointing them out: Texas Acres, Little Oklahoma, Dee's Camp, as if they were actual communities instead of a large, loose grouping of desperate men, women, and children. They all seemed to run together, making the area larger than Ragtown and McKeeversville combined, with the dwellings more tightly clustered and without the benefit of a river nearby.

As we continued to drive the dirt road leading to Las Vegas, the number of camps dwindled until we were in open desert again. Three Las Vegas police cars passed us, heading back toward the Pass. Shortly after, two more followed. "Looks like there might be some trouble," Mr. Emery said.

"With all these people, how could there not be?" I asked. "They all came for jobs at the dam? I know it's a big project, but are there that many jobs?"

"No, there aren't. But I guess things are worse everywhere else. At least here, they have a chance at a job."

Although I had been excited, even optimistic, about seeing my dad when we left Ragtown, I felt a horrible sense of dread cover me. He had to be okay. He had one of those jobs, and if he lost it…

As we pulled into Las Vegas, the streets were thick with unemployed men and their women and children. It was barely nine o'clock in the morning, and they were already lining up for a Red Cross soup line.

Mr. Emery continued driving through the populated town then turned onto a paved street. "This is Fremont Street, kind of the main road."

We passed a bakery, a hardware store, a meat market, a drug store, and a restaurant—pretty much everything anyone could have wanted was on the main street. There were also casinos, the Las Vegas Club and the Northern Club casino. It was almost like two cities had merged into one: the hustle of a city of entertainment and prosperity, mixed with the obvious presence of the desperate and unemployed.

He turned left on 2nd Street then parked the truck in an open spot in the middle of the block. He pointed at the post office on the corner. "I need to run in there real quick. Then I'll take you to the hospital. It won't take me but a minute."

I smoothed my dress and placed my hands in my lap to wait. Across the street, a three-story structure loomed on the corner. The Apache Hotel, one of its signs said. I was still staring when Mr. Emery came back to the truck.

"Just opened two days ago. I hear it's already full," he said as he got in the truck. His face was lit up like a kid with a new pair of shoes. I briefly wondered if Mr. Emery was a gambling man. "Look at those signs. Neon, I think they call it. I bet they are something to see at night. And those canopies didn't come cheap. Keep the sun off the patrons, I suppose. Wanna go look?"

I trusted Mr. Emery. I'd never been given any reason not to, and I knew he was trying to be nice and show me a little bit of Las Vegas, knowing I hadn't been out of Ragtown. And I appreciated it. But I didn't think my daddy would be too happy to know that I went there to see him, dressed in my pretty yellow dress, and ended up in the Apache Hotel. I was curious, but I had seen enough for one day. "No, I think I just want to go see my dad."

Mr. Emery started the truck then turned around and headed back down 2nd Street in the opposite direction. "Fair enough. Maybe another time."

Yes. Another time. I was sure of it.

AUTHOR NOTE: ONE OF my favorite exchanges in this book is between Mr. Emery and Helen about the prostitutes in the shacks behind Railroad Pass. Their differing opinions about the relationship

between prostitution and the economy is shown in their age, gender, and socioeconomic differences.

Chapter 21: He Was My Daddy

Helen

THE LAS VEGAS HOSPITAL was a two-story building, white with curved arches at the front, situated in the middle of the block on 2nd Street, right off Fremont. It was as big as the Apache Hotel but not nearly as flashy. It was difficult to tell whether the tents on the front grounds were additional space for patients or simply those of families who had made camp. Mr. Emery parked his truck in front of the building, and I didn't move.

"Are you sure you don't want me to go in with you?" he said.

"No, I'll be fine," I said. I felt like I'd already put Mr. Emery out by coming with him, and I didn't need him holding my hand while I visited my dad. I was a woman, I reminded myself, and I needed to start acting like one.

"Okay. It's almost 9:30. I'll be right here in two hours. You tell that daddy of yours to hurry up and get well. I'm sure there's a house with your name on it in Boulder City, and the sooner he gets back, the sooner you can be in it."

I smiled when I thought of the pretty little town by the river. The city park, the movie theatre, the company store. We were almost there. "I will, Mr. Emery. Thank you," I said.

The entrance to the hospital was blocked with people, and I squeezed by women holding babies to get in the door. Organized chaos was the first thing that came to mind once I was inside, and I didn't know where to go or who to ask for directions. I looked around for a reception desk and saw several women taking information from people who were most likely wanting to be seen. There was a sign that read Take a Number, so I did. Mine was thirty-two, and I sat on the floor in the waiting area, since all the seats were full.

A *Las Vegas Age* paper lay on the floor next to me, so I picked it up and scanned the headlines: "Midwestern Drought Worsens," "Number of Failed U.S. Banks Tops 2000," "Unemployment Doubles Over Last Year." I didn't want to read that. I could just look outside to see the sad state of humans, and I doubted the words in print could show the true suffering that was going on. I flipped through and settled on the want ads, but after scanning a dozen ads with titles like "Woman Seeking Husband," I folded the paper up and placed it back on the floor. I wondered if any of the ads I'd read were Betsy Allen's, and then I thought of Pepper. I needed to take him up on the mountain again, let him feel the warm air and the sun on his face before he and his mother went off to start anew. He had really grown on me, and I would miss him.

One of the women at the desks called number twenty-five, and I tried to lose myself in thoughts of better days to come while I waited. I waited almost an hour until another woman called my number. I quickly made my way to her post and sat in the chair before her.

"State your name," she said without looking up from her pad. She was an older woman. Gray wisps of hair strayed from a bun tied on top of her head, and her eyes looked heavy, as if she hadn't slept very well.

"Helen Carter," I said. "But I'm not a patient."

She stopped writing and looked at me. "What can I do for you, Miss Carter?"

"My father, Ben Carter, was brought here on Tuesday from the dam. I'm here to see him," I said.

"Tuesday, you say." She flipped back in her notebook, scanning the names. She grabbed another sheet of paper and scanned it as well. "Give me a minute," she said then got up from her seat and went out of my sight.

I sat, trying to be patient, although my stomach was turning circles with the excitement of being so close to seeing my dad. It had been a difficult few days, and I just needed him to smile and tell me everything was going to be okay.

The woman returned with a taller, younger woman who was wearing a white dress with light-blue sleeves and had a white cover over her blond hair. "This is Nurse Sandy," the first woman said.

Nurse Sandy came from behind the counter and held out a hand to me. "Your name is Helen? Can you come with me?"

I smiled tightly and followed her down a long hall with doors on either side. She opened the last door on the left and ushered me inside. There were lockers on the wall, and a few nurses were putting their caps on in front of a mirror over a sink. I looked back at Nurse Sandy.

"I've got the doctor coming to talk to you. It'll just be a minute. In the meantime—"

She stopped when the door opened, and a tall man wearing white came in. He looked at Nurse Sandy, and she placed her hand on my shoulder.

"This is Helen, Dr. Reed. She's here about her father, Ben Carter."

She handed Dr. Reed a chart with a piece of paper clipped to the front, which he read carefully. When he finished, he turned his attention to me and motioned for me to sit on the bench in the middle of the room.

"Is he okay?" I was hoping he wasn't contagious. I'd come all that way to see him.

"Where's your mother, Helen?" the doctor asked.

"It's just my dad and me. Please, tell me what's wrong."

He looked at Nurse Sandy, who sat next to me on the bench and reached for my hand. I let her take it. Her hands were warm and steady but did little to stop mine from shaking.

"I'm sorry, Helen. He passed yesterday morning. There was nothing we could do."

His words echoed in my head so loudly that I felt them pounding at the base of my skull. What? I shook my head slowly. I tried to speak, but the words were stuck in my throat. This couldn't be happening. I swallowed hard, the ache piercing my heart as it burned its way to the pit of my stomach. "But he was..." I whispered. He was my daddy.

Nurse Sandy released my hand, put an arm around me, and said something, but all I heard were the words of Dr. Reed, over and over again. "He passed yesterday morning. There was nothing we could do."

The doctor wrote something on a sheet in the chart he still had in front of him then pulled it out and handed it to me. I couldn't look. The walls in the small room were starting to close in on me just as an overwhelming smell of antiseptic that I hadn't noticed before hit me, adding to my queasiness. I had to get out of there. My heart was beating faster, and I started to sweat.

I stood, and Nurse Sandy steadied me as my legs threatened to buckle. I could feel my body filling with a mixture of sorrow, anger, and disbelief, and I stumbled back down the hallway, oblivious to those around me, fueled only by my need to be outside the confines of the hospital.

I fought the tears that were building inside of me, knowing that if I let them flow, they would never stop. As I collapsed on the grass outside, I wiped the moisture from my eyes and willed myself to hold it in, hold it down, allow the numbness to settle in my soul. The families who passed me by couldn't see my agony, most likely blinded by their own. I was one girl, wounded, invisible, and alone.

AUTHOR NOTE: I SPENT a lot of time researching the layout of downtown Las Vegas and the Las Vegas hospital in order to make this section as descriptively accurate as possible. I had even found a brief reference to a Dr. Reed in my research, so I used his name for my fictional doctor. As for the layout of Fremont Street, I found a 1931 Las Vegas phone book and, using the addresses shown for various businesses, drew a map from the Apache Hotel to the hospital, putting in the business names along the way.

Chapter 22: Far from Paradise

Helen

WHEN MR. EMERY PULLED to the curb, I walked to his truck without looking back at the hospital. I didn't say anything, just handed him the paper that Dr. Reed had given me. I looked straight ahead at the throngs of people wandering the streets as he drove me the three blocks to Palm Funeral Home, the same one that had come to pick up Grace and the baby over a month before.

Mr. Emery sat with me in a small waiting area, and I tried to focus my attention on the green curtains and brown tiled floors, ignoring the painting of Jesus that dominated the room and the instrumental music that softly played on the radio. The funeral director didn't make us wait long. He was a tall man about my daddy's age, with pale skin and a black suit. He offered his condolences and explained that notification had been sent to Six Companies yesterday, and it wasn't unusual for it to take at least twenty-four hours to get the word to families, especially those that lived in the desert. Sometime that day, Ranger Williams would be coming to my camp to tell me about my dad.

"Since he was an employee of Six Companies, his burial will be paid for," he explained. "It's tentatively set for Saturday at Woodlawn Cemetery north of town, unless you want something else done with his body." His body. Not him. I shook my head and signed the release, giving my consent to put my daddy in the ground in two days.

"Would you like to see him?" he asked.

His question caught me off guard, although I knew I should have expected it. It caused a fleeting sense of hope that was quickly replaced by the pinprick of reality. I would have loved to see him. But he wasn't there. Just his body. I closed my eyes and pictured Daddy on the day we were in town at the coffee shop, the way he smiled at me and winked, and the pride and love that showed in those simple gestures. I shook my head. No, I would rather remember him that way.

As we left town, Mr. Emery repeatedly told me how sorry he was. He tried to make me feel better, but I wasn't sure I'd ever feel better.

"Death is natural, Helen. We all have to face it. And your daddy is at peace now," he said.

I knew Mr. Emery was a faithful man, and being raised a Baptist, I tried to hold strong to my own beliefs. But I was angry at Mr. Emery for being so upbeat, angry at Six Companies for letting him get poisoned in the tunnels, and angry at God. I knew it was best not to say any of that, so I stared out the window and watched the world go by.

When we got to the pass, traffic was backed up to the casino. "There must be an accident," Mr. Emery said.

I didn't care. I looked at the little outhouse shacks behind the casino and wondered about the women who worked there. How many of them were once in my same situation and saw no other way to provide for themselves? Wondering how many dreams had died on that hill made me ill.

Traffic moved slowly, and as we got to the front of the line, a Las Vegas deputy sheriff was talking to every car. Most, he turned away. He questioned Mr. Emery about why he was going to town.

"I run the ferry at the river," he said. "I live there."

The deputy didn't ask about me. It was as if I was assumed to be his wife or his daughter, basically invisible. He continued to question Mr. Emery, who didn't seem happy about having to explain himself.

"I assure you, I've been at that river longer than the government has. You need to call whoever you have to, because I'm going to my home," he said.

After much discussion with a few other deputies present, checking lists, and talking into their radios, the deputy came back to us. "Go straight to the river, Emery. And I suggest you stay there for a while. Next time, getting back in won't be so easy."

"Getting back in? It's a public road," Mr. Emery said.

"No, it's a government reservation. We're trying to keep the troublemakers out, at least the ones who aren't already there."

"Has there been some trouble? Should I be concerned?" Mr. Emery asked.

"The dam workers went on strike. It's a madhouse down there, and I suspect it's going to get worse before it gets better."

The road back to the river was backed up with traffic, and it took us almost an hour to get back to the Wash from Railroad Pass. Mr. Emery was riled up and talking nonstop. "This is going to be a mess… These men better have a good plan… I don't like this at all…" When he turned to me and said, "Don't worry. These men will be back to work soon, and they'll all be looking for a pretty girl to marry," I felt all that emotion boil up in me again. I forced it back down and tried to fake sleep to avoid talking to Mr. Emery anymore. The only person I wanted to talk to was Ezra.

When we finally parked at Mr. Emery's store, I thanked him and started walking through Ragtown. There were groups of men everywhere, talking, yelling, even fighting. I kept my head down, hoping to stay invisible. I felt alone and empty, walking through a thousand people.

I went straight to Ezra's tent, but it was gone.

Panic rose in me, and I turned in every direction, thinking I must have wandered in the wrong direction. My camp was right there, the Goons' three back, and Ezra's... gone.

I ran to the Goons'. Miss Smitty saw me and met me halfway. "How is your dad?" she asked.

I shook my head, unable to answer, but she seemed to understand. She wrapped her arms around me, but I pulled back. "Where is Ezra's tent? Where is he?" I tried to hold my voice steady, but I could hear it crack.

"He didn't leave with the rest of the men. Ranger Williams came and gathered his stuff and took it to him, I guess. I hear they are making them stay in the dormitories or at River Camp. Oh, Helen, this is bad, and here you are with your own problems, and—"

I held my hand up to stop her. I couldn't take any more. My head throbbed, and I wanted to jump in the river, but I was afraid if I went near the water, I might go under and never come up. Instead, I walked slowly back to my own camp, crawled into the backseat of Daddy's Model T, and let the tears fall.

AUTHOR NOTE: RIVER Camp was a government dormitory built into the side of the mountain. It housed 480, all single men, and was the only government housing available to workers until accommodations were built in Boulder City. Since it was for single men only, workers with families, those who were waiting for a job to become

available, and overflow of single workers were forced to make do in the desert, in camps like Ragtown.

Chapter 23: Building Fences

Ezra

I LEANED ON A TIMBER post, wiped my brow, and looked up at the clear night sky. The clean air away from the tunnels tasted good, and I took another deep breath. It was almost midnight, and we'd been working since nightfall, but I was not complaining. Frenchie had said the fence needed to be up before dawn, and if Pete ever got back with some water, we might get our section done.

Two teams of Negroes were to my left. They seemed to be working as a team of four instead of as two pair, which doubled their assignment but seemed to allow a better use of labor. I'd been watching them work while I waited for Pete. The man closest to me continued to shovel but looked up at me every few minutes. He wasn't moving at the same hectic pace as Pete and me but had completed twice the work. Finally, he quit shoveling and turned to face me. "Whatcha lookin' at?"

I could barely see his face in the darkness. The only light was provided by the Railroad Pass Casino to the south and the few lanterns that had been randomly placed along the fence line. He was a tall man, as tall as me, and thin as one of the posts he was digging holes for. When he spoke, the other three Negroes stopped working, too, and stared at me.

"Whatya doing, Yank, picking a fight with the darks?" Pete said as he returned.

"No. Just wondering how they are getting so much done, and we don't seem to be moving much," I said.

"Did you ask them?"

I shook my head.

Pete yelled to the tall man, "My friend's wondering how you are getting so much done, when we don't seem to be. You guys must have more of this rock than we do, seeing as you're closer to the mountain."

The tall man looked at Pete then at the other three men on his team, who had approached from the sides.

One of the men, short and stocky, walked a few feet closer. "Maybe we're better at it than you."

Pete laughed and walked a few feet closer to the four men. "Maybe. Or maybe you'd like to show us what you're doing different."

All four men laughed. "Now why'd we want to do that?" the short one asked.

Pete shrugged and scratched his chin. "Maybe because I have a girlfriend working over at the Pass, and maybe she's going to bring a couple bottles of whiskey out here in a few hours, and maybe, the six of us being so far away from the shack down there, no one would notice if we took a little break." He paused as they looked at one another. "That is, if we are all far enough along to take a break."

The tall man was the first to respond. "It don't work right with two of you. Three of us dig, one does the pickin', then we switch off so the picker don't get too tired. The way you's doin' it, you gotta rest after every hole."

"You got something there." Pete scratched his chin again. "So, saying there were four diggers and two pickers, how long would it take six of us to finish our lot?"

The tall man looked around at his friends, who talked among themselves, then they collectively shrugged.

"Probly 'bout as long as it'd take some woman to round up two bottles of whiskey, I guess," the tall man responded.

Pete walked up to the men with his hand outstretched. I followed at a distance.

"Pete McGee. This here's Easy."

The tall man smiled but did not take Pete's hand. He looked straight at me. "Easy, huh? You and Shorty can pick first."

"DON'T YOUR FRIEND NEVER shut up?" Shorty asked as we stood waiting for the last post to be placed. The two other Negroes—I'd heard their names but had not taken note—were rolling out the last forty-foot section of fence while Pete and Jimison, the apparent spokesperson for the group, secured the chain link to the poles with chain ties.

"No, he don't." I walked to a large boulder and sat down to wait.

"I ain't never seen fence like this," Jimison said as he stretched the drape tight while Pete tied it to the pole.

"Yeah, this isn't chicken wire," Pete said.

"It sure is stronger than that old chicken wire, though. Keep a lot of critters outta there, for sure."

Pete smiled. "I'm figuring it's the two-legged kind they are trying to keep out. What do you think, Easy?"

I shrugged. "Sure is a lot of work to decide to do all of a sudden."

"All of a sudden?" Shorty laughed. "This stuff ain't layin' aroun', ya know?"

"Yeah, they's had to be a-planning this for some while, having this fencing here," Jimison added.

A sudden commotion at the half-built guard shack caused all six of us to turn. Three armed men guarded the shack and searched a truck that was trying to pass. The driver and the four men sitting in the back weren't too happy about being held up and were very vocal in their protests. The driver waved a paper at the guards, and after one glanced at it, they let the truck pass.

Jimison pointed. "Another truckload of them Vegas boys." He shook his head. "I hate to know what's goin' on in that little town tonight." He looked at Pete. "How come you two ain't in there?"

Pete finished the last tie and stood back to admire the job. "I figure I'll get whatever those strikers get, and if they don't get anything, I'll be better off for not walking off the job."

"Why aren't you guys striking?" I asked before I really thought about it.

"You sound as if ya think we get that choice," Jimison said.

The others joined me at my boulder, and when Pete sat down, I handed him the two bottles of whiskey that Marguerite had brought earlier. Pete opened one, swigged it, then handed it to Shorty. After Shorty took a drink, he passed the bottle to me, and I waved it off.

"Not drinkin' with us?" Jimison asked.

"I'm afraid if I start, two bottles won't be enough," I said.

"What's her name?" Shorty asked.

"Who? Oh, Helen, but it's not what you think."

"Yeah, it is," Pete said. "Hair the color of fire and eyes like green sea glass. Isn't that what you told me, Easy?"

Shorty laughed. "Yeah, if you describe her like that, it's definitely what I think."

I promised her I'd take care of her until Ben got back, and there I was, not even allowed to go collect my own gear from Ragtown. After the strikers were cleared out from the job site, the rest of us were loaded up, sent to the dorms, and told to get some rest for the night shift. I wanted so badly to make my way to Ragtown to see how her visit with Ben had gone, but I didn't think all those strikers wanted to see my smiling face. She'd be fine. Cotton was there, and the Goons, and the strike wouldn't last more than a few days. I was sure of it.

Nobody said anything for a while. Pete opened the second bottle and passed it in the same direction.

"So, that was your girl?" one of the men asked as he passed the bottle back to Pete.

"One of 'em."

"She sure looks familiar," Shorty said. "She ever work up in Vegas?"

Pete shot him a sharp look. "Yeah, she did for a bit. But I doubt you'd have seen her."

"Don't know. You'd be surprised the girls we get on our side of town when they's hungry."

The other two men started laughing.

"Enough," Jimison said. "You're mistaken. She seems like a fine lady there, Pete. No offending our bartender."

Pete stood and wiped his hands on his pants leg. "You enjoy the rest of that. Our piece is done, and I'm going home. It's going to be a long day tomorrow."

I stood as well. I'd have to catch a ride with one of the deputies to get back to the dormitories, but I was hoping in the morning, I might see one of the guys from Ragtown who could at least get a message to Helen for me. If they would. Damned if the minute I said I wasn't walking off the job, my friends didn't seem so friendly anymore. Cotton had spit at my feet and didn't look back.

But it was all about business, really. I had my reasons, they had theirs, and I'd do whatever it took so I'd have a job the next day, next week, next year.

AUTHOR NOTE: The original contract for the dam specifically stated that American citizens were to be hired. The only race that was excluded was "Mongolians." However, of the first 1000 workers hired, none were African American. Pressure from the government saw the hiring of some African American workers, but even then, by 1933, only 24 African American workers had been hired, and they performed the most labor-intensive jobs at the dam.

The few African American workers who were hired on the dam project were not allowed to live in Boulder City, the government town established for the workers. Instead, they were bussed in and out each day from West Las Vegas, a 33-mile journey that took about an hour each way.

Chapter 24: My Little Scab

Ezra

I WASN'T SURE WHAT was going on in town while I was out building that fence, but I had a pretty good idea. The sheriff's deputies, the Vegas police, and a lot of other guys that seemed to be on the company's side flowed back and forth through the checkpoint all night. They drove in empty but came out with the beds of their trucks and the backseats of their cars loaded down with men. It was 4:00 a.m. by the time I caught a ride back into town with one of the deputies, after showing my temporary badge and explaining that I was supposed to report back to the dormitories. As we drove into town, a town that was usually going twenty-four hours, I got an eerie feeling that something wasn't right. There was still activity—a lot of it—but it wasn't construction like it usually was. It was union busters looking for Wobblies.

It looked like most of the men that had returned to the dorms had taken the opportunity to catch up on some sleep. That sounded good to me, too, but I was hungry. The mess hall was open, so I thought I'd grab a bite before taking a shower and heading to my new room, with a new bed, in the dorms. Why the hell I hadn't applied for a dorm room right after Grace died was beyond me.

The deputy dropped me off in front of the mess, with a warning to get off the streets if I knew what was good for me. I was not a troublemaker, not playing for either side, and all I wanted to do was eat and sleep. I'd be fine. The mess was empty except for a few guys who looked at me hard when I walked in. I could tell they were busters, sporting the toy badges that they were given and calling themselves deputized. I walked straight to the food line, grabbed a to-go box, and started to fill it, paying them no mind. They were just putting out some hot food, so I grabbed a couple of biscuits for my box and waited for whatever they were bringing out next.

One of the busters yelled at me, "Hey, you, come over here."

I ignored him, smelling bacon, thinking of bacon and biscuits smothered with strawberry jam.

"I'm talkin' to you."

He had moved right behind me, and I was too tired for this. I turned around, and he was close enough to steal my biscuits, so I put my to-go box on the table behind me and turned back to him. His two friends were behind him. One of them slapped his palm with his fist, trying to look intimidating, and I laughed.

"What's so funny?" the lead man said.

I was a good-sized guy, and I'd been working in the diversion tunnels for a while. These guys, even though there were three of them, looked like they'd been sitting on a barstool in Vegas for just as long. The lead guy even had on shiny shoes, which made me laugh again. I heard one of the cooks walking out of the kitchen behind me, and I could smell the bacon.

"Why don't you guys go play in the street. I'm just a workin' man trying to get some food before my next shift." I looked up and saw someone in uniform walking into the mess, and I recognized him as Bud Bodell.

He walked straight to us and looked at the three men and then to me. "What the hell is going on?"

"I've been out building a fence at the Pass all night and just getting some food so I can be ready for my next shift, sir," I said. I knew better than to laugh at Bodell. And tonight, he looked like he'd had about enough of anybody that didn't do what he said.

He looked me up and down then turned to the three deputies. "What are you guys doing in the mess hall? You're supposed to be out there looking for groups. One man grabbing breakfast ain't exactly what we hired you to worry about."

"Yes, sir," the lead man said and turned while the others followed him. I turned back to my to-go box and filled it with the fresh bacon. Then I grabbed an apple to top it off. When I turned back around, Bodell was still standing there, watching me.

"You say you just got back from the Pass," he said to me.

"Yes, sir. Rode in with one of the real deputies. Now I'm going to bed, if you don't mind." I started to walk past him, but he grabbed my arm. Damn, I just wanted to eat and sleep.

"You best stay in that dorm. These guys are having too much fun rounding up troublemakers, and I wouldn't want you to lose your bacon." He turned me loose, and I headed for the door, thinking, yes, all the rumors I heard about him must be true. He was a real ass.

I was between the mess and the dorm when a pickup truck pulled up too close to me, blocking the view from the mess hall. The three guys that had just left me jumped out, this time two of them holding baseball bats. "Didn't you hear what your boss said?" I probably shouldn't have been mouthy to them now that they had a little backup. One bat, I could take, but two might be a problem.

"You look like a troublemaker to me. Don't you think, boys?" the lead guy said.

I looked around and wondered if running might be a good idea; I saw someone coming around the front of the truck and kind of hoped it was Bodell.

"Not today, boys." Moose Martin grabbed one of the baseball bats and took it from the man as easily as pulling a straw from a Nehi soda. The other two turned, but when they saw the size of him, they backed up.

"There's a group of men at the equipment barn, getting ready to cut the brake lines on the trucks. Shouldn't you boys be over there? Or would you rather take an ass whippin' with one of your own bats?"

The three men scrambled for their truck, and I was so glad to see Moose, I almost hugged him.

"What the hell, Moose? Has this place gone crazy?"

He waited until the truck pulled off then threw the bat on the ground and pointed me toward the dorm. "Yeah, it has. Those Wobblies are as crazy as the busters. Trying to tear up the equipment and get some of the scabs killed out there. I didn't sign up for this," he said.

"I thought you were striking," I said as we walked toward the dorm.

"I am. We came up with a list of demands last night, and we're supposed to give them to Crowe in the morning. It's a good and reasonable list, so we should all be back to work in short order. But in the meantime, those IWW boys have got them a group of rogues, and the law has gone vigilante. It ain't safe out here for nobody. This ain't how a strike is supposed to be. I don't like the scabs, but I don't want to kill 'em."

"You know I'm not striking, right? I've been working all night." I figured he had a right to know.

He shrugged. "We all got our own reasons for what we do. I just want to get back to work. All of us. And I damn sure don't want no wannabe sheriff's deputies beating up on any of my friends." He put an arm on my shoulder. "And besides, you're my little scab; after this is all over, I'll kick your ass myself."

AUTHOR NOTE: ONE OF my favorite things to write is the evolving friendships between men. There is such a contrast between male friendships and female friendships—how they talk to each other, their physical actions, their advice to one another. Maybe it's because I grew up with brothers and, as an adult, had two sons and two stepsons. I have been surrounded by testosterone my entire life! I love the relationship Ezra has with Moose and, in contrast, the relationship he has with Pete. I hope you do as well!

Chapter 25: Believe in Myself

Helen

AFTER I GOT BACK TO Ragtown from Las Vegas, I stayed in my camp and cried. Cotton came in to check on me a few times, but I sent him away, not wanting to talk to anyone. I didn't want anyone except Ezra, but he wasn't there. I cried until I had no more tears, and then I lay in the backseat of the Model T and looked at the ceiling liner until it was too dark to see the threads.

I'd always thought my dad had planned for everything. Maybe that is what all little girls think about their fathers, because as I lay there, I realized that so many things couldn't be planned for. When the mine closed in Kansas, for example, we ended up here. It wasn't that he had ever planned for us to move to Nevada. We were in a bad situation, an opportunity presented itself, and he had to make a quick decision about our future. There weren't many options available at the time, so even if moving to the middle of the desert wasn't ideal, we made the best of it. He remained optimistic about better days ahead, and I believed him. I believed in him. Now I had to believe in myself.

Cotton came in and lay down in my dad's spot and was snoring like a tractor, but at least he took to the lye this time and didn't smell like raw onions. I snuck past him only to find several cans of goods outside my tent entrance, offerings from those who had heard the news and didn't want me to starve to death right away. Some people, regardless of their own situation, find a place for charity. I set the cans on the inside of the tent flap and made my way to the river.

The camp wasn't as quiet as usual. With no one at work and most people on edge about the strike, that should have been expected. But I really wanted my time alone and could feel the eyes on me with each step I took. I heard the words "I'm sorry" at least ten times between my camp and the water's edge, and I nodded to those who offered their condolences, and watched as they turned back to their lives. I was sorry too.

I knew with Daddy gone, I had to figure out what I was going to do to survive on my own. The trip to Vegas did little to raise my level of optimism. In fact, it had opened my eyes to the reality of life, especially for a single woman. Daddy had had two dollars and forty-eight cents in his pocket, half a week's pay, that the undertaker had given to me. I had the car, the scraps for the tent, my camera, and my uncle Dwayne's gun. And about two weeks' worth of canned beans and other goods. That was my inventory. That was my survival kit.

I sat close to the water with my feet in and looked at the stars. I hoped wherever Daddy was, he had found my momma and my grandparents, and together, they would all watch over me. I could use some angels.

My mind was going a million miles a minute, but I didn't want to think, to plan, to organize anything right now. I just wanted to sit and watch the stars, think about the good times I had had with Dad, and feel a little sorry for myself. I figured I got one night of that.

Tomorrow, I'd worry about the rest of my life.

THE FIRST THING THAT hit me when I woke up was that Daddy was gone and I was alone. I lay in the backseat of the Model T and looked at the lining. It was faded and worn and could have used a good cleaning. It was mine now, so I should make sure I took care of it. Mine. A car and two dollars and forty-eight cents.

I peeked out of the backseat and was relieved that Cotton had rolled up his bedroll and was not inside. I changed clothes quickly and made my way out of the tent. There were more cans at the entrance, and I placed them in the food pit. I had enough food for a few weeks; then I'd need to figure out how to eat.

Betsy Allen had told me when Clive died that filling out the papers for Six Companies to receive Clive's death benefit was simple, and they handed her the money right there. I knew with the men striking, there would probably be a lot more confusion at the Administration Building, but I wanted to get there as early as possible. I knew that most likely they wouldn't give me anything for his death, but they did owe him a final paycheck, which I intended to collect. The sun was barely out, so I figured it was as good a time as any to make my way into town. I didn't make it thirty feet toward the highway before Cotton was by my side.

"Where are you going?" He sounded irritated, and it wore thin on me.

I let out an exasperated breath. "I'm going to town to get my dad's last paycheck," I said as I continued to walk.

"You need to wait for Ranger Williams. I hear there was a lot of trouble in town last night," he said.

"I don't care, and I'm not waiting." I waved a hand in the air. "You guys have your problems, and I have my own."

He tried to argue with me, but I kept walking. It was none of his business anyway. Finally, he threw his hands up in the air. "Fine. I'm going with you, though."

I shook my head but didn't say anything. He was like a bug that kept buzzing around, and no matter how many times I swatted, he kept coming back.

When we got to the highway, a police car from Las Vegas stopped, and after I explained my situation, the officer gave us a ride straight to the Administration Building. "Hurry up," the officer said as we got out of his car. "You need to get back down to the river as quick as possible."

Men, I thought. I wasn't worried about all the activity going on in town. I was concerned with one thing. Myself. Cotton stayed on my heels as I entered the building and made my way to the woman behind the front counter. She wasn't smiling.

Thirty minutes later, I walked out with eighteen dollars and some change. After explaining to the woman—whose name I didn't bother to get—about my dad, she gave me two pieces of paper to fill out and verified his time for the week. That was it. Apparently, they'd already gotten the notification from the hospital and were ready to file Benjamin Carter away. I fought back the knot in my stomach that seemed to be growing by the minute.

"One more place," I said to Cotton as we left the Administration Building. Again, he tried to argue with me, but I paid him no mind. He could follow if he wanted, but I was going to talk to the woman my dad had told me to find if something happened to him. Ida Browder.

"Who is this woman?" Cotton asked as we made our way down Utah Street.

"A friend of my dad's," I said. He didn't need any more of an explanation, and the truth was, I didn't know how she knew him. I assumed she owned Browder's Café, where my dad had taken me to eat on my birthday, but that didn't explain his relationship to her. I only knew that he told me to see her, and that was what I intended to do.

A man was leaving her house when we arrived, and she stood on the porch as we approached. She was a tall woman with soft features and kind eyes. After I introduced myself and told her about my dad, she took my hands in hers. "Oh, I am so sorry. He was such a nice man."

"Thank you," I said. I had no idea what her relationship with my dad had been and didn't really know how to ask. So I just stood there, waiting for her to say something.

She turned to Cotton, eyeing him hard. "And you are?"

"I worked with Ben," Cotton said.

She continued to look at him, her face twisted as if she were contemplating what else to say.

"I didn't know he had a gal."

"Ben and I were friends," she said. Then she turned to me, as if gauging my reaction. My brow furrowed. I had no idea what kind of friends they were.

Another man was standing on the sidewalk as if waiting for us to leave. Cotton saw him and smiled. "Oh, I see. Okay." He turned to me. "Can we go now?"

Ms. Browder stared at me, as if trying to convey something with her eyes that I couldn't understand. "Well, it was nice to meet you. My dad just wanted you to know."

"Helen," she said. "Come back and see me." She glanced at Cotton and then winked at me. "Girl talk, you might say."

I told her I would but knew I wouldn't be back. My dad had asked that I tell her if something happened to him, and he seemed to think she could help me. But with men lining up at her door, I was afraid her help might come at a price I didn't want to pay. My heart ached. Did my dad really think that my only hope would be an in-town prostitute? What could she possibly do to help me, other than give me a job I didn't really want?

"Damn," Cotton said as we turned to leave. "I had no idea Ben had that going on." He laughed.

"Shut up," I said.

Ms. Browder was a pretty woman but older than what I assumed a typical prostitute would be. It was silly to assume that was what she was, even if when we got to her house, one man was leaving, and another was waiting on the curb. Someone to talk to, maybe? He'd only had the men at the dam and me to talk to, and I knew there were women who did that kind of thing. The fact that she said we should have a "girl talk" made me think that was more logical than her being a prostitute. I shook my head as I beelined back to the highway. I didn't need someone to talk to and help me through my grief, if that's what my daddy had been thinking. I needed... something else. Right then, I just wanted to be back in Ragtown, where at least something was familiar. I wanted to forget about Ida Browder, and I definitely wanted to get away from Cotton.

When we walked back into the Wash, the camp was alive with too many people, too many of them watching me. Cotton stopped to talk to two men I didn't recognize, and I went straight back to my camp. I grabbed my canteen and my ballcap and headed back out. I wanted to escape, to think, and the best place for me to do both was in the mountains.

The men were in the two open-roofed tents that were used as a makeshift community hall. During the week, it was used for classes for the children. On Sunday mornings, it was full of men, women, and children raising their voices to ask for God's mercy; today it was just the men, trying to gain a little mercy themselves.

As I walked by, Cotton saw me and excused himself from the talk to catch up with me. "Where you goin' now?" he asked.

I shivered, thinking it was none of his business.

"To the mountains. I need to think," I said.

"You shouldn't go up there alone. That Indian is up there somewhere, and I'm sure he'd love to get hold of you." The way he looked at me, staring a little too long when he said that, made me uneasy.

"I'll be fine." Which I knew I would, but I should stop and see if Pepper needed a break from all the commotion as well. I had felt sorry for him for the past weeks since his father died, but now I could really empathize with him. I pointed at the tents. "Strikers?"

He glanced back then returned to me. "We're all going into town. Crowe is going to hear our demands, and then he'll decide what he's going to do for us. They can't build this thing without us, so we'll be back to work real soon." He seemed sure of that, and I guessed it shouldn't concern me as much anymore.

I turned, but Cotton caught my arm, his grip a little too tight. "Helen, I need to talk to ya."

I looked at his hand on my arm, and he released me.

"I said I'd take care of ya. So as soon as we get back to work, I'm willing to marry ya. I can get on the list for one of them houses, then," he said.

"Us... marry?" I couldn't believe Cotton was asking—no, telling me that he was willing to marry me, like it was a privilege I should jump all over, even though his proposal sounded to me like a way for him to get one of the houses in town. My upper lip started to sweat, and all I wanted to do was turn and run toward the mountain, but I was too shocked to move.

He must have sensed my hesitation. He pointed back at the tent. "We're getting ready to go, so you go on up the mountain and think. Think real hard, now," he said, staring at me with his eyes squinted.

He turned to go back to the other men, but I stopped him. "Cotton? When you go back into town, will you do me a favor?"

He turned around, smiling.

"If you see Ezra, will you tell him I need to talk to him?"

His smile disappeared, and he turned back toward the others without even acknowledging my request.

AUTHOR NOTE: HELEN knows the situation she is in, but she still wants to try to find a way to do things her way. She is a strong, independent young woman, but that doesn't mean she can't cry by the river and feel a little sorry for herself. I think that makes her more human.

Ida Browder was a remarkable woman, but I can't tell you much more about her at this point without it being a spoiler for Helen's story. I will say she probably deserves her own book. Maybe someday...

Chapter 26: She Ain't Fine

Ezra

THE DEMANDS OF THE strikers were simple and not unreasonable: improved living conditions for the workers, an ample supply of cold water, an eight-hour day camp-to-camp, strict enforcement of Arizona and Nevada mining laws, no wage reductions, and amnesty for strikers. Frank Crowe listened to all these with his hands behind his back, and when the strikers said their piece and handed him a list, he told them he would need twenty-four hours to consider all their demands, and he'd let them know by the next morning.

Strikers from all the camps were present, and everyone seemed optimistic that we'd all be back to the work site by the next day, the day after that at the latest. I was glad it was all civil, especially after everything that went down the night before. I didn't know where the Wobblies and troublemakers had been taken during the night, but I assumed it was to the Las Vegas sheriff's infamous jail. Pete had told me about the holding pit in the Las Vegas jail known as the Blue Room: one room, about fifteen by forty feet with no bathroom. The floor was slanted from both ends so that the prisoners' waste accumulated in the center. On the weekends, they put a hundred or more men in there, standing room only. If you were lucky, Pete had said, you wouldn't be pushed down to the middle and be standing knee-deep. It didn't matter anyway, he had said. The stench from anywhere in there was enough to make you think twice about disobeying the law.

I searched the crowd of strikers for a familiar face from Ragtown. I needed to get word to Helen. I had promised her I'd watch out for her until Ben got back, but things had gotten crazy, and at least I knew that Cotton, the Goons, and Mr. Emery wouldn't let anything bad happen to her. I found Cotton over by Browder's Cafe, talking to Molly Woodward. They both gave me a look when I walked up like I wasn't quite welcome.

"Well, look here, a scab. Why ain't you at work?" Molly said.

"How's Helen?" I ignored Molly's dig and looked at Cotton.

He looked me up and down, and I wanted to knock the smirk off his face. "I'm watching out for her, so she's just fine." He turned to walk away from me, but I grabbed his arm.

"How's Ben?" I caught the look between Cotton and Molly, and the air went out of me.

"They are burying him tomorrow in Vegas," Cotton said.

My face was hot when he said this without much emotion. "Then how the hell can you say Helen is just fine? You know damn good and well she ain't fine." I ran my hand through my hair, grabbed a handful, and tugged. I need to get to Helen, I thought. She must be devastated right now.

"She's fine because I'm taking care of her," he said.

"No, no. This is all wrong. I've got to go see her." I was supposed to report for my shift in two hours, but I needed to get to Ragtown, let her know... something. I looked around town, crawling with at least a thousand men, none of whom, I was sure, were too keen on giving a scab a ride down to the river.

"She went up in the mountains this morning," he said. "Said she has some things to think about. I suspect she won't be back down until afternoon."

"By herself? Cotton, those mountains aren't safe, and that Indian is up there somewhere. How could you let her go up there alone?" I was getting angry, and honestly, I was feeling a little bit too protective of Helen, almost possessive. I couldn't feel this way. I didn't know what to feel.

"She's fine," he said again. "Besides, she don't have to listen to me. Not yet anyway."

"What the hell is that supposed to mean?" I wasn't liking this conversation at all.

"This morning, I told her I'd marry her. So she'll be just fine. You don't need to worry about her anymore. I'm taking care of her from now on."

AUTHOR NOTE: THE DESCRIPTION of the Las Vegas jail's infamous Blue Room is fairly accurate. For anyone who ever spent the night there, the thought of ever going back was enough of a deterrent to make them think twice about committing a crime.

Chapter 27: Pepper's Fate

Helen

BETSY ALLEN SAT ON a large boulder outside her tent, putting a patch on a pair of Pepper's blue jeans. She seemed lost in her task, focused, and I watched her delicate hands play the needle and thread like an instrument. When she noticed me, she gave me her warm smile, stood and wrapped her arms around me, and hugged me tightly. It felt good. Motherly.

"I'm so sorry, Helen," she said. Her long blond hair was pulled up in a twist and her blue eyes had lost some of their sparkle, but she was still, in my eyes, a beautiful woman.

"Thank you, Mrs. Allen," I said. "I thought I'd take Pepper with me up in the mountain today, if that's okay?"

"Of course. He'd love that. He ran down to Emery's to get our final bill so we can settle up, but he'll be right back. He's been worried about you." I felt bad that Pepper, a twelve-year-old who had just lost his own father, had been concerning himself with me.

"It's still unreal to me," I said.

Betsy sat back down and patted the boulder for me to join her. I did. "Oh, I know. I thought Clive and I would be together forever. But change happens quickly," she said.

"But I..." I didn't know how to say all I was thinking, and if anyone would understand, I thought Betsy might. She had just lost her husband, which wasn't the same as a father, but maybe it was even worse? And she had a child to look after. At least it was only me I had to worry about.

I took a deep breath. "I just don't know what to do. I have no family in Kansas—anywhere, for that matter—and the only advice anyone has given me is to find a husband. Quickly. I wish I had prepared myself for something like this. I wish..." I wished it had never happened. But it had.

"It's hard to be prepared for everything. Plans have to be flexible enough for change, but you already know that. Wishes..." She stopped and looked off toward the mountain. "I used to wish for a ranch, with horses. Oh, I love horses. And I wanted to teach Pepper to ride, because I wanted him to love horses too. And, well, now I'm getting my wish." She looked down at her hands folded in her lap. "But I had to lose someone precious to get it."

"You're going to a ranch?" I asked.

She looked back up at me. She looked tired but not defeated. "A man answered my ad, and I met him in town yesterday. He has a small ranch and two boys and no one to cook and clean. I can do that, and I can do all the other things a wife needs to do. And although I'll be adding two more mouths to the mix, I've got one hundred dollars to add as well. So, an arrangement, of sorts, which is how a marriage is, I guess."

"I didn't know you were leaving." I had been so wrapped up in my own problems, I hadn't even known what was going on in Pepper's camp. I felt like a bad friend—just another thing to add to my loneliness. My hopelessness.

"Pepper is dealing with it in his own way. He misses his daddy so much, it hurts me deep down in my heart. But this will give him a chance. He can learn about horses, and he can finish school, and he won't starve. And I'll be there for him. It's the best I can do."

"But you don't love him. I always thought I would marry a man I loved," I said.

"Well, I had one that I loved very much, and I may not have had him long, but I'm lucky to have had him at all. I figure it would be kind of selfish of me to wait for another when so many women never get one in their entire life. And besides, I will love him, for different reasons. I'll love him for taking Pepper and me in, and I might grow to love him in other ways too."

I bit my lip, trying to think how her words, her choices, could apply to me. She must have noticed my confusion. She put a hand on my knee. "Here is my advice to you, sweet Helen. You are young and beautiful, kind, and one of the smartest girls I've ever met. And you've got a head full of dreams, and that's good too. Keep going after those dreams, but along the way, you'll have to give some things up in order to keep going. But you can always change your mind and go another way. You'll just have to give something else up to do it."

My freedom. My ideal of a man I loved for a man that would allow me to pursue other dreams. I didn't like it, but I thought I understood. "Thank you, Mrs. Allen. I'm going to miss you and Pepper."

"We're going to miss you, too, Helen. But I'm sure our paths will cross again. It's one of the things I'll be wishing for."

I heard the crunch of small feet on pebbles and turned to see Pepper coming toward us, chewing on a licorice whip. "Mr. Emery said we didn't owe him anything," he said.

Betsy shook her head. I knew Mr. Emery was known to wipe out the credit of some people who fell on really hard times, and I assumed that was what he'd done for Betsy and Pepper. She looked back at me. "One more thing," she said. "There are also angels out there, like Mr. Emery. You never know when or who will be your angel."

AUTHOR NOTE: BETSY marrying in order to keep Pepper and herself from starving was not uncommon. Sometimes, those arrangements worked out well for all parties involved. However, many times the women and children were victims of abuse, taken in as servants or slaves under the guise of marriage.

Chapter 28: Queho and the Rattlesnake

Helen

THE FIRST DAY I GOT to Ragtown, I went up the mountain, and it was that first day I discovered the mountain sheep. I was fascinated with their size and how they were able to bounce from rock to rock at the top of the mountains. They had two large toes on their hooves, which I could tell by the tracks they left, and somehow that must have allowed them to grip the rocks, because they never fell. Maybe like the chuckwalla, they were made from the mountain, and that was what kept them safe. While some people thought the high-scalers working at the dam were a sight to watch, they didn't realize that nature had its own high-scalers, and to me they were much more fascinating.

The more I watched them, the more I learned about their ways. They could be fierce if they needed to be, but usually, they just wanted to go about their lives and not be bothered. But their lives were changing. As more people moved to the desert, and more started coming to the mountain, their home was being compromised. But they stuck together and continued their routine. I figured it was their togetherness, their keeping with the herd, that made the changes they were going through tolerable. As they walked slowly by Pepper and me, we didn't remain entirely out of sight. They knew we were there—they could sense us—and it would be silly to hide. They tolerated us at a distance, and although I would have loved to get closer, I knew better. Even though Pepper was with me, after they passed, I felt alone. Why couldn't I have been a mountain sheep?

"Come on," I said to Pepper as I continued up the trail, keeping a keen eye out for rattlesnakes, which tended to come out in the morning. By afternoon, most had gone back underground, the sun even too hot for them. Just like the sheep and the other critters on the mountain, they wouldn't hurt you if you just stayed out of their way. Nature was all about respect.

Pepper stayed close but was being quiet. I felt sorry for him, and I knew he was going through his own changes. But his silence gave me some time to think, and I figured he needed his own time as well. We walked to the music of our own footsteps.

Almost twenty-one dollars, five more in company scrip that could only be used at the company store, an old Model T, two pairs of overalls, a fancy dress and two day-dresses, some plyboard and canvas, a Smith and Wesson .38 revolver, a camera, a canteen, *The Great Gatsby*, and a few weeks' worth of food. That was what I had to work with. Now I had to figure out how to use that to support myself and not have to look for a husband or accept Cotton's offer.

Cotton. I shook when I thought about what he said that morning. I knew he was being nice, and it was very honorable of him to be willing to marry me when I'd done nothing but shoo him away. I guessed there were a lot of worse things that could happen to me, but I still thought there had to be something I could do to avoid having to marry someone I didn't love.

I let out a deep sigh.

"What?" Pepper said.

I shook my head. "Nothing. Just thinking."

He stopped walking, squatted down, and picked randomly at a pile of small stones. "Where are you going?"

"When Mr. Emery and I were driving to Vegas, I noticed children standing by the side of the road, selling bat guano they had found in the caves around the camps. Mr. Emery said they get a little spending money. I found a big cave full of it up here one time when I wandered too far from camp, and I'm trying to remember where it was." The guano, Mr. Emery had told me, made great fertilizer, and in the desert, anything that would help something grow was important. "And while I'm up here, I can get more brittlebush for my salve," I added.

"That's not what I meant," Pepper said.

"Oh. I don't know."

Maybe, just maybe, I should move up into the mountains, like the chuckwalla or the mountain sheep, and I could go down and sell guano and my salve to buy what food I couldn't find in the desert. I could learn to trap rabbit, and I was sure rattlesnake meat would keep me from starving. Or maybe I'd become a legend, like the Indian. Helen-in-the-Mountain.

If only it were that easy.

Pepper shrugged. "You could come with us." His voice was barely above a whisper.

I put a hand on his shoulder. "You'll be fine, Pepper. And I'll be fine. And one day, we'll see each other again, and we'll talk about all the adventures we've had after we left this place."

He nodded weakly.

"Come on, let's go this way," I said, pointing at an incline that was off the usual trail. I could hear men in the distance, and I was trying to avoid them. They were loud and had no respect for the mountain, so it wasn't hard to stay out of their sight. I wished they'd all just go back to work.

We wandered for about an hour, stopping to take a few pictures with my camera and noticing different plants than we had seen closer to camp. We started to smell the guano, and we knew we were getting closer. Pepper didn't seem concerned that we were in unfamiliar territory. It was like our own adventure—our last adventure—and he would go wherever I wanted. I knew my dad worried, or had worried, about me going too far, but as long as I could see the river, I could always find my way back to Ragtown. I made sure I was always aware of its presence.

I stopped and took my water flask from my overalls and gave it to Pepper, who took a drink. Then I tipped it back, taking only a small drink to conserve what I brought.

I heard a faint sound, a snap of a weed, somewhere above me, and I froze. I was not afraid; it was just the desert talking. I knew that fear was something that the animals could smell, so I tried not to give them something to stir about. I put a finger to my lips to tell Pepper to be quiet, and he pretended to zip his mouth shut to show he understood. I still had my flask in hand, and as I slowly turned toward the sound, I heard the familiar rattle of a western diamondback to my left. I turned too quickly and lost my footing and found myself tumbling backward. I hit the ground hard and slid upside down along the rocky terrain, only to be stopped suddenly when my foot caught between two rocks.

My flask continued to tumble, spilling what was left of my water, but I didn't care. The pain in my ankle was so excruciating, I couldn't even scream. My eyes watered, and I tried to bend upward to release my foot but couldn't do it without pulling back on the ankle, causing more pain.

"Pepper!" I said. "Help me."

There was no response. No sound.

I shut my eyes, trying to push the pain out of my mind long enough for me to release my foot. When I opened my eyes, I caught a glint of something below me, and I turned, expecting to see Pepper. Instead, I saw a tall, thin man with long black hair, taking my flask and hobbling back up the mountain. He stopped briefly, close to where I had fallen, took out a long knife, bent down, and sliced at something on the ground. He stood back up, holding a headless rattlesnake.

Queho.

He glanced at Pepper and then looked back to me briefly.

I held one hand up to him. "Please," I said.

He turned to go the other way then suddenly turned back to me. He tucked my flask in his pants, wrapped the rattlesnake carcass around his arm, and made his way to me. Roughly, he grabbed my foot and pulled it free, which sent me tumbling down a few more feet.

I heard the loud men in the distance and could tell they were coming this way. Queho was watching me, and I pointed toward the sound of the men. Then I pointed in the other direction. "Go," I said. He ran, navigating the terrain with a clubfoot as deftly as a mountain sheep.

Pepper stood right where he'd been when I fell. He hadn't moved. His mouth hung open, and he stared at me, his eyes as wide as two moons. A large wet spot covered the front of his blue jeans.

"Pepper, come here. Snap out of it. I need you!"

Looking back toward where the Indian had gone, he moved slowly toward me and sat down on the ground next to where I lay.

He pointed toward the top of the mountain. "That was—"

"Shhh," I said. "Don't say his name."

"But—"

"Pepper. I'm hurt." My eyes started to water. I tried to pull myself up to a sitting position, but I was almost paralyzed with pain. Pepper reached out and gently touched my ankle, and I squealed, which made him pull his hand back quickly.

I heard the men, closer, and knew I would only be able to get back to camp with their help. "Pepper, I need you to do something very important. I need you to go get those men. Can you do that for me?"

"But the Indian..."

"He won't hurt you. Or me. I need those men to get me back to Ragtown. I can't walk," I said.

"How do you know he won't hurt us?" Pepper was scared. Terrified. And as much as I hated to send him after the men, I had no choice.

"I just do. I just know." I closed my eyes for a second, and when I opened them again, Pepper was crying.

"I need you to help me, Pepper. You're the only one who can. Will you help me?" I said. My ankle was starting to go numb, and as long as I didn't try to move it, I could tolerate the pain.

He wiped his eyes and nodded.

I forced a smile. "Good. Now go find those men, follow the sounds of their voices, and bring them back here. And Pepper? Don't say anything about the Indian. You hear me? That has to be our secret."

He looked at me with his face twisted up and cocked his head.

"I know you don't understand, and I'll explain it later, but you just have to trust me. Do you trust me?"

His voice shaking, he whispered, "Yes."

I reached out and squeezed his hand weakly then closed my eyes again. When I opened them, Pepper was gone, and the mountain was silent.

AUTHOR NOTE: ENTERTAINMENT *for those living in the Hoovervilles around the dam was limited. However, several of the*

men used their spare time to hunt Queho. By this time, he had become almost legend, and the reward for him was significant.

Chapter 29: A Federal Reservation

Helen

IT WAS PAST NOON WHEN we got back to Ragtown. Instead of going to Boulder City with the rest of the strikers, the three men on the mountain had decided to spend their day off work on an Indian hunt. I guessed I should have been more thankful, because I would have had to crawl back, without water, had Pepper not found them. But being carried most of the way, listening to them tell me how dangerous it was for a girl in the mountains, may not have been worth surviving. If it weren't for me telling them how to get back to camp, we'd have been wandering around for hours, if not days.

"I come up here all the time," I told them as we made our way back down the bighorn trail. "Don't you think if there was some Indian hiding up there, he would have killed me by now?" I wasn't about to tell them that I actually saw Queho, and Pepper never said a word about it, as promised. The Indian may have taken my canteen, but he freed me from the rock, and if he was a murderer like they all said, we'd both be dead right now. Something about him made me feel sorry for him. Maybe it was that he was being hunted, had been for several years. And yet here I was, someone who could easily tell where he was, and he only took my canteen. I felt as if I owed him something, if not any more than a thank-you for releasing me from the rock. But also, it was as if I understood him in some way. He was trying to survive, and he'd done so for a lot of years. Or maybe the pain from my swollen ankle straining against my boot was making me dizzy enough to be a little crazy right then. Either way, I just wanted to get my boot off, rub some of my homemade salve on my ankle, and figure out how I was going to get to the bat cave now that I would have a bad ankle for at least a week.

And talk to Pepper, alone. I had to explain to him why we couldn't say anything about seeing Queho. I knew he didn't understand my reasoning, but he'd keep the secret for as long as I wanted him to.

Which was forever.

Miss Smitty saw me being half carried, half dragged through the camp and came to my rescue.

"What happened?" she asked as she put her arm around my waist while one of the men stood me upright. I put my arm on her shoulder and tried to put pressure on my bad foot, but the pain was too intense. I ended up limping my way with her, with Pepper close behind.

"Silly girl got up there and got herself hurt," one of the men said. "She'd have died if we hadn't found her."

I rolled my eyes to Miss Smitty but thanked the men properly. Now if we could just get back to my tent without Cotton—

"What the hell happened?" Figured.

"I just twisted my ankle. I'll be fine," I said, attempting to hide my grimace with each step I tried to take.

He reached for my arm, but I held up a hand. "I'll be fine. Miss Smitty and I can handle this," I said. "I thought you went to town?"

"We did. Crowe said he needed to think about it. It won't take him long; I bet we're back to work tomorrow."

He walked with us, and as we got to my spot, I'd never been so glad to see my dusty camp. Miss Smitty helped me sit on the large flat boulder outside my tent. Pepper went to tell Betsy we were back, and I gave him a look that said, "Don't tell her anything else." He nodded in understanding.

"Cotton, would you run over to Mr. Emery's and see if he has a small chunk of ice?" Smitty winked at me, and I wanted to hug her.

He hesitated, as if he wasn't sure if he'd been asked to help or been dismissed, then said, "Oh, sure," and took off toward Mr. Emery's.

"Thank you, Miss Smitty. I just can't handle him right now," I said.

She took my boot off. My ankle was black and blue and swollen to twice its normal size.

"Oh, Helen, this is bad," she said. She gently lifted my foot and looked at it from several angles. "But it doesn't look broken."

My eyes watered from the pain, and I tried to move my toes, which just made it worse. "Inside my tent, in the food pit, there's a Mason jar that looks like brown fatback. And there should be a rag of canvas in the front seat of the car."

Miss Smitty retrieved my salve and a piece of canvas and handed them to me. I dipped my fingers in the jar and rubbed the salve gently over my foot and ankle. I could feel it penetrating and sat back, hoping it would relieve some of the pain.

Miss Smitty returned the jar to the food pit and joined me at the boulder. She gently lifted my foot onto a large rock and grabbed the canvas. "I'm going to have to wrap this tight. It's going to hurt."

I gritted my teeth and shut my eyes tight. The pain was so intense, my head started swimming, and I caught myself with my palms on the rocky ground to keep from falling over. Cotton returned with a small chunk of ice, and Miss Smitty told him to find a bowl and go fill it with river water. He opened his mouth as if to protest then, seeing the stern look on Miss Smitty's face, did as he was told.

"Now we'll get some ice on it, and you need to stay put for a while," Miss Smitty said. She tilted her head in the direction that Cotton had gone. "He's telling everyone that you two are getting married."

"What? Oh, no!" I started to get up, ready to have it out with Cotton at the river's edge, but my ankle protested, and instead I yelled out in pain.

"That's what I figured. Settle down. You can deal with him later. Let's worry about this for now," Miss Smitty said.

But I didn't want to deal with him later. When he returned, he set the bowl of water down next to me, and Miss Smitty put the ice in it.

"Cotton, we need to talk," I said.

A commotion started in the camp, and before I could go any further, I spotted an old red bus and three dump trucks moving into the Wash.

"What in hell?" Cotton said.

He walked toward a large group of men that had been meeting in the community tent. They stood together and watched as the convoy made its way to them. The bus stopped at the group, stirring up a choking dust.

Miss Smitty helped me up, and together we hobbled toward the growing crowd around the bus and the dump trucks. Pepper and Betsy joined us. The man Daddy told me to stay away from when we were in town got out of the bus. I remembered his name, Bud Bodell, and that he was Six Companies' Chief of Security. Bodell raised a megaphone to his mouth, calling for every man to report to one of the vehicles immediately.

Ranger Williams walked up from the back of one of the trucks with two other marshals. All of them were visibly armed. Ranger walked among the men, talking quietly to them. As he reached a man standing close to Miss Smitty and me, I heard him whisper to him, "Do what you're told."

Once the men were gathered, their families not far behind, Bodell put the loudspeaker down and instead yelled his orders. "This here is part of a federal reservation, and as of now, the government is shutting it down." He paused as the grumbling began, raised his hand for silence, and continued. "I need every man to get in one of these trucks and bring what you need with ya. If you got a job, you'll be let back on the reservation. If not, well, you'll have to move on."

"Move on? What does that mean?"

"Where are you taking us?"

"What about our families?"

"I suggest you tell them to pack up and meet you up the road, 'cause I doubt any of you will be getting back in. This reservation is now officially closed," Bodell said.

"But wait a minute. We got jobs. We're striking! Just waiting on Mr. Crowe to make some decisions."

"News travels pretty slow down here to this hellhole, don't it?" Bodell said. "Crowe already made his decision. The job is shut down indefinitely. You're all fired."

Miss Smitty got me back to my rock and went to find George while I soaked my bandaged foot in the ice water, which was such a relief even amid the unsettling news. Betsy and Pepper sat with me while the rest of those in camp moved quickly to do as they were told. Mr. Emery stood close by, watching the chaos unfold, and I motioned him over to sit on one of the boulders with us. Ranger Williams and the other deputies walked through the camp, urging the men along, while Bodell continued to yell commands over and over throughout the camp.

"You got fifteen minutes to grab your gear and kiss this place goodbye," he said. "This entire area from the casino to the other side of the river is a federal reservation. After today, no one is allowed on the reservation without a pass."

He saw our group sitting on our boulders, watching while the others were scrambling to pack what they needed. "You better get busy," he said to Mr. Emery.

"I own the ferry. You can't fire me, and President Hoover is about the only one that can kick me off the river."

Bodell looked him up and down then turned to Betsy then me and did the same, hesitating when he got to my foot. "That looks like it hurts," he said then turned back to the crowd.

"What about my family?" one of the men asked, his wife holding his arm with one hand and a small child with the other.

"Everyone with a job will get a pass. If you got a pass, your family has a pass. If you're not working, you're not getting back in. It's that simple," Bodell said.

"But you said we're all fired," another man said.

"An employment office has been set up at the gate. If you want a job, you'll have to reapply. Personally, I wouldn't hire a one of ya back."

Cotton appeared in front of me, carrying his rolled-up tent and bedding. "You stay with Smitty. Wherever she is, I'll find you, you hear?"

I let out a long sigh. I had every intention of staying near Miss Smitty but not because he was requesting it. "Cotton, don't worry about me—"

He gritted his teeth and almost spit out his words. "Dammit, woman, you need to listen to me!"

Ranger Williams put a hand on Cotton's shoulder. "Come on, Vaughn, let's go. He's not going to ask nicely beyond his fifteen-minute mark."

Cotton let out a defeated sigh, and as the two turned to leave, I asked, "Ranger, what about the men in town? The ones who didn't strike? Are they still there?"

Cotton shook his head at me and stormed toward one of the trucks.

"They fired everybody. They're clearing out the dorms right now. It's going to be a ghost town in the next hour."

I helplessly watched the scene before me: men folding tents quickly with the help of the women and children, families dividing, men climbing in the trucks with what they could carry. Ragtown deflated right before my eyes.

As the trucks pulled away, leaving the women and children and scraps of their camps on the desert floor, the cries and the fears of those left behind echoed eerily off the canyon walls.

AUTHOR NOTE: AND THIS was the response from Six Companies to the strikers' demands: shut the job down, fire everyone, and start over. In the process, they cleared out all of the Hoovervilles in the area. This was a drastic move, but in doing so, they were able to "lock down" the area as a federal reservation and, with the town of Boulder City almost built, start accepting dam workers as residents. Boulder City was designed as the "ideal American city," and it seems clearing out all of the unemployed living in the desert was the easiest way for them to make this a reality.

Chapter 30: That Ass Kickin' Goes Both Ways

Ezra

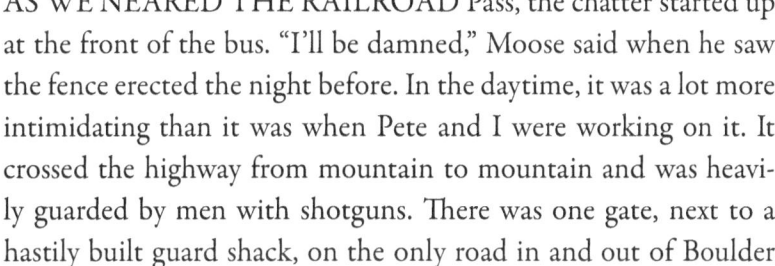

AS WE NEARED THE RAILROAD Pass, the chatter started up at the front of the bus. "I'll be damned," Moose said when he saw the fence erected the night before. In the daytime, it was a lot more intimidating than it was when Pete and I were working on it. It crossed the highway from mountain to mountain and was heavily guarded by men with shotguns. There was one gate, next to a hastily built guard shack, on the only road in and out of Boulder City. The Railroad Pass Casino was on the other side, looming high above a throng of men already waiting.

After the strikers made their case that morning, Frank Crowe said he needed time to think about their demands, which sounded reasonable to me, so I didn't think much more about it at the time. In fact, I was more concerned with what Cotton had told me about Helen. I went back to the dorms to brood a little, even though down deep, there was a little relief that I wouldn't have to take on a responsibility that I wasn't sure I wanted.

I was barely out of the shower when the deputies showed up and told us all to get our gear because we were all fired.

"But I wasn't striking," I protested to no avail.

"Well, you can thank your buddies that were for getting you canned. Now get your things and load up in one of those buses before we do it for ya."

Apparently, Frank Crowe didn't need much time to make a decision. Instead of considering the strikers' demands, he shut the entire project down.

I sat next to Moose on the bus, with Tex Mahoney and Beau Dandy riding up toward the front. Damn them. They wanted to strike, not me. I didn't want to lose my job.

"Hey, Moose, you know that ass kickin' you promised me last night?"

"Still comin'," he said with a little less conviction.

"Yeah, well, it goes both ways now." I doubted I could take someone as big as Moose, but I really wanted to hit something about now.

We crossed through the gate and went a few hundred feet before stopping. One of the deputies at the front of the bus stood and faced us. He pointed at a one-room wooden building near the opening in the fence. "That there is where you can apply for a job. Now go on."

Moose, Tex, Beau Dandy, and I started walking toward the shack, but another guy approached us from the other direction. He shook his thumb over his shoulder. "Don't even try. Ain't nobody there. Just a sign that says they'll start taking applications tomorrow."

"Tomorrow? What the hell we s'pose to do 'til then?" Moose said.

Beau Dandy spit on the ground. "I got a cousin that stays out here at Texas Acres."

"Yeah, I guess I can hang out in the casino for a bit and find a spot somewhere for the night," Tex said.

Moose looked around at the hundreds of men hanging out between the gate and the casino. "I think I'll stay out here and try to find out what's goin' on."

I shook my head. I hated to say this couldn't get much worse, because I knew it could. "I'm going to go find me a place to pitch my bedroll before all those squatters from Ragtown and McKeeversville get here," I said to Moose.

"I thought you was from Ragtown?" Moose said.

"I was." But after talking to Cotton that morning, I didn't think there was anything there for me anymore.

"HEY, EASY, WAKE UP."

I uncrossed my arms and legs and tried to focus on the familiar voice. I had found a rare shaded spot under a sparse tree and claimed it as I watched truckloads of men come through the gate throughout the day. I must have fallen asleep, and I looked over to my roll, making sure that it was still with me, which it fortunately was. Too many men out there to trust anyone. Too many unemployed men. I took Pete's outstretched hand and stood, brushing the dust from my pants. "I guess you were smart for staying outside the gates last night," I said.

"Well, I told ya. I like the setup I got out here. And besides, it doesn't look like it mattered much where we were, striking or not."

I looked around at the growing crowd. "They're clearing everybody out. This ain't gonna be pretty out here tonight."

"It's temporary. They'll start rehiring tomorrow," Pete said.

I shook my head. "It ain't gonna be that easy for all of us. I hear they are going to hire veterans first, like they were supposed to be doing in the first place. That leaves us younger guys out."

Pete smiled and scratched his chin. "We'll see about that. Grab your gear. You can stay at the mansion."

"The mansion? That's what you call your camp?"

"Come on, I got plenty of room." Pete winked at me as I grabbed my roll. "By the way, you don't have anything against pretty girls, do you?"

"The mansion" was an apt nickname for Pete's camp. It was one of the largest tents in the area, a rectangular structure built with railroad tie planks as supports, covered with five large pieces of canvas, which enclosed it on all four sides and provided a roof of sorts. It sat high on the side of a hill, with the railroad tracks above and the rag camp of Little Oklahoma below. From that vantage, the camp offered an unobstructed view of Railroad Pass and the newly built gate beyond to the left, the road to Las Vegas to the right, and the thousands of campsites—dirty sheets, tents, and boxes—of Texas Acres, Little Oklahoma, and Picher before it. It looked like a giant rag pile that covered both sides of the main road and continued far up the highway.

I knew there were other Hoovervilles this far from the work site, but I'd only seen them once, at night, when I'd snuck away from Ragtown to visit the shacks. From where I stood, I could see it all, and I guessed I wasn't prepared for the number of people who traveled to the desert looking for work. There couldn't be more than a few thousand jobs available, if that, and there were at least four times that many men right here. Damn, why couldn't the guys have just been happy they had one of those jobs?

"I think I'll wander around a bit and see if I can find anyone from Ragtown," I said. Helen might not be my responsibility, but I was still concerned about her.

"There aren't many men out here working, and they haven't got much use for those that had jobs and gave them up," Pete said. "You might be better off to stay close until this is over." He turned back toward his tent and gestured toward a slit in the canvas that acted as the only door.

Inside, the tent was divided with sheets, with a room on each end and a common area in the middle. An old couch sat in the main room, covered with clean sheets and a fresh pillow.

"I figured I'd find you out there, so I already made up the couch for you." He grabbed my bedroll from me and threw it on the dirt floor.

"How do you have a couch?"

"That's not all I got out here," he said.

I caught a whiff of roses strong enough to make me sneeze and turned in time to see a large woman almost as tall as me lift one of the faded yellow sheets. Her flowered robe barely closed in the front and revealed a glimpse of a black nightie and nylons rolled at the thigh. Long blond hair fell in ringlets around rounded cheeks and continued until it lay atop her ample bosom.

She extended a strong yet delicate hand, her nails tipped with bright-red polish, and in a husky voice introduced herself as Mae. Her face was made up like she was ready for a night on the town—eyelashes thick, eyes and cheeks painted, and lips as red as holly berries—but I could still see the lines that the makeup didn't cover and figured her to be quite a bit older than me. "I've got coffee made, and I'm gonna cook some eggs and bacon. Anyone else hungry?"

My mouth started to water at the thought of eggs and bacon. "I'd be glad to pay you for your time and the food."

She laughed. "Don't worry about it. How about you, Pete?"

"Sounds good," Pete said.

As Mae slipped through the slit in the canvas, I turned to Pete. "I thought you lived with Marguerite."

"I do," Pete said. "A man can live with two women, can't he?"

At the mention of her name, Marguerite came out from behind the other curtained area, dressed in the same sequined conductor's uniform that she had been wearing the night before. It hugged her body, revealing a tiny waist and an impressive bust. She was tall for a woman, just a few inches shy of my six-foot frame, with eyes as brown as coffee. Her olive skin was dark, like she'd been out in the sun too long, and her short hair was fashionably styled. When she smiled, two small dimples appeared in her cheeks that added an innocent quality to her otherwise exotic looks.

She kissed Pete on the cheek. "I'm going to work. You coming to walk me home tonight?"

"Definitely tonight. A lot of riffraff out there today."

Marguerite cocked her head. "What makes that different from any other day?"

Pete said to me, "Mae works up behind Railroad Pass. Marguerite works inside as a waitress. Out here, you can't leave your tent for the day and go to work if you want anything to be here when you get back." I hadn't said much, and I guessed Pete felt like he had to explain. He didn't. He could live with fifty women if he wanted to. It was none of my business. He continued, "With the three of us living together, there's always someone here to keep the bums out. And besides, it's nice having the ladies around after being around men all day long."

"I'm not going to work tonight." Mae had come back through the slit, not bothering to close her robe that had opened a little farther. She flashed me a toothy smile when she caught me looking then turned to Pete. "Those men out there got no money, and I'm not giving out any free feels tonight. That'll make four of us to guard our spot. I think we can handle it."

Behind her, I caught a glimpse past the sheet into their sleeping area. "Is that a real bed in there?"

"Full-size brass bed with rails and a foundation."

"But—"

"There are times when Mae trades goods for services," Pete said. "And she doesn't work cheap."

AUTHOR NOTE: DURING the strike, everyone was fired, even those who refused to strike. There were already shantytowns around the Railroad Pass casino, such as Little Oklahoma, Texas Acres, and Dee's Camp, but with the influx of those from Ragtown and McKeeversville, these areas grew quickly. While Ragtown and McKeeversville had federal marshals responsible for keeping order, the areas on the outside of Boulder City did not.

Although the people were desperate, it's interesting some of the items they brought to the desert or otherwise obtained to add to their meager possessions. From oral histories, I've read of one man and his wife whose entire tent was occupied by a king-sized brass bed, and at Dee's Camp, one man landed his small aircraft and lived under it.

Chapter 31: Billy Green and Four Roses

Ezra

I SLEPT MOST OF THE evening, or at least tried to. I was nervous about not getting my job back, pissed off at the guys that went on strike to get us fired to begin with, and still thinking about Helen for some reason. I couldn't believe she had agreed to marry Cotton, but I guessed he stepped up, and she saw the opportunity. It was easier to imagine her with him, I guessed, than doing what Mae did, which, for an unmarried woman, seemed like a logical way to eat. I decided to get out of the tent and go with Pete to walk Marguerite back from work.

This place was a lot different from Ragtown. Sure, we had some rough ones down there, but for the most part, it was families and guys that weren't trying to make too much trouble. The camps out here had a little bit of everything going on. It was loud twenty-four hours a day, and sometimes I wondered if people ever slept. There were families, but there were a lot of fights and a lot of thieves. I'd heard estimates that there were ten thousand people living out here, which was ten times the number there were in Ragtown. From what I'd seen, that was a pretty low guess.

Marguerite stopped walking the second she came out of the casino and took a deep breath of night air. She let it out through pursed lips. The white brick building looked yellow in the dark, the only light provided by the bulb lights above the painted sign that said simply Railroad Pass Casino. She leaned against the rough exterior and rubbed her forehead.

"Tough night, huh?" Pete asked.

"You have no idea. I swear there's a million of 'em in there. Little money and no manners."

Pete took her hand, and we started walking back to Little Oklahoma. A man in a worn blue jumpsuit passed in front of us, and the smell of body odor mixed with too much whiskey lingered well after he'd passed. Six men sat under one tree, their backs to the trunk, angling for more room. Those who weren't trying to sleep in the open were either drunk or trying to get that way. The ocean of men began at the gate and waved back over the Pass, through Texas Acres, trickling into Little Oklahoma.

"Did you get a chance to check on those applications?" Pete asked.

Marguerite rubbed her temples again. "One of the other waitresses said she could get a handful from the hiring office in the morning. I don't know why you'd need more than one, though."

Pete shrugged. "Not everyone's going to get their jobs back. Veterans will get the first shot this time around. I'll try the regular route, but if I don't get hired, I'll fill out a few more. Say I'm a veteran. Who's going to check? A lot of these guys aren't working under their proper names anyhow."

"If I don't get my job back here, I think I'm going to join the army," I said. I'd been thinking a lot about what Helen said the night we stayed up talking, which was only a few nights ago but now seemed like forever ago. I had no responsibilities other than to myself, so why not follow my dream?

"The army?" Pete let out a chuckle, but I didn't see what was so funny. "Hell, they aren't even able to pay the pension they promised from the last war; I doubt they are trying to build up a new force right now."

A large fight involving a few dozen men broke out at the edge of Texas Acres, some men standing, some on the ground, bodies tangled in a mass of movement and blood. Another dozen circled around, cheering and yelling. The sound of fist to bone was as powerful as the yells of the bystanders.

A young girl, not more than twelve, ran in front of us wearing a dirty night slip and holding a half-empty bottle of Four Roses whiskey. She stood at the edge of the crowd and hastily handed it to a man old enough to be her father. His hair was matted, and his face and bare chest covered in blood. The man took a long swig from the bottle and then broke it on the ground and stepped back into the fight.

"What a waste of good whiskey," Pete said.

I looked around at the crowd, who seemed eager to see bloodshed. A gladiator complex, I'd heard it called before, some form of violent contest as entertainment to help them escape the reality of their own lives. A familiar face caught my eye from a distance. I squinted, trying to picture the bearded man without his facial hair and with a few more pounds on his scrawny frame. "Son of a bitch," I said. Billy Green.

I began pushing my way through the crowd, trying to keep my eye on the little bastard that had gotten my sister pregnant and then denied his responsibility. Of course nothing would bring Grace back, but I had vowed to make him feel the pain—at least some of the pain—that she went through as she died in childbirth. Pete was yelling at me from behind, but I was focused. The fight continued beside me, but I blocked out the cheers and yells from the crowd, my prey in sight. He turned and saw me, just as I was pushed by someone in the crowd and found myself inside the ring of those fighting.

I felt something hit my head, reached up, and pulled back a hand covered in blood. I tried to focus on Billy in the crowd, but he was gone. And suddenly, everything went dark.

I CAME TO, PROPPED against a boulder, with Marguerite wiping the side of my head with my own shirt tail. Her closeness startled me, and I reacted, but Pete caught my hand before it connected with Marguerite's face. "Whoa, there, killer. If you hit my gal, we're going to have a problem," Pete said.

My head was swimming, and I could hear the angry yells and excited cheers of the ongoing fight in the distance. "Billy. That son of a bitch," I said and tried to stand, but I was unsteady on my feet. Pete grabbed me under the arm.

"Billy?" Pete said. "So you were going after someone. Damn, Easy, we were watching the fight, and next thing we knew, you were in the middle of it."

"I gotta go. I need to find him," I said.

"No can do. You took one helluva hit, and that head needs wrapping, or it might never stop bleeding. Billy's going to have to wait," he said.

I was weak and had a headache that made me see double, so reluctantly, I let Pete and Marguerite guide me back to Pete's mansion.

Mae was sitting on the picnic table, her long hair piled loosely on her head, barely contained with an oversized ballcap. When she saw us, she jumped up quickly and rushed to help. "What happened?" she said as she guided me to the bench of the picnic table.

Marguerite shook her head. "Ezra got in the middle of a fight."

Mae held the candle that had been sitting on the table up to the side of my head. "Looks like he lost. Maggie, get that peroxide out of my room and some clean rags. And a needle and thread."

"It's not that bad," I said, the idea of being sewn up by Mae by candlelight not very appealing. "I just need to cover it and lie down."

"Not going to happen. You need to stay awake for a little while, make sure they didn't knock you silly, and without a stitch or two, it's not going to stop bleeding." She stood and looked at Pete. "Go grab that bottle of whiskey you got stashed. He's going to need it."

I SPENT A GOOD PORTION of that night talking to Mae and Pete. Marguerite had to work the next day after she scrubbed all my blood out of her uniform, so she went to bed early. I had a good amount of whiskey in me, which still didn't numb the pain from getting my head sewn up, and my tongue got loose. I told them about growing up in New Hampshire, my abusive father, my mother I couldn't save, and my sister, my best friend, who I had tried so hard to protect. "But she died," I said. "Trying to give birth to that bastard Billy's child, a child he had no intention of claiming."

"He didn't kill her," Mae said softly. "It happens, and I'm sorry, but it's not this Billy's fault she died. And beating him to death won't bring her back." Mae was probably in her midthirties and not what I would expect of one of the women working in the shacks. Pete told me she was in high demand, though, so I guessed experience paid well. She was motherly, in an odd sort of way, and her words were full of compassion, not condemnation.

I shook my head. "You don't understand."

"I do," Pete said. "And I don't blame you. You came all the way out here to help your sister find that guy, and then he turned his back on her. I'd want to beat him into the ground too. But after you do that, then what?"

"What do you mean?" I asked.

He shrugged. "Then what? It sounds like you don't want to go back to New Hampshire, and after you find this Billy guy, you have to have some idea of what kind of future you want."

I didn't say anything. Pete snapped his fingers. "Oh, yeah. The army."

"Why the army?" Mae asked.

"I guess since I was little, I liked the idea of it. Getting away from home, working with a bunch of guys that were like brothers, women drooling over the uniform." It sounded kind of silly when I said it out loud. "But I'm not saying that's what I'm going to do. It's just a dream I had as a kid. I don't know if that's what I want now."

"Well, what do you want to do now?" Mae asked.

Again, I said nothing. I knew they wanted to keep me talking to make sure my head was okay, but I was tired, broke, and out of work, living in a desert in the middle of summer. Dreaming about my future wasn't high on my list.

"I'm buying a house," Mae said. "My story is quite a bit different than yours, but I can't go back home either. So I'm doing what I do for the money, saving all I can, and then I'm going to buy myself a little house and get a job like Maggie's. And who knows, maybe I'll find someone I can't live without along the way. But I have a plan. You need one too."

I tried to picture Mae in a little house with a picket fence, planting flowers in the yard and chatting with neighbors on her front porch, and I could see it. I smiled.

"She's right," Pete said. "What are you, about twenty? Right now, the only person you have to consider is you. So maybe you should do that."

"What about you and Marguerite?" I asked.

Pete scratched his chin. "Well, Marguerite's story isn't mine to tell, but she'll be going back to New York when she has enough money saved. She's got something to prove to a lot of people, and she will.

"Me? I can't go home, and to be honest, I like it here. Sure, the work's hard—for now—but I know when the economy comes back strong, people are going to trust banks again, and those banks will be needing guys like me that know how to run them."

I realized I didn't know much about Pete other than that he had worked in a bank somewhere in Iowa before coming here. "You don't have any family?" I asked.

He laughed. "Oh, I have a brother. He's in prison for trying to rob a bank. Don't think he'll be out too soon, and when he does get out, I doubt he'll want to see me."

"Why? Just because you work in a bank?"

"No, Easy, because it was my bank he tried to rob, and I'm the one that turned him in to the cops."

"Oh," I said.

"But the point is, we all have a sad story. And unless we want it to get even worse, we have to do something about it. We could run around beating up everyone who wronged us, or we can work toward something else," Mae said.

"I feel like I just got a lecture from my parents," I said. I was joking with them but not entirely.

Mae laughed. "How about advice from two friends?"

"A woman of the world and your much wiser, much more handsome, and not so much older brother." He slapped me on the shoulder, and in that instant, I did feel as if Pete and I were, in a sense, brothers, or at least family, in a way that wasn't born of blood.

AUTHOR NOTE: *AS I STATED earlier, the camps were rough and dangerous, but there were families living there. At about this time, a small school was established at the edge of the camps, built by*

several of the men who lived there, which offered the children some sense of normality. The school was a small, one-room building and at one time had fifty-six students of all ages enrolled.

Something interesting to read about this time in history is related to the Bonus Army protests that happened in Washington, which is what Pete is referring to when talking about the military. The United States had issued certificates to World War I veterans that would draw interest and could be cashed out in the '40s, similar to a pension plan today. However, with the Great Depression, so many were out of work that protests were held in Washington demanding early payment on these certificates. The "Bonus Army" was a name given by the media to a group of forty thousand protestors in 1932.

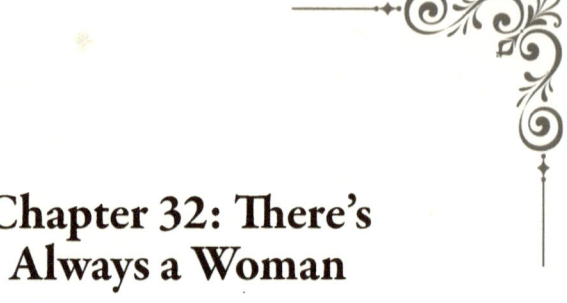

Chapter 32: There's Always a Woman

Ezra

WE MADE OUR WAY THROUGH the crowd to the employment office early in the morning. Few of the men from the previous day's roundup had left their spot near the office, and they became angrier by the minute for not being allowed access to the reservation.

I thought about what Mae and Pete had said last night, and they were right. I needed to decide what I wanted, and then I needed to make a plan. Working on the dam for the next few years would give me the money and the freedom to do—whatever I wanted, to a point. I felt a sense of optimism I hadn't felt in a while. A small bit, at least.

But looking around at all the other men—family men, veterans, men a lot more experienced than me—I was filled with a sense of dread, not to mention a good portion of anger. Why the hell did they have to strike? I had had a good thing going, at least by comparison to doing nothing, and now I would have to compete, somehow, for a job I had already had. I took a deep breath and pushed down my emotions as a guard that was circulating through the crowd handed Pete and me applications.

"Fill those out and get in line," he said. "Hiring begins at noon."

We made our way back to Little Oklahoma, deciding it would be best to get a good breakfast to hold us for the long wait that lay ahead.

After we ate, we sat at the picnic table in front of Pete's camp, filling out the applications to get our jobs back. There were easily thirty men for every job at the dam, maybe more like fifty, and as I filled in blanks and checked boxes, I couldn't think of many reasons that made me more desirable than most. I wasn't a veteran like Moose Martin. I didn't have a college degree like Pete. I didn't have a specialty like Beau Dandy or George Goon. I was just a twenty-year-old nobody needing to work so I didn't starve. About halfway through my application, I slammed my pencil down on the table and got up. "Walker Young's done said veterans would get hired first, so I ain't got a chance of getting my job back."

"Keep checking those little boxes. We need to fill out these papers like everyone else. And if we don't get hired, Marguerite will have us a stack of new papers this afternoon. We just fill them out differently and keep trying," Pete said without looking up.

Frustration and a general sense of being pissed off were running through my body, my optimism after the sermon last night wearing off fast. I broke the lead on my pencil when I sat back down and tried to complete the application. I took my pocketknife out and whittled the pencil back to a tip. I huffed loudly, feeling as though I could spit fire.

"Yank, I'm mad as hell, too, but that isn't going to get our jobs back," Pete said.

Mae came from behind the tent opening wearing a long gown that was sheer enough to leave little to the imagination, and I wondered if she had any real clothes or just chose not to get dressed. She sat at the picnic table with us and began filing her nails but was quiet. Pete got up about halfway through his application to get rid of some water, leaving Mae and me alone. I slammed my pencil again, this time cracking it in two. "Damn," I said.

Mae set down her emery board and put a hand on my shoulder. "I think your frustration has to do with more than the job and that man you wanted to beat up last night," she said. "Who is she?"

"Who said there's a woman?" I asked, wondering if Pete had said anything, although I doubted it.

She smiled. "There's always a woman."

Pete returned, but when he saw us talking, he went the other way.

I ran my hand through my hair, stopping short when I touched the wound on the side of my head. Talking to Mae the night before had been easy, and I had to admit, Helen had been on my mind, although in the back of it. I was so unsure of my feelings for her, but maybe talking it out would help me see things more clearly.

"There's Helen." Her name came out as a whisper, but after I said it, the words tumbled out so fast that it was like I'd been uncorked. I hadn't realized they'd been bottled up so tight. "The first time I met her, I knew she was something different, something special. She's pretty and all that, but she's smart. Real smart. She'd walk around Ragtown, and it was obvious she deserved a better place. But she never complained. In fact, she was about the brightest spot in the desert. I swear, that first day I met her, I wanted a taste of her, but then I quickly pushed that down. The last thing I needed was to get mixed up with a girl. She and Grace became friends, and she and I did too. But now that Grace is gone, well, we're still friends."

I didn't know how to explain what I felt for Helen. I wanted to care—I did care—but something was holding me back from giving in to those feelings. Maybe it was the idea I'd always had of being free but never really getting to that point. But if that were true, then my idea of freedom had more to do with not having responsibility, and I didn't think that was quite it either. How could I put into words what I couldn't even define myself?

"Her daddy died a few days ago. He was real sick, and I know she's hurting. And like I said, she's my friend. I thought about marrying her because she's seventeen and alone, and I don't want to see her..." I stopped, remembering I was talking to a whore, but she understood and just nodded. "Anyway, she is marrying someone else, so I'm off the hook." I thought of Helen with Cotton, and my stomach ached. I'd worked with Cotton for a year, and he was a hard worker, and the guys didn't seem to mind him. I felt he thought he had something to prove, but then again, I thought all men were that way to an extent. It was Cotton, not me, that remembered to give Helen money for her trip into Vegas. It was Cotton that remembered her birthday, when I had to slip away and make up some story about Mr. Emery not getting my package back in time.

She leaned back a little and steepled her hands. "Oh, I see. So she took someone else's offer other than yours." At least to hear Cotton tell it. He may not have worded it that way, but I was pretty sure Helen wouldn't have said yes if he hadn't demanded it.

"Well, no, I didn't offer. I haven't seen her since her daddy died, and honestly, I don't know if I would have asked her anyway. I was thinking about it, but—"

"But you're off the hook. A hook you put yourself on anyway."

I looked at her and said nothing. She stared into my eyes, as if she could see deep into my soul, and I had to turn away. "Yes, I guess so," I said.

"She was never your responsibility, yet for some reason, you chose to make her your responsibility. And now that she's marrying someone else, you're upset about it. Why do you think that is?"

"I'm not in love with her," I said almost reflexively. It was as if the words came out before I had a chance to really think about it.

Mae laughed. "Oh, love. What a dangerous little word. Harder to find than gold, more work than building a dam, and as fleeting as the beauty of youth. And unnecessary, to be honest." She leaned forward and asked more seriously, "What would truly make you happy, Ezra?"

Her words struck me, as they didn't seem like something a woman might say. Most women I'd known talked about love as if it was the ultimate goal in life, and yet Mae spoke of it as something far away, unattainable, and not worth the effort. Maybe her profession had something to do with her cynicism, or maybe her experiences had led her to this truth.

I thought about her question for at least a minute. Seriously thought about it. When had I truly been happy? And what would sustain it for a lifetime? "I don't know," I said.

"Well, I'm glad you didn't say love," she said. "Now, about this girl—"

"Helen." I could see her standing next to the soda box at Emery's, her red hair falling down her back, smiling at me as she held the book I had given her for her birthday.

"Yes, Helen. She's marrying another man, most likely not because she loves him. She's getting married because her only other choice is to join the other girls and me or starve."

"I want her to be happy," I said. I couldn't imagine how she must be feeling right now, and I wished I could hold her, let her cry, or scream, or whatever she needed to do to mourn Ben.

"And you think she'd be happier with you than the other guy? Well, who knows, right? I guess she's made her choice."

"She didn't have a choice," I said. I felt a knot in my stomach, which rose into my throat.

"Exactly."

I shifted nervously on the bench, and for some reason, I thought about Grace. Everything I'd done, everything that led us here, I had done so that Grace could find happiness, and my own was never considered. Thinking about Mae's question, what would make me truly happy, I realized I didn't know because I'd never considered it. I had always been too busy trying to help others find theirs. Maybe that was exactly what I was feeling for Helen; I liked her, and given enough time, maybe could fall in love with her, but at the moment, I felt sorry for her and just wanted her to be happy. I was hiding behind the façade, a martyr of sorts, willing to sacrifice my own happiness so others could find theirs—and only because I couldn't define my own dreams. Maybe I was afraid to dream, or maybe I was just a mess, needing to work out my own life before I thought about blending it with another's.

I picked my pencil back up, an indication that I was done talking, and Mae went back to her nails while I continued to work on my application. I needed a job. Then I would figure out where I wanted to go from there.

AUTHOR NOTE: INITIALLY, veterans were supposed to have preferential hiring status. This didn't happen. So when the strike occurred and everyone was fired, it allowed the company the ability to screen all the applicants better and hire veterans first. However, a lot of men filled out several applications in different names and claimed different statuses in hopes of one of the applications going through and getting them a job, so it didn't really help much.

Chapter 33: It's Our Secret

Helen

IT WAS THE NEXT MORNING before I got Pepper alone. I was having a hard time getting around with my ankle, and he had come to my camp to check on me. The silence in Ragtown, with all the men gone, was eerie, the sense of worried desperation thick in the air. I hadn't eaten since the day before, too worried about my problems to think about food, and I was thankful that Betsy had sent a can of Peter Pan and some soda crackers with him.

"You didn't say anything about yesterday, did you?" I asked as he opened the peanut butter and held it out to me. He shook his head.

"Good. We can't turn him in," I said. I knew there was a big reward for Queho. I'd thought about it most of the night, among the other things I had to think about. But I was a girl, and Pepper was a child; there was no way either of us would ever see any reward money if we said something. All we would be doing would be condemning a man, to death most likely, when he had helped me. I explained this to Pepper, who still wasn't so sure.

"But he stole your canteen. And it was his fault you got hurt in the first place," he said. "And he's a bad guy, right?"

"It wasn't his fault I got hurt. But he did get my foot loose. And he killed that rattlesnake, which was close enough to bite me. He might have done some bad things, but we don't really know what all he's done, right? We do know if he wanted to kill us, all he had to do was—" I slid a finger across my throat in a cutting motion. "But he didn't. He just wanted to get away, to be left alone."

Pepper cocked his head and looked off in the distance, as if he were thinking. I dipped another soda cracker in the peanut butter and took a big bite. Pepper did the same.

"It's our secret, then," he said.

I let out a relieved breath. "Yes. Our secret." I didn't know why, but deep in my soul, I knew I couldn't say anything about him. Maybe it was Betsy's talk the day before about angels, or maybe I just felt sorry for the guy.

"We were supposed to leave today, but the man we're going with can't get down here to get us," Pepper said. "Maybe he'll never come, and we can all just stay here."

I dipped another cracker in the peanut butter and held it out to him. "It won't be all bad, Pepper. You'll see."

"But you won't be there," he said.

We heard something outside my tent, and Pepper went to see who was there, since I had my ankle to deal with. Mr. Emery stuck his head in and, with his face filled with concern, said, "I'm sorry about today, Helen. But there's no way we can get into Vegas and get back here with all that's going on."

It was Saturday. The day they would be putting my daddy in the ground. Two days ago, Mr. Emery had said he'd take me so I could be there for his burial. But now if we left, we couldn't get back in without a pass. As one of a handful of men left in Ragtown after the roundup, I thought Mr. Emery felt somewhat responsible for the women and children that remained. I was glad someone was trying. I knew Daddy would understand.

"What about going to Boulder City?" I asked.

He indicated my ankle. "I think you need to stay off that as much as you can. And besides, I've heard without a pass, getting up there and back isn't so easy. Better to wait a few days until the guys are back to work."

I let out a slow breath. I knew he was right.

A supply truck came to the Wash about noon with food and provisions, but I thought it was there for the benefit of the news cameras that had come with it and not so much for the hungry families left behind. The reporters talked about the men striking and how Six Companies had shut down and was now trying to hire back some of the workers. They called us "the real innocents in the whole mess" and looked sad for the camera, then they packed up with the supply truck and left.

As the sun began its downward slide across the west canyon wall, Mr. Emery sat on a large boulder with a group of children in front of him. They sat quietly, their eyes wide as he told them stories about the canyon. I sat with them for a while then went back to the river to turn the Model T. Daddy had always tried to do it at least once a month to keep the wood spokes on the wheels from drying out too much in the desert heat. I had to soak the back wheels in the water all day, and Mr. Emery said if I soaked the front ones all night, it should be fine to drive.

Ranger Williams was walking from camp to camp with a list and some orange papers. He was giving passes to those whose husbands had been hired that day so the families could come back in the gate once their husbands, or brothers, or fathers, had secured a house. He spent a long time talking to Miss Smitty, which had me a little worried for her, but either way, I had to get the car ready. I knew what was coming. I turned the car, and he was standing beside my Joshua tree when I got out of the water.

"How are you doing, Helen?"

I was limping on my bad ankle, but the salve had really helped. At least I knew it wasn't broken, though I was sure it wasn't the ankle he was asking about. He knew about my dad, of course. He had been given the news from Six Companies in the middle of all the striking, and by the time he had gotten to me, I'd already been to Vegas. He seemed really concerned, but there wasn't much he could do.

"I'll be fine," I said. "I've got options." I couldn't even look at him as I said that. He knew my options as well as I did.

He let out a sigh. "If you can, just hold on out there for a little bit longer. I'm sure if it weren't for this strike, you'd have had someone want to take you as a wife. Once they get back to work—"

I liked Ranger Williams, but I was so tired of hearing that my only option was to get married, even if in my heart, I knew that to be true. "Well, I must be special, because I've already had two proposals even with the strike," I said. I wasn't sure seven-year-old Richie Warner's counted, but Ranger didn't need to know that.

"Good! Well, I won't worry about you, then. I'll wish you luck instead. And I'm sure I'll be seeing you around town. Be sure and tell the fella you choose that he needs to get you one of those orange passes as soon as he gets a place secured." He handed me a white paper, an eviction letter saying I had to be out of there by the next morning, signed by some government official.

I hobbled back to where Mr. Emery was telling stories to the young kids while their mothers packed up what was left of their lives. I'd spent the last year helping at the makeshift school, teaching these same kids to read, and I was worried for their survival as much as my own. As if they didn't have a hard enough time trying to stay alive, now they were being pushed from someplace that they'd grown to see as their home, even if it was a dangerous place to be. I looked around at the small faces, several sallow with the first signs of starvation or dehydration. The danger wasn't only the heat and the lack of food. They also had the local wildlife to worry about. The mountain cats and rattlesnakes sometimes entered the camp, desperate as any of the other riffraff, looking for food. But at least a person could see them coming. The centipedes, fire ants, scorpions, and spiders were harder to defend against, so the kids had learned to shake their clothes and bedding and to be extra careful if they used the privy.

Getting out of this hole would be good for them, if they had any place to go.

Mr. Emery gave each one a licorice whip as they headed back to their camps. I watched him watching them; he released his forced smile and wiped his face when they turned away. When they were all gone, he lowered his head. I felt like I'd done everything but pray. So I lowered my head, too, said a prayer for us all, and hoped—not for the first time—that the canyon's walls weren't so high that God himself couldn't see us.

AUTHOR NOTE: HELEN had a real dilemma with Queho. She knew, as a young woman with no father or husband to claim the reward for her, she would never be able to get the money being offered for Queho. But it was deeper than that. Helen felt she was part of the mountain, and in a way, she related to Queho. The fact that he didn't try to kill her only solidified her perceived bond between them.

Chapter 34: The End of the Wobblies

Ezra

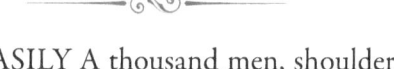

THERE WERE EASILY A thousand men, shoulder to shoulder, pushing their way toward the gate. As Pete and I neared the hiring shack, a parade of trucks led by a Las Vegas sheriff's car divided the crowd. A deputy with a loudspeaker instructed the men to move off the road to let the convoy pass.

"Was that Jimmy Baker?" Pete asked as we stared at the dirty men tied together in the beds of the trucks. None appeared to have slept in the past few days, and most looked as if they had been beaten pretty badly.

The convoy stopped shy of the gate to unload the men. Standing them in line, the sheriff's deputies pointed them south, down the side of the fence, toward the road to Nipton, California.

The deputy with the speaker turned to the crowd.

"Before any of you get back in, you need to know that no trouble will be tolerated." He motioned at the bound men. "All the Wobblies are cleared out of there, and they ain't never coming back. If any of you want to join them, jump right in line here. Otherwise, you'd best get your applications in and hope you'll be getting back to work."

With that, the deputy got back in the car, positioned it behind the last man in line, and started to drive. The group was forced to walk, their hands bound behind their backs with coarse rope, their bodies tied together at the waist.

I recognized several of the men, but my gaze fell on Jimmy Baker. His face was swollen, his exposed upper body covered in a black grime, and he was limping, wearing only one boot, trying to keep pace with the others.

"Where are they going?" I asked no one in particular.

One of the drivers from the trucks smiled. "California. Got out of jail if they promised to never cross that state line again. Sheriff said we needed to make sure they know where that line is."

"It's a good hundred and ten degrees out here. Nipton is at least thirty miles."

The driver shrugged. "More like forty." He laughed. "What you wanna bet they don't never come back to Nevada?"

As one man stumbled, the others continued to walk, dragging him between them until he righted himself. The line continued to move forward, and I couldn't help but watch Jimmy, head lowered, trying to keep up with the men beside him. I knew Jimmy had a sister, who lived with him in a shanty in McKeeversville. I shuddered, trying to forget what I was seeing; I had my own problems to keep me up at night.

"We're up, Easy," Pete said.

The tiny shack had one small table set in the middle of the dirt floor. It had been hastily built, and the sunlight shone through the two square openings on the north and south. The windows did little to provide any ventilation; the sour smell of body odor lingered in the air. Three men sat at the table, taking applications without looking up from their work. Several others stood behind them, holding bright-orange five-by-seven squares of paper.

"Are you a veteran?"

"No," I replied.

"You one of the ones that got laid off?"

"Yes."

"Who was your supervisor?"

"Bouchard. Claude Bouchard."

From behind the seated men, Frenchie leaned forward. It took him a spell to recognize me, my face black and blue from the night before, then he gave Pete and me an orange square. Looking at the three agents, he said, "These two. Deal and McGee. They're mine."

The agents each made a mark on our applications and placed them to the side in a small pile. "Bring those passes back in the morning at six a.m. and be ready to work. You'll have an hour to check in at the dorms before first shift."

I looked to the pass and back at the agent sitting before me then over at Frenchie.

"Crowe stepped in. Said us supervisors could hire back the guys that weren't troublemakers. The good workers. Glad to have you two on my crew."

Pete and I let out a loud yip. Pete tried to get behind the table to hug Frenchie but was stopped by the agent. "Get on outta here. We got a lot of men to get through. Stop at the ranger station up by the casino and show them your pass to get your dorm assignments. If you go in that gate, you stay in a dorm or one of those houses they're building. Otherwise, you stay out here. The squatters are being cleared out," the agent said.

"Don't need a dorm," Pete said. "Got a fine place right here."

"The squatters? You mean all the people still at Ragtown?" I figured all the men had already been cleared out, but the women and kids... Helen.

"Cleaning them all out. After tomorrow, there ain't no more Ragtown."

"HOW ARE MY FAVORITE scabs?" Moose asked as he climbed into the back of the work truck and joined Pete and me. We stood against the sun-worn wooden planks on the passenger side and looked out across the desert. The once-red paint on the truck had worn and peeled, and the planks looked as if they'd been bleeding.

"Ready to get back to work," I said. "These guys out here are giddy as squirrels."

Moose grabbed my chin roughly and turned my head to look at my wound. "Looks like you tried to cut down their tree."

The sun cast a purple glow over the desert as we passed through the reservation gate. Molly Woodward was squeezed into the middle of the truckload of workers. He made his way to the side as the truck bounced over the rocky, now-deserted highway. I stood beside him. "Looks like that was a wasted few days."

Molly shook his head. "Not wasted at all. At least they know where we stand. It's a start. Ya gotta trust."

"Trust? How you gonna trust Crowe and his gang? Sure, we got our jobs back, but remember, nothing has changed."

"Crowe? Not him. You gotta know there's three things worth puttin' your trust in: God, your family, and yourself."

I winced at his words. He knew about Grace and the baby, and even though I hadn't talked much about my family, or lack thereof, he probably figured there was a story. But he said this anyway.

"You got a job, a place to live, and food to eat. That right there is God at work. We're your family, and you damn sure better trust us. You're the only one left."

Although Molly had gotten his nickname for being as slow as molasses, not only physically but in his head a little, he sure seemed to be talking sense.

Pete slapped me on the back. "And now that you are a working man again, if you want to go after that little filly, do it. Like Molly said: trust yourself."

After talking with Mae yesterday afternoon, I thought a lot about what she'd said and came to a few conclusions. What did I want? I wanted to work hard and be proud of what I did. I didn't want to work hard for nothing, and when I came home at night, I would like a warm body that could make me laugh, make me dinner, and keep me focused on what was important. I thought Helen could do all that, and in return, she'd be taken care of. But the problem was, I wasn't sure I wanted it all right now. I had a choice, and as much as I cared about Helen, I felt I needed to take a chance on myself. Cotton would take care of her. I needed to take care of myself.

But she was my friend, and I wanted to check on her, tell her how sorry I was about Ben, and make sure she was going to be all right. She might not have been my responsibility, but I still cared.

"I do trust myself," I said to Pete. "And I think I'm going to stick around to keep you out of trouble for a bit, then when the army decides they can't live without me, I'll see the world." Or maybe not the army at all. I had time. I'd figure it all out.

After stopping at the dormitories for our assignments, we were back in the truck, heading to the work site. "Anyone see Cotton this morning?" I said.

Moose shook his head. "He didn't get hired back. Neither did Sam. I guess Frenchie didn't vouch for all of us."

Damn! It had been so easy to convince myself that Helen would be taken care of, and now, with Cotton not getting hired back, the entire situation changed. I couldn't let her starve, and I needed time to rethink this, but I didn't have time. I let out a long breath. I knew they were clearing out the camps yesterday and finishing up today, but I also knew Helen would hold out as long as she could. As the truck pulled slowly down the highway toward the work site, I hopped out at Hemenway Wash.

"What are you doing?" Pete yelled.

"Tell Frenchie I'm riding the ferry. I got something I need to take care of here."

I walked through the Wash, littered with the debris of what was left of the families that lived there. There were still fifty or so, and I weaved my way toward the front, where my camp once stood and where Helen's camp would be. The car was gone. Helen was gone. I looked toward the mountains then to the river and turned toward the ferry. And even though I felt a pang deep in my abdomen that I didn't get a chance to tell Helen goodbye, I also felt something else. Freedom.

AUTHOR NOTE: THE SCENE of the men tied together and being forced to walk to the California state line in one-hundred-and-ten-degree heat is gleaned from an oral history account. It was a torturous way to let the union know they weren't welcome, but it worked. The IWW caused no more problems at the dam after this short but very important strike.

Since the dam was six months ahead of schedule at the time of the strike, Six Companies could afford to shut down for a week. Not only did it force the hand of the strikers but gave Six Companies time to reorganize and prepare Boulder City to be "the great American city" instead of a desert full of homeless families. Conditions didn't change much after the strike.

Chapter 35: Goodbye to Ragtown

Helen

WITH A TRUNK FULL OF canvas and blankets, Miss Smitty and I drove across the rocky wash out of Ragtown just as the sun began to rise. There were very few people left; we had waited as long as possible but didn't want to be traveling in the heat of the day. Pepper cried when we left, and as I looked back, I saw Betsy wipe her face as well. I told him we'd see each other again, somehow, and I truly believed that. We shared a secret, and that was our bond.

We stopped in town at the company store, where I bought a new canteen and stocked up on supplies with the company scrip I had. With all the donated cans I had received, I had enough food for several weeks, more if I rationed it well. The service station took my last dollar of company scrip and gave me seventy cents worth of gas and said that would be enough to get me to Vegas if that was where I wanted to go.

I thought of Vegas, the stores and shops and casinos, and the thousands of others trying to get those jobs as well. I couldn't imagine being alone there, and Miss Smitty wasn't going any farther than the Pass. Ranger Williams had told her last night that George had been assigned a two-room house and had put her down as his family, so she had a pass. It'd take two to three days for him to get settled, and then she could ride the bus back in from Railroad Pass. I could tell she was excited, but she didn't want to make me feel bad. I was just glad she'd be with me for a few days before I had to decide what to do.

I had almost twenty-one dollars and a car, which was enough to get me all the way to Kansas, if I had any place to go once I got there. That was my problem: I had the means to travel, just nowhere to go. I had a few days to figure it out, then I'd be on my own for good.

Truckloads of men passed us as we left Boulder City behind. For those that got their jobs back, I guessed it would be back to usual, only living in town now instead of the desert. For the men and families that didn't get their jobs back, it would be a different story. I took a deep breath as we crossed through the gate that now separated Boulder City from the rest of the desert. I couldn't worry about those others anymore. It was only my story I needed to write now.

Since I'd already been this way just a few days before, I wasn't as shocked to see the mass of camps set up, and I had already pretty much decided I would go down the highway a little bit away from the casino to find a spot to pitch camp. There wasn't anything for me at the casino, and if I did need to go down there, I didn't mind the walk. As kind as Miss Smitty was, she didn't say a word. I guess she'd been hardened to all this despair herself.

We pulled off the highway about half a mile from the casino on the opposite side, near a place I remembered Mr. Emery called Dee's Camp. I didn't know who Dee was, but I guessed if he minded us being there, he'd let us know. Children were running wild, some wearing not more than a diaper. Others, boys and girls both, were in nightshirts and overalls.

"Is that an airplane?" Miss Smitty pointed toward the mountain.

I followed her gaze, and there was a small airplane parked in the middle of the camp. "I guess that would be hard to steal," I said.

It took us over an hour to get my camp set up, similar to what I had in Ragtown, keeping the car in the center. I took several breaks because of my ankle, which still hurt, but at least the swelling had gone down. We saw some women walking from the mountain behind the camp with jugs of water and figured there was a spring of some sort back there, so maybe this wouldn't be so bad after all.

As soon as we got all set up, it wasn't five minutes before a woman with a baby was asking us for food. I gave her a can of garden peas, then Miss Smitty gave me a stern talking-to.

"You can't be doing that. When you're out of food, who do you think is going to give you any?"

I knew she was right, but with the baby, I couldn't say no. I would have to learn I came first.

We took turns exploring the area, not wanting to leave our camp unattended for one minute. We didn't know anyone out there, and from what we'd seen, the people were a little less respectful and maybe a little more desperate than they had been in Ragtown. I found the spring and filled my canteen with fresh water then made my way back. Miss Smitty had found two big rocks and managed to place them at the entrance to our camp by herself.

Together, we sat and watched the sun go down over the mountain before climbing in the car, me in the backseat, her in the front, trying to sleep with the sounds of people, never stopping, around us.

AUTHOR NOTE: THE AREA known as Ragtown, or Williamsville, is now under Lake Mead. Important fact: Water levels at Lake Mead have been monitored closely since 1934. Currently, because of a megadrought sweeping the West, water levels are at their *all-time low. Considering Lake Mead provides about 90 percent of the drinking water for Las Vegas, this is a serious issue. It is possible that these decreasing levels will one day soon make it impossible for the dam to generate electricity year-round as it has since it was built.*

Chapter 36: When Your Only Hope Is Cotton

Helen

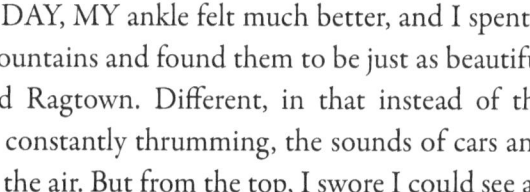

BY THE THIRD DAY, MY ankle felt much better, and I spent a little time in the mountains and found them to be just as beautiful as the ones around Ragtown. Different, in that instead of the sounds of the river constantly thrumming, the sounds of cars and people below filled the air. But from the top, I swore I could see all the way to California on one side and Arizona on the other. I was sure at night I would be able to see Las Vegas to the west, but it would be a while before I was comfortable enough to wander up at night.

I spoke to the woman I'd given the can of peas to on our first day here. Her name was Myra, and the baby was Kade. They lived somewhere at the back of the camp, but the only way Myra could keep Kade silent was to walk with him. He found comfort in the motion, she had said, and I understood that. She also agreed to watch my camp for me while I walked Miss Smitty up to the casino so she could get on the bus to Boulder City. She didn't want me to leave my camp, but I had to trust someone, and Myra would be happy to have a few cans of goods in return for her watch.

"I'm going to miss you, Helen." Miss Smitty had a large pack, and I carried another bundle of her wares. It seemed like a lot, but it was so little when it was everything you had. "But it's temporary, right? As soon as the men get back to work, things will be fine. You and I can go have coffee at that little café we saw in town, and this will just be a bad memory." I thought about Browder's Cafe and the day Daddy and I sat there on my birthday, talking about the future. A future that would never happen now.

"Sure," I said, trying to sound optimistic. "I did apply for several jobs last week; maybe I'll get one." Although I didn't know how they would find me if I did.

We stood by the side of the highway, waiting to cross. Whirlwinds of dust fell over us each time a car passed. "Helen, I don't want to tell you what to do, but if Cotton is willing to marry you, it won't be all bad. You'll have a home, and things will get better and better."

I let out a long sigh. As much as I wanted to try to survive on my own, I had been thinking a lot about Cotton's offer. Gathering bat guano and selling it by the road might be enough for me to eat, but then what? For how long? What if I got hurt again? At least if I was in town, in a house, I'd be safe. My idea of romantic love was slowly being replaced by a need for security.

"I know. I just—"

"You just want someone else. I know. I can see it. But someone else didn't step up, and you've got to give Cotton some credit for that."

We finally made it across the highway and wound our way through Little Oklahoma. It didn't look much like Oklahoma to me, except for the dust. Now that most of the dam workers had been hired and had been moved inside the gate, there weren't nearly as many people as there had been three days ago. The ones left, however, were unemployed and desperate. I was glad we chose to make this walk in the daytime, because I didn't think I would be safe at night.

There was a guard shack set up behind the casino, and they seemed to be in charge of giving passes to families and handing out information on housing. We stood in a long line with other women, and when we got to the front, Miss Smitty showed her pass and told them that she was there to go to her house. Her house. It sounded so wonderful.

Miss Smitty was lucky. Since she was a schoolteacher, she couldn't get married, at least not if she wanted to have a job. And because of that, George got to say that he was responsible for her, which I guessed until she got a job, he was. Maybe I should go to school like Daddy always said. Maybe I should be a schoolteacher and not have to worry about getting married. But school, like everything else, was nothing more than a dream that couldn't be reached. This was supposed to be my last year of high school, but without Miss Smitty to sign off on my education, and without the ability to get to Vegas to finish at a real school, that wouldn't happen either. I let out a long sigh and pushed it all back down.

Miss Smitty got a new slip of paper and was told to stand with several other women who were waiting for the bus to take them into town. I pictured them in the little white houses, putting up curtains, planting in the yards, taking walks through town, and watching the construction men build the theatre and the city park. I wanted to be there. I would do anything to be there.

I'd even marry Cotton.

The bus arrived, and Miss Smitty gave me a tearful hug. "Is there anything you need me to do? I will if I can. Just tell me."

"No," I said. "Take care of yourself."

Miss Smitty gave me another long hug. "You take care too. Everything will work out, and when you get to town, come find me."

I promised I would, hoping it was a promise I'd be able to keep, and waved to her as she got on the bus. After it pulled away, I stood there, looking around the casino parking lot and toward the camps, suddenly feeling very alone.

"Helen."

I heard my name and turned quickly. Cotton was leaning against the guard shack, wearing a pair of clean slacks and a white shirt. His hair was slicked down, and if I didn't know better, I'd have thought it wasn't Cotton at all.

"What are you doing here?" Of the thousands of people milling around, I didn't think I'd run into the one person that said he'd help me. But there he was, and I didn't know if what I felt was annoyance or relief.

He pushed himself off the wall and smiled. "I told you if you stayed with Miss Smitty I'd find you. George told me before he went into town that she'd be here today to get moved in. I figured she'd know where you were."

I kept walking, and he kept pace with me. "You were looking for me?" I reminded myself that this was not what I wanted, but could it really be that bad?

"I was serious when I said I'd marry you and take care of you. I'm still serious," he said. "But I'm not going to hunt you down forever."

"Why aren't you at work?" I said, changing the subject so I didn't have to answer right away. His clothes were ill-fitting, and he looked like a teenage boy playing in his daddy's Sunday clothes.

He held his hands out, and they were cleaner than I'd ever seen them. "I am at work. I got a good job, and I don't have to kill myself to do it," he said.

I stopped at the highway and waited for a break in the traffic to make my way across. He was right in step with me. When we got to the other side, he grabbed my arm and stopped me from walking, turning me to face him. He dug in his pocket and pulled out a roll of bills.

"Cotton, where did you get that?"

He smiled. "I told you: I got a job. A good one. I met some guys at the casino, and I've been doing things for them. This is eighty dollars, Helen."

"Eighty dollars?" I said in a hushed tone. "Cotton, put that back in your pocket. Someone will kill you for that."

He laughed. "This ain't nothin', Helen. I've got a job waiting for me in Vegas. All I gotta do is get there, and I'll make a lot more than this."

We started walking back to my camp, where I had a few weeks' worth of food and barely twenty dollars to my name.

"So you're going to Vegas?" I said. The stores, the casinos, the people. They weren't all covered in soot and grime like the dam workers, and if you had a job, I could see where you could live pretty well. But it wasn't Boulder City.

"We, Helen. We're going to Vegas. If you'll go with me." I was still walking, limping a little as my ankle started to hurt again, and Cotton took my arm, trying to help. I was thinking, so I didn't respond right away.

"Look," he said. "I'll be making enough money to take care of us, and you won't starve."

"Why me?" I said. "There are a thousand women out here wanting just what you are offering, but you keep coming for me. Why?" I didn't mean it to come off as confrontational. It was something I'd been thinking about a lot. He didn't take it that way, and he didn't take long to answer.

"Because I saw the way you took care of your daddy, and I want someone to take care of me like that. I'll do the working, and you take care of the house stuff. And besides, it doesn't hurt to have the prettiest wife in all of Nevada."

I felt myself blush. I thought that was the first time any man, other than Daddy, had called me pretty.

But he didn't say he loved me. And although those were the words I longed to hear, I was relieved they didn't come from Cotton's mouth.

When we got to Dee's Camp, I waved my arm in front of it. "Well, this is home." There were so many people, and I had a hard time finding my camp. I knew it was right toward the front. I looked around for Myra and didn't see her.

"Is that your car?" Cotton said.

I turned in the direction that he was pointing, and my heart dropped in my chest. All my canvas and plyboard were gone, and the Model T sat by itself, the trunk pried open. I ran to the car and looked inside the trunk. Gone. My clothes, my food, my new canteen. Everything gone. I dug in my pocket for the keys and prayed that whoever did this didn't get to the inside. Fortunately, I needed the keys to unlock it, but just to be sure, I dug under the front seat and felt the holstered gun and the rolled pack that held my money. *The Great Gatsby* lay on the backseat next to my camera, my jar of salve that I had used in the night on the floorboard.

I looked around the camp, and no one would meet my eyes. I realized without Miss Smitty, if I had to leave—for fresh water, food, to gather bat guano—what little I had would be exposed. I hadn't been gone long, and someone took almost everything. Another thirty minutes, and I was sure they would have been inside the car, and I would have had nothing left.

I couldn't do this alone. The realization was heavy, and I felt like I hadn't slept in days.

I sat in the passenger side of the Model T and let the tears fall. What was I doing? I couldn't keep living like this, not having anyone to trust, not knowing how I was going to eat, especially now that all my food was gone. I cried, and then when I couldn't cry any more, I hit the seat with my fists several times.

"Helen." Cotton stood before me, all dressed up with eighty dollars in his pocket. He looked around at the shambles of my camp and opened his arms wide with his palms up. He was offering me a chance.

I wiped my face with the back of my hand and looked at him, remembering what Daddy had said: "You need a good man that will take care of you." I nodded, hoping Cotton was that man.

"Let's go." My voice echoed from the hollow abyss of my soul. Then I threw him the keys to my daddy's car and shut the passenger door.

AUTHOR NOTE: THIS CHAPTER concludes Part I of Ragtown. Part II begins a year later in Las Vegas, October 1932.

Chapter 37: Las Vegas, October 1932

Helen

THE SMELL OF BACON and coffee pulled at my stomach as I served another table, this one, two men and a woman. The men were dressed in fine clothes, their hair slick and their shoes shiny. The woman laughed with an open mouth at the men's words, her bosom rising and falling under her green dress, which left little to the imagination. A short table, I thought as I set their plates in front of them. They'd expect dime service and would only leave a nickel tip.

"What's your name, honey?" one of the men said as I refilled his coffee.

I stood up and pointed at the name tag clearly displayed on my apron. "Helen," I said. Nothing more.

"You should smile, Helen," the woman said. "You'd get more tips that way."

I gave her a crack of a smile and a half curtsy. "Yes, ma'am," I said. That was all they'd get. Too much smiling, and the men took it as an invitation, and when I pulled away from their advances, I would get no tip. I'd been there almost nine months, and I knew how this worked; I didn't need some fancy woman in half a dress telling me how to get my nickels.

The clock above the counter said 9:28, and I was counting the seconds until my shift ended at ten. Cotton was just getting home when I had left for my morning shift, so I knew he'd be sleeping all day, which meant I could sneak off to the desert, take some pictures, and gather some more creosote and brittlebush to make my salve.

My friend Sally came in and sat at the counter, and I let out a sigh of relief. She normally came in earlier in the day, and considering the hazards of her profession, when she was late, I worried about her. I'd never had a best friend before, and although I might have thought it odd a few years ago that a prostitute would take that role, Sally had grown to be very important to me. A sister, in a very short time.

I poured her a cup of coffee and handed her the sugar bowl.

"Thanks, Hel. I need coffee this morning," she said.

"Rough night?" I asked.

Her eyes were red and puffy, and I knew she hadn't slept at all. She was wearing one of her fancy dresses, a blue one that was cut a little too low, and matching strapped three-inch heels. Rarely did Sally come in still dressed from her job. Once in a while she did, but Ralph, my boss, said he didn't like that kind of advertisement going on in his place, so she usually cleaned up and came in looking like any other young girl in a modest dress or pants. But Sally was too pretty to be any other girl, and even dressed in her loose shirt and dungarees without any makeup, the men couldn't help but stare.

"Clinic day," she said as she took a long sip of her coffee then added more sugar. "They made me wait half the morning, but I'm papered for the next week," she said with a weak smile.

I was not naive enough to not know what happened on Block 16. Everyone in town knew that if you had five dollars and a hankering for sex, Block 16 was a playground. All the establishments on the block, including the Arizona Club where Sally worked, required the girls to get an exam each week to show that they were free from disease and fit to work. I guess the clubs didn't want their reputation tarnished by passing out venereal diseases instead of blow jobs.

She set her coffee down and clapped her hands, changing the subject. "Well, let me see your diploma!"

I laughed. "You are assuming I passed and further assuming that I am carrying it with me."

Sally cocked her head and pursed her lips, and I went behind the counter and got the high school diploma out of my purse that the schoolmaster had handed me yesterday. I didn't see what a high school diploma would do for me working in a coffee cafe, but it was a promise I had made to my dad, and I had kept it.

Sally ran her fingers over the words. "I don't know what it says, but it sure is pretty."

Ralph, my boss, came up behind me. "It says, 'If Helen doesn't bus that table over there, she'll be selling that piece of paper for rent money.'"

"Oh, stop, Ralph. This is a big accomplishment. Let her have her day."

Sally took another sip of her coffee while I headed to table number three. Three cents. I swear, the people who dressed the fanciest seemed to be the stingiest with their coin.

After cleaning the table, I wiped my hands on my apron and carefully put the diploma back in my bag. Once I'd checked on table number one, I busied myself wiping the counter so I could talk to Sally while she ate her breakfast.

"So, what did Cotton say about your diploma?" she asked in between bites.

"I didn't tell him. He'd just say it was a waste of time getting it anyway." Just like he said everything I wanted to do was a waste of time.

"He's one to talk," she said. "Oh!" She paused with a forkful of egg halfway to her mouth and laid it back down on her plate. She dug in her pocket and laid a dollar on the counter. "I sold those two jars you gave me in one night," she said. "If you got enough for five more, I can sell them on the weekend."

I waited until Ralph and the other waitresses weren't looking and picked up the dollar and put it in my apron. "That's what Ralph pays me for a day," I whispered to Sally. Two small jars of my homemade salve, which cost me less than a nickel to make, and Sally sold them for fifty cents each.

When I first met Sally, she was in Monroe's Pharmacy, looking at different kinds of salve that promised miracles and offered no relief. It was hard not to notice her, a tall blonde dressed in a skimpy party dress at nine a.m., and I had gotten closer to see if her hair really was that white, or if she smelled of bleach like I knew some of those women did. I hadn't expected her to notice me. "Excuse me," she had said, "do you know which one of these is good?"

She kept rubbing her left upper arm, and I could tell she was in pain. "Are you hurt?" I asked, pointing at her arm.

She shrugged and lifted the sleeve of her dress to reveal a dark-purple-and-red bruise in the shape of a handprint. "It's not as bad as it looks," she said, trying to smile.

I had a little of my salve with me—I tried to keep a small jar in my purse for emergencies—and I pulled it out and held it out to her. She unscrewed the lid, took a whiff, and handed it back. "That's okay. I'll go with the stuff that doesn't smell like a barn."

"None of that other stuff works as good as this. Really. I have some more at home, so you can have this. If you put it on now, it will feel better before you leave the store."

She raised one of her finely manicured eyebrows and took the jar back from me. "That's so nice of... Are you sure?"

I smiled. I knew that a lot of the women who worked on Block 16 were shunned by some of the women in town, and getting a little kindness from some of those that professed to be keepers of the community morals, whatever that meant, could be difficult. But I wasn't one of those. In the past two years, I'd seen women do a lot of things to keep from starving, or keep their kids from starving, and I wasn't about to claim that I hadn't sold myself out for a different price.

I had gone back to the feminine hygiene aisle and was lost in thought when Sally walked up behind me and handed me a bottle of Lysol. "None of that other stuff works as good as this," she had whispered.

I was a little embarrassed to be caught looking for products that everyone knew were to keep me from getting pregnant, but as a married woman, I guess it wasn't that unusual. And if I were going to take advice on the subject, I figured a prostitute would know best.

I saw her again a week later when she happened to be in the coffee shop, and she introduced herself. We'd been friends ever since. I kept her in salve for the times her customers got too rough, and she had given me the priceless gift of the wonders of Lysol, which kept me from getting pregnant with Cotton's baby. It was a fair trade.

"I'm going out to the desert today for more plants," I said to her.

The desert right outside the Vegas city limits was pretty, in its own way, but it was nothing like the desert closer to the river. At Ragtown, the creosote and brittlebush had been everywhere; here I had to hunt for it. But it'd been almost a year since I'd been that far away from Vegas, and I was sure Cotton would have a fit if he thought I'd gone out that way. He wasn't thrilled that I went out to the desert at all, and other than my weekly visits to Woodlawn to visit Daddy, he liked me to be right under his thumb. He probably wouldn't have let me work if he didn't spend all his money at the casinos every night.

With five more minutes left on my shift, the little bell on the front door rang. I turned to see Cotton, still in his expensive but wrinkled suit that he had worn the night before, unshaven, and his hair so slick it looked like he'd fallen headfirst in a bucket of tar.

"Speak of the devil," Sally said under her breath.

I tried to catch him before he got too far in the door. "You aren't supposed to be here!" I looked around to make sure Ralph was in the back and tried to push Cotton out the door.

He put his hands on my hips, and I stood straight up. "It's payday, darlin', and I've come to collect."

He stuck his hands in my apron pockets. "Got any tips in there?" he whispered in my ear. His hot breath against my neck reeked of whiskey. I slapped his hands hard.

"Get out of my pockets," I said.

He backed up and laughed. "Fine, keep your pennies. I'm here for the real money."

He went to the counter, slapped it hard, and yelled toward the back. "Hey, Ralphie, isn't it payday around here?"

"Stop it, Cotton. You're going to get me fired!" Ralph had already warned me twice about Cotton being in the cafe. When he was drinking, which seemed to be all the time, he was loud and could be downright mean. He was not good for business, Ralph said. He was not much good for anything.

When I had first agreed to marry Cotton and come to Vegas, I felt I had no other real options. He went to work every night, and I didn't know what he did at first, except that he was making some real money. Good money. He'd bring home almost fifty dollars every week, and although I didn't love him, I felt at least it wasn't so bad. He kept me fed, bought me some new clothes, and didn't lay a hand on me until we went to the courthouse and said, "I do." Even then, he was quick, so I only had to lie still and let my mind wander back to a place where Cotton wasn't. We had a nice little apartment over the pharmacy, and I cooked dinners, kept the place straightened up, and made sure his clothes were clean. It wasn't a bad arrangement. At first.

But Cotton had a problem, one that I couldn't have foreseen. Living around the dam site, where alcohol and gambling were banned, I had no opportunity to realize Cotton was what my dad would have called "a mean drunk." And he was horribly mean when he drank. We hadn't been in Las Vegas two months before he came home, barely able to stand up alone, and screamed at me all night about how much of his money I spent and how I didn't do much to earn it. The next morning, he didn't remember any of it, said he was sorry, and went about his day as if it was nothing to be concerned about. But I was concerned, and when I told him I didn't want him drinking, it made him drink more and made him even angrier.

"How do you get drunk at work!" I remembered screaming at him one night, when he'd come home smelling so bad of whiskey and vomit I didn't think I'd ever get the stench out of our apartment. He didn't answer me, but he didn't have to. I knew how he did it. His job required him to be in and out of the local casinos all night, doing God only knew what for a local gangster, and the casinos were happy to give out free alcohol. For someone who had a taste for it, that was like turning on a water hose.

By Christmas, he was drinking every night, and I felt as if I were living with two different people: one that I tolerated and one I downright hated. Even though he was still, supposedly, making decent money, I got a job at the cafe because the money he was making wasn't making it home every week. That was when I realized Cotton's other problem.

Cotton with money in his pocket was like a loaded weapon. Rent, bills, food, and I became a lot less exciting to spend his money on than more booze, women, and gambling. The problem was, you can't win at any of those, and the more Cotton played, the harder he tried to prove that wrong. We lost our apartment just as the heat of summer began and now lived in a studio over the feed store that smelled like hay and wasn't much bigger than a horse stall.

"No, Cotton, I need that money to pay the rent." I pulled on his coat sleeve, but he shrugged me off and slapped the counter again.

Sally was sitting at the counter, not two feet from Cotton, and muttered, "Jackass."

He turned quickly toward her and yelled loudly enough for the people in the bakery next door to hear, "Whore!"

Ralph was behind the counter, his face red but his voice controlled. He handed me five dollars. "Here, Helen. Now get him out of here."

Cotton grabbed the money out of my hand.

My eyes started to burn with tears. "Cotton, we can't lose this apartment too."

He counted the money, licking his finger as he separated each bill. "I got it taken care of."

"No! You can't gamble my pay. You'll lose. You always lose!"

He stuffed the bills in his pocket and smiled at me then reached out and touched my cheek. I pulled away. "I'm not gambling to pay the rent. I've got a big payday coming tomorrow. I got a job, too, you know. One that pays better than this shithole."

"Enough," Ralph said. He reached under the counter and grabbed the Louisville Slugger he kept for troublemakers. "Get out of here, Cotton, and don't come back."

Cotton gave Ralph a mock salute and sauntered toward the door, not looking back at me or anyone else. There were only a few patrons in the diner, and they were all staring at me. I covered my face and let the tears fall freely.

When I looked back up, Sally handed me a napkin to wipe my face. Ralph handed me a five-dollar bill.

"What's this?" I said.

His voice was quieter. "It's your first week's pay that I held back. I'm sorry, Helen. You're a good girl, but I can't have the likes of him around. He's bad for business."

"You're firing her?" Sally said. "Come on, Ralph. It isn't her fault." She put an arm around me, and I was thankful, because my head was spinning, and I couldn't decide if I wanted to fall down or throw up.

Ralph walked back to the kitchen without a word. I hated losing my job, but I couldn't blame him. There were young single women in here all day trying to get a waitress job who would work more hours for less money and not have any drama from men.

"Shh," Sally said. "We'll think of something. Helen, you need to get away from him. I'm afraid for you."

I pulled myself together, not wanting to be the morning show for the customers any longer. I wiped my face as I took off my apron then folded it neatly and laid it on the counter. I grabbed my purse and came back around to Sally. "I'm afraid for me too."

AUTHOR NOTE: THIS CHAPTER begins one year after the death of Helen's father, the closing of Ragtown, and the previous chapter when Helen makes the decision to trust Cotton and leave with him. But a lot can happen in a year, and Las Vegas, then and now, has a way of bringing out the worst in some people.

Chapter 38: Marriage and Criminals

Helen

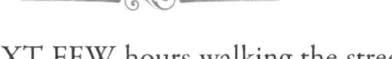

I SPENT THE NEXT FEW hours walking the streets, asking at various businesses if they were hiring. I got two offers for "personal services," which I knew was a legal way to ask for what Sally did, and that was the closest I got to anything at all.

It was not that I hadn't considered it before. I could leave Cotton, join Sally, and get paid for letting men do what Cotton did for free every other night. Sally taught me how to keep from getting pregnant, and she taught me how to let my mind wander while Cotton did what he wanted. It was not much different from cleaning toilets, she had said. You did it, got your money, and didn't think about it. But the more I tried not to think about it, the more I did. My heart still wanted to feel, and I knew if I trained it not to, it would never be able to again.

It'd been three hours since I had been fired from a job I didn't love but that kept me busy, and I went back to our apartment, thinking that surely Cotton was asleep. I could change clothes and still make it to the desert, where I could at least have a little peace. If Sally could sell five or six jars of my salve every week, maybe I could make enough to leave Cotton. If I had somewhere to go.

Our apartment had a sink, a stove, and a bed in the main room and a powder room off to the back, which doubled as a pantry. I had four dresses now, a pair of overalls, three blouses, and two pair of dungarees, which I guessed was more than I had when I left with Cotton. I also had my old Brownie camera, although buying film had become a luxury that I used my tip money for. Cotton said it was a waste of money, but he didn't understand how free it made me feel, being in the desert, finding something beautiful, and taking its picture.

Cotton was passed out in the bed, still in his clothes. I wanted to get my money out of his pocket, if it was still there, but didn't want to risk waking him up. Instead, I snuck past the bed and grabbed a pair of dungarees and a shirt out of the closet then quietly closed myself in the powder room. I could still hear him snoring, so I carefully moved the sack of flour on the floor and lifted the floorboard. I pulled out my money jar and put the dollar Sally gave me and the five from Ralph in the jar. I kept the thirty-two cents I made in tips in my pocket, in case the car was out of gas, like it always was, and put the jar back under the floorboard, next to my uncle Dwayne's revolver. Then I replaced the board and flour sack quickly. After changing my clothes and twisting my hair in a braid, I tried to make it to the front door without waking Cotton.

He grabbed my arm roughly as I passed the bed. "Where you goin'?"

"Job hunting," I lied. "Ralph fired me this morning, thanks to you."

He rolled over and sat on the side of the bed without letting go of me. "It wasn't much of a job anyway. And besides, I have another job lined up for ya."

I rolled my eyes. The last time Cotton said he had a great job lined up for me, it turned out to be a stand-in waitress at a fancy party that his boss was having. I didn't see a dime from that, but waited on a bunch of greasy men and their painted women while Cotton stood at the door, checking people's pockets as they came in. Everyone in town was afraid of his boss, Tony Badamo, and his group of henchmen that he called bodyguards. I knew who they were; I read the papers when there was a break at the diner, and Sally told me all the rest I needed to know.

"I don't want to work for Tony Badamo. He's a criminal, Cotton," I said. It was bad enough I was married to one of his pawns.

He gritted his teeth and tightened his hold on my arm. "Tony wouldn't have you. He likes loyal employees."

I tried to pull away, but he pulled back. "You're hurting me, Cotton, and I don't like it."

He let go of my arm and held his hands up, palms out. "My friend Johnny Sparks is coming over after dinner, and I expect you to be real nice to him. Do you hear me? He owes me a favor, and he's willing to hire you, as long as you can keep your words to 'yes, sir' and 'no, sir.'"

I put my hands on my hips and stayed outside his reach. "What happened to the big payday tomorrow?"

He tensed and untensed his hands at his sides. "Oh, it's coming. And as soon as I pay Tony the money I owe him, we'll be back on track. I quit gamblin', and I—"

"You owe Tony money? How much?"

He took a deep breath. "I was stupid, Helen. Okay? I admit it. But I promise—"

"How much?" I asked again.

"A hundred dollars," he said.

I grabbed my stomach, which felt like someone had filled it with cement. My mouth was open, but no words came out. My whole body was shaking, but I headed toward the door. I needed out of there.

AUTHOR NOTE: FOR A nineteen-year-old woman during the Great Depression, thoughts of leaving your husband, no matter how bad the circumstances, were bold. There really wasn't much opportunity for a woman, much less a single woman, and a divorced one, even less. The fact she is even considering prostitution at this point, one year after she first saw the cribs behind Railroad Pass, is a great indication of how her life and her worldview are changing. On reflection, I'm not sure Helen realizes how lucky she is to have a street-smart friend like Sally.

Chapter 39: Block 16

Helen

THE ENTIRE APARTMENT smelled like creosote, but I didn't mind the smell at all—it reminded me of the desert. I put the fifteen jars of salve I made for Sally in a box and put them in the pantry then looked through the closet for something decent to wear to meet Cotton's friend. I didn't care what the job was. I needed it, and I'd be nice to the man, if the job he was offering was paying. The note Cotton left me that afternoon said he'd be home around seven, which gave me thirty minutes to air out the apartment and make Cotton a sandwich.

After clearing my head while looking for brush, I made a few decisions. The first one, and the big one, was that no matter what, I had to get out of this marriage to Cotton. He owed Tony Badamo money, which meant he probably owed others money, too, and these were dangerous men. And then there was the drinking. I'd never been around anyone who drank like Cotton did, and as long as it was so readily available, I didn't see it getting any better. Maybe it would, but I didn't feel it was safe for me to stick around and find out. He wouldn't listen to me when I told him he needed to stop; it just made him angrier. I had to get out.

Fortunately, I could get a Reno Cure without having to go to Reno. I'd just have to come up with the money to pay a divorce lawyer. According to Sally, if you had the money, it took the judge about five minutes to stamp the paper, and you were divorced. Eight hundred dollars was the going rate, if there wasn't any party contesting. Sally said she had a customer who would do it for two hundred dollars, which was still a small fortune to me. I needed work, to sell some of my salve, and to save as much as I possibly could—and hope Cotton didn't get us both killed by Tony Badamo in the meantime.

Getting Cotton to sign off on the divorce was a whole other problem, but I'd worry about that when the time came.

The second decision I made was that I was leaving Nevada. I had Daddy's car, and even though it was getting older and could use some work, it would make it to California. It had to. I'd heard there were jobs there for men and women, working on farms, and even though they were scarce, the weather wasn't as hot. If I had to live in the open for a while, I could handle it. They had just had the Olympics there, so they couldn't be totally broke. And besides, Roosevelt was going to be president soon—I just knew it—and he would make everything better.

Once I had the money, I'd throw everything I owned into a milk crate—my money jar, my clothes, my camera, Uncle Dwayne's gun, my high school diploma, and the copy of *The Great Gatsby* that Ezra gave me for my birthday last year—and I'd drive off in my daddy's car and start over in California.

I let out a long sigh. Once I had the money.

I often wondered how different things would be now if my dad hadn't gotten sick. I heard people in the diner talk about Boulder City, its cute little stores, the movie theater, and the houses all lined up in a row. Maybe I'd be up in the mountains, taking pictures every day and gathering supplies to sell my salve for money to buy things for our house. Maybe I'd be working at the candy store, handing out licorice whips and peppermint sticks, or maybe I'd be dating someone I really cared for.

Like Ezra. I had thought at one point Ezra would offer to marry me, like Cotton had. But he didn't even come to see me after my daddy died, and he had to have known. I had been heartbroken and angry and still was to some degree. I really thought we had the start of something, but it was just another fairy tale, better left to my books.

A knock at the door brought me from my thoughts. When I opened it, a man dressed in a sharp suit, his hair as slick as Cotton's, smiled at me with a toothpick stuck between his teeth. "You Helen?" he said.

I knew Cotton would be there any minute, but I didn't like the idea of having a man in my apartment without him being there. "Cotton isn't here yet. Could you come back a little later?" I said it nicely, real nice, with a smile as big as Texas.

He pulled a watch from his pocket and looked at it. "Well, this won't take long, and I got other things to do. If you don't want the job—"

"No, no, I do! I just—" I took a deep breath and held the door open for him.

He stepped in and took his hat off while looking around the room. I set his hat on the counter in the kitchen area and grabbed our one chair for him to sit on. He turned it around and straddled it. I sat on the edge of the bed with my back straight and my hands placed perfectly in my lap.

"Cotton said you had a job for me, and I can do just about anything." He was looking me up and down, and it was making me a little nervous. I wished Cotton would hurry up.

"Your husband didn't mention how pretty you were. How long you been married?" he asked.

I shifted uncomfortably on the bed. "We've been married for about a year. What is the job, exactly?"

He crossed his arms on the back of the chair. "Well, I manage a club. You might have heard of it—the Golden Room, over on Block 16."

I stood up and moved toward the door. "Oh, no. There must be a mistake. I'm not a prostitute."

He waved me back toward the bed, but I stayed standing. "Sit down. I know you're not a whore. I need someone who can wash the sheets and keep the place clean. I pay three dollars a night." He winked at me and added, "And if you decide to make any extra on the side, you keep half of it."

I raised my chin. "There won't be any extra. But I can wash sheets and clean." Three dollars a night was a lot of money, and if I could work every night, I might be able to stash enough in the next six months to get out of here. Six months. I could do this.

He winked at me and stood. "Okay, then I'll see you tomorrow night. Shift starts at midnight. Don't be late."

I moved out of his way as he went to the door, then he turned and snapped his fingers. "Damn, I'm always forgetting my hat." He walked to the counter and grabbed his hat, and as he walked back by me, he wrapped his arms tightly around my waist and pulled me close. "And any extra I get, you keep it all."

I tried to move out of his grasp, but he pulled me tighter, his breath heavy on my neck as he brushed his lips across my cheek.

"Let go of me!" I yelled as his hand drifted down my back.

I pushed him with all my strength, and he let loose. "Loosen up, girl. Cotton said you'd be nice to me."

"Get out," I said. I was shaking, both from anger and fear, and I wished I had put Uncle Dwayne's gun under the mattress before I let that man in my apartment. He laughed at me as he tipped his hat and sauntered carelessly out the door.

I was fuming by the time Cotton got home thirty minutes later. "You're late," I said.

He waved a hand at me. "Yeah, yeah. So were you nice? Did Johnny give you the job?"

"I'm not working for that man. He molested me!" I could still smell his cologne, and all I could think about was taking a bath.

"What? What happened?" Cotton crossed his arms over his chest and gave me a smirk.

"He wrapped his arms around me and pulled me to him. He doesn't have that right," I said.

Cotton laughed. "That's it? That's hardly considered molesting you. Honestly, you need to grow up. Johnny treats his girls good."

"I'm not one of his girls. And I'm not working for him." I thought of my plans to get away from here and shook my head. I'd figure out something else.

Cotton moved closer, took a deep breath, and let it out slowly. I could smell the whiskey on him and turned my head away. He grabbed my braid, pulled me toward the bed, and threw me down on it, then straddled me with his knees holding down my arms.

"Get off of me!" I screamed and tried to buck him off, but he was too strong.

"You listen to me. You are my wife, and you will do what I tell you to do. You will work for him, and if he grabs a feel every now and then, you'll smile and nod your head. Do you hear me?"

"How dare you!" I struggled with all my strength, but it wasn't enough to move him off me.

He was smiling at me and raised his hand as if to hit me, and I shut my eyes and waited for the blow. But it didn't come. Instead, he got off me and grabbed my car keys off the counter. "I gotta get back to work. If you have anything in that car that you need, you better get it now. I finally found someone to unload that pile of steel on."

"You're not selling my car. It's mine." I jumped off the bed and tried to take the keys from him.

"It's Tony Badamo's now. And besides, it was time your dowry was paid."

AUTHOR NOTE: WHILE most people think of Las Vegas as the marriage capital of the world, Nevada was once considered the divorce capital of the world. A "Reno Cure," as you may have deduced, was a slang term for a quickie divorce. In 1931, in an effort to boost the economy in the state, Nevada reduced the residency requirements to six weeks in order to file. The divorce rate in the state skyrocketed, and "divorce ranches," places where women would stay for six weeks to establish residency and gain their quickie divorce, sprang up all over the Reno, Nevada, area, and to a lesser extent, Las Vegas.

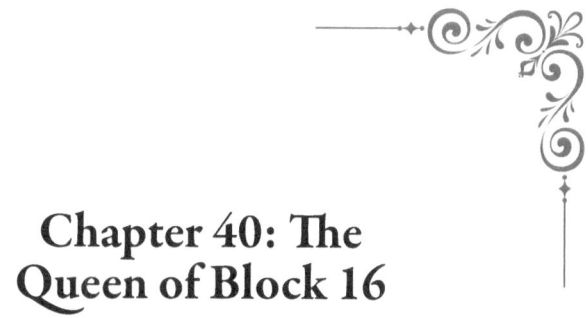

Chapter 40: The Queen of Block 16

Helen

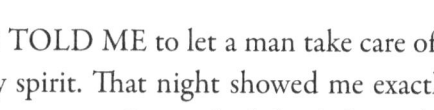

MY DAD HAD TOLD ME to let a man take care of me but not let him break my spirit. That night showed me exactly what he'd meant. Over the past year, Cotton had slowly been chipping away at me, at my very being, and I didn't even realize it was happening. It had been a slow descent into a shell of who I was just a year ago. With his final attempt to give me to Johnny Sparks—and that was exactly how I interpreted it—his taking my car to pay his gambling debts, and his attacking me on the bed, I knew it was only a matter of time before he would let that hand fall. And that wasn't going to happen.

After he left with my car, I cried until I had no more tears. I felt defeated. My coin jar held $19.11, not nearly enough to get me out of my marriage and out of Nevada, but it didn't matter. I'd starve to death in the desert before I'd let Cotton touch me again, and if I had to use Uncle Dwayne's gun to keep him away, I would. I rolled my belongings in a towel and slung it over my shoulder, keeping my hands free for Sally's box of salve, and made my way to Block 16.

The Arizona Club was packed with men, the smoke so thick I had to squint to see. Women with painted faces and thin dresses walked confidently through the crowd, sitting on laps and laughing like they were having a good time. Once in a while, one of the women took a man upstairs and disappeared down the hall. The entire place smelled of whiskey, smoke, and sex.

"Whoa, there, where do you think you're going?" A large man stopped me at the door, but I didn't let him see me sweat. My hair was tucked under my ballcap, and I had on one of Cotton's old shirts with dungarees. I hoped I looked like a gangly teenage boy.

I showed him the box in my hands and said in a deep voice, "I have a delivery for Sally Garland."

He tried to take it from me, but I pulled back. "Sorry, my boss said I have to give it to her myself."

He crossed his arms over his chest and looked down at me. "Well, I don't know who your boss is, but he sure as hell—"

"Tony Badamo. He's my boss, and he said no one touches this box but Sally."

No matter how big and mean a man was, there was always something, or someone, he was afraid of. My intuition was right. Tony was a much scarier man than I thought, as the minute I said his name, the bouncer dropped his arms and his jaw at the same time.

"Hold on, I think Sally's in the pool room," he said.

I waited by the door, and within a minute, Sally came back with him, with a concerned look on her face. When she saw it was just me, her face cracked for just an instant, then she went along with my story.

"Oh, thank you! I didn't know he was sending this over tonight." She turned to the big man that stood close by, watching us both. "Bruce, you can't tell anyone about this. Tony would have my skin if anyone found out he was sending me gifts."

Bruce smiled. "You owe me one, Miss Sally."

She moved closer to him and put a hand on his chest. "And as long as this boy can carry the box to my room, you'll get what's due."

Sally's room was very similar to the apartment Cotton and I lived in, at least in size. She had more furnishings—two chairs, a small round table, and a vanity—and her bed had big fluffy pillows with red satin cases that matched her bedspread. The walls were covered with framed prints, mostly nature scenes, and instead of it smelling like a hay barn, it reeked of rose perfume.

She sat quietly and listened as I told her everything that had happened. When I finished, she let out a long sigh and leaned back in her chair. "I know Johnny Sparks, and he definitely wasn't going to let you clean sheets. This is real bad, honey."

Pointing at the box of salve, I said, "I've got to get out of here, but I need to stay in Nevada until I get my divorce. I'm going to Reno, then I'll get word to you so you can send me the money when you sell those. I really appreciate it, Sally."

"Reno? How are you going to get to Reno? You can't hitch. You'll get yourself killed or worse."

"I'm taking my car. I saw it parked out back at the Apache, and I intend to take it and get out of here." One thing my dad had taught me about a car was you didn't have to have a key if you knew what the wires under the dash were for. Cotton, or Badamo, if that was who he'd really sold it to, would never suspect that it was gone until I was miles down the road.

"You can't steal a car!" Sally said.

"It's my car, and I—"

"No," she said. "It was your daddy's car, and now that you are married to Cotton, it's his car. He owed Tony money, and that car was the only way for him to get it. So I guarantee you if you take it, you won't make it to Beatty before they'll have you and probably throw you in jail. You're better off to hitch the train in the morning and take your chances there." I could tell she was thinking about what else I could do, and I was glad for it, but there was no way I was leaving Daddy's car to some gangster.

"I won't go through Beatty. I'll take the long way and go through California. I'm not leaving my car with him. It's all I have left of my dad." And I was not going to start crying thinking about it. I was tired of crying.

She leaned over and took my hands in hers. "Listen to me. Tony can do anything he sets his mind to, you hear me? Anything. And if Cotton had given him that car, and you take it... he'll be looking for you too. Please don't take the car. Just disappear and—"

I shook my head. "No. I'm tired of men deciding what is mine and how I live. I don't care who they are. I'll starve if I have to, but if anyone sells my dad's car, my car, it will be me."

She took a deep breath and shook her head. "If we can get your divorce here without going to Reno, I guarantee it will be cheaper. But you'll have to hide somewhere for a while. At least until we see how serious they are about finding you. Do you have a friend you can stay with for a few days that Cotton doesn't know? I'd hide you here, but this is the first place he's going to look."

"You're my only friend," I said. I remembered the tent cities at Railroad Pass and the thousands of souls living in tents that all melded together into a sea of humans. The only people I knew other than Sally were in Boulder City, but if Cotton wanted to find me, that was where he'd go. I thought of the mountains and how I was always able to melt into the landscape when I sensed others nearby. There was no one in Ragtown as far as I knew, so there would be even fewer people to avoid. "But I know where I can go."

AUTHOR NOTE: BLOCKS 16 and 17 of the early 1900s Las Vegas plan were the only blocks originally set aside for liquor sales with-

out licensing requirements. Block 16 quickly became the red light district, so to speak, with most of the bars hosting rooms or cribs in the rear dedicated to prostitution. Around 1912-1913, the Arizona Club, one of several drinking establishments in the area, built an upstairs on their bar to house a bordello and became known as "the Queen of Block 16." I tried to recreate it here based on very few historical records and a lot of how I imagined it would have been.

Chapter 41: Definitely a Circus

Ezra

"HEY, WATCH IT!" MOOSE Martin screamed to the men above him as a screwdriver sailed by his head and landed with a loud clunk in the bed of the widow-maker. Tight as a pack of Luckies in the small tin box, we rode with our hard-boiled hats on, three hundred feet down the canyon wall to tunnel number one, while construction debris, rock, and dirt rained from above. The widow whined on its steel track as it strained to carry us.

"A little jumpy this morning. You aren't a little afraid for the fight, are you?" I asked.

Since the recreation center had opened in town, amateur boxing had become one of the main attractions on Saturday nights. Moose had a natural spinning punch and had been undefeated for eight straight weeks. When the pool of opponents started running thin, Bud Bodell decided to up the stakes and bring in an outsider for the bout.

Moose dismissed my words with a wave of his hand. "Afraid? Of that skinny little brownie? Pfft."

Chief Dan Buck laid a hand on Moose's shoulder. "He's no skinny little brownie. I hear he's big as me. Never lost a fight."

Moose shrugged. "I'm not small myself, but I'll be careful not to let him land on me when he's going down."

"You be careful. I hear this guy has killed people in the ring," I said.

Moose raised his chin. "I work here, don't I? I ain't afraid to die."

The widow-maker screeched, metal to metal, as we crossed two hundred feet, marked by a cable that ran from the Nevada side of the canyon across the river to the Arizona side. A wrench bounced off Moose's hard-boiled hat, followed by a flurry of small rocks, before they fell to the river below.

"But if I'm gonna die, I'd like a man's death. Not because some hack from Indiana can't hold his tools."

"Smile, boys. This one's for the history books." Ben Glaha, a photographer hired by the Bureau of Reclamation to document the building of the dam, clung to a steel ladder that had been bolted to the side of the cliff. His left leg and arm were wrapped around the side of the ladder like a monkey on a vine while he held his big camera in his right hand. As the widow-maker descended the mountain, passing within five feet of him, he snapped off numerous shots.

Several men tipped their hats to Glaha as we passed.

"I swear," Moose said, "this place gets more like a circus every day."

It'd been a year since the strike ended, and aside from the faces of the crew, little had changed at the work site. We blew through the solid mountain wall to the other side about six months ago, a year ahead of schedule, and I would never forget that day. As the blue-green haze mingled with smoke, dust, and debris, sunlight exploded through the wall, and we all had to shield our eyes from the overpowering light that poured into the darkness. Together, we stood in the giant hole and yelled and waved to the high-scalers working above and the muckers and general laborers below. A small colony of bats flew by, their wings beating in a chorus, silhouetted as if suspended in flight against the orange background of the sun for a few seconds before flying off to find another cave. It was eerie and beautiful all at the same time, and I could finally breathe.

When the concreting of the tunnels began, we were all reassigned, and of the old crew, only Moose and I had stayed together. Pete was assigned to the beach, a large protrusion of rock near the water's edge, a place large enough to house the construction of the concrete frames that we used in the tunnels. He considered it a step up from working in the tunnels and never let us forget it.

A lot had changed outside the tunnel too. Ragtown was nothing more than a memory. Living in the dormitories, I got clean sheets and daily showers, luxuries that were unheard of in the desert. Anderson's mess hall provided me with fresh meals, and the company store offered necessities and teasers. The recreation center was a place to unwind and play a little eight-ball. There were plenty of girls to dance with, and Mae's friends took care of my other needs. And that was just the beginning. The town was growing every day, twenty-four hours a day, with construction nonstop on new homes, businesses, and roads, all for the purpose of making the lives of us dam workers tolerable.

Guys were already talking about sticking around after this thing was built, and I had to say starting a family here wouldn't be so bad. But like Pete said, "There are girls to play with, girls to lay with, and girls to marry," and I was doing just fine with the first two. I could have stepped up with Helen last year, and I might have let a good one go, but I wasn't ready to settle down. Mr. Emery had seen Cotton a few months ago in Vegas, and he said Helen was working, going to school, and making friends. I was glad to hear it. But I did still think of her.

The cable box stopped with a jerk. I held tight to the side while the cattle gate opened.

"If it ain't the fight that's got you rattled, it must be Smitty," I said.

Tall and thin, Smitty Goon was a direct contrast to Moose's thick frame. Her skin was as white as milk, and aside from her starched skirts and shirts she wore every day, she seemed to take little care of her appearance, rarely wearing any sign of makeup and hair always forced into a severe bun. Moose, however, was quite the ladies' choice, with dark hair, blue eyes, and skin browned from the sun. His worn blue jeans and ill-fitting shirts, usually covered in soot from a day's labor, were no deterrent to their attention.

While Moose walked with the swagger of a man carrying a lot of extra muscle, Smitty walked tall and erect—proper. She always seemed very sober to me, but Moose said she had quite a sense of humor; she just didn't share it with everyone.

On St. Patrick's Day, Moose had intervened as three men tried to convince Smitty to join them in Vegas for an Irish celebration. He could tell she was uncomfortable in the situation by the way she looked around, her gaze landing pleadingly on Moose a half block away. Since that day, he started walking her to the store, taking her to the picture shows and dances, and claimed he was protecting her from the riffraff. Although thanks to Sims Ely, the new city manager, the streets of Boulder City were the safest in the United States.

Moose let out a long sigh. "She ain't like other girls. Refined, you know? And smart. Real smart."

"Ezra, Chief, you two are swinging the bucket today. Moose, you're on measure."

"Ah, give me something else, Frenchie. A girl could measure. I won't even break a sweat," Moose said.

"You save your sweat for tonight. I got a week's pay on you."

I climbed the scaffold on the gantry crane and stood next to Chief. He took the line from the cement truck and attached it to the trough.

Chief double-checked the tubing while waiting for the trough to fill. "Hey, Frenchie, I hear you been telling around town that Moose here has a gimp leg. Got no chance against that big ol' Mexican tonight."

"That's right," Frenchie said. He pointed a stern finger at Moose and said, "And if you find yourself anywhere near those wetback puddlers, you start limping, you hear? The more hurt you look, the better the odds are going to be."

"Hell, he's already the underdog. That Mexican's got a reputation, you know. He's brought down some mighty tough fighters." Chief signaled to the cement truck to stop pumping and started detaching the lines.

"That's right. He's an underdog," Frenchie said. "But I got a ton of Franklins on him, and the higher the odds, the better."

Moose shook his head and started measuring for the first pour of the day. "A circus, I tell ya."

I laughed. Definitely a circus. But our circus.

AUTHOR NOTE: WHILE Helen's past year has been fraught with a troubled marriage, Ezra, an hour away and still working on the dam project, seems to be thriving. One line in this chapter, "I could finally breathe," says a lot about Ezra's life and probably why he so easily convinced himself that Helen was doing just fine in Vegas, without ever checking on her. Life in Boulder City, the town built by Six Companies to house the dam workers, was a model small town and offered everything a young man like Ezra needed at the time. He was fine, and Helen was far from his mind. But how quickly things can change.

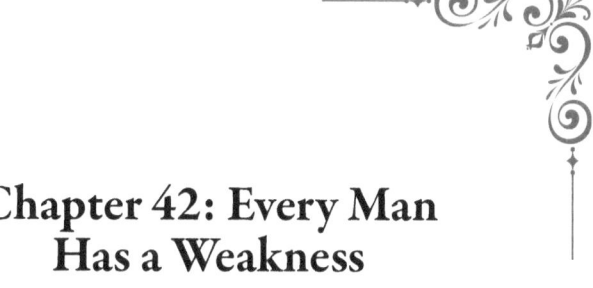

Chapter 42: Every Man Has a Weakness

Ezra

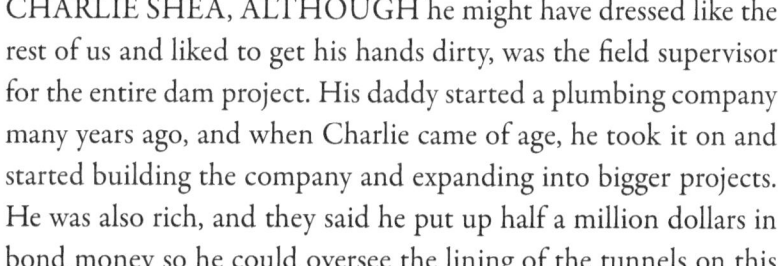

CHARLIE SHEA, ALTHOUGH he might have dressed like the rest of us and liked to get his hands dirty, was the field supervisor for the entire dam project. His daddy started a plumbing company many years ago, and when Charlie came of age, he took it on and started building the company and expanding into bigger projects. He was also rich, and they said he put up half a million dollars in bond money so he could oversee the lining of the tunnels on this project, directly under Crowe himself.

Charlie sat on an upturned bucket, watching the progress of the men on the beach. His worn shirt and tattered jeans were accented by his boots, which looked like he'd been puddling all morning. Charlie's idea of supervising was to show, not tell, and he was rarely just sitting on a bucket while his men did the work.

"Well, if it isn't the tunnel boys," Charlie said as we get closer. He signaled to the crew that it was time for lunch. "You're early."

"Driver had to go back to Lo-Mix," I said. "They had the wrong concrete again." I sat on a flat rock next to Shea.

Chief sat down under the shade of an overhanging boulder and opened his sack lunch. "Morning, Mr. Shea," he said.

"You may be twice my size, Chief, but if you call me Mr. Shea again, I'm gonna knock the red off ya. You hear me?"

Chief cleared his throat. "Yes, sir, Mr.—I mean, Charlie."

"That's better. Now, Moose, tell me how you're gonna beat that Pedro tonight."

Moose, squatting next to Chief, was already halfway through his turkey sandwich. He shrugged. "I guess the same way I beat the rest."

Pete stood with his face aimed at the sky and took a deep breath. "Smell that, boys? No gas fumes. Nothing but dust."

"You look like a giant fire ant working out here in the sun." I held the tip of my hat as I looked up at Pete.

"I guarantee it isn't as hot down here as it is in those holes. No puddlers down here, and once in a while, we get a little breeze coming off that water. Damn near paradise. Right, Charlie?"

Shea motioned at Pete. "Sit down and eat, Banker. We're talking about fighting, not working."

Pete sat next to me and looked at Moose. "I got about every man's pay in my pocket to take to the book at the Pass. You better beat him good. For your sake."

"He ain't no Jack Sharkey, so I figure he'll go down fine," Moose said. He finished his sandwich, wiping his mouth on the back of his hand.

"Sharkey? You crazy, boy? Schmeling's the man right now," Charlie said.

"Not for long," I said. "Sharkey's gonna take him to school next week."

"I have to agree with Ezra," Chief said. "There's only one man who's going to take a beating worse than that big German this year, and that would be President Hoover."

Pete lay back, supporting himself on his elbows, and stretched his long legs in front of him. "Well said, Chief. At least we all agree on something."

EVERY MAN HAD A WEAKNESS. It might be as complicated as a woman, but sometimes it was as simple as a perfectly placed punch above the second rib. A good fighter could find that sweet spot. A great one knew how to take advantage of it. By the last round of the fight, Moose's left eye was bleeding and damn near shut. Doc wanted to call the fight, but Moose wouldn't let him. He must have known that Ponce was going for his left eye, trying to close it completely. He waited until Ponce made that stretch, turning slightly, and Moose stepped in, half spinning his body to the left and shifting his weight to the right. A short, straight punch to Ponce's left abdomen, and for a split second, Ponce dropped his guard and his chin. Long enough for Moose to connect with a left uppercut.

Ponce stumbled, and Moose hit him with another combo. Right jab, left uppercut. The big Mexican tried to pull away, but Moose dropped his guard, daring him to make a move. Ponce went for a left overcut, hitting Moose in his good eye. He took the punch, but his opponent had again left his side exposed. Moose put all his weight behind a right hook into Ponce's side—I swear I heard the give of a rib or two—and followed it with a brutal left uppercut as Ponce dropped his guard. Ponce went to his knees.

Moose never took his good eye off him. The thirty-second bell rang. Ponce rose slowly. Moose had one more shot, and to hear him tell the story after the fight, all he could think about was all the money us guys at work would lose if he didn't take this guy out. Dropping his own guard, Moose planted his left foot and wound up like a windmill. His right connected. Ponce doubled over, and his jaw met Moose's upward left hook, a punch with enough force to snap the Mexican's head back. He stood motionless for half a second before falling backward onto the mat.

That was all the talk in the morning at the work site. How Moose took that big man down and made us all a lot of money. The final odds were fifteen to one against him, and although those two bills Pete handed me this morning felt good in my hands, they sure weighed heavy knowing the price Moose had paid.

"I talked to Charlie, and he said Moose is going to be in the hospital for a few days. If it makes you feel any better, I'm sure those nurses are treating him like a god," Pete said.

I put my money in my pocket. "It don't. He needs his job, and you know they aren't going to hold his spot forever."

"Just a couple of days. He's in the company hospital, so his job is safe. Have you talked to his girl?"

"Smitty. She lives with her brother, George, and I talked to him this morning before he went up top. I told him to tell her if there's anything I can do to let me know." I shook my head. What the hell could I do?

Pete patted me on the back and headed back toward the beach just as Frenchie called for me to crawl in the tunnel. Chief and I were pouring again, and even though most of the men were in a good mood after the fight last night, Chief and I weren't talking a whole lot about it.

While the puddlers got to work on the third pour, Frenchie called my name, and I headed to the mouth of the tunnel. My stomach dropped when I saw Bud Bodell standing there, and my first thought was that Moose took a bad turn. I took off my hard-boiled hat, wiped the sweat from my brow, and prepared myself for the worst.

Bodell looked me up and down as if he were scrutinizing a bug. "You Ezra Deal?" he said.

I took a deep breath and suddenly thought this might not be about Moose at all. I rubbed the scruff on my chin and stood up straight. "What can I do for you?" I asked.

He smiled and hesitated, which I knew was his way of making me worry more about what he was going to say. It was a game that those in power used quite a bit, and from one who had always been a minion, one I was familiar with. I waited, keeping my face unreadable. I could play the game as well.

"You know a woman named Helen Vaughn?" he asked.

Helen Vaughn. It took me a hot second to realize he was talking about my Helen. "I knew her by Helen Carter. Is she okay?"

"Well, her name is Vaughn now. When's the last time you seen her?" He was watching me closely, and I refused to lower my eyes.

"It's been at least a year. Right before the strike. Is she in trouble?" I figured he wasn't going to answer me, but I was worried about her now, and those old feelings of guilt started to creep back into my body.

"Assault. Kidnapping. Stolen car. Depends on your definition of trouble. She hightailed it out of Vegas in the middle of the night."

My mouth fell open in disbelief. Assault? Kidnapping? Helen?

"Her husband thought she may have come to you. Now, my question is, why would he think that?"

Damn you, Cotton. She married you. "We were friends when we lived in Ragtown, then she married Cotton and left. I doubt she'd come to me if she was in trouble, and I don't know why Cotton would think that either."

He stared at me, as if trying to decide if he believed me or not. "Any idea where she'd go, then?"

I shrugged. "She was from Kansas, but I don't know if she had any family left there or anywhere else. Like I said, I didn't know her like that."

He scratched his chin, looking at me hard, then puffed up his chest. "Well, if you hear from her, I'm the first person you tell, you hear?"

"Yes, sir," I said.

He dismissed me toward the tunnel with a wave of his hand and motioned for Frenchie to walk with him. As I headed back to work, all I could think about was what could have possibly happened if Helen was mixed up in all that Bodell had listed. Cotton, that was what. "Yes, sir, you'll be the first person I tell if I hear from her," I whispered to myself as I made my way back to the gantry. Hardly.

AUTHOR NOTE: RACISM was rampant at the dam, just as it was pretty much everywhere in the US in the 1930s. I tried representing dialogue in a way that would have been historically accurate, and in doing so, this chapter, in particular, might be difficult for some to read. Boxing was not only a popular spectator sport during this time but also was very popular in Boulder City amongst the dam workers. I'm also a boxing fan, and the scene of the fight was a lot of fun for me to write.

Chapter 43: Saving Pepper

Helen

BEFORE LEAVING VEGAS, Sally traded my change jar for paper money, which made it a lot easier to carry. Using a thin blanket instead of the worn towel I took from the apartment, she rerolled my personal items and secured each end with cord, leaving enough slack for me to slip my arms through so I could carry it on my back. When I told her I could hide out in the mountains beyond Railroad Pass, Sally told me she had a friend named Mae that worked in the cribs, and she made me promise to find her in one week. In the meantime, Sally would get as much information as possible and would try to sell all fifteen jars of the salve I'd left her.

It wasn't much of a plan, but it would at least get me away from Cotton, and that realization alone made me feel a little lighter. It was the beginning of fall, so living in the desert would be tolerable. If no one was looking for me, I could just leave, a poor-man's divorce, and go to California and start over.

But I didn't want to just leave. I wanted a divorce. I wanted to be Helen Carter again. Without the divorce, I would forever be looking over my shoulder for Cotton. Without a divorce, everything I had would only be mine until Cotton took it from me.

I made my way from Block 16 to the Apache Hotel, sticking to the shadows of the bright neon lights. Men and women, dressed in everything from overalls to their fanciest suits and dresses, walked the streets as if it were three in the afternoon, not three in the morning. The sounds of cars on the streets, people talking and laughing, were only equaled by the sounds of music and the constant ding-ding of slot machines from within the casinos.

A sense of panic struck me as I approached the Apache and saw Johnny Sparks standing at the entrance, smoking a cigarette. He turned and looked right at me. I froze, but he didn't seem to recognize me with my hair up and dressed in men's clothing. He finished his cigarette and went inside, but I chose to go around to the back anyway, not wanting to take my chances on Cotton possibly coming out of his drunken stupor and showing up too.

Hesitantly, I walked down the darkened alley behind the Apache. There were muffled sounds, from the inside of the casino, from the city beyond that, but also from the shadows of the dark alley. I heard murmuring, someone in the distance sobbing, and voices coming from the cracks. About halfway down the alley, moving toward the parking lot, a man appeared from behind a trash dumpster. He was fastening his belt and didn't notice me until he looked up. His eyes crept over me from head to toe. "Damn, I should have waited a few minutes," he said.

My skin crawled, and I kept my head down and brushed past him. I was minding the man behind me and not paying much attention to what was before me when I ran head-on into a young girl coming from behind the same dumpster. She was small, her hair cut short, wearing a dingy brown dress. She fell when I bumped into her.

"Oh, I'm so sorry," I said as I held a hand out to her. I heard the man behind me laugh as he continued down the alley in the opposite direction.

"Helen?" I heard the young girl say.

When I looked down and into her face, it wasn't a girl at all. It was Pepper Allen, my friend from Ragtown, dressed as a girl.

"Pepper?" I said. He hadn't taken my hand, so I crouched down next to him and put an arm around him. It had been over a year since I'd seen Pepper, the day I had left Ragtown. His mother and he had stayed, waiting for a man that was to take his mother, Betsy, as his wife and provide them with a home on his ranch and a life beyond Ragtown. He must have been thirteen by now, I thought, but had the build of a ten-year-old. He smelled of stale cigarettes, sweat, and lavender. "What in the world..."

He sniffled and wiped his face with the back of his hand. I pulled him closer, as I had when his father had died, and felt ill. He wept openly in my arms. "Where is your mother, Pepper?" I whispered as I stroked his slick hair, which smelled like a mixture of hay and oil.

"She's gone," he whispered between his sobs.

I closed my eyes and felt my own tears trail down my cheeks. No. No.

"When you two are finished..." I looked up to see another man standing before us, waving a dollar bill.

Anger boiled up from inside, and I stood, one hand on my hip, and waved at him. "Go home to your wife," I spat.

He hadn't been prepared for my words and started to grab me, but Pepper stood and got between us. "No, don't touch her," he said in a cracked voice. "I'll go with you," he said.

Pepper turned to me and said, "Go, Helen. I have to make my five dollars so I can go back home tonight."

"Yeah, get out of here, Helen," the man mocked.

He grabbed Pepper's arm and dragged him behind the dumpster. I stood there, filled with anger and disgust. Pepper was not my responsibility, but he was a child, and I couldn't just leave him there. I dropped my pack and grabbed my uncle Dwayne's gun and walked behind the dumpster. I held it out, pointing it at the man. "No, I'm not leaving without him," I said.

The man chuckled until I cocked the hammer and pointed it straight at his private area. He hesitated for a minute, as if thinking, then waved a hand at us both and turned and walked back down the darkened alley from which he came.

"Helen," Pepper said. "I'm going to be in so much trouble..."

I crouched next to him again. "Pepper, I'm leaving. I don't know where I'm going, but I'll take you with me if you want to go."

He looked up at me with dull eyes. Then, without having to think more than three seconds, he held his hand out to me. I helped him up, and together we made our way to the parking lot and to my daddy's car.

I didn't have to hot-wire it after all; Cotton had left the keys in it. I told Pepper to lie down in the backseat, which he did without a word. I knew the people coming and going in and out of the casino wouldn't even question a sole teenage boy driving out of the lot in an old car. I drove to a part of the desert between Vegas and Boulder City, an area I had found one day looking for brittlebush. I carefully drove the car off the road about a half mile to a small ravine that I knew would hide it from anyone that wandered out this far, and I was thankful that I remembered how to find it. Pepper hadn't moved or said a word, and I didn't push. I grabbed a pair of overalls from my pack, knowing they would be too large for Pepper, but he needed to get out of the dress he was wearing. He silently changed in the backseat and only got out when I instructed him to. He took my hand and held tightly, then we backtracked to the highway and slowly began walking.

Pepper didn't say a word, and he didn't let go of my hand.

By the time we got to the casino, it must have been four a.m. I knew better than to start a journey across the desert before daybreak, and I was tired, so I found a spot on the other side of the highway, near a small general store that hadn't been there the last time I had been in the area. I spread my pack so it was long enough for two to lean on. "Let's sleep for a few hours. We have a long walk," I said and patted the spot next to me. Again, Pepper did as he was told without question and lay down next to me.

One of the things about being in Vegas for the past year that had kept me from feeling so alone was my weekly visits to Woodlawn, the cemetery where my dad was buried. I would sit and talk to the ground, knowing his body was somewhere below me, and it made me feel sad but somehow better at the same time. I had plans to one day buy him a nice headstone, instead of the small wooden cross that I had carved his name into. I hoped that I still could, one day. But it would have to wait. I had to take care of the living first.

I wondered what had happened to Betsy, if she, too, was at Woodlawn, where I knew Clive, Pepper's dad, was. Where Grace and her baby were. I knew Pepper would tell me in his time what had happened, so I wouldn't push. Right now, he needed a friend.

I looked at the stars and tried to imagine my dad and Betsy looking out for us. I had little to no plan as it was, and now, I had a kid with me, a kid that had obviously been through something very traumatic, for God only knew how long. Last year, I was scared, afraid of what would happen to me alone in the desert. That was why I had gone with Cotton in the first place, so I would have some help—have someone to take care of me, like Daddy had said. But a lot had happened in a year, and instead of feeling afraid, I felt determined. Determined to not only find a better way for myself but to save Pepper from whatever hell he had been living in. I would be his angel.

Pepper was tucked in close to me, and just before my eyes closed, I heard him whisper. "Helen? You have a gun?"

"Yes, Pepper, I do."

"Good," he said.

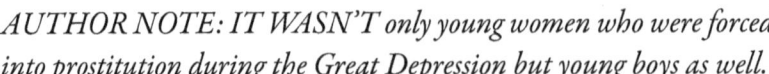

AUTHOR NOTE: IT WASN'T only young women who were forced into prostitution during the Great Depression but young boys as well.

I have read several true accounts of young boys, especially those like Pepper who were small and frail and may have had some developmental limitations, who were used by their adoptive or foster parents for prostitution. Writing the scene about Pepper was hard for me, but I felt it was something that should be mentioned.

Chapter 44: Teenie Weenies and a Little Peace

Helen

I SLEPT HARD WITHOUT dreaming and woke up in the shadow of two kids, a boy and a girl. They stood over us, just looking down, and when I opened my eyes, they ran off toward the small store that looked out of place amongst the tents and boxes. I woke Pepper from a restless sleep. Our destination was about a five-mile walk over the mountain and through the desert, and I figured with the heat and the terrain, it would take most of the day to get there. It would be a lot quicker if we could go through Boulder City, but unless I knew someone who could sneak us through the gate, that wasn't an option. I checked my pack and my pockets and told Pepper to stay put while I went to the little store that was just opening.

I kept my hair tucked under my cap, and although I would have loved to get rid of Cotton's shirt, the only other shirts I had were women's, and they wouldn't do if I was trying to look like a teenage boy. The man running the store called me "son" twice, so my disguise must have been good, or at least satisfactory. I spent $3.50 and bought a canteen, a bar of lye soap, six cans of pork and beans, six PayDay candy bars, a box of saltines, a can of peanut butter, two forks, a box of matches, and six cans of Armour sausages, what Daddy used to call teenie weenies. The storekeeper let me fill my new canteen from his cooler, and as I was leaving, his wife came out with fresh bread, so I spent another dime and bought two bananas that were starting to turn and a chunk of the bread to eat for breakfast, which the woman kindly buttered for me. I hated to spend the money, but we would need a lot of energy for the hike today, and I could ration the rest out for a week. I'd have to get supplies to make more salve, but I'd wait until I knew Sally sold the other jars first.

I used one of my shirts to make a pack for Pepper to carry and repacked my blanket roll with the new items. It was significantly heavier with so many cans but manageable. We ate our bananas and bread and watched the sun rise a little higher on the mountain. Then we crossed the highway, headed due east over the mountain and the desert, toward Hemenway Wash. Back to Ragtown. Back to where I first landed two years ago.

ABOUT TWO MILES INTO the desert, I found a natural spring coming from seemingly nowhere and stopped to take a break. Pepper had stopped looking back every two minutes, as if someone might be following us, and he looked exhausted. He still hadn't said more than a few words, and I was beginning to wonder if his trauma was more than I had initially thought. It was still morning, and I knew we couldn't dally long—best to move while the sun was still low, or it would just slow us down.

I could see the town of Boulder City in the distance to my right, the houses and buildings tiny dots that seemed perfectly placed. How Daddy and I had wanted to live in that world, and thinking about the dances and the movie house and the city park made me long for some normality in my life. But I was not sad. The desert and the creatures that inhabited it, the heat, the immensity of the mountains made me happy, and I felt more alive than I'd felt in a year. I wondered if maybe what I had thought would be a satisfying life in the small town of Boulder City was just another facade. Maybe this was my place.

Pepper immediately took off his worn boots and thin, dirty socks and put his feet in the water. I smiled at him. "You remembered."

He shrugged. "Always keep your feet clean," he said. I noticed he winced slightly, and I told him to hold his feet up for me to look at. They were red and a little swollen, but there was no broken skin. I pulled a pair of socks from my pack, laid them next to his boots, and stuffed his old ones inside the pack. I only had two extra pair, but Pepper had nothing. We could wash them every day. We'd make it. I also had half a jar of salve but chose to keep it until we made it to Hemenway Wash. It had to last an entire week, and I thought it best to save it.

I took my boots off and joined Pepper at the spring. The water was warm and soothing. Pepper and I scrubbed our faces and our arms and drank our fill. A sharp crack in the distance, and Pepper turned his head quickly, his eyes wide with terror.

I put a hand on his small thigh. "He's not coming. And if he does, I'll protect you."

"Mr. Cromwell," he said, turning back to me. "His name is Mr. Cromwell." He lowered his head, and I saw him flinch.

"Well, if Mr. Dumbbell comes along, you leave him to me." I didn't know exactly what I'd do if confronted with Pepper's stepfather, but there was no way I was going to let him take Pepper.

I saw a hint of a smile at the nickname, and he slowly nodded.

We rebooted, refilled my canteen from the spring, readjusted our packs, and headed toward the sun, staying alert to the sounds around us. I heard a few rattles to my left and hoped the animals still recognized me as one of their own. Or maybe I smelled differently now. Maybe I smelled like Cotton. If that was the case, they'd probably attack me in my sleep.

I shouldn't be surprised that Cotton turned on me. At first, I thought he really liked me, even if I didn't necessarily feel the same. I tried, but there was always something there, something about him that made me hold back with both my heart and my head. When we first got to Vegas, Tony Badamo had him doing all kinds of things, every night, and he came home happy, with his pockets full of bills. Then he didn't come home as much, choosing to stay out with some of Tony's other guys, and that was when the drinking and gambling started.

Sally said he probably didn't have many friends in his life, and once a few took an interest, he'd do anything to please them. That made sense to me, and I'd seen it happen before with men and women alike. I thought that was how some people became powerful, by taking advantage of the Cottons of the world, befriending them, and getting them to do what would please the bosses. Tony Badamo. Johnny Sparks. Damn them all.

Tony Badamo was a bad man, even though Sally seemed to be all right with him. To hear her talk, he always followed through on his promises, and he treated women, all women, like ladies. Even the prostitutes, she said. He took advantage of their services but paid them extra and didn't abuse them like some of the other men did. I guessed that meant he had some sense of honor, at least as defined by whatever code he followed. It was a shame that he didn't use what power he had to do something good. He was just a gangster in fancy clothes to me and, from some of the things I had heard around town, could be downright mean. He wanted to take my car because Cotton owed him money. He only wanted to do that to hurt Cotton, to show he was in charge, because there was no way that a man like him would really want a ten-year-old Model T. I laughed out loud. I guessed, since I had the car, I was the one in charge.

"What's funny?" Pepper asked. He hadn't talked much on our walk, but he was starting to at least say a few words.

"Oh, I was just thinking about that day you picked up that baby rattlesnake."

"I'm not afraid of them now. I killed a hundred on the ranch," he said.

"You killed a rattlesnake?" I said.

"I had to. Mr. Dumbbell locked me in the barn with a bunch of them and told me if I didn't kill them, they'd kill me. He said that's how you learn things."

I looked at Pepper, so small and so frail, who a year ago wouldn't have hurt a fire ant, and tried to imagine how terrified he must have been.

I could feel myself slowing and forced my legs to pick up the pace. I didn't know how or when I was going to be able to leave, but I knew I was going to do it, regardless of what Tony, Cotton, or any of his other men had to say about it. Or maybe I'd just stay on this mountain forever, like Queho.

While I was in Vegas, I did a little research on Queho and decided to tell Pepper what I had learned to take our minds off the heat and the walk. I'd found that he was a renegade, possibly Paiute and Cocopah, whose mother had died in childbirth and whose father was nowhere to be found. In addition to his mixed blood, he had a clubfoot, and none of the tribes really wanted him, so he grew up an outcast. I pictured the poor little Indian boy that no one wanted and felt sorry for him at once. As I relayed this bit to Pepper, he nodded as if he understood too.

"They say he killed another Indian when he was eighteen, the same age as me, and after that, started a life on the run, a criminal and murderer roaming the area between Nipton and Searchlight, all the way to Las Vegas. The accounts I read didn't say why he killed the first man, but I want to think that he was tired of being treated so badly, and it finally all blew up for him. He's over fifty years old now and has been hiding in the mountains ever since." He must find some peace here, I thought—I could understand that as well.

"I'm not afraid of him," Pepper said.

Pepper had definitely changed in the year since I'd seen him. I knew he had his reasons, and when I said he had changed, I didn't mean he was now some fearless warrior, no longer afraid of rattlesnakes or renegade Indians. What he wasn't afraid of was any of those things killing him. In fact, I felt as if he'd rather that happen than Mr. Cromwell find him and take him back to his ranch.

"He had the chance to kill us once, and all he wanted was my canteen. I think if he sees that we're not a threat, just two more renegades like him, he'll leave us be," I said.

"And if not?"

I shrugged. "If not, I'll shoot him," I said. But I didn't think it would come to that. In fact, he was probably long gone from where we had last seen him, moving around so as not to be caught by the men that still hunted him.

And although I knew he was a criminal, I really wasn't afraid of him. In fact, I took some inspiration from him. I figured if Queho could hide out and not be found for several decades, Pepper and I could certainly do it for a few months. I knew how the desert worked, I knew how to live in it, and I was determined to get out of the mess I was in and find some peace.

AUTHOR NOTE: DOES ANYONE else call these little sausages "teenie weenies?" I used to love them as a kid, as well as PayDay candy bars, and was so glad to find they were available for Helen and Pep-

per when I researched food available during the 1930s. The two items seemed like the perfect combination for the two to take on a long hike through the desert.

Chapter 45: Stray Puppies

Ezra

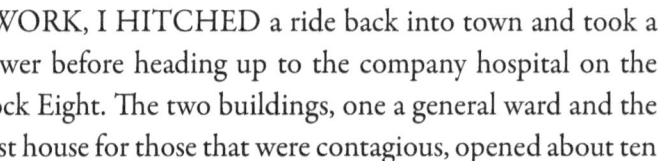

AFTER WORK, I HITCHED a ride back into town and took a quick shower before heading up to the company hospital on the top of Block Eight. The two buildings, one a general ward and the other a pest house for those that were contagious, opened about ten months ago and had been full ever since. I headed to the L-shaped brick-and-stucco main building, needing to check on Moose, and, if Smitty was around, needing to talk to her about Helen.

After Bodell left, I took my morning break and headed to the beach to see if Pete and Charlie could find out more information about why Bodell would be looking for her. By lunchtime, they had a full report, and it wasn't good. They said she threatened to shoot some man behind the Apache Hotel and then stole a car owned by some gangster named Tony Badamo. Helen and the car were gone, and no one had seen her since.

"He also mentioned kidnapping," I said.

"Yeah, some guy named Cromwell said he lost track of his little girl on Fremont, and a man said he saw her with a young woman at the Apache," Charlie said. "He said the little girl called the woman Helen."

"Why would some guy have his little girl on Fremont Street in the middle of the night?" Pete mused.

"None of it adds up to me. I knew Helen. She isn't a criminal," I said.

"Well, she was married to one," Charlie added. "Seems her husband works for Tony Badamo, and the guy that she threatened to shoot was another one of his minions, a guy named Wally Woods. That friend of yours is in a world of trouble," he said.

I couldn't imagine what could have happened for her to do any of that, but something told me the roses that Cotton painted to Mr. Emery about his life with Helen were one-sided as hell. Maybe I should have checked myself, but I didn't have any reason to think Cotton wasn't taking care of her, or any responsibility to see to it that he was. I bet she was scared right now, and although I didn't know what I could do to help, I wanted to. After Grace died, Helen was there for me, and I never returned the favor.

Smitty was sitting with Moose when I got to his bed, and he looked like he'd been run over by the Jumbo. His left eye was completely shut, and he had stitches on his eyebrow and a few on his lip. The other eye was swollen and barely open, and his entire face was various shades of purple, red, and black. He attempted a smile when he saw me, but it looked more sinister than happy, thanks to the swelling and stitches. "You should see the other guy," he said.

"You look like hell," I said.

I lit up a Camel, took a drag, and handed it to him. He stuck it in one corner of his mouth and drew lightly.

"I sure needed that," he said. "Everybody get paid?"

"Yeah," I said with my head low. "Don't look like it was worth it."

Smitty stood up and straightened her skirt. "If you two are going to talk about the money you made last night, I think I'll wait in the lobby."

"Actually, there is something else I need to talk to you about, Smitty. If you are up to it?"

"Figures," Moose said. "Man waits until I'm down then goes after my girl."

Smitty swatted a hand at him. "Oh, stop." She reclined in the straight-back chair next to his bed. "Bodell came to see you too," she said.

"Yeah. And it ain't good." I told her and Moose everything that I learned from Pete and Charlie that afternoon then finished with "I just wish I knew where she was so I could help."

Moose tapped Smitty's arm and then made a motion with his hand like he wanted a drink. She looked around and pulled a flask from her purse and handed it to him. He took a long swig and laid his head back on the pillow. "Damn, I wish they'd let me go back to the dorms where I can get something for this pain." He took a few deep breaths then said, "I thought you were over that girl?"

"I was. I mean, I am. There never was anything there anyway," I said. "She married Cotton, remember?"

"She married him because she didn't have much of a choice," Smitty said. "I told George we should have gone to Vegas and tried to find her. I just knew something wasn't right." She started wringing her hands, and Moose reached out and put a hand on top of hers.

"Both of ya. Not your responsibility," he said.

"This from a man that let himself get almost beaten to death so his friends wouldn't lose a few dollars," Smitty said.

Moose held up both hands. "Okay, you got me there. So, you two want to help an old friend who tried to shoot a gangster, stole from the boss, kidnapped a little girl, and is running from the mob. And you don't even know where she is. Sure, sounds like fun. Just as soon as I can see again—"

"This is serious, Moose. Helen is a good kid, and whatever has happened—"

"*Was* a good kid. It's been a year since you seen her, and anything could have happened. And didn't you tell me she was eighteen? And married. She ain't a kid anymore." Aside from Moose's rough exterior, I'd learned over the past year or so that he was one of the kindest people I'd ever known. If he knew Helen, and if he weren't wincing every time he opened his mouth, I was pretty sure he'd be right there with Smitty and me, wanting to help. But he also had a point, and maybe I was letting my emotions get the better of me. She was not only a woman but a smart one, and if she was trying to leave, I was sure she'd have had a plan.

"She's long gone by now," I said, not sure if I was trying to relieve Smitty or convince myself.

"Exactly," Moose said. "California most likely. It's a big place, especially if you want to get lost."

A nurse came by to tell us that it was time to leave so Moose could rest, and I volunteered to walk Smitty back to her house. I knew Moose appreciated it, but I also wanted to talk to Smitty alone. I thought she might have felt the same way I did about Helen, not completely convinced that she went rogue and left for California, or wherever else people ran to when they'd done wrong. I figured most just came to Nevada, but after that... maybe Mexico.

"You ever been to Mexico, Smitty?" I asked as we entered the rows of houses that made up the workers' homes. Little white boxes, from one to three rooms, perfectly spaced and separated by dirt roads.

"No, and I know what you are thinking. That would be quite a journey, don't you think?"

"Yeah. You know, I really wish she had come to me. I wish I knew a little bit more about the situation, but damned if I know how to find out."

"I don't know, either, but if I did, I'd certainly want to help." She paused. "You knew her better than anyone, Ezra. If Kansas wasn't an option, where else could she go?"

I had been thinking about that all day, and we hadn't really talked about any other family or friends that we had. Surely she had someone. "I don't know," I said.

Smitty let out a long sigh as she reached her porch. "Thank you, Ezra. I'm glad Moose has a friend like you."

"I'm your friend, too, Smitty. Don't forget that. If you need anything—"

"How's he doin'?" George came out the door as we were standing on the stoop. In contrast to Smitty's sternness, George was a guy with a big smile and a hello for everyone. He liked to drink, liked to gamble, and liked the ladies, but he seemed to have all three under control, unlike some of the other guys who worked in the canyon. I heard the ladies liked him too. He was dressed in wide-legged trousers and a white shirt and smelled like he fell in a bucket of Pinaud's aftershave lotion.

"He's playing the tough guy," Smitty said. "He also asked if you would sneak a bottle of Roses back through the gate for him if you're going out to the Pass soon."

"That's where I'm headed. Meeting a little doll out there for some dancing. Wanna come?" he asked her jokingly.

Smitty smiled and shook her head, but I spoke up. "Mind if I ride out there with ya?"

George gave Smitty a peck on the cheek then slapped me on the back and started walking toward his car. "Not at all. Hell, I think every man in town made money last night, so the place will probably be hoppin'. But those darlin's got to eat, too, right?"

I followed George. I didn't particularly care to visit the cribs on busy nights, but maybe I could catch Mae before she went to work. Me asking questions about Helen might raise some eyebrows

I didn't care to raise, but Mae seemed to know the news before it happened. And if anyone could get information about what really happened, I'd bet money on her.

AFTER I TOLD MAE WHAT little I knew, she promised to get me more information and report back in a few days. "I'll see what else I can find. Men's lips get real loose when their pants are down."

Pete was just coming back from walking Marguerite to her shift at the Railroad Pass. He sat at the picnic table with us and shook his head. "I swear, we sat right here a year ago and had this same conversation. You ready to be a martyr again?"

"No. It's not that. She's in trouble, and she's my friend. Last year it was about marrying her—"

"And this year, it's about getting her out of the state because she's a criminal. Oh, things have definitely gotten better," he said.

I felt the heat rise in my face but didn't say anything.

"Leave him be, Pete. Ezra is right. She's a young woman, probably being accused of something she didn't do, and if she needs help and we can give it to her, we should," Mae said.

Pete shook his head again. "I'm sure glad there aren't a lot of stray puppies around here. Between you two and Marguerite, I have a feeling we'd have a tentful by now."

AUTHOR NOTE: I MAY have mentioned this before, but I love writing male characters. I particularly enjoyed writing this chapter, since Ezra, Moose, and Pete all have such a different take on Helen's situation. It was a great character-building chapter, especially for Moose and Pete, who have a much larger role in this half of the story. Pete, incidentally, is one of my favorite characters I've ever written.

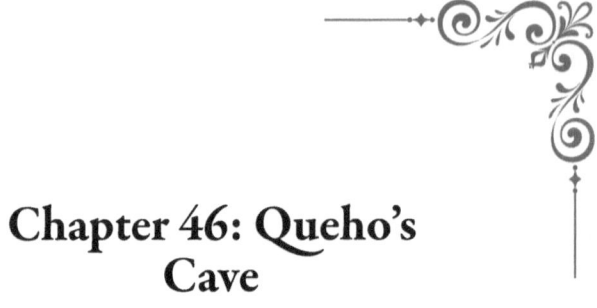

Chapter 46: Queho's Cave

Helen

LIVING IN TOWN HAD made me soft. After hiking five miles through the desert, we made it to the mountains above Hemenway Wash by late afternoon. My feet were swollen and blistered, and I was happy I had half a jar of salve with me. I could hear the river below us and saw the open ground that was once Ragtown. It looked foreign to me without the tents and makeshift camps, and I was so tired; all I wanted was to find a place to set up a small camp for the rest of the evening, eat, and, I hoped, get a good night's sleep. But I needed to fill my canteen, wash my feet at least, and, while I was in the water, get rid of Cotton's stench from the clothes I was wearing.

"What now?" Pepper said. He looked tired, too, and I was sure his feet hurt as badly as mine, but he wasn't complaining.

"Clean up, eat, and make camp," I said.

Pepper raised his eyebrows and gave me a questioning look. "Is this where we are going to live now?" I saw a flicker of hope in his eyes, and the realization that he was relying on me to give him that hope struck me. That mixed with the heat and my exhaustion wore down on me, and it was almost more than I could bear.

I tousled his hair and gave him a weak smile. "For now." I had no plan. But this was my thinking place, and I hoped I would come up with something soon.

Finding one of my old paths to the river was easy. By staying on the paths that the bighorn sheep followed into the canyon and staying a little bit to the north, we could get down to the river and still be upstream from Mr. Emery's ferry. He was always friendly to me, but I didn't know if he'd turn me in or take me across the river, and I wasn't taking any chances until I found out more from Sally about how bad things were. It would be tempting to drive my dad's car right back to Kansas and find some way to make a living, but if I did that, I'd still be married to Cotton, and regardless of anything else, I needed to remedy that mistake. I didn't want to go through life as Helen Vaughn. Not to mention that Pepper was a runaway, and I had no idea the trouble I could get into taking him across state lines. Pepper was a complication, but I wasn't going to sacrifice him for myself. I'd just have to figure it out.

After finding a pool that was calm enough to wade into, we took off our boots, and I examined our feet. They weren't as bad as I thought they would be, and I was glad I still had two extra pairs of socks with me to protect them. Daddy had always told me to take care of my feet, and although I'd never had to worry much about that before, now I could see why it was so important to him. I took the bar of soap out of my pack, broke it in half, and handed a piece to Pepper. He walked upstream until he found another pool and walked in fully clothed. I found a large rock to sit on in the middle of the pool, scrubbed my socks first, then threw them back on the beach to dry. Cotton's shirt was next, then my dungarees, and soon I was sitting in the pool, wearing only my underwear. I washed my hair and scrubbed my body until it felt raw then lay back in the water and let it wash away what it could.

Walking through the desert, I had had a lot of time to think. Last year I was scared, unsure of what would happen to me alone in the desert, and still hurt and sad over the loss of Daddy. I wanted to do things on my own, but it didn't take long for me to take Cotton up on his offer, to fall for the idea that as a girl—as a woman—I needed a man to take care of me. But over the past year, I had realized that I was the one doing the "taking care of." Sure, Cotton brought in the money, at least at first, but it was me that made sure we had food to eat, soap to wash with, and other necessities when we needed them. When the rent came due, and there wasn't any money left, it was me that worked extra hours and explained things to the landlord. I figured without Cotton, the money I made would have gone a lot further, and I wouldn't have had to act like a wife.

I also saw that in Vegas, there were some single women who made it on their own. Of course there were the Sallys of the world, but there were also women who were not prostitutes. There were women working in the cafes, the bakery, even the library. I knew they didn't get paid half what the men did, but they still made it; they were still surviving.

Lying in the water, I imagined working in a library all day, surrounded by books, getting to choose the new ones as they came through the door. At the end of the day, I would go home—to my home—however small or sparse it might be, feed only me, tend only to me. I didn't imagine I would be lonely, since I was sure there were plenty of other women, like me, that I could befriend. I could tell people Pepper was my little brother and send him to school and find a way to make a little extra money, respectable money, to give him some kind of a chance.

Or maybe I would one day fall in love.

Pepper was sitting on the beach, letting the overalls I had given him to wear dry on his body, looking out across the river, when I finally crawled from my dream. I put on one of my thin cotton dresses and decided to eat on the beach and give our socks and my dungarees time to dry. It was tempting to sleep here, but I knew animals came to drink, especially at night, and I didn't want to be sleeping when a coyote decided to sniff out my food roll. We ate beans and Vienna sausages and split a candy bar in silence. After eating, I washed our forks and rinsed out my bean can, thinking I could use it to put bat guano in if I could find the cave. Then I rubbed a thin layer of salve over my feet, Pepper did the same, and we put on clean socks.

After storing the soap and dried clothes, I rerolled our supplies, and we hoisted them on our backs. I looked up at the mountain and let out a long sigh. I felt at home. "Ready?" I said.

"Ready," Pepper replied, and he led the way.

We followed the same path we had taken down to the water and began searching for a small shelter for the night. The higher we went, the better the view was of the valley, and the closer we got to the bat guano cave that I knew was up here. We passed an endless supply of brittlebush and creosote, and I decided I'd collect the plants this week and buy the penny jars, honey, and lard to make more salve when I got back to the Pass on Saturday. That way, if Sally needed more to sell and if her friend Mae could get the salve to her, I'd have it ready. I was feeling confident and happier than I had in a long time when I noticed a large amount of brittlebush off the path. I pointed it out to Pepper, who left the trail before I could stop him and headed straight for the patch.

"Pepper, be careful. Rattlers like to hide in the brittlebush," I said.

I couldn't see him—he had gone beyond the patch—and I heard him yell, "Helen, come here!"

My stomach did a quick turn, and I quickly made my way beyond the plants to where Pepper stood before what looked like a stone wall against the mountain with holes in it. It was peculiar, and I would have passed it by as nothing more than an anomaly in the mountain, but Pepper went straight to it and looked in one of the holes.

"There's a cave behind this!" he said.

I put a finger to my lips, and we stood in front of the wall, listening, but heard nothing out of the ordinary. There was a thin break between the wall and the mountain, one that no one would think to enter if they didn't realize there was something behind it. I made my way slowly between the wall and the mountain with Pepper close behind. We stood at the mouth of the cave and carefully, cautiously peeked around the corner.

The cave was littered with papers, cans, dishes, and other used goods. And in the back against the wall sat the body of Queho, his mouth open and his dead eyes welcoming us home.

He didn't carry the stench of fresh death but instead smelled more like old dust. His skin was dried up and shriveled, mummified as opposed to decayed, and I figured he'd been dead for quite some time, probably not long after we saw him last year. From the looks of things, a rattler got him in the good foot. I imagined him getting bitten, making his way back to his cave, and sitting against the wall, waiting for death to take him. I hoped it wasn't long, but I was sure it was painful.

Pepper walked slowly toward the body, silently, and examined it from head to toe. He didn't seem afraid at all, which surprised me. I watched him, the faint light of the setting sun casting an eerie glow around us, one direct ray seeming to reach out and envelop Queho in its light. Pepper reached out a hand to touch his face—

"Don't," I whispered.

Pepper pulled back, his brows twisted up. "He's dead. He can't hurt us."

"I... I know, but don't touch him. Please." It was so quiet in the cave, almost peaceful, and I had a strange feeling that as long as we didn't disturb him, we'd be safe here. It was as if he were a sentinel, protecting us from whatever we had to fear.

Pepper smiled. "Can we stay here? It's a great cave," he said.

"This isn't a little creepy to you?" I asked.

He shrugged. "He's like us. And I figure there's a reason we found this cave."

I thought of the angels that Pepper's mother, Betsy, had told me about the first time I saw Queho in the desert. At the time, I had thought that he could be one of those angels she spoke of. His presence gave me a little comfort in a strange sort of way.

"Sure," I said. "But don't touch him."

AUTHOR NOTE: I TOOK some creative liberty with the location of Queho's cave. When it was found in the mid-'30s (Queho's final story is in the epilogue), it was a mile or so farther down the canyon. However, I moved it to a location above Hemenway Wash for the purposes of this story. Some of the items I mention that he had in his possession were some of the actual items he was found with.

Chapter 47: The "Monster"

Helen

WE STUCK CLOSE BY THE cave for the first two days to let our feet heal. It was October, which meant the nights weren't as hot, and that partnered with being in a cave made it downright cool. I slept better those first few nights than I had in a year, and Pepper, although still restless, seemed more relaxed. Even if we did have a dead Indian watching our every move.

We gathered brittlebush and creosote, careful to store them away from the cave as to not attract any rattlers. I had decided that even if Sally couldn't sell my salve, I was going to stockpile it and take it with me, wherever that may be, and have it to sell along with the bat guano—if we ever found the cave. We could smell it—it seemed to fill the air—but we hadn't been able to find it. Yet. Pepper was determined to fill all our bean cans with guano. It was as if he could see our future, selling salve and guano and living somewhere in the outdoors, surviving on beans and Payday candy bars. Of course, I wanted more, but it was a place to start.

We'd taken to looking through some of Queho's possessions, trying to place them exactly as we found them, unless, of course, there was something we could use. I was sure he didn't mind. We found my old canteen, the one he had stolen the year before. We took his blankets to the river, washed them with lye, and used them to make sleeping pallets, mine at the front of the cave near the false wall, Pepper's closer toward the back, not far from Queho's body.

On our third night in the cave, I woke one night in the darkness to the soft sound of Pepper talking. I thought he was talking in his sleep, but in the darkness, I could see two shadows, sitting side by side. He was sitting next to the body of Queho, talking to him, as if carrying on a conversation. I remained still and listened.

"...and my daddy is up there too. You'd like him. And if you tell him you're looking out for me, he'll like you too… Oh, I know what people say, but bad things happened to you, and you just wanted to hide… just like me… Of course we're friends…No, I haven't killed anybody, but I would. If I had to…"

A chill ran up my spine. Pepper had some real problems, and he'd yet to open up to me and talk about them. But at least, I thought, he was talking some now, even if the person he trusted most with his secrets was a dead renegade.

The next morning, I thought we should get out of our usual routine and do something different. Pepper was excited at the thought of an adventure, and I was too. "Let's go check on the tunnels," I said. I knew Pepper's dad had died in one of the tunnels, and mine basically had, too, but I thought it would be a good way for us both to put that behind us. At least I hoped so. The last time I'd been there was when Smitty and I went to watch George swing on his bosun's chair high above the river, and I knew in a year a lot must have changed. I'd been keeping up with its progress, reading the news when I could in the diner, and I knew the tunnel my dad used to work in had been blown through and the men were now concreting and readying it for use in less than a month. The Colorado River would be diverted from its path, leaving the bed dry. Then the work of building a dam could begin.

Pepper had found an old man's shirt in the cave and had taken to wearing it over my overalls. It was long enough to be a dress on him, but he liked it, and it made him look like a young boy, dressed in his daddy's clothes. I wore my dungarees, a ballcap, and Cotton's shirt, and to anyone not getting too close, I looked like a boy too. We grabbed our crackers and peanut butter, my camera, my new canteen, and the one Queho "borrowed" from me last year and went to the river to get water first. Not wanting to be recognized, we waited until Emery's ferry was downriver then made our way across Hemenway Wash, the now-deserted area where Ragtown used to be, to the path my dad and Ezra had used to walk to the site. We make it to Lookout Point by midmorning and were surprised by the number of people that were there watching the men work. Some had brought their kids, and many had packed a picnic lunch. We found a couple that looked to be in their early forties and got close enough that any onlookers might think we were with them. The woman smiled at us as we sat down a few feet from them. I smiled weakly back, lowered my chin, and focused on the work site. It didn't take me long to see what the attraction was.

There were four tunnels, two on either side of the river, one seemingly on top of another. Trucks and men were wandering in and out, back and forth. The man next to us was pointing these out for his girlfriend, telling her that they were each about a mile long and fifty-six feet in diameter and that the concrete wall that was built between them and the river, which extended the full height to cover both tunnels, was there to protect them from flooding while the men bored the holes. "They weren't supposed to be finished until next year," he said, "but they've worked those men to the bone to get it done ahead of schedule."

Some were worked to death, I said in my mind.

Pepper was silent, too, listening to the man explain as if he were talking for our benefit but not taking his eyes off the site.

From their conversation, I learned that there were two concrete plants, one called Hi-Mix at the top of the canyon, and one down closer to the bottom, Lo-Mix. I watched a concrete truck from the Lo-Mix plant weave along the trails to a tunnel and disappear inside of it, while dump trucks came out loaded with debris.

"They call that 'the Monster,'" the man told his girl, pointing at the spiderweb-like network of pulleys and cables that ran across the river from one side to the other. The Monster carried cable cars hauling men and supplies, and there were even cable cars mounted on the side of the mountains, moving up and down. Some whined loudly on their tracks and didn't exactly look safe, but they didn't stop moving: back and forth, up and down.

Men dotted the shore on either side of the river, working on building concrete forms, and the high-scalers blasted the walls with dynamite and jackhammered out the debris while dangling six hundred feet above the river on a tiny wooden chair. That hadn't changed much since Miss Smitty and I came to watch over a year ago. I tried to pick out George Goon from the high-scalers, who seemed to be putting on a show for those watching, but they were all covered in a fine gray powder, and they all looked alike from this distance. From the water to the top of the canyon, men worked at various tasks, their movements in coordinated groups like a dance. The river ran boldly through it all, powerful and unyielding, unaware that the work going on around it was intended to temper its movement.

"They never stop working," the man said. "Well, except when they had that strike last year, and when the place flooded last month. When they are ready to turn the river, they'll blow up that big wall in front of the tunnels on the Arizona side so the water can go in there."

The woman squealed and said something to the man that I couldn't hear.

"November thirteenth," the man told his girlfriend. "That's the date they say they are going to be done with the tunnels and will start turning the river. We gotta come back for that. Going to be one helluva show."

Pepper looked at me when the man said this, his eyes sparkling like I hadn't seen them in over a year. I nodded, and he grinned.

We watched the work for hours, long after the man and woman next to us left, long after the picnickers packed up their baskets and went back to their homes. I was captivated, and all thoughts of looking for the guano cave or gathering more brush were pushed to the back of my mind, as if watching the construction had become my reason for being here, my purpose. I had a fresh roll of film in my camera, but only took one picture—Pepper smiling as if his innocence was still intact, with the monster cableway in the background.

November thirteenth, the man had told his girl sitting next to us, was the date set for the diversion of the river. I wasn't sure of the date, but I knew it had to be mid-October, so a month away. Pepper and I chattered about it all the way back to our cave, Queho's cave. Our daddies had both been a part of this project, and November thirteenth, when they stopped the river, we planned to be here to watch. Nothing was going to stand in our way.

AUTHOR NOTE: PEPPER having nighttime conversations with the corpse of Queho may be a good indication of how damaged Pepper is. Helen wants to be his "angel," to somehow save him, but she is starting to wonder if that is possible. Lookout Point is the place where people would come from all over the area to watch the men build the dam. It was a very popular spot, and watching the work being performed was a favorite pastime.

Chapter 48: Black Widows, Aspirin, and Four Roses

Ezra

IT WAS STILL DARK OUTSIDE when Moose and I climbed into the back of a dump truck with thirty other men. He had gotten out of the hospital the night before and looked like he could use a few more days to heal, but he wanted to get back to work and not lie around the dorm, wishing he had somewhere to go. Transportation to and from the work site was limited, so to ensure a ride, we got up early. The work site was a few miles from town, but it took an hour to get there. The winding road was thick with traffic. Work trucks going back and forth to town mingled with the cars of those who drove themselves. It was a long ride, thirty men standing in the back, clanging together like soda bottles, but it gave me time to think. And my thoughts were of Helen.

I hadn't heard any more about her. In fact, I had been checking the papers, and there was no mention of Helen Vaughn, or any of the other things that Bodell had mentioned. I was beginning to wonder if she had been found, or if she was still out there, somewhere, and her problems weren't nearly as severe as Bodell had made them sound. But something wasn't right about it, and just from what I knew about Helen, her free-spiritedness, and I might say hard-headedness, led me to assume she was hiding. Somewhere.

"You got something on your mind?" Moose said as we moved to the back of the truck. The sun had started to show its colors, and in the morning light, Moose's face looked like a piece of aged steak.

"Nah, just wondering if you could get any uglier," I said. I knew he didn't feel up to speed, and I figured he didn't want to hear my theories about Helen.

Chief pulled into the parking area in his sedan as I jumped from the truck. I landed with one foot in a hole that went down a foot deep and hit the bottom of the hole hard. A sharp pain ran from my foot and up my left leg as I felt the bone in my ankle compress against the force. "Damn!" I fell to the ground and pulled my knee to my chest, holding my leg.

Chief must've seen me fall; he knelt beside me as pain radiated through my entire body. Then I felt what seemed like a hard jab from the end of a sharp stick penetrate my leg at mid-calf. "Something bit me!" I yelled through gritted teeth. I rolled around on the ground, trying to keep my ankle in the air while swatting at my calf.

"Damn spiders. You must have picked him up on the truck. Moose, help me get him in the car. I'll take him down to the clinic and let Doc take a look. Them damn brown ones will kill you quicker than the black ones will."

I shook my head. "No. I can't go down there from here."

"He's right," Moose said. "If he isn't in the hospital, they'll replace him if he doesn't check in for work."

"Hell they will," Chief said. "He's at work."

Moose tried to take off my boot to see my ankle in the dim light. "Can't go down to Doc's clinic unless Frenchie sends you. Otherwise, you're counted as a no-show." Moose looked around at the hundred men standing at the edge of the canyon. "That's what those guys are waiting for. They'll take your job before you can say 'black widow.'"

"Get me up," I said.

"Get on the other side, Chief. We've got to get him down the widow-maker before he passes out on us."

Moose and Chief lifted me, and I draped my arms over their shoulders. I yelled again.

"Sorry, kid," Chief said. "This isn't going to be a trip to the fair."

My head spun, and I felt sick to my stomach. Sweat formed on my forehead and neck as the stabbing sensation in my leg burnt its way up my body. I focused on getting to my check-in point, but everything was beginning to blur. Even if I died, I had to make it to Frenchie first.

One hundred steps to the widow-maker then three hundred feet down to the tunnel. Chief and Moose tightened their strong arms around my waist. I bit down hard on my bottom lip, drawing blood, and braced myself for the first step.

I DIDN'T REMEMBER ANYTHING after that. I woke what appeared to be several hours later, the sun high in the sky, lying on a stretcher at the back of the clinic with a wet cloth on my forehead. The air reeked of antiseptic mixed with body odor, and I took short breaths, resisting the urge to heave.

Someone had taken my boot off and cut my pants leg up the outside. My foot, swollen to twice the normal size, lay on top of a thin bed of ice with my ankle tightly bandaged. Halfway up my calf, a red knot with a half-moon bruise above it had been cut open to bleed out the poison. The opening was packed with salt, the tiny white crystals giving off an unnatural shine. It looked like a half-chewed gumball.

"Did you bite the bastard back?" Pete's voice startled me, and I looked over to find him kneeling beside me. I didn't know how long he'd been there. I managed a weak smile.

"Sprained ankle and a black widow bite," Doc Jensen said as he approached, wiping his hands on a clean rag. "He's going to be hurting for a few weeks. How are you feeling now, Ezra?"

My voice cracked as I spoke. "You got anything else for pain, Doc? That aspirin must be for kids." I held out my left hand. "And my hands are still shaking."

Doc examined the bite on my leg. "Aspirin's it, son. Don't want any addicts down here, so that's what they give me. Everything will get better as more of that poison comes out. I got you a box of Arm and Hammer and a box of Morton's. You mix those two together and keep putting it on the bite. As for the ankle, keep it on ice as you can."

I shut my eyes, and Doc continued, talking to Pete now. "He's lucky. Hell, it took him damn near two hours to get down here. Limping on that bad leg and shaking like he was having fits." I opened my eyes and saw Doc motion at the door. "Bud Bodell's next door at Administration. Volunteered to take him back to the dorm. I'll give him another few minutes or so, and then you can help him out to Bodell's car."

"He looks pretty bad. Why isn't he going to the hospital?" Pete said.

Doc knelt beside Pete and lowered his voice, speaking to me. "Look, if I send you to the hospital, they're going to give you aspirin and a few days off. You're probably better off going to work and trying to find your own medication." He looked around before continuing. "I know whiskey is illegal in town, but a good friend might try to sneak some in tonight. It'd sure help with the pain."

I wiped the perspiration from my lip. "No hospital," I said.

Pete helped me up and supported me on my bad side. We wove our way through the small clinic, my head spinning and my leg on fire. The clinic was full. Bodies filled the few gurneys; others lay on the floor. Outside the clinic, two dozen more men lay on stretchers on the ground, most in the open sun. A man grabbed Pete's leg as we worked our way through.

"My daughter," the man said, his words coming out in a gurgle, his mouth full of frothy white bubbles. Pete stopped walking, propped me against a rock, and rolled the man on his side, allowing the spittle to roll across his cheek, just as his body went limp.

Murl Emery walked up to us just as Pete stood up and took my arm again.

Pete inclined his head toward the masses. "What the hell happened?"

"An entire tunnel crew got sick. I picked them up on the ferry and hauled them down here," Emery said.

Pete looked back at the men on the ground. "They don't look very good."

"Hell no," Emery said. "They got gassed. Two of them died on my boat."

Pete snapped his fingers. "Damn. That was Four Roses."

"What?" Emery asked.

Pete pointed at the dead man he had rolled on his side. "I know that guy. He lives at Texas Acres. Has a daughter."

Emery removed his hat and fanned it in front of his face. "You don't look too good yourself," he said to me.

"Better days," I said.

"He got bit by a widow," Pete said. "And not the kind that feeds you breakfast the next day."

"Sorry to hear that. I'll say a prayer for ya. Say, I guess you heard about Helen Carter and Pepper Allen," he said.

"Pepper?" I said.

"Yeah, they said she had kidnapped a little girl named Pepper. I figure you and I both know who that little girl is." He stopped and looked around to make sure no one was listening. He motioned his head toward Pete, and I motioned for him to continue. "And you and I both know that boy would follow her anywhere. Especially up in those mountains."

Of course. Even in my pain-filled haze, I knew the one place Helen would feel safe was the mountains. I cleared my throat, but before I could ask if he'd seen or heard from them, Bud Bodell walked out of the admin building.

"Let's go," Bodell said.

Pete had me on one side, and Murl Emery took the other, and they walked me to Bodell's car.

As they helped me get in, Emery got close and whispered to me, "If you hear from her, tell her I'll get her across the river, no questions asked."

I smiled weakly and then laid my head back against the seat of the car. As he shut the car door, I yelled to him out the window.

"Emery." I dug in my pocket and pulled out two dollars and handed it to him. "That should pay off my tab," I lied for Bodell's benefit. Emery's eyes locked on mine, and then he took the crumpled bills from my hand.

The narrow road leading from the administration offices out of the canyon was nothing but a path of dirt and rocks, with a few potholes scattered for sport. Although Pete and Emery were careful to situate my leg to avoid the most aggravation, it had been in vain. I felt every pebble.

The pain was so intense, though, that I couldn't move at all, not even to reposition my bandaged leg and swollen ankle. By the time we made it to the top of the canyon, where the dirt road met the highway, I was covered in sweat and was slipping in and out of consciousness.

Bodell slowed the car. "Oh, hell," he said, and reached under his seat. He pulled out a mason jar of dark-amber liquid and gave it to me. "Here. Compliments of the bootleggers I broke up last night."

I fumbled with the lid and took a drink, letting the whiskey burn as it went down. I took another long swig and replaced the lid, waiting for the warmth to spread throughout my body.

As we started on the highway, the numbing sensation began in my leg. I got the lid off one more time and took another big gulp from the jar.

"Careful now," Bodell said. "That's the real thing. It ain't been watered down."

I let out a deep breath and let the warm breeze from the window wash over me. "Thanks."

"No problem. That's gotta hurt like hell. By the way, how's that friend of yours doing?"

I leaned back against his seat. "Which one?" I mumbled.

"That girl. Helen, that's her name, right?"

The pain and the whiskey had muddled my mind. I was not in the mood to talk and definitely not in the mood for any of Bodell's games. I kept my head against the seat and didn't respond.

"Still ain't seen her, huh? Well, if you do, you be sure and tell me. Harboring a criminal is a bad deal, but I'm sure I can pull some strings and keep you out of that Blue Room."

"I haven't seen her," I said.

But after talking with Emery, I was pretty sure I knew where she was.

As we entered town, I saw the dormitory a few blocks away. My thoughts turned to my bed and how the hell I was going to get up the stairs to it. Then I saw Moose, looking half-dead himself, waving to Bodell to pull over.

"Now that's a tough guy there," Bodell said. "And tuck that jar in your shirt. You don't want anyone to see it."

He slapped my shoulder. "Hey! You with me? That spider didn't make you go deaf, did she?"

"No," I said as Bodell pulled over.

Moose opened the passenger door to help me ease out of the car.

"Thanks," I said again to Bodell. My mind was fuzzy but not so bad that I didn't know that I owed him one now. Damn.

"Come on, I'll get you up to your room," Moose said. "Sleep off what you can. That seven a.m. shift comes mighty early."

When we got to the lobby area of the dorms, I motioned to Moose to sit down on one of the benches. They were usually filled with women, waiting for their boyfriends to come down, since they weren't allowed in the rooms. They were empty, and I needed to take a break before tackling the stairs to my room.

"Moose, I think I know where Helen might be hiding," I said.

He sucked in a deep breath. "Smitty has been really worried about her. I don't know the girl, but between you and her..."

I looked him in the eye and tried to hold my gaze steady.

He studied me for a minute then slapped his thighs lightly, stood and hauled me up by one arm. "Sleep first. I'll try to find you something for the pain. Tomorrow, we'll worry about the girl."

AUTHOR NOTE: BLACK widow spiders are often depicted as much more lethal than they actually are. In the 1930s, about five percent of those bitten died, and of those, most were either children or medically compromised adults. Today, the number is even less. Their venom is for small prey, not usually potent enough to kill humans, and they don't "go after" humans; mostly their bite is defensive. A bite will, however, hurt like hell and make you very, very sick for quite some time. During my many years as a nurse, I took care of one young man who had been bitten by one of these beauties, and Ezra's reaction

and symptoms were gleaned from those of that young man. The "damn brown ones," as Chief mentions, are downright evil, in my opinion. I've seen them move toward humans, and I've seen some bites that left horrible, permanent scarring after months of treatment to remove necrotic tissue and treat infection in the wounds, not to mention the systemic reactions one often experiences. Black widows are black with a red hourglass shape on their undersides. Brown recluses are brown with a darker brown violin shape on their heads.

From historical records, aspirin was the drug of choice during the building of the Hoover Dam. Six Companies didn't want anyone addicted to anything more potent, and liquor was not legal in Boulder City, so workers often sought other ways to get relief. The scene of the men being "gassed" in a tunnel is a true event taken from oral histories, fictionalized for this novel.

Chapter 49: The First Noel

Helen

AFTER SPENDING MOST of the day at the Point, watching the men work on the dam project, I wished I had learned more about it when I was in Vegas. The mountain and the river were living, breathing things, and I always thought what they were doing was destroying the beauty of it. Now I wasn't so sure. To watch them engage with the mountain, it was as if they became a part of it, helping it change with the times. I had taken my Brownie and used almost all the film I had left, wishing I could get closer but satisfied that I was, in some way, part of it at all.

I had sent Pepper down to the river to wash. He was so much older than he had been when we lived in Ragtown—older in a sense of experiences that he still wouldn't talk about. He wasn't afraid to be on the mountain alone, and he seemed to want some time to himself. I understood that, and although I worried about him by himself, I could respect his need for some privacy to think and, ideally, dream.

Alone in the cave, I looked over Queho's possessions. Some I would use, or borrow, as we needed. Of the many goods, supplies, and trinkets that we'd found in Queho's cave, nothing was as precious as the small silver box that was sitting next to his body. I didn't want to touch it at first, it was so close to him. But as I got nearer, the small porcelain inset on the top of a woman and man, holding hands and walking through the snow, drew my attention, and I really wanted to see what was inside. When I picked it up, a small turn key on the side told me it was a music box. I slowly cranked it, and when I opened the box to reveal nothing inside, "The First Noel" rang through the small cave. I closed my eyes and let the music wash over me and smiled. "Thank you," I said to the corpse beside the wall.

I didn't know what waited for me at the Railroad Pass. I'd promised Sally I would go to meet her friend Mae on Saturday, and I trusted Sally but didn't know what to expect. I was not sure what she or Mae could do to help me, other than selling my salve so I could get money to leave. I held the small music box in my hand as I laid out the supplies for our five-mile walk back across the mountain and debated whether I should take it with me. No, I decided. I'd be back, and if not, it was not mine to take in the first place.

Nothing was, really, except the extra canteen that replaced the one he had stolen from me, and I'd been very respectful of the items in the cave. I knew they were all stolen, but somehow, some of the things, like the music box, seemed more personal. His death must have been painful, and of the things he had, he chose to have the music box next to him when he died. I imagined him listening to the tinny tune and it bringing him some comfort in his last hours. Nothing in the cave was mine; however, there were a few things that I would borrow while I was there.

I laid out the two wool blankets to pack for our hike to the Pass. I needed to find a woman named Mae, and I knew she worked at the cribs behind the Pass, so nighttime would be the best time to find her. I didn't want to go through the mountains at night, so I was planning on leaving the next afternoon, getting there just as the sun set, and finding a place to lay out our blankets for the rest of the night. In the morning, I could grind the plants and shrub pieces Pepper and I had gathered during the week and put them in the bean cans we had been saving for guano. I had enough easily for fifty penny jars. Once at the pass, I could get the honey, lard, and penny jars from the little store across the highway, then make up the jars in the mountain, maybe by the little stream we had passed, and return them to Mae to give to Sally. The extra supplies would cost me almost three dollars, but if Sally could sell the fifty jars, it would be twenty-five dollars. If she could sell them, I reminded myself. If nothing else, we could come back to the cave and figure something out. Queho's cave. Our cave.

I packed my extra clothes and our last can of Vienna sausages. I took a few pictures in the cave to finish off the roll and threw my film in as well. Maybe Mae or Sally could get it developed for me. I knew it was a waste of what little money I had, but I wanted to look at the pictures at night, and I wanted to have them to take with me when we left.

I still didn't know how I was going to get my divorce from Cotton. Maybe Sally had some other ideas, or maybe I would just have to go on being married to him until he died. I knew there were women out there that had left their husbands and changed their names, hoping they wouldn't one day show up and claim them. I didn't want to be one of those. I wanted to be Helen Carter again. "I'll figure it out," I said to the corpse against the wall. Somehow.

"Helen, look!" Pepper bounced into the cave, carrying a sack. "I saw Mr. Emery put it under your tree, and after he left, I went and got it!"

"Pepper, that's stealing! We can't do that! We—"

He shook his head excitedly. "No, it's for us! Look," he said as he opened the sack and began pulling items from inside: a box of crackers, a can of peanut butter, four orange Nehi sodas, and six licorice whips.

I put a hand on my chest. Mr. Emery. One of our angels. Then a disturbing thought crossed my mind. He knew we were up here? How? And if he knew, who else did?

AUTHOR NOTE: ALTHOUGH several of the items I mention in this manuscript are items that were actually found in Queho's cave with his corpse, the music box was not. As a child, my grandmother had one similar to what is described, and when I needed an object that made Helen feel safe, that gave her a sense of home, Grandma's little music box came to mind.

Chapter 50: He's a Good Snake

Helen

EVEN THOUGH OUR TREK was in the late afternoon, and we were heading into the sun, we made much better time and weren't totally exhausted the entire way. I remembered the mountain stream we had found on the way and stopped there for a good rest, including washing and drying our feet and applying a layer of salve. I had very little left but knew I'd be making a new batch tomorrow and planned on keeping plenty for myself. I fell asleep next to the stream, listening to the sound of the water as it lazily made its way through the mountain, but Pepper made sure I didn't sleep too long. After we ate our dinner, Vienna sausages and the remaining box of crackers and peanut butter that Mr. Emery had left the night before, we put our boots back on and continued on our way. I felt revived, which may have been why we got to the Pass in time to watch the sun set.

We found ourselves in a place above the Pass away from the congestion of those in the camps. A few others were camped in the area, but most didn't like to wander too far away from the false security of the other squatters. I'd take my chances on the wildlife any day.

"I still don't understand why we had to leave," Pepper said. He had grown comfortable in the cave in a very short period of time, and I had noticed the closer we got to people, the more anxious he became.

"We need money, Pepper. And the only way I know to get it right now is to make my salve and let Sally sell it. Also, we need to know if Cotton and Mr. Cromwell are looking for us," I said.

"Dumbbell," Pepper replied. "And he don't have no right."

I put my arm on his shoulder. "I told you I'd protect you. Don't worry."

He bit his bottom lip and leaned into me.

We were out of food but could wait until morning. The thought of the storekeeper's homemade bread made my mouth water, and I tried to turn my thoughts back to the sun, watching the red, purple, and golden streaks across the sky as they cast a rainbow of hues on the mountain. My peace was interrupted by the screams of a small boy.

"Snake, snake!" he yelled as he pointed at a rocky area about thirty feet from where we had dropped our wares. He stood still, too scared to move, and a woman not much older than me ran up behind him and pulled him back by his shoulders. Another woman followed her, and together they stood looking in the direction of the snake, neither making a move to kill it.

I didn't really want to talk to anyone that I didn't have to, but they appeared to be alone and probably didn't realize that rattlesnake meat was actually very tasty. My stomach growled as I thought about it. Maybe if we offered to share the meat with the women and boy, they'd have the means to make a fire.

"Be careful!" they said to me as I headed in the direction they were pointing, Pepper staying close by. I was always aware of my surroundings, and knowing there was a snake nearby was half the battle. I put a finger to my lips to tell them to hush and listened for the telltale rattle that meant the snake felt threatened. It didn't come.

Slowly, we moved farther away from the trio and into the rocky haven. I spied the snake, and even with the sun dying, I could tell that it wasn't a rattlesnake. It was a gopher snake, which didn't have the rattle tail but did look similar to its poisonous cousin. He was not only harmless but was good to have around. He kept other critters, including rattlesnakes, away. I reached my hand down toward him and placed my palm on the ground next to him. He turned toward me then slowly wrapped around my arm.

"Hello, there," I said as I sat down and put my arm in front of me, looking into his beady eyes. Pepper sat next to me and reached out to pet the snake. The trio behind us collectively gasped, and I said over my shoulder, "Don't worry, he's a good snake."

I heard one of them say, "Ain't no such thing," and the two women headed back toward their camp. The little boy remained, watching us interact with our new friend.

"He won't hurt you," I said. "Come say hello."

He took two steps forward and then stopped. I turned around on my rock and looked at him. He looked to be about five or six and had on a dirty T-shirt that hung to his knees and a pair of worn boots that looked three sizes too big.

"How do you know?" he said.

I lifted my arm up slowly, the snake's head bobbing next to mine. "See his tail? No rattles. And his body is shiny, like it has oil on it. A rattlesnake is dull looking." I turned my arm so the snake's head was clearly visible. "And see his head? It's smooth, almost the same size as his neck. A rattlesnake has a head that is shaped like a triangle."

He walked closer, and Pepper put his hand in front of the snake's mouth and let it tickle him with its long, forked tongue.

"See? He'll still bite if he's scared, but it won't kill ya. He's just out here looking for food like everyone else."

"I'm Jay," the boy said as he moved within five feet of us, never taking his eyes off the snake.

"I'm... Henry," I said.

Pepper giggled when I called myself Henry and said, "And I'm Ford."

I lifted the gopher snake toward the boy. "And this is... Gatsby." I smiled, thinking about the book that I'd read at least a hundred times.

"He likes you. Whatya gonna do with him?" Jay asked.

The snake twisted on my arm and looked at me, as if asking the same thing.

"I guess I'll keep him around tonight, to scare off the real snakes," I said. I did remember to put Uncle Dwayne's gun in my pocket, but a lot of men would be more afraid of looking a snake in the eye than the barrel of a gun.

"Jay, get over here!" one of the women yelled.

"Don't forget, a triangle head and rattles on the tail. That's the bad one out here," I said.

He bobbed his head vigorously and waved to me as he ran back to his mother.

Pepper and I went back to our packs and sat down. Pepper held out his hands. "Can I hold him?" he asked.

I slowly unwrapped him from my arm and laid him in Pepper's, and he coiled around his arm and tickled his neck with his tongue.

Pepper giggled. "I've never had a pet before," he said.

I lay back, shut my eyes, and listened to Pepper talk to the snake as he would a kitten. As sleep found me, I took comfort in knowing that Gatsby was nearby and would keep the real animals at bay.

AUTHOR NOTE: I HAVE to admit, I've always been like the majority of the population in that snakes basically creep me out. Sure, I know the difference between a rattlesnake and a gopher snake, but I'd never get close enough to check it out. However, my oldest son and his husband have blessed me with "grand-snakes," and I'm starting to warm up to them.

Chapter 51: Where the Ladies Are

Helen

I WOKE UP TO A NIGHT full of stars. It was cold, and I sat up and rubbed my arms. I took a drink from my canteen and splashed a little of the water on my face. I should have asked Jay last night about a water source so I could fill up, but surely Mae would know.

I was putting a lot of trust in someone I didn't know, but I didn't have a lot of options. I thought I could trust Mr. Emery and Smitty Goon or Ezra, if I could find either one, but after watching the work at the dam and seeing Boulder City from the mountains, it would be hard to find them and still stay undercover. I did trust Sally, and she trusted Mae, so I was taking a leap of faith. I looked up at the stars, a million tiny lights in a clear sky. Once in a while, you just had to jump, Daddy would have said.

I nudged Pepper, but he didn't want to go. "We talked about this, Pepper," I said.

"Please? I don't want to go where the ladies are," he said. I remembered where I had found Pepper, and my heart sank. I gave his shoulder a gentle squeeze.

"You don't have to. You can wait on the path with Gatsby, and I'll go up there. I'm not leaving you here," I said.

He let out a long sigh and sat up. We repacked our packs and found Gatsby curled up underneath one of the blankets, looking for warmth. Pepper stuck him in his pack, and after a little fuss, he found a spot and settled down.

We moved down through Texas Acres, which wasn't as lively as I remembered it a year ago but still not as quiet as Ragtown was at night. I found a good tree for Pepper to wait at, and I slipped behind the Railroad Pass and found the dirt incline that led to the cribs.

There were four small shacks that didn't seem big enough for two people and three small canvas tents lined up like a street. Three wick lamps were placed on poles to provide enough light to keep from tripping on the gravel path that ran through the shelters but not enough to truly see.

A few men were waiting, and two of them laughed as I walked by. My first reaction was to lower my head, but I knew I looked like a boy right now, so I kept my head high and eyes forward. One of them asked me if it was my first time, and I ignored him, just as I ignored the proposition from the other. A young blond woman crawled out of one of the tents, followed by a much older man who stood and buttoned his trousers. I swallowed hard and approached the woman before she had a chance to grab another customer from the line.

"Are you Mae?" I asked, trying to keep my voice steady.

The young woman looked me up and down. "If you want a job, you need to speak to Babe."

"I'm looking for Mae. Are you her?" I asked again.

The young woman placed her hands on her hips. "No, I'm not. Aren't you a little young to be up here?"

I didn't flinch as two more women came to stand next to the blonde. The shortest one stepped forward and reached toward my ballcap, but I pulled back. "Unless, of course, you want a job. We had a boy about your age up here once. You can use my shack for the night."

One of the men behind me yelled at the three women to hurry up, and two of them walked toward the group, leaving me standing alone with the tall blonde. She spoke softly and motioned toward her tent. "Are you sure you wouldn't rather see me? Mae is a lot older, and I'm sure I could–"

I shook my head and smiled. "I'm not a customer. I'm a friend. I hate to bother her here, but I didn't know how else to find her."

She pursed her lips and cocked her head, eyeing me from head to toe again. "Stay here," she said.

I did as I was told and watched her walk toward a large, older woman sitting next to one of the shacks on a wooden chair. After saying a few words to the woman, she turned and motioned for me to follow, and as I approached, the big woman stood and eyed me so hard I could almost feel it in my bones. Then she focused on my eyes and suddenly smiled.

"I'm a friend of Sally's," I said.

Mae turned to the blonde. "Tell Babe I didn't feel well and went home." She raised her long skirt to just above the knee and pulled a small change purse from her boot. She retrieved a few coins from it and handed them to the woman. "And don't tell anyone about the boy."

The woman looked at me one more time before walking back toward her tent. I followed Mae to the end of the little gravel lane of shacks to a steeper, rockier incline that led away from the cribs and the casino. The tree where I had left Pepper was just off to the south, and I asked Mae to hold up while I went to get him. When we got back to her, she looked at him. I could see the puzzled look on her face, but she said nothing.

She was a big woman, wearing a long dress and boots, but seemed to be able to maneuver down the trail easily and quickly in the dark, and I struggled to keep up. Once we reached the bottom, we were at the edge of the camp to the north of the casino, and she finally turned to me.

"My camp is just a little ways up the hill. We'll talk when we get there," she said.

I silently followed her, all the while keeping sharp that Pepper was right by my side. Her large canvas tent had a picnic table in front, but she held a flap open, and we went inside. Mae followed and lit a small candle then motioned us toward a couch in the middle of the tent. It was sectioned off with two other rooms, one on either side of the common area. Pepper and I put our packs on the ground and sat on the couch. I enjoyed how soft it felt and realized how tired I was, even after sleeping for a few hours in the desert.

Mae went to one of the curtains and raised it, said a few words to someone on the other side, and came back to us. In the corner of the common room, she lifted a lid on the floor and pulled out two sodas and a couple of candy bars. Pepper's stomach growled, and he said, "Sorry." He tore open his candy bar and took a ravenous bite.

"I'll get you something decent in the morning, but this should help you sleep a little better tonight."

I took my ballcap off and let my long red braid fall down my back. "Thank you," I said.

She watched us eat for a minute. "Helen, I tell ya, this is one heck of a mess. Sally told me everything, and Pete filled me in with some details he'd found out, and of course the word coming from Tony Badamo is a little different. I can't say that I'd be willing to get involved if it weren't for Sally and Ezra."

"Ezra?" I stopped chewing and swallowed hard.

She smiled. "Yes, it seems we have a couple of mutual friends."

I heard someone coming from behind and turned quickly to see a tall man with hair as red as mine coming through the back curtain. I reached for my pack and wrapped my hand around Uncle Dwayne's .38.

The man saw my reaction, stopped short, and smiled. "I'll be damned. I thought you were just a legend, but here you are, sitting in my living room. What do you think, Mae, blond or bald?"

"What?" I said.

Another woman, tall and slender and wearing a cotton nightgown, was behind him and smacked him on the shoulder. "Don't mind him. He thinks he's funny. I'm Marguerite. The tent clown is Pete. Sit. Eat. You're safe here."

Pepper hadn't said a word, but I noticed him sink into the couch when Pete came in the room. I sat back down next to him and realized he was shaking.

"I am funny," Pete said, "and I've got to get to work. I expect you to be here when I get back, because I don't want to drag Ezra out here for nothing. He's not having the best of days right now, but I think he'll make do if he knows you're sitting on my couch."

"He's not well?" Ezra. I had been thinking about him all week, wondering if I should even bother trying to find him, and I didn't realize he'd been looking for me too.

"He'll be fine," Pete said. He kissed Marguerite on the cheek and started toward the entrance then turned back slowly. "I knew both of your daddies. They were good men," he said.

"Thank you," I said. Pepper said nothing.

"Don't move," he said.

The sudden change in the tone of his voice caused Pepper and me both to sit up straight. He was looking toward my pack, and I shifted my eyes to see that Gatsby had crawled out of Pepper's pack and found a spot near the back of the tent.

"He's with us," I said.

AUTHOR NOTE: THERE is such a difference between the establishments in Las Vegas where the prostitutes, like Sally, worked and the desert cribs of the Railroad Pass prostitutes. I tried to recreate the scene from the few pictures I've seen of the actual cribs, including the wick lamps, the rocky incline, and the tents and small shanties.

Chapter 52: The Girl with Green Sea-Glass Eyes

Ezra

LAYING A SLAB OF CONCRETE three feet thick normally required days, even weeks, to dry and set properly. This could be altered by changing the mixture ratios of the cement, using more of the aggregate and less of the Portland, or a bit more or less water. The combinations were virtually endless, but with each one, there also existed a difference in strength as well as how the concrete might handle other forces, such as time and stress.

The Bureau of Reclamation experimented with concrete for years on other government projects but none as big as this one. A friend of mine from the dorms who worked at Lo-Mix said that the government had close to a hundred different formulas they tested to find the right one—the one that would set quickly and last for a thousand years.

One thing the concrete formulas had in common was the unusual amount of heat they gave off. When it was freshly poured, it was at its worst. The puddlers, who stomped the air bubbles out of a fresh pour, sweated so much they didn't wear shirts and had to stop each hour to take off their boots and wring out their socks. The tunnel held the heat, making it one of the more unpleasant jobs. If you were close to the floor and the wet concrete, it was unbearable.

Tubing ran through the slabs, with water constantly flowing through to cool the hot cement while it cured properly. After laying the lines on top of a fresh pour, the lineman lay on the ground on the most recently set piece and watched closely as the puddlers went to work to make sure none of the lines were kinked by their efforts. When I showed up to work, barely able to walk and drunk on cough syrup, Frenchie had switched me down to lineman to keep me off my leg as much as possible.

I lay still on the ground as the concrete truck slowly moved forward after filling the gantry trough with a fresh mix. Sweat poured from my face, and I didn't bother to wipe it, knowing it would be replaced as soon as I moved my arm. As the truck pulled away, I turned my head and looked along the bottom of the tunnel, barely able to distinguish the light at its entrance.

Hell was lined with concrete.

A small stream of water showered me from above. I rolled over, opened my mouth, and let it wash my face and chest.

Moose stood over me, holding one of the cooling lines. "Come on, Ezra. It's time to go home."

Moose and Chief lifted me from the floor and helped me to the waiting cement truck that took us the half mile to the entrance. As I sat on the sideboard, holding on with my left hand, I pulled out a bottle of cough syrup that was tucked in my pants waist, unscrewed the lid with my teeth, and took a long drink. After tipping the bottle upside down and draining the last bit, I tucked the empty back away and leaned my head on the side of the big truck.

As the truck came to a stop outside the tunnel, Chief handed me the cane Miss Smitty had found in the company store for me last night. He reached down to help me up.

"I'm okay. I can do it." I stood, wincing, and reached for Chief's shoulder as I put a minimal amount of my weight on my left leg.

Chief pointed at the cane. "Pete said if you don't use that thing, he's gonna beat you with it."

I took the cane and leaned into it, taking some of the pressure off my ankle. "I got it, Chief. It's hard to work the cane and the damn boot."

Chief's wife, Donna Sue, had given me one of Chief's old boots. It was at least three full sizes bigger than mine, but she had also given me a thick piece of foam to wrap my foot and ankle in before sticking it in the boot. It didn't take the pain away, but it allowed enough cushion to walk.

"How are you doing, Ezra?" Frenchie had been watching me all day. He explained that although he knew I was hurting, if I couldn't be of any use on the job, I'd have to go home.

"I'm great, Frenchie. Thinking I'll go dancin' tonight."

Moose stepped up. "Frenchie, you gotta get him off that floor. The heat is going to kill him. Put the damn Mexican back down there."

"No problem," Frenchie said. He looked at me. "Can you get up that ladder?"

"I'll get him up there," Chief said. "Hell, he can lean against the frame if he needs to."

Frenchie continued to talk to me. "You still drinking cough syrup?"

"I got a cold," I said.

Frenchie pointed a finger at me as if scolding a child. "Well, look here. You show up here sober tomorrow, without your 'cold,' and we'll try you back up on the gantry. I can't let you put these other guys in danger."

"I'll be fine," I said.

After a long ride up to the top of the canyon in the widow-maker, Moose walked with me, giving me plenty of time to get to Chief's waiting car. I'd been concentrating on walking but needed to take my mind off the pain.

"When's the next fight?" I asked.

"No more for me. It's hard enough staying alive down here without pushing my luck any."

Chief was standing in front of his car, in a heated discussion about the upcoming election with one of the guys from Lo-Mix. "I'll be there in a minute," he said as Moose helped me into the back of Chief's sedan, allowing me room to stretch out my leg.

I reached under the seat and pulled out a fresh bottle of Jameson Irish. "Thank you, Pete," I whispered as I broke the seal and took a long swig.

Right on cue, Pete stuck his head in the side window. "How's the leg, Easy?"

"Fine, Pete. Now a shower, and I'll be ready for a night of liquor and ladies," I said as I took another swig off the bottle. I felt the throb in my leg start to numb and waited for the alcohol to completely take hold.

"Good," Pete said. "Because after your shower, George Goon is going to give you a ride out to the Pass. Bring a change of clothes—you'll be staying at the mansion tonight."

I gave him a weak laugh. "I was kidding, Pete. I'm going to rinse off this sweat and go straight to bed."

"Nope, not tonight. And don't get yourself drunk before you get out there. I have a surprise for you," Pete said.

"Pete, there ain't no way—"

He leaned in the window and whispered to me. "She's got red hair and eyes the color of green sea glass. Isn't that the way you described her?"

"Helen? What—"

"Just get yourself cleaned up and get out there. She won't be there forever." Pete and Moose exchanged knowing glances, and then Pete headed off toward the train.

As he walked away, Moose asked, "What's Doc say?"

I shrugged. "He thinks the bite hit a nerve or something. Said I'll have a limp. Not much, but I'll have one."

Moose climbed in the front seat of Chief's sedan. "That's not too bad. It could have been a lot worse."

"Funny," I said, "you get thrown around by some big old Pedro and heal in a week. One little spider bite and a twisted ankle, and I'm gonna walk sideways for the rest of my life."

Moose sat quietly for a minute. "Can I tell you something, Ezra? You can't say anything. If anyone else knew, they wouldn't trust to work with me."

I didn't reply, giving him time to finish.

"It's my left eye," Moose said. "The one old Ponce kept beating on. I can't see out of it. Doc said I probably never will."

I leaned my head back on the door and looked up into the car's black headliner. After a few moments, I uncapped the whiskey bottle and took a long, deep swig and then passed the bottle to Moose. He took a drink and handed it back.

"So, Pete found Helen, huh?" he said.

"How did you know that?" I asked.

"It's my eye that doesn't work. My hearing is excellent. Look, you know Smitty and I will do what we can to help you—to help her—but you need to be careful. You gotta take care of yourself before you start thinking about taking care of someone else."

Moose was my friend. I knew he meant well, and I trusted that if anything happened to me, he'd be there, just as he was then. But I thought he wanted me to walk away from Helen, which would be easy to do, except somewhere deep inside me, I just couldn't. I knew she wasn't my responsibility, but I also knew that if the tables were turned, she'd help me. I'd not had many friends in my life, and working in the desert had taught me when you found a few that would always have your bad side, you were best to have theirs too. Sure, I had problems of my own right now, but maybe focusing on Helen's might keep my mind off my own.

I took a short swig off the bottle then put it away, remembering what Pete had said. The numbing wasn't complete, but it was tolerable, and I needed to shower and change if I was going to get out to the Pass with George.

"I'm going with you tonight," Moose said.

"No, really, you don't—"

"You'll never make it through Little Oklahoma by yourself, and besides, Smitty would kill me if she knew I didn't go with you and make sure Helen was okay. To be honest, I can't wait to meet this girl that everyone seems to want to help. I can ride back with George when he's done entertaining the ladies." He said it with finality, and I knew there was no point in arguing.

AUTHOR NOTE: WRITERS often have their "darlings," and I have to say this particular chapter is one of mine. I think it shows the extremely harsh conditions experienced by the men who worked in the diversion tunnels and the choices they had to make to keep working, whether sick or injured. This chapter also has my favorite line in the entire book. Hell is lined with concrete.

Chapter 53: What is That Smell?

Helen

I WOKE TO THE SMELL of bacon. It took me a minute to remember where I was, and looking around the small camp, I thought it was heaven. I fell asleep shortly after Pete left for work, and someone took off my boots and put a clean sheet over me. It had been a long time since anyone tried to take care of me, and I felt a pang of longing for a family that I no longer had.

I stretched and sat up on the couch, looking around to make sure Pepper and Gatsby weren't getting into any trouble. Gatsby was in the far corner, stretching too. I could hear Pepper outside with Mae.

"Put your hat back on before you come out to breakfast," Marguerite said. "That red hair stands out."

I put my braid up in my cap and stood then fell back on the couch. My feet hadn't fared as well as I thought, and I pulled my socks off and saw the blisters forming on my soles. I really needed to wash them before I dressed them, but I'd have to wait for that. I got my last jar of salve out of my pack and massaged my feet then put my dirty socks back on before putting on my boots.

"What is that smell?" Mae said as she came in from outside. She wore a light cotton dress, and her hair fell in ringlets around her face. If I were to guess, I'd have said she was in her late twenties, but she acted much older, and in a way, I was sure she was. Sometimes, experience weighs more than years.

"Sorry, it's the salve I put on my feet. I know it isn't the sweetest scent, but it works."

She snapped her fingers. "That reminds me. Sally gave me ten dollars for you. Said to tell you she sold all the bottles you left with her in just a few days. It must work."

"Ten dollars? That's... amazing." I didn't figure she'd sell all the salve I left her in a week, but I was certainly glad she did. If I weren't running from Tony Badamo and Cotton, I could probably live in Queho's cave and make salve for the rest of my life. "I brought enough brush to make fifty more. I just need to run over to the store and get a few supplies."

"Give me a list of what you need," Marguerite said. "You best stay right here."

Pepper popped in the tent and was literally bouncing up and down. His hair had been cut down to almost his scalp, and he had on a pair of dungarees and a shirt that almost fit him. "Can I go with you?" he asked Marguerite.

She rubbed his stubby head. "Sure. Let me get you a ball cap to wear. You can help me carry everything back." She looked at me. "He'll be safe."

"She's right," Mae said. "Let's eat, and then let's talk."

The bacon and biscuits melted in my mouth, and I felt like I ate more than my share, but Mae and Marguerite didn't seem to mind. After we finished and cleaned up our spot, Marguerite took my list and three dollars and, holding Pepper's hand, headed out to the store.

"I don't know how to thank you for everything," I said to Mae as we settled on the couch.

She softened her voice and leaned closer to me. "I didn't want to ask with him around, but what's the deal with Pepper? Everyone is looking for a thirteen-year-old girl, not a ten-year-old boy."

I shook my head in disgust. "His stepfather, Mr. Cromwell, dressed him up like a girl and had him... doing things... for money, in the alley behind the Apache. I saw him... I—"

She held up her hand. "That's why he was afraid of Pete this morning. Poor kid. How old is he?"

"He is thirteen. He's just small. And acts younger," I said.

She squared her shoulders and lifted her chin. "I don't blame you for taking him. But it just adds to your own mess," she said.

She took my ball cap off again. "You're a much prettier girl than you are a boy," she said. "But you are in a lot of trouble. And we need to figure out how to get you out of it."

I clutched my hands in my lap and tried to sit up straight. "I have to get a divorce from Cotton. I've got the car hidden, so once I get enough money to leave and—"

"You'll never make it that far. Tony Badamo is mad as hellfire, and he's got a cop in his pocket in every town from here to San Francisco," she said. "Kidnapping, assault with a weapon, and stealing a car. Those are serious crimes."

"Assault? I didn't assault anyone!" I thought back and realized the man in the alley that I pulled my gun on must have claimed I had hit him with it or was going to shoot him. I was—I would have—but I didn't try to kill him. I felt myself deflate. "I don't know why they would say that. Pepper came with me; I didn't kidnap him. And the car is rightfully mine, and it's not me that owes Tony Badamo a thing. It's Cotton. Maybe if I just talk to Mr. Badamo—"

Mae laughed. "Honey, they had to say something to get the police to help them find you. And it ain't about whether you owe Tony or not. You're a young girl, and you made him and his men look real stupid, and that makes him look weak. He doesn't care about your car, or your marriage, or Pepper at all. He cares about his reputation."

She was right, and although I could possibly hide in the desert for quite some time, sooner or later, I was going to have to figure out a way to get Tony Badamo and Cotton out of my life. And get on with my life. "So what do I do?"

"Change your look, get some money in your hands, and smuggle you as far away from this desert as we can." She put a hand on my knee, and it was the most maternal feeling I'd had in a long time.

"I want the divorce. I don't want to feel like I'm running my entire life. It's not fair. If I were a man, this wouldn't be happening," I said.

"You're right. But if you were a man, you'd have different problems. Life isn't easy for anyone right now, and we all make our own choices about how we're going to make it through. As much as I'd like to help you run away, I have to respect that you want to do things right, no matter how hard it's going to be. It will take us a while to get enough money to pay off Tony Badamo. But if you bear with me..."

"I can sell salve. And bat guano. And anything else I need to do." I looked at my hands folded in my lap and thought about how quickly I could get the money I needed if I would just swallow my pride and work the cribs with Mae for a few months. I'd had sex with Cotton for free, and it couldn't be much worse. I felt moisture gather in my eyes and wiped away a tear before it had a chance to fall.

Mae put her arm around me, and I leaned my head on her bosom. "Can I ask you something?" she said.

I cleared my throat. "Of course."

"Have you ever had sex for money?" She said it so calmly, like it was something most women did.

I shook my head. I could do this, though. And never look back.

She pulled away from me, held my face in her hands, and looked me in the eyes. "Good. And you're not going to either. I'll get your money, and we'll get you out of here."

"I don't understand. You don't even know me. Why are you being so good to me?"

She smiled. "I had your sparkle once, and I let that fire go out. I don't want that to happen to you. And don't think I'm doing it for nothing. You are going to owe me a big favor."

"Anything," I said.

She laughed. "You need to watch that word 'anything.' It's going to get you in trouble someday."

Marguerite and Pepper returned with a large bag and set it on the ground a little too close to Gatsby. He reared his head and looked at her, and she gasped. "Does the snake have to stay?" she said.

Pepper picked up Gatsby and sat on the ground with him. "Really, he won't hurt you, and I promise to take him back to our cave."

I looked at Pepper, hoping he hadn't told Marguerite everything about our cave. He winked at me, and I trusted that he hadn't. I looked through the sack and found that she had gotten me double the supplies I asked for.

"I figure that would save a trip next week," she said.

"Thank you," I said.

She reached out and twirled a strand of my hair. "We need to cut your hair and peroxide it. There was a man in the store asking about two young girls. I figure someone cares enough to be looking for you."

"What did he look like?" I asked.

Marguerite shrugged. "Short, skinny, dark greasy hair, half-drunk."

I let out an exasperated breath. Cotton.

Mae tilted her head toward the sack in my hands. "You get to making your stuff, and then we'll do your hair and get you cleaned up and into some fresh clothes. You've got company coming tonight."

AUTHOR NOTE: PEPPER'S character is one of the most tragic to me. While we often focus on the hardships and the challenges that the men and women faced during the Great Depression, sometimes the very real abuses of the children are left unsaid. He was also a very complex character for me to write. I want Pepper to be okay, but his past experiences and the things he still must go through make it hard to believe that will happen.

Chapter 54: Ezra Would Never Betray Me

Helen

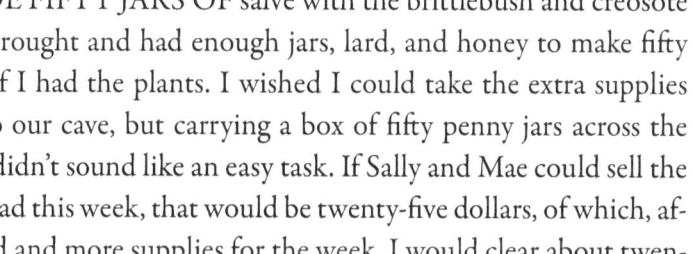

I MADE FIFTY JARS OF salve with the brittlebush and creosote I had brought and had enough jars, lard, and honey to make fifty more, if I had the plants. I wished I could take the extra supplies back to our cave, but carrying a box of fifty penny jars across the desert didn't sound like an easy task. If Sally and Mae could sell the fifty I had this week, that would be twenty-five dollars, of which, after food and more supplies for the week, I would clear about twenty dollars. It was a dent in what it would take to buy Tony Badamo off and have him out of my life. But I still needed my divorce. And money to leave town.

Thinking back, I probably never should have waited so long to leave Cotton. I should have just left, taken what little I had at the time, and made my way out of town instead of waiting until things escalated. But looking back never seemed to do much good. I needed to focus on looking forward.

After I closed the lid on the last jar of a fresh batch, Mae brought me two slop buckets with water and some soap so I could finally clean up. It was not as soothing as lying in the river, but the water was much cleaner, and the soap smelled like roses. I wanted to wash my hair, too, but I didn't have a brush and was afraid of what kind of a mess it might be if I unbraided it. So I used some of Mae's Rosebud talcum and powdered my head to soak up some of the oiliness and considered Mae's offer to cut it off. I knew I needed to disguise myself somehow, but I just couldn't bring myself to cut and dye my hair. Not yet. Instead, I promised to keep it braided and hidden, either with a ball cap or a scarf that Mae had given me to wear.

I felt girlish again in the light cotton dress that Marguerite had put out for me. She was a lot taller than I was, so it was a little too long but fit me well otherwise. I scrubbed my dungarees and shirt and put them outside to dry. I hadn't intended to stay two nights, but it sure was nice to have people to talk to. Pepper loved the attention he was getting. I could easily get spoiled with Mae and Marguerite, but I couldn't let that happen right now. And although the human contact was nice, I did miss the solitude of the desert. The quiet gave me time to think, and I needed that.

I was anxious to see Ezra but didn't know what to expect. Mae told me he had been bitten by a black widow, and I couldn't imagine the pain he must be in. I knew the course of a black widow bite—I'd seen it before in Ragtown—and a day or two was not nearly enough time for the agony to be bearable. He should be resting, I thought, not traipsing out here to see me. A sudden sense of panic washed over me. What if this was all a ruse, a chance for Mae and Marguerite, Pete, maybe even Ezra, to trap me into a sense of security then turn me in? It was desperate times, and none of them knew Pepper or me. Was there a reward of some kind?

I shook the thought away. No. No. Sally would never do that to me, and she had sent me to Mae. It was nothing but coincidence that she knew Ezra, and he wouldn't betray me. Would he?

I'd been angry with Ezra for a year because, as Cotton had said, if he were really my friend, he would have at least come and told me that he was sorry about Daddy. But after chatting with Mae today and having some time to reflect, I had realized that sometimes even our best intentions didn't always work out the way we planned them to.

"He went to Ragtown to see you, but you were already gone," she said. And that made my stomach hurt even more. I used to dream about Ezra, his easy smile, and the way my whole body warmed when he touched my arm. But I let go of those dreams a long time ago. Or maybe I just tucked them away somewhere to keep me safe.

No. Ezra would never betray me.

When Pete came into the tent, I expected Ezra to be with him. He must have noticed my disappointment, because he said, "Usually the ladies smile when they see me come through that canvas slit."

Pepper grabbed Gatsby and allowed him to wrap around his forearm then huddled close to me on the couch. Pete stared at the boy and the snake but said nothing.

I was not sure what to think about Pete yet. Mae and Marguerite told me that he tried to be funny, but he had a heart of gold. I knew he was friends with Ezra, and he'd also worked with my daddy. "Mae is taking a nap, and Marguerite is getting dressed. Sorry, I..."

He waved a hand at me. "Don't worry about it. I'm just glad you seem to be as happy to see Ezra as he is to see you. As hardheaded as you both are, I'm surprised you two ever talked to each other at all."

"I'm not hardheaded," I said. Just protective.

"Yeah, and Hoover ain't still president," he said.

"Not for long," Marguerite said as she walked out from behind the curtain, dressed in her sequined conductor's outfit. "Another few weeks, and Hoover will be but a bad memory." She kissed Pete passionately, and I turned my head, feeling like I was intruding.

Pepper kept his eyes lowered but did not turn away. He was watching Pete intently.

"I'm going to walk Marguerite to work. If Ezra gets here before I get back, take it easy on him," he said.

After they left, Pepper relaxed, and I settled back on the couch with *The Great Gatsby*. I'd read the book so many times, I almost had it memorized. I was lost in the pages, wondering if I'd ever see New York City or go to a place like Long Island, when I heard my name and was torn from my thoughts. I dropped the book, stood, and turned quickly.

"Ezra."

AUTHOR NOTE: IT'S BEEN a long time since Helen and Ezra have seen each other, and in the previous year, their lives have changed drastically. The fact that Helen still believes, or hopes, Ezra is the man she thinks he is has a lot to do with her youth. But she is also starting to understand that maybe her original dreams of a happy marriage, a family, and a picture-perfect life may not be the only life there is.

Chapter 55: A Black Widow Couldn't Keep Me Away

Ezra

BY THE TIME MOOSE AND I made it through Little Oklahoma and to Pete's camp, the alcoholic numbness in my leg and ankle had subsided, and I took the last twenty or so steps as lightly as possible, leaning on my cane and on Moose, hoping I didn't pass out from the pain. My brow was soaked, and I didn't want to risk wiping it for fear I'd lose my balance. As much as I had hated the thought of Moose babysitting me, I was thankful he was there.

On the ride out, George gave me a hard time about needing to see a girl so bad that I wouldn't let a black widow keep me away. Pete had apparently not told him who I was coming to meet; if he had, maybe he'd have understood. But I also considered that maybe it was better to let as few people as possible know that Helen was nearby. Moose, however, had told Smitty, who, as he had said, wanted to go, too, but was relieved that Moose would go and report back to her. Their relationship was at a point that they were open with each other and trusted each other, and although I was a little envious, I was also happy for them.

I pulled back the piece of canvas that acted as the entrance to Pete's mansion. Pepper sat in the corner, holding a snake, of all things, and I smiled and put a finger to my lips, telling him to be quiet. He didn't smile, his gaze turning to Moose, who stood behind me.

I saw her sitting on the couch, facing away from me, one long red braid trailing down her back, reading a book. Other than being on a couch, it was just the way I always pictured Helen: a book in hand, lost in another world. I didn't want to disturb her, but I said her name.

She stood and turned toward me, and I didn't know if it was the pain in my leg, the alcohol I'd been drinking too much of, or something else that sent my head on a spin like a ride at the state fair. She looked skinnier than I remembered, if that was even possible, but in some way more womanly too. She said my name, and I limped slowly toward her, trying not to wince with each step.

"You're hurt," she said, reaching for my arm and helping me to the couch.

"Black widow and a sprained ankle, not a great combination," I said.

"I've got just the thing," she said and started to take off my boot. I wanted to stop her, but I did want the damn thing off. "Where's the bite?" she asked, and I pointed at the spot mid-calf that still felt like a hot poker was attached to it at times. She pushed my pants leg up gently, but it still hurt. "That looks awful," she said.

Pepper had sidled over next to her to look at my leg. He stuck out a finger to touch it but stopped when Moose cleared his throat from the front of the tent.

I waved toward him. "Oh, this is Moose. He's a good friend. Smitty is his girl," I added, as if that gave him a little more credibility in Helen's eyes.

"Oh, I miss her!" She turned to Pepper. "You remember Miss Smitty, right, Pepper? Moose is her boyfriend, so he's okay." I'd never known Pepper to be anything but open, friendly, and talkative to everyone, but there was something different about him. It was as if he had a shell, something he could crawl into and safely hide away from... something. I didn't know what had happened to Pepper and his mother after Ragtown, but from his behavior and Helen's words of encouragement to him, I could tell it wasn't good.

Pepper looked Moose over from head to toe, keeping close to Helen and keeping that snake wrapped around his forearm. Then he looked Moose in the eye and giggled.

Moose smiled. "What's so funny, little man?"

"You don't look like a Moose."

Moose twisted his face up in an overexaggerated way, as if he were thinking. "Well, you don't look like Pepper to me." Then he smiled again.

I shook my head to try to clear it. I was a little drunk, sure, but if Pepper was hiding, his old personality seemed to come out with Moose.

Helen, too, I could tell, was taken a little by their interaction and, for a few seconds, said nothing. Then she said, "Pepper, grab me a jar of salve and see if there's a piece of cloth I can use for Ezra's leg."

Pepper put the snake down in the corner, went behind the couch, and returned with a small jar of what looked like brown lotion. "Here," Moose said as he handed her a handkerchief.

She opened the jar, and from the smell, I could tell it was the same salve she used to use on her dad. She started rubbing it on and around the bite area. I wanted to scream; it hurt so bad every time she touched it.

After taking off my boot and removing the foam piece I had my foot wrapped in, she rubbed more goop on my ankle.

"You still haven't found a way to make that stuff smell good, I see."

"Hush. You know it works."

I leaned back against the couch and smiled. I knew I came to see how I could help her, but it sure felt good letting someone take care of me right now. And she was right. The area around the bite was lessening to a dull ache as the goop penetrated deeper into the wound. When she finished, she wiped her hands on my other pants leg and sat next to me on the couch.

"I didn't do what they say," she said.

"Yes, you did," Pepper said. "Kind of."

She shrugged. "Okay, kind of. But I had to. It's my car, and I had to get away from Cotton. And that man in the alley, he was going to hurt Pepper, so I pointed my gun at him, and Pepper came with me. I didn't kidnap him."

Moose sat down on the ground and didn't say anything. But I could tell he was concerned by what she had said and wanted to hear more. Me, too, of course.

"Tell me what happened with you."

She sat back against the couch, put her hands in her lap, and told us all about living with Cotton, living in Vegas, and the events that led up to her being here. She had glanced at Pepper when she got to the part about finding Pepper and didn't go into any detail, but Moose and I glanced at each other when she mentioned it, as if we both knew what she was talking about. I could feel my face warm, wanting to find Cotton and knock him into next Tuesday, and Moose's face was beet red, but we both stayed quiet and waited until she finished. Pepper had sat quietly in the corner, playing with his snake.

"You've been living in the mountains for a week?" I said.

She shrugged. "We don't mind it, actually. I mean, it's peaceful, and I get along well with the desert, and there's no one to worry about but Pepper and me. I did miss going to the cemetery this week, though. I've gone every week since…" She looked at me and gave me a weak smile, and I felt a ball of guilt well up inside me.

"I've gone a few times. I saw the flowers on Grace's grave the last time, and I figured they were from you. Thank you," I said.

Pepper spoke up but almost in a whisper. "That's where my daddy is too. I think my momma. I've never been there," he said.

Moose scooted a little closer to him but not enough to make Pepper pull back. "Well, maybe we'll just have to figure out a way to get you up there to say hello."

Pepper cracked a small smile without looking up.

Pete came through the canvas slit and smiled when he saw us sitting on the couch. "Did you meet her pet snake yet?" He set a sack next to us and called out to Mae, who was dressing in her room for work. "Dinner, compliments of the Railroad Pass. But Marguerite will have a fit if we eat in here. You need help getting out to the table, Easy?"

Mae came out of her room, took the bag off the couch, looked inside, and told Pete, "Grab some plates and get those extra biscuits out of the cooler." She smiled and motioned for us to follow her outside. Helen helped me put my boot back on, and I leaned on her while I stood up instead of using the cane. Helen's salve helped a lot. It was not painless, but it was tolerable.

"Where do they get all the food?" Helen said.

I leaned toward her and caught a scent of roses. "Pete has a dorm room in town, which means he gets 'all-you-can-eat' at the company mess hall. He doesn't sleep in his room much but uses the shower and takes all the extra food he can manage."

"That's right," Pete said as we sat at the table. He put a tin plate in front of each of us. "I take what they give me, and I share with my girls."

Mae rolled her eyes as she set a soda in front of me and passed the bag of chicken around the table. Once we all had food on our plate, Mae nodded toward Pete. "Okay, Pete, tell her."

"Tell me what?" Helen said, mid-bite.

I was curious what she was talking about, too, and quit eating and looked directly at Pete.

He kept eating and spoke in between bites. "I talked to Charlie today."

"Who's Charlie?" Helen asked.

"A friend of mine at the dam that has a lot of connections," Pete said.

"Dammit, Banker, you trust that guy too much," Moose said.

Pete pointed a chicken leg at him. "Settle down. I didn't tell him everything. I just told him I hadn't seen anything in the papers and wondered if it were as bad as Bodell made it sound. He said he'd call around and find out by end of day. He was a little curious too."

Moose rolled his eyes. He didn't trust Charlie because he was one of the big bosses. I could see it going either way, but what was done was done, so I gave Pete the benefit of the doubt.

"What did he say?" I asked.

"Good news and bad news. No attempted murder, but there is an 'assault with a deadly weapon' complaint against you, and you are 'wanted for questioning about a kidnapping.' No charges filed or report of stealing a car," he said.

"But I can tell them that those two didn't happen. She didn't assault anyone, and she didn't kidnap me," Pepper said.

"You can't go anywhere near it. If you show up, they'll send you right back where you were. And that ain't gonna happen," Moose said.

Pepper smiled at him, and I thought everyone at the table was surprised by the way Moose was protecting him.

"Actually," Mae said, "it's the car that worries me most. It wasn't reported to the police, which means Tony wants to handle it himself."

"What does he want?" Helen said.

"What do any of them want? I would guess money," I said.

"That's too easy. Sally knows him. She's going to see what she can find out for us," Mae said.

Helen looked at her lap. "I don't want her to get in any trouble."

"She'll be fine. In the meantime, we need to start gathering as much money as we can. To pay these people off and get you where you need to go," Pete said.

I felt a little stab in my chest. "Where are you planning to go? I mean, if everything gets taken care of, why can't you stay here?"

She looked at me, and for a moment, our eyes locked. I saw so much pain in them that I almost looked away. Then she shrugged. "Someplace... else," she said.

"Say, you wouldn't happen to have seen that Indian in the mountains, would you? That bounty on him sure would take care of things," Pete said jokingly.

It was just for a moment, but I saw something pass between Helen and Pepper that made me uneasy. I didn't think anyone else noticed while they were laughing at Pete's jab, but I did. Their eyes met, and Helen gave a slight shake of her head.

"There ain't no Indian up there," Pepper said.

Helen's mouth twitched in a quick smile.

Then Pepper winked. He winked! What the hell did that mean?

Pete slapped his hands on the top of the picnic table. "Okay, so while we wait for Sally to come up with something, let's get some of that salve sold. If it's as good as you say, those guys at the dam will buy it like crazy."

"What about the two charges?" Helen said. She seemed to be more worried about Pepper than about what a gangster wanted with her.

"One charge. The assault. The kidnapping is just questioning," Pete corrected. "And with those, you're right. Probably throw some money at them, and they will go away."

"If I could get more supplies to the mountain, Pepper and I could make salve all week long," Helen said. I knew what she was thinking. Selling her salve was a great idea, but it was going to take a while to save.

"I've got some money," I said. Between the money I had made off Moose's fight and what I'd been saving since working at the site, I had about four hundred fifty dollars saved. I would do what I could to help.

Helen shook her head. "Oh, I couldn't—"

Mae held up a hand. "Well, let's see what we're looking at first, sell some of that miracle goop, and then we'll figure out what we can all pitch in to help."

Helen shook her head but didn't refuse Mae's offer, which I wasn't sure I understood. Sure, Mae was like everyone's mother, or maybe an older, wiser sister, but Helen had only known her for a day, and she'd known me for almost two years. I wasn't surprised that she told me no so fast because she was hardheaded and liked to think she was independent. But I also didn't think we'd be able to sell a few hundred dollars' worth of Helen's salve in a few weeks. And something told me Tony Badamo wouldn't wait much longer than that for whatever he wanted.

I raised my hands, palms out. "Okay, fine. Tell me what I can do to help."

Pete smiled. "Oh, you are definitely going to be helping."

AUTHOR NOTE: FINALLY, *after a long separation, Ezra and Helen are back together. They are both a little older and a little wiser, and both have a little more baggage to carry. But the emotional ten-*

sion between them is still there. Ezra does want to help her. But whether it is out of guilt, some strange sense of responsibility, or maybe something else, he'll have to figure out. Helen has changed a lot, and Ezra will soon find out just how much.

Chapter 56: WANTED: Dead or Alive

Helen

THERE WAS A CERTAIN amount of comfort that came with having friends that seemed to be willing to help. By morning, Marguerite had two days' worth of food ready for me to pack, and Ezra had already planned to leave me supplies at Mr. Emery's dock for the week. They wanted us to stay with them, but Pepper and I needed to stay out of sight, and after two days, I was already stir-crazy from being inside the tent. Instead of walking the five miles back through the desert, though, we rode the train with Pete and Ezra to the work site, with the intent of walking back to our cave from there. Pete slipped the conductor two dollars and said Pepper was his little brother who wanted to go sit at Lookout Point for the day and that I was another worker filling in for someone. Ezra hovered over me in the corner of a boxcar, so no one gave me a second look. Except Ezra. He seemed to be looking quite a bit, and I couldn't say that I minded. As the train moved unsteadily through the mountain tunnels, our bodies were constantly pressed together, and I couldn't say that I minded that either. He was very different than he was a year ago, as if anything left of boyhood had gone, and now there was nothing but man. He was also very different from

Cotton; when Ezra touched me, I didn't cringe. Instead, I craved more.

When the train stopped, we were near a gravel parking area that I assumed was for the workers. The sun was just making its first appearance of the morning, casting a dim light over the desert. The never-ending sounds of machines and men from the site were muffled by distance. The top of the canyon was lined with men, looking, watching, waiting for someone to get injured and need replaced. It was a horrible existence when you relied on the misfortune of others to survive.

Ezra hesitated before we parted and went our separate ways. If I weren't dressed as a boy, and there weren't a hundred men around, I would have sworn he was about to kiss me. It was a good thing he didn't, because I was afraid I would kiss him back. Instead, he touched my cheek quickly and turned away, hobbling with his cane toward a group of other men. I watched him go, thinking about what might have been, and shook my head, knowing dreams weren't always what you expected when you tried to live them.

Instead of going straight back to the mountain, we headed to Lookout Point. It was so early, there were only a few people there. Pepper pulled Gatsby from his pack so he could grab what little sun there was, and we sat and watched the morning crew take the place of the night men. The work didn't seem to stop, and just like my other visits here, I was entranced watching them and, in a way, wished I could be there with them. I watched the man driving the tool truck from tunnel to tunnel, site to site, passing out various tools and checking in others. I could do that. The small clinic at the bottom of the canyon, I knew, was passing out aspirin and tending to small wounds. I could do that too. From what Ezra had told me about working in the tunnels, I thought I could do some of that as well. But I was a woman, so getting a real job that would get me a real paycheck was just another dream.

We knew Ezra and Moose were in tunnel number one, and we tried to pick them out from a distance. A dynamite blast shook the entire mountain, and I trembled with it, feeling the mountain fight to maintain its form then finally relent and give pieces of itself to the men who persisted. Small pieces, necessary pieces so that the mountain and men could coexist, fell to the river below. I followed a truck from Lo-Mix to Hi-Mix, and I thought of my daddy and realized that the men were giving pieces too.

After watching for at least an hour, my mind suddenly reverted to dollar signs and my current problem. I'd done nothing wrong—well, not in my eyes—and yet I needed to pay a mobster and two other grubby men more money than I made at the cafe in six months just to be able to live my own life. And I barely had thirty dollars. Our friends said they could help me get the cash Pepper and I needed to escape Nevada, but I hated to think their plan involved any of them using their own money.

And Cotton was looking for me. I knew from the description Marguerite gave of the man in the store that it had been Cotton. From what Ezra had said, the Boulder City policeman, Bodell, had talked to him almost immediately after I left, so Cotton knew Boulder City was about the only place I had to go. Now, a week later, he was at Railroad Pass, asking questions. It was just a matter of time before he figured out I was up in the mountains. I'd have to deal with him sooner or later, but I preferred later. I just wanted to leave.

After everyone retired last night, Ezra asked me why I wanted to go to California instead of staying in Nevada. After all, he'd said, "You'll get divorced from Cotton and be able to do what you want on your own." I had told him, as a woman, I needed more opportunity, opportunity that just wasn't available to me here. He jokingly said maybe I should go to Mexico, and although I didn't know much about it, maybe that wasn't such a bad idea. Sun, the ocean, mountains. I felt a weight in my stomach when I thought about going anywhere, because it meant I wouldn't see my friends again. I wouldn't see Ezra again. Maybe... just maybe, he'd consider going with me...

I pounded my hands on my thighs. Damn, I couldn't be thinking like that. I was not a child, needing a prince to carry me away into a happily ever after. And Ezra was not a prince. He was just a man, flawed, with problems of his own. He didn't need another one. And neither did I.

"What's wrong?" Pepper asked.

I let out a long sigh. "Just thinking about money."

Pepper was silent for a moment. "Are you going to turn him in?" he asked. "It's a lot of money."

Yes, I had been thinking about the reward for Queho. I couldn't lie. But I still didn't know that if we could trust someone, a man, to say he had found it, whoever had originally offered the reward would even pay. The reward had been established way before everyone in the country became poor, and it just seemed like a lot of "ifs" to me. But it was a lot of money.

"What do you think we should do?" I asked. After all, it wasn't just my find. "You're the one that found the cave, so it's really up to you," I said.

He seemed to think about that and after a few moments said, "It's a lot of money."

Gatsby hadn't traveled far from us, so I picked him up and let him coil around my arm. A woman and a small boy were just making their way to a spot to watch the work. She gasped when she saw the snake, but I paid them no mind as Pepper and I lifted our packs and walked back toward Hemenway Wash. My mind went back to Ezra. He was older now, smarter, stronger. And he made my stomach do backflips when he smiled.

I shook my head. Men. I didn't need a man. All I needed was money.

WE SPENT THE AFTERNOON gathering root for salve. In my heart, I knew it was like poking a bull with a small stick, but Mae had said I should make as much as possible in the next few weeks, and I intended to do as she said. I had a feeling she had other plans for getting me money, yet when I asked, she told me not to worry about it; make salve. There were some people you meet in your life that you instantly want to believe, and you want to trust. Mae was one of those.

There weren't a lot of prostitutes her age, at least not successful ones. There were always young ones, my age, willing to do whatever a man wanted for a few dollars. From what Sally had told me, some women in her business saved their money and then took off, starting over without saying where they made their money. Some got married. And many died young, from abuse, neglect, starvation, or venereal diseases. I couldn't imagine the first two options would have been much easier five years or so ago, before our country was thrown into an economic disaster.

Women like Mae were kind of stuck at that juncture where they were still young enough and healthy enough to make a go on their own, but the country seemed to be against them. Mae was a survivor and didn't seem to let her situation own her. She had dreams—I could see it in her eyes—and most of all, she had a heart full of love that she liked to share. I was glad she had taken me as one of her own.

I could tell from Pepper's silence that he, too, had been thinking while we collected creosote and brittlebush, and I figured it was probably about Queho. When we first saw him last year, he hadn't understood why I didn't want to turn him in but had kept our secret simply because I had asked him to. Now, I gave him the decision, and I could tell it was weighing on him.

When we got back to the cave, Pepper released Gatsby to catch the last of the day's sun. It was a shame Queho hadn't had his own Gatsby around earlier. I unpacked my haul for the day and placed it in a corner of the cave away from my sleeping pallet. The strong odor from the creosote seemed to appeal to Gatsby, and I didn't mind it. It reminded me of wet earth after a rain. Then I remembered that rattlesnakes also liked it, and even though most should be hibernating, I didn't want to take any chances, so I moved it outside and found a spot to store it under a large overhanging boulder.

We sat outside to eat our dinner and watched the sun go down behind the mountain. The purples and reds were especially bright that evening, their rays reaching out and touching the tips of the mountains, painting the area in various shades of pink. I tried to imagine it as something tangible, something I could wrap around me, and let it cover me from head to toe.

I SPENT MOST OF THE morning by the river, washing our clothes from the past few days and taking a long bath. Pepper stayed in the cave, saying he wanted to organize it some, but I knew what he was doing. I'd had a fitful night, probably from sleeping on the ground again after sleeping two nights on Pete's couch, and had heard the conversation he had had with Queho while he thought I was sleeping.

"I met some people that were real nice... I think they are going to help us get some money so we can leave... No, I thought about it all day, but it's not right to sell somebody. That's what Mr. Cromwell tried to do with me... I know you're dead, but it's still not right... But you don't really need all these things, do you? Just a few, to sell so Helen and I can leave..."

Pepper still hadn't told me about his year living with Mr. Cromwell, and I hadn't pushed. I knew that bad things had happened, and although I was sure he probably needed to talk with someone about it, I wasn't sure that someone was me. I'd had my own problems, but they weren't comparable. Maybe talking to Queho was a way for him to begin thinking about it, talking to someone without judgement. Or maybe he had bigger problems than I had suspected, since it seemed he was actually having a conversation in which Queho talked to him as well. Maybe getting out of Nevada would be the best thing for Pepper, or maybe it wasn't what he needed at all.

Ezra would be leaving a package for me today on the north side of Emery's store, and I was not sure if I wanted to talk to him or not. I could just show up later in the evening, take the box, and come back to my cave, or I could send Pepper. I was torn between wanting to hide from him and wanting, desperately, to be close to him.

When I got back to the cave, Pepper showed me some of the things he had decided we could sell in the cave: two guns, a few knives, a porcelain teapot, the music box. Stolen items, things that Queho had taken from others. I knew some were from people he had killed, and although I didn't want to turn him in, I also didn't want a record of his actual crimes to be taken away from the cave. Someday, someone would find him, and the items he had told a part of his story. I held a tarnished badge with the number 896 on it, the badge number of the security man Queho was accused of murdering many years ago.

I explained my feelings about this to Pepper, and although I was sure he didn't fully agree, he said he'd keep looking. There was so much stuff in the cave, he was certain he'd find something that we could use that wouldn't be missed.

"I also found this," he said, holding a yellowed piece of paper out to me.

It was a "wanted" handbill with a picture of a young Indian man and the words Wanted Dead or Alive plastered across the top. "Queho the Killer," it read, "wanted for murder, kidnapping, thievery."

I looked at the picture then looked at the corpse in the corner. "It doesn't much look like him."

"It says a thousand dollars," Pepper said.

I glanced at the paper once more and handed it back to him.

I put on one of my thin dresses, leaving my Henry persona behind, needing to feel like a girl for the day. No one had seen me out here, even though there had been male voices on the mountain, most likely looking for Queho. They didn't go high enough to find the cave, driven away by either the smell from the bat guano nearby or the threat of rattlesnakes, coyote, wild cats, and mountain sheep. Pepper and I had gotten good at listening for them and staying at a good distance to avoid being seen while we collected our plants, sticking to the mountain sheep's paths to get back and forth from the river. By evening, when the snakes and coyote were more active, they had all gone home for dinner, and it was just us, Queho, and the rest of the inhabitants of the mountain. Peaceful. Soothing. Lonely.

AUTHOR NOTE: AGAIN, Helen is a dreamer. She still holds on to the idea of love, and the tension between her and Ezra is growing again. But her experience with Cotton has also hardened her somewhat. Going to Lookout Point, being in the mountains again, act as diversions for those thoughts, but they are weighing on her.

The idea that Pepper finds some comfort in his conversations with the corpse of Queho lends a lot to how damaged the boy truly is. But

Helen understands that sometimes you have to find comfort and peace where you can. It's also important to remember at this point that Queho was a real person, a murderer, who was the target of one of the largest manhunts in Nevada history. When Queho's body was eventually found, special deputy badge 896, that of the murdered L.W. "Doc" Gilbert from the Gold Bug mine, was among his possessions.

Chapter 57: A License to Dream

Helen

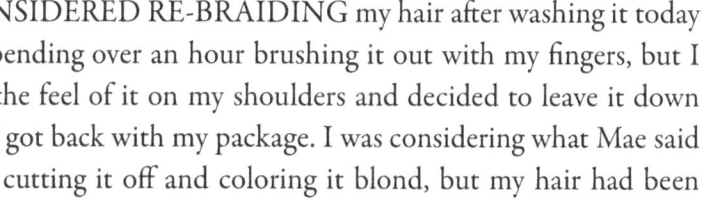

I CONSIDERED RE-BRAIDING my hair after washing it today and spending over an hour brushing it out with my fingers, but I liked the feel of it on my shoulders and decided to leave it down until I got back with my package. I was considering what Mae said about cutting it off and coloring it blond, but my hair had been long since I was a little girl, and I imagined that bits of me would fall away with every severed lock. I knew that the hair would grow back, but would my lost pieces?

Pepper didn't want to go with me to get the package from Ezra. He knew Ezra from our time in Ragtown, but I'd noticed while at Mae's he was leery of the men, except for Moose. I still didn't know what that was about, either, but I respected his feelings and left him with Gatsby and told him I'd go meet Ezra. I decided to hide behind a boulder once I got to Emery's, and when he arrived, I could decide whether I wanted to let him know I was there or wait until he left. Maybe just seeing him would be enough contact for me. I grabbed my canteen and slowly made my way down the mountain, ever on alert for predators or other dangers, including the two-legged kind. When the mountains glowed golden in the early-evening sun, I stopped a few times to lift my face to it and let it caress my skin. I reached a good vantage point and saw Ezra, sitting on a boulder with a large parcel next to him. He was waiting for me. I took a deep breath, let it out slowly, and continued down the mountain. When he smiled at me, my heart melted a little, and I was even more undecided about whether I should be meeting him or not.

"Now you look more like the woman I remember," he said as I approached him.

I absently touched my hair and looked down, unsure if the knot in my stomach was from being uncomfortable or appreciative of his gaze.

He gestured toward the package at his feet. "I brought you two dozen jars, the other things you asked for, and enough food for three to four days. And I dropped your film off to be developed. It will be ready Thursday, so I'll bring that and bring you more stuff."

"Thank you. What do I owe you?"

He smiled, dug in his pocket, and produced a roll of bills. "I took it out of this. Between Moose, Pete, and me, we had no trouble selling thirty jars of that goop. Pete said Mae sold all of hers too."

I took the money and counted out forty-two dollars. "This is too much. Thirty jars should have only been fifteen dollars, minus the money for my supplies... Ezra, you can't just give me your money," I said.

"Relax. Your fifty-cent price wasn't enough, so we sold it for one dollar a jar and told the guys it was to help two kids who'd lost their daddies at the dam. Some of them put in a couple of dollars, and if we'd had enough, I think we would have sold a thousand."

I felt a pang of guilt and longing for my daddy. I missed his easy smile, the way he used to put his arm around me and tell me how everything was going to be fine. I took that for granted when he was alive, believing his plans were infallible. The realities of the past year had taught me that "fine" was a golden ring on the carousel, just out of reach. "That's... amazing. I can make more, a lot more. I can—"

"And if I want to give you my money, I will."

I flinched, his words sounding more like something Cotton would say, but he was smiling, so I pushed the feeling of annoyance that was roiling inside me down.

I knelt beside the package and started looking through it. "There's enough food here for a week," I said as I pushed through the canned goods, breads, and fresh apples and pears that looked so good my mouth started to water. I opened a sack that had three single-use plates full of roast beef, potatoes, and carrots, and a healthy dose of cherry cobbler covered with a paper food wrap.

"I figured I'd eat dinner with you tonight. Maybe we could talk some," Ezra said.

"This is what they feed you?" I asked. It smelled like Sunday afternoon at the diner, and as I put it all back in the sack, my stomach growled in protest.

He smiled again. "They feed us pretty good." He reached for the packages and motioned for me to guide the way.

He was still limping, and he winced as we made our way across the rocky floor of the wash, so I moved slowly around the shore until we were in a secluded area by the river north of the ferry. I took the packages from him and helped him sit on the rocky ground.

"Where's Pepper?" he asked while looking around.

"He stayed to watch our things. I think he likes living out here," I said.

"Well, you can't blame him. You found him in an alley in the middle of the night with a dress on. I can imagine being out here would be paradise."

"Are you still using the salve?" I asked, abruptly changing the subject.

He let out a long breath as he stretched his long legs out in front of him. "Yes, I've got a few more days' worth." He pointed toward the bags. "That will last me until I get some more."

I took two of the plates, complete with disposable utensils, sat next to him, and handed him one. The food was warm, and the roast melted in my mouth as I savored each bite. I wanted to save some for later, but once I began eating, there was no way I could stop until I was full. I lay back on the rocks, one hand on my stomach and the other on my forehead, and smiled.

"This reminds me of when we used to sit by the river in Ragtown," I said.

The sound of the river flowing by and the day's heat on my skin, not to mention my full stomach, was comforting, and I felt relaxed and somewhat at peace. I closed my eyes and took a deep breath, taking in the scents of the desert, with a bit of Ezra's mixed in.

"The guys and I came up with a plan to get you a lot of money, if you're interested," Ezra said as he leaned back on his elbows beside me.

My eyes shoot open. "What? How?"

"Smitty came up with the idea to wrap the jars with a little ribbon and call it some cute name and sell it to the people who come to watch us work. They are expecting thousands on the day we turn the river, and they'll all want to take a piece of it back with them."

"Sounds like Smitty came up with the plan, not 'the guys,'" I said under my breath. Typical. This was exactly the reason I couldn't trust any of them with Queho. I wanted to be angry, but it was a good idea—no, a great idea. I thought of the man and woman I had seen at Lookout Point the first day we went to watch. I could imagine them buying a jar, or two, of something to take home with them, something that made them feel a part of the project long after they left. "How would we sell it?" I asked.

He pointed at his bad leg. "My friend Chief's wife made me this boot. She and Smitty are friends, and Smitty said they could set up a little table at Lookout Point. And Chief has four little kids that are pretty cute that they can send through the crowd with more. We'll sell it, Helen. We'll sell all you can make."

I did a mental inventory. I had fifty empty jars at Mae's, twenty-four jars that Ezra had just brought, and enough supplies to fill those in a day. "'I can make a lot," I said.

A guy named Chief, his wife, Moose, even Mae and Pete—all these people I didn't know or had just met, and I was relying on them, simply because I trusted Sally and Ezra. I felt uneasy, but then I thought of Smitty; I did trust Smitty.

"You really think this will work?" Five hundred dollars. That, I decided, was my goal. That would buy back my car, pay for my divorce, and still leave me two hundred dollars to go somewhere and start over.

He shrugged. "It's not just a novelty. That stuff really works, if it just didn't smell so bad. You know, you could just plan on staying here and making it until the dam is completely built." He looked down at me and wiped a piece of cobbler from my chin. My body tightened when his fingertips brushed my skin.

"I like the smell," I said. "It reminds me of rain." I ignored his reference to staying here. I loved it in the mountains, but I couldn't live here forever.

He moved a little closer to me. "Helen, I wish things could have been different," he said. He looked at me, and I became lost in those blue eyes, how I imagined swimming in an ocean would be. I couldn't speak. He had no idea how many times I wished things could have been different.

He took a deep breath and pushed himself up. "Well, I need to get back. I have to get off this foot for a while. You sure you're okay out here?" he asked.

I stood and straightened my dress then helped him get up. When he stood to full height, he was so close to me I could feel the heat coming off his body, pulling me toward him like a magnet.

"I'm fine," I said.

He pushed a tendril of hair from my face, and when I looked up, he leaned down and brushed his lips against mine. I didn't pull back—I was frozen—and he kissed me. His lips were soft and full, and I didn't want to stop. I put my hands on his arms and felt a jolt from my fingertips that went to my core. Then I slowly pushed back.

"I—" I didn't know what to say.

He ran a hand over his head and leaned on his cane. "I'm... sorry. I just—"

"Don't be sorry," I said. "It was nice." I reached down and picked up the parcels, wanting, needing to get away from him as quickly as possible. If only things had been different.

As I made my way back up the mountain, juggling the heavy packages, I heard a sound off the path to my left. I almost dropped my load when Pepper jumped out from behind a large boulder.

"Pepper, you scared me!" I said.

He shrugged and reached for one of the bags. "Sorry. You were gone for a while, and I was worried about you," he said.

I smiled. "Thank you. You should have come down with me. Ezra brought us dinner."

He nodded. "I saw. It looked good."

I slowed. "How long have you been here?" I asked.

"For a while," he said.

A while. He had been watching, listening to Ezra and me. I thought back to our kiss and was a little embarrassed that he had been watching. He got a little ahead of me, and I noticed the handgrip of my uncle Dwayne's gun sticking out of the back of his dungarees.

"Pepper. Stop."

He stopped.

"Is that my gun?"

He looked me straight in the eye. "I told you I was worried about you. What if Cotton or that gangster had found you?" he said.

"I don't want you carrying my gun around. No matter what. It isn't safe," I said. "You don't know how to use it and—"

"Yes, I do. My daddy taught me how to shoot a gun when we were still in South Dakota. I'm not afraid to use it either," he said.

I shook my head. "Fine. Just don't take my gun. It will get you in nothing but trouble," I said, thinking back to my own situation.

I put our supplies away while Pepper ate his dinner, and then we talked about our plan for collecting plants and making salve. We were both excited because we had a purpose—a job—that would get us enough money to go anywhere we wanted. Pepper told me about South Dakota, I told him about Kansas, and we both shared what we had read about places like Washington State, Chicago, and San Francisco. It was as if we had been given a license to dream again.

AUTHOR NOTE: WHEN I was a small child, I remember my grandmother slathering me with her homemade salve any time I had a cut or a pain or anything, really. I have no idea what ingredients she used, and I'm not sure, in retrospect, if it even worked to any degree. What I do remember is it smelled so bad my eyes watered. Helen's concoction is made from brittlebush, creosote, and a few other plants from the desert, and therefore, it would have a very distinct odor. The ingredients, however, were used by Native American tribes medicinally, so her mixture, I'm going to say, would be a little more effective than my grandmother's.

Chapter 58: High-Scalers and Cherry Cobbler

Ezra

CABLE BOX NUMBER SEVEN moaned softly as it carried Moose, Chief, and me from the Nevada side of the project to the Arizona side. With the opening of the diversion tunnels scheduled in a few weeks, activity had escalated to a new level, and men had been reassigned to help in deficient areas. Although we were almost two years ahead of schedule, a new schedule had emerged, and its deadline was fast approaching.

Looking down over the side of the cable box, I saw only specks of the men working on the beaches on either side. I couldn't make out any crew but knew Pete was on the Arizona side, not far from Doc Jensen's clinic. Through a maze of pulleys and cable cars, the trucks traveled the gravel and dirt roads loaded with debris and cement. The men working on the upper cofferdam were in constant motion, like ants on a floating hill. Those going in and out of the tunnels were much slower—the result of the excessive heat and lack of clean air to breathe. The high-scalers were scattered throughout the canyon, laden with jackhammers and dynamite, shearing the walls.

I couldn't help but smile when I thought about how far we'd come on this project since I had gotten here—and to think the first phase was almost done. We were going to move a river. Or at least give it one helluva try.

I glanced up at the ridge of the mountain as the car carried us across. The project itself had become somewhat of a novelty, and spectators came from all around to watch us build, particularly to focus on the circus-like acts of the high-scalers like George Goon. They had become celebrities, performing six hundred feet above the river below. At the top of the canyon, on the Nevada side, Lookout Point was full of people. I scanned the crowd for Helen and Pepper. I hoped they were there.

Two nights ago, I had kissed her. We were talking, like we used to, and yet she was so much more than the teenage girl I remembered from a year ago. She was smart, resourceful, determined, and funny. Being with her brought out feelings that I didn't know I had, or that I had forced deep down into my core. But alone with her, next to the roaring river, surrounded by the silence of the mountains, I couldn't help my instincts, and pulled her closer and kissed her. She tasted like cherry cobbler, and I wanted to eat my fill.

I shook my head at the thought. Bad idea, Ezra. She was a married woman and was currently hiding out from a gangster. That was a dangerous combination.

Moose was next to me, looking out across the site too. "This is really going to be something."

"If it works," I said.

Moose raised his eyebrows. "Oh, it'll work. Crowe ain't no dummy. We will be diverting that river in no time. And then we can get to some real dam building."

"I still don't see how we're going to ram a slab of concrete between these two peaks. It doesn't seem possible."

"That's just it. We are going to do it, and everybody is going to say, 'Now how the hell did they do that?' But we are. You and me. And someday I'm going to be able to tell my kids, 'Yeah, me and your uncle Ezra did that.'"

"Kids? You better get married first." I teasingly punched him on the shoulder. "Ain't that right, Chief?"

Chief sat cross-legged in the bottom of the cable box, his back to a corner, and held on to two sides. His face had gone pale, and his eyes were closed.

"Leave me alone until we are off this damn circus ride," he said.

"Oh, come on, Chief. Jump up here and look over the side with us," Moose said. "It's only a little ways down."

"I haven't decided if I'm staying around for the next phase," I said.

Moose gave me a slightly puzzled look. I hadn't ever said I might leave my job, and if I were honest with myself, I hadn't considered leaving until the words were out. I guessed he'd figured I'd just help Helen get the money she needed to leave and go on with my life, and I guessed that was probably the best for all of us. But still, something inside of me would regret never seeing her again.

The cable box slowed and screeched on its line, sending sparks onto the passengers below. It stopped at a rocky ledge, and we began making our way down the steep path that led to the mouth of tunnel number three.

As we stood outside number three, waiting for our assignments, Moose slapped me on the back. "This is it. Where you and I started."

I smiled. "Yeah, we should have stayed over here. Then this one would be done like the rest of 'em."

"It would be a shame after all this work not to see it through," he said. Ah, he had heard me.

We were told to go to the exit side of the tunnel on the south side of the canyon. To get there, we had to go halfway back up the little path we had traveled down, walk three-quarters of a mile along the dirt and gravel road used by the trucks, and catch a widow-maker down to a rock shelf large enough to hold fifteen men. A considerable rock protrusion kept us from reaching the tunnel itself, and we stood with several others, waiting for the transportation that would take us to the exit side.

Louis Fagan, one of the high-scalers, swung to us on a bosun chair. "Okay, who's up?"

Moose stepped forward. "I guess I am. What are we doing there, friend?"

Fagan smiled and wrapped his arms and legs tightly around Moose and lifted him off the ground. They swung freely toward the solid wall that was behind Moose, and he was trapped between the man and the mountain.

"Hey! What the hell?" Moose yelled.

"You better quit fighting and hold on. I haven't dropped one yet, but some say that means I'm due." With that, Fagan pushed off from the mountain with his legs, sending the two men swinging high out over the canyon. He kicked at the protrusion to gain more speed and distance and twisted around as they cleared the rock. He deposited Moose on the other side and was back to the rest of us in less than a minute.

"Who's up?" Fagan asked.

Chief backed up against the rock wall. "You must be crazy! Not me. You go ahead, I'll be sitting right here waiting when you get back."

I thought of Helen on Lookout Point, watching the entire operation, and hoped this wasn't something she was missing. I held my arms up and braced my legs for the wrap. "I'm all yours. Just don't try to kiss me."

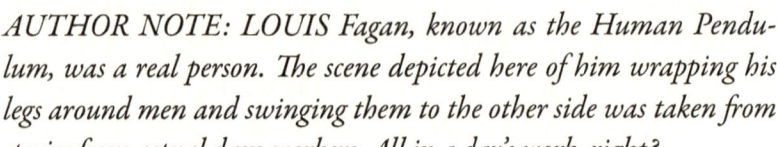

AUTHOR NOTE: LOUIS Fagan, known as the Human Pendulum, was a real person. The scene depicted here of him wrapping his legs around men and swinging them to the other side was taken from stories from actual dam workers. All in a day's work, right?

Chapter 59: A Helluva Shot

Ezra

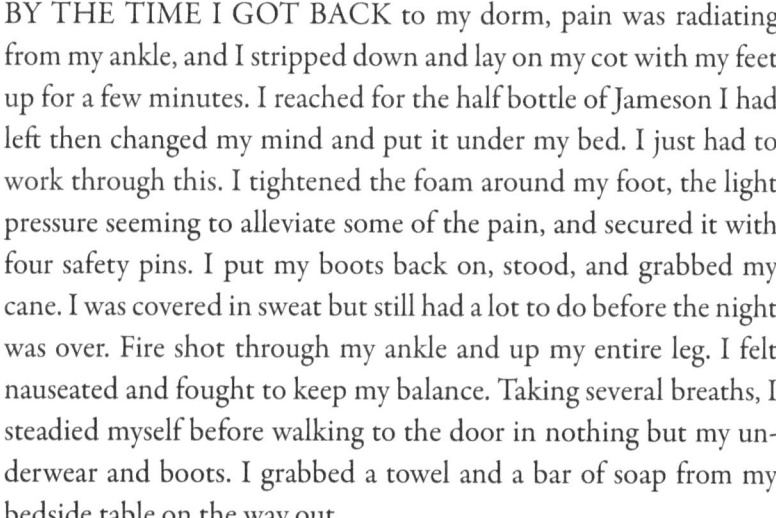

BY THE TIME I GOT BACK to my dorm, pain was radiating from my ankle, and I stripped down and lay on my cot with my feet up for a few minutes. I reached for the half bottle of Jameson I had left then changed my mind and put it under my bed. I just had to work through this. I tightened the foam around my foot, the light pressure seeming to alleviate some of the pain, and secured it with four safety pins. I put my boots back on, stood, and grabbed my cane. I was covered in sweat but still had a lot to do before the night was over. Fire shot through my ankle and up my entire leg. I felt nauseated and fought to keep my balance. Taking several breaths, I steadied myself before walking to the door in nothing but my underwear and boots. I grabbed a towel and a bar of soap from my bedside table on the way out.

The shower was full. I counted fifteen men in a shower room that had twelve spigots, some doubling up to avoid waiting in line. I leaned against the wall in the hallway, taking the weight off my left leg, closed my eyes, and waited.

It had just been two days since I saw Helen, but I missed her. I felt guilty for not stepping up last year when her daddy died, leaving her to Cotton. I wouldn't do that again. There was something so different about her now. She was a woman, for one, and she seemed so strong, but I wanted desperately to protect her. I always liked the girl, but now, it was more than that. I wanted to touch her face, her hair, every part of her. And it was more than just physical. She was fresh and bright—such a contrast to what I saw in the tunnels all day. I couldn't explain the feeling I had when I was around her, and I wouldn't try. Maybe it was me that had changed.

The man at the first spigot—I couldn't seem to remember his name—tilted his head toward me as he wrapped a towel around his waist. "Come on, Ezra. You're up."

In the shower, I leaned against the wall to remove my boots. I left the foam wrap on, knowing it needed a good cleaning too. I washed with one hand, needing the other to hold my cane.

I had said something to Moose this afternoon about not hanging around for the next phase of the dam building. At the time, I didn't know where that came from, but as I thought about it, I considered it even more. Helen would be divorced soon, and why couldn't I just leave with her? Or maybe she'd want to stay here, marry me, and move to Boulder City.

Marry me? I turned the water to cold and let the shock of it needle its way into my skin. What the hell was I thinking?

I had to put my boots back on in order to make it back down the hallway, which wasn't an easy task while standing up holding a cane. With a white cotton towel wrapped around my waist, I made my way back to my room and took my boots off again. This time I slid the foam off and rubbed some of Helen's salve over my ankle and lower leg. The numbing was almost instant as the salve penetrated my skin. I gave it a few minutes and then got dressed. Regardless of whether I should or shouldn't be falling for Helen, I was excited to see her this evening. Part of me wished she were in Boulder City, going to dances and the movies with me, but there was something so natural about meeting her by the river, just the two of us, talking, and ideally, getting a little closer.

"You about ready?" Moose said as I made my way back down the hall. He was going with me tonight because he wanted to see Pepper. I had been in awe of Moose's interaction with him at Pete's, especially since Pepper seemed so inside of himself. Moose told me later that he had a lot of sympathy for Pepper, said he had been made fun of as a child because of his size. He said he knew what that felt like. Also, from what little Helen had told us, we kind of figured out that Pepper's stepfather had been dressing him as a girl and prostituting him. Moose said he hated more than anything to see kids taken advantage of, and he would do what he could to help him. He didn't mention Helen.

"I need to run over to the store first. I'll meet you outside in ten minutes," I said.

In the company store, I made my way through to the camera section and gave the clerk my ticket to pick up Helen's pictures. I knew the money could be used better, but I also knew how much she loved taking her pictures, and I wanted to see her smile again.

When he handed me the small packet, I couldn't help but open it and see what Helen had been seeing. There was a picture of the high school in Las Vegas, a smiling, pretty blonde sitting in a diner, four or five of the desert, some animals, and several of the work site taken from Lookout Point. Of all the photos, there was only one that was bad—that I would consider bad, anyway. It looked like a collection of small items taken in the dark. I flipped back through and settled on a shot of a coyote, standing on top of the mountain, looking down. He was a skeleton of a dog, his patchy fur stretched tight across his ribs. His lips were slightly lifted, exposing canine teeth. A bushy round tail sagged downward between his spindly legs.

"That's a helluva shot. What kind of camera you using?"

I hadn't noticed anyone behind me and had been so absorbed in the pictures that I hadn't realized anyone was looking over my shoulder. I turned, and the man stuck out his hand and introduced himself as Ben Glaha, the photographer that worked for the government. "Sorry," he said, "but pictures are kind of my business, and I can't help but be a little curious."

"No problem," I said. "A friend of mine took it. She's got a little Brownie." I hand him the stack of pictures to look through, curious as to his thoughts.

"A Brownie?" Glaha laughed. "I'll be. If she can do this with a Brownie, I'd sure like to see what she could do with a real camera." He stopped on one shot and whistled, a view from the edge of the Point looking straight down to the river beach below. "This is a doozy," he said.

I pointed at the camera around his neck. "What's one like that cost?"

"This one cost a hundred dollars. It's a beauty, though. You looking to buy one for your friend?"

I shook my head. "That's a lot of money."

"Tell you what," Glaha said, "I got an old one. It's not like this, but it did a good job. Has a long lens, too, so she won't have to get so close to get a good shot. Comes in handy if she wants to shoot a mountain cat. Fifteen dollars for the whole setup."

"I'll have to think about it, but thanks. It's good to know I'm not the only one that thinks her pictures are pretty good." I tucked them in my shirt pocket and started to walk away.

"Pretty good? A nice camera, and she could sell some of those. Newspapers and magazines are always looking for shots, especially ones their guys can't get." He leaned in and whispered to me, "Don't tell Six Companies I said that, though."

I walked the aisles of the store, picking up more things I thought Helen and Pepper might need. I saw Glaha in line and got behind him. "So, I'm curious, how much would someone pay for pictures?"

He shrugged. "Depends on who's buying and what the picture is of. Newspapers would love some of those ones from the work site, and there's plenty of nature magazines that would buy those desert shots. Not a lot of people taking pictures out there. The bigger the paper, the bigger the pay." He rubbed his chin and looked up. "I'd say a dollar to five dollars, depending on what they like."

"Five dollars for a picture?"

He laughed. "You don't think I do this for free, do ya?"

I had twenty pictures in my pocket that cost twenty cents for the film and a quarter to develop. If Helen sold just one picture out of the bunch, that was a helluva return. I knew she wouldn't accept my money flat out, but maybe I could help her in another way.

It didn't take me but seconds to decide. "Say, how soon can I get that camera from you?"

SHE WAS WAITING FOR me in the same spot that I had met her last time. She had on the same dress as before, and I wished she had one that fit a little better, one that would outline her thin body underneath. One long red braid fell from under her ball cap and down her back. She scooted behind Emery's building when she saw us pull up and only came back into view when Moose and I got out of the car.

"Whose car?" she asked.

Moose hefted the packages, and I hobbled toward her with my cane in one hand and a box of penny jars in the other. "George Goon's. He loaned it to me so I can go to Vegas this evening," Moose said. He looked behind Helen, toward the mountain. "Where's Pepper?"

When he heard his name, Pepper came running, as if he'd been hiding somewhere, watching. "Hi, Mr. Moose!" he said.

Moose smiled. "Mr. Pepper, I'm going to Vegas on some business. Would you like to join me?"

Pepper looked to Helen and back to Moose. "Do you think…"

"I promise you, Pepper, ain't nobody going to mess with you while you are with me."

"But what about the kidnapping thing?" Helen had one hand on her hip and her head cocked to one side.

Moose shook his head. "It's you they want for questioning. And besides, we aren't going to be hanging out around the casinos."

Pepper looked at Helen, his eyes pleading.

"You don't need my permission, Pepper," she said.

He bit his lip and turned back to Moose. "Where are we going?"

Moose exaggeratedly rubbed his chin. "Well, I need to pick up a bunch of jars for Helen, because we've pretty much drained the company store. I have to pick up something at the jewelry store, and I thought we might stop by Woodlawn Cemetery and see if there's anyone we know."

Pepper's bottom lip started to quiver, and I thought he was going to cry. Then he smiled and enthusiastically nodded.

"Okay, then. We'll be back around eleven," Moose said. He handed Helen the packages he had, and turned toward the car with Pepper next to him.

We watched them drive out of the wash, and then I followed her toward our spot near the river. She wasn't smiling, and I hoped she wasn't offended by my kiss from the other night. My chest tightened at the thought that she might not have appreciated it as much as I did.

"What's wrong? Don't worry about Pepper," I said as I set the large box that Glaha had given me next to the package of other supplies.

"No, I'm not. He needs a friend... other than just me... Moose seems like a nice man, and Pepper likes him." She frowned and looked toward the mountain. "We can't find Gatsby."

I suppressed a laugh because I knew the snake was important to them both, even though I couldn't imagine why anyone would want to have a pet snake. But it was Helen and therefore not your average girl. Woman, I reminded myself.

"He'll come back," I said. "How could he resist not being with you?"

She was looking in the package and didn't see me roll my eyes at my own words. I couldn't believe I was openly flirting with her, especially when I knew it wasn't a good idea, and yet, just seeing her made me want to take her in my arms and kiss her again.

She motioned to a package that she had brought with her. "There are twenty jars there. I didn't know if you wanted to take them with you or wanted me to store everything here. We can make about twenty a day if we have all the supplies."

"I'll take them back as you get them and store them in my dorm room," I said. "They'll be safe there. We brought you thirty jars, and Moose is going to try to get a few hundred tonight."

"I still can't believe you're getting a dollar a jar. When I worked at the diner, I barely made a dollar a day. Maybe I have a new job," she said with a laugh.

I smiled. I could picture me going to work every day, Helen in the mountains gathering plants and making salve to sell in town, and us meeting in the evening in our own home. Where did that come from?

I sat down on the rocky ground, stretched my legs out, and reached for the box next to me. "And I got you a birthday present."

She cocked her head and raised one brow. "My birthday was in August," she said.

"I know. And I missed it this year." I held the box out to her, and she took it reluctantly. She sat down next to me and placed the box in her lap.

"You really shouldn't have," she whispered without looking at me.

I put my arm around her and whispered in her ear, "Maybe you should open it first and see if you like it before you start with all that."

She sucked in a deep breath, and I couldn't help but watch her chest rise as she did. She slowly opened the box and then looked at me with those green eyes sparkling, her mouth wide open. "Ezra, this is too much." She ran her hand over the camera as if it were a sleeping child.

"No, it isn't. I talked to Ben Glaha today, and he saw your pictures." I pulled the picture envelope out of my shirt pocket and handed it to her. "He said you have a natural eye, and he also said you can make money, real money, from your pictures. So it was an investment more than anything else."

She thumbed through the pictures, stopped at the one of the blond woman, and smiled.

"Who is she?" I asked.

"Sally. My friend. That's how I knew to go to Mae. She's a friend of hers too."

I told her all about the newspapers and magazines and what Glaha had told me about them paying for pictures. She finally picked the camera up and looked through the eyehole, adjusted the long lens to focus, and turned in every direction. When she put it down, her face was lit up like the sun, and I wanted to kiss her again.

But instead, she leaned over and kissed me. It was quick and just a peck on the cheek, but it surprised me. She immediately looked down at her lap again, focusing on the camera.

I had to adjust myself so she didn't see how that little kiss affected other parts of my body, so I reached for the bag of supplies and changed the subject. "Let's eat," I said. "And then I'll help you find your snake."

AUTHOR NOTE: BEN GLAHA was an employee of the Bureau of Reclamation, and it was his job to photograph and document the building on the dam. When you see historical photos or images of the dam during this time, chances are they were taken by Mr. Glaha himself. However, according to his contract, he was not given personal credit for the majority of the images he took during this time. The importance of his work as a historical record, however, cannot be denied.

While making salve and selling it to tourists and dam workers may be a nice short-term fix for Helen's money issue, Ezra realizes that there may be other ways for her to one day make money and pursue her passion for photography. While his gift to her is definitely a way for him to show her how much he cares about her, it also opens up possibilities for her life that neither of them have considered. Yet.

Chapter 60: Snake Hunting

Helen

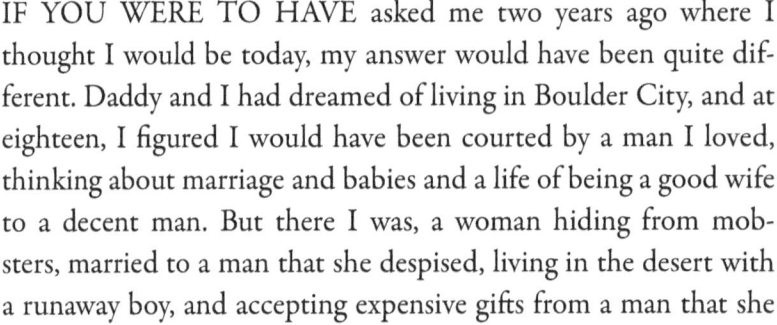

IF YOU WERE TO HAVE asked me two years ago where I thought I would be today, my answer would have been quite different. Daddy and I had dreamed of living in Boulder City, and at eighteen, I figured I would have been courted by a man I loved, thinking about marriage and babies and a life of being a good wife to a decent man. But there I was, a woman hiding from mobsters, married to a man that she despised, living in the desert with a runaway boy, and accepting expensive gifts from a man that she wouldn't mind getting a lot closer to.

After the other evening, when Ezra kissed me, I thought about it most of the night. Since Pepper had been spying on us, he saw and teased me about it, which in a way helped me work out some of my own feelings about it. It would have been nice to have Sally to talk to, or even Mae, but in the end, I knew that nothing real could happen for us.

As I sat next to Ezra, eating dinner by the river, talking about my new camera, the dam work, and the election, it seemed so natural that I couldn't imagine it could be wrong. But I knew better. That feeling in my stomach that I got when his arm brushed close to mine should be a warning. I needed to handle my business right now and not let another man get in the way of what needed to be done. Even if it was Ezra.

When we finished eating, I gathered everything back up and repacked it—everything except the camera. I loaded it with one of the rolls of film that Ezra had also bought for me and put it around my neck, adjusting the leather strap so it rode comfortably on my chest. Its weight felt like a natural extension of my body, and I couldn't wait to use it.

Ezra struggled a little to get up, but he seemed to be walking much better, wincing only occasionally. "Let's go snake hunting," he said.

I shook my head. "You don't have to help me find Gatsby. I figure he'll come back if he wants to."

He shrugged and glanced at my camera. "I don't mind. And besides, I'd like to see if you really know how to use that thing."

He knew better, but I figured it wouldn't hurt to pal around with Ezra in the desert for a little while before the sun went down. I did like his company, maybe more than I should. "Fine. We'll leave this stuff here, and I'll pick it up after I introduce you to the real desert."

Holding my new camera close so it didn't sway too much, I climbed the rocky terrain, slower than usual so Ezra could keep up. I stopped at a large creosote bush and pointed at the small lavender flower it was protecting. "It's a desert aster. Pretty, isn't it?"

"Kind of strange, so much color on that ugly old bush," Ezra said.

"That ugly old bush is called creosote and is tougher than any man in this state. Older than you, judging by its size. The Indians used to crush the leaves. It's said to cure a lot of things, from female problems to snakebite poisoning. It's also the main ingredient in my salve," I said. He leaned over to touch the flower, and I grabbed his arm and pulled him back. "It's also a favorite hiding place for rattlesnakes—they seem to like the smell. So unless you check for them first, you probably shouldn't be touching it."

He took two steps back from the bush, which made me giggle. "And this is what you do all day? Look for rattlesnakes so you can steal their shelter and make salve?"

I shook my head and rolled my eyes. "You make it sound so... Most of them are hibernating right now, and I'm very careful. If it were springtime, it would be a lot more difficult."

I caught movement out of the corner of my eye, and Ezra jumped back.

"That's Chuck. He won't hurt you," I said. I crept closer to the large lizard, holding my camera up to get a picture. "This will probably be the last time I see him. He should be hibernating by now too."

"Chuck?" Ezra asked.

I looked through the eyepiece, waited until Chuck looked my way, and snapped, careful to not jiggle the camera, then I lowered it back to my chest. "He is a chuckwalla. So I call him Chuck."

"Aren't those giant lizards poisonous too?" he asked.

"You're thinking of the Gila monster. They are out here, too, but they're real slow. So as long as you don't try to pick one up—"

"And you know the difference between the lizards?"

"Of course."

We didn't talk about our problems while we headed farther up the mountain. Instead, I continued to tell him about the various plants and creatures. He seemed genuinely interested, not taking his eyes from mine as he asked questions, and I wished we had done this before. I felt very much at peace with Ezra in the desert and, for a moment, wished there were a way for us to scamper around the desert, like Chuck, forever.

I stopped when I got the first scents of bat guano and knew we were getting too close to the cave. I trusted Ezra, to an extent, but

I didn't want him to know where I was living and definitely didn't want him to know about Queho. "Let's go," I said. "You need to get off that leg."

As we began our descent back down the mountain, Ezra asked, "Helen, where do you sleep?"

I shrugged. "I have a good spot. But sometimes I sleep by the river. I like the sound of it."

He put his arm across my shoulder and pulled me close to him, and I let him. Then I saw a movement in the distance and stopped. I carefully removed the camera from around my neck and dropped to my knees then my stomach. Ezra followed and looked in the direction I was pointing.

In an area that was fairly flat and circular, there were two gopher snakes. They seemed to be dancing. They twisted their bodies around each other, rising together, then separated and repeated the same pattern over and over again. They ascended straight up, belly to belly, each trying to lift its head higher than the other, then they collapsed together, falling on the desert floor before continuing their ritual, gracefully winding and unwinding to some unheard music of the mountain. I'd never seen anything like it before, and Ezra, like me, couldn't turn away from their lovers' dance.

Suddenly one spun its head toward us, and the other followed. Sensing a threat, they raced away, side by side, hissing as they went.

"Was it Gatsby?" Ezra said, trying to follow their escape.

"I don't know," I replied. I had to catch my breath, lying there on the skin of the desert, trying to stamp the memory of what I'd just seen on my brain. I didn't think I'd ever seen anything so raw and beautiful.

We lay on our stomachs on the warm desert rocks, watching until the snakes were out of sight. Ezra looked at me, his face brighter than I'd ever seen it, and I smiled. He reached for me, rolled on his back, and pulled me on top of him. I didn't resist—in that moment, I couldn't—and as our bodies crushed together, I was a prisoner to nature. He kissed me, and his hands roamed greedily over me, lifting my dress over my head, until our bodies were intertwined. We danced to the same unheard music as the snakes, until we, too, collapsed on the desert floor.

AUTHOR NOTE: MAYBE not a lot of people see snakes and become aroused, but for Helen and Ezra, it seemed to work. But I did have to take some liberties to write this scene. For example, this chapter takes place in late October, while gopher snakes typically mate in spring. An interesting fact about gopher snakes: one of the ways they try to imitate rattlesnakes is "rattling" their tails. They don't actually have rattles, but they shake their tails against the ground in an attempt to fool predators.

Chapter 61: Find Ida Browder

Helen

WE MADE OUR WAY BACK to our spot by the river, and after Ezra got situated on the ground, I took the box of jars, said, "Wait here," and turned to scurry up the mountain.

"Helen, wait," he said behind me.

But I kept moving. I didn't want him to follow me. "I'll be right back," I said as I moved out of his sight.

When I got back to the cave, Queho was staring at me. "Oh, you are no one to judge," I said to the corpse. "I may be a married woman who just made love to another man in the open, but at least I haven't killed anyone," I said. I avoided his gaze while I gathered two blankets, deciding Pepper and I would sleep by the river when he got back. Traversing the trail at night was more difficult; adding to that, carrying the packages would make it more so. We had done that only a few times since we'd been here, too afraid of being seen by anyone, but no one seemed to be looking for us out here, and our spot north of Emery's was well hidden from any random eyes. I also didn't want Queho staring at me all night tonight.

Ezra sat where I had left him, looking across the water through the lens of my new camera. When he heard me coming, he laid the camera next to him and smiled. His eyes were warm, his face relaxed. He was happy. He was Easy. I laughed.

"What's so funny?" he said, holding his hand up and pulling me down next to him.

"Easy. That's what Pete calls you. I like it. I think I'm going to steal it," I said.

He shook his head but was still smiling. "You can call me anything you like. Just don't run off like that anymore, okay?"

The way he said it, the way he pulled me closer to him, melted my heart. I wanted to say, "Okay, I won't ever run away," but I knew it wouldn't be the truth. I had run from Ragtown and run from Cotton, and I had every intention of running away from here as soon as I had the money to do so. I didn't respond to his question but simply leaned into him, taking in his warmth and his scent.

We talked away the hours, laughing, kissing, and skipping rocks across the river. It was as simple and as perfect as I could ever have imagined life to be.

He yawned.

"Oh, am I boring you?" I said.

"No, not at all. It's just been a long day, and tomorrow comes early," he said.

"It's got to be close to eleven. Moose and Pepper should be back soon," I said. I didn't want to worry, but there was a piece of me that felt overly protective of Pepper, and that must have come out in my voice.

"He's fine. Moose really feels sorry for him," he said.

"I can tell. And Pepper seems to like him."

He cleared his throat. "Moose told me he lost both of his parents when he was young and was moved all over, from one relative to the next, a bunch of people who didn't want him. He finally left when he was sixteen and has pretty much been on his own. He said he isn't complaining, but he wonders how different his life would be had he had someone... Anyway, he sees that in Pepper, and he wants to do what he can."

I smiled. "I see why Smitty likes him. By the way, he said he was going to a jewelry shop?" I raised one eyebrow and one side of my mouth in a half smile.

"He did, didn't he?" He smiled, and I knew he was faking, hiding a secret for his friend.

We were silent for a minute, while I thought of Miss Smitty, living the dream that I had clung to my entire time in Ragtown. I was happy for her.

Ezra pulled me closer and kissed me on the forehead. "I was thinking about what I said earlier about not running away."

I frowned. "What?"

"Sometimes running away is the only way," he said. He turned to me and took both my hands in his. "Helen, let's go. I've got a little money. We'll take your daddy's car and just drive. We can go to Los Angeles and get lost, or maybe we can go to Mexico, and no one will ever find us. We'll just leave all this behind and start over somewhere."

His words came as a shock. There was a part of me that wanted to stay with him forever, fueled by the warmth still running through my body, but another part told me to run far away. We'd only just become close. How could he think he wanted to spend the rest of his life with me?

"But the dam. You've got a good job. You can have such a good life here," I stammered.

"But you won't be here," he said.

Me.

I shook my head slowly. "I don't want to be on the run for the rest of my life. I want to start over, but the only way to truly do that is to straighten out the problem I have with the police and Tony Badamo and get a divorce."

He looked at me, his gaze never wavering. "Fine. I understand that. And then, once all of that is straightened out, I wouldn't have to leave my job. You could move into Boulder City with me."

I was saved by the sound of a car entering the Wash.

He stood and looked at the sky. "Just think about it," he said. "I'll check with Ms. Browder tomorrow to see how much I have in savings for sure, and if you're willing, we can make a plan. Run off together or set up housekeeping. Your choice."

"Ms. Browder?" I sat straight up and looked at him.

"Ida Browder. She owns the cafe in town and keeps money for a lot of us guys so we don't lose it or spend it. Kind of like a bank until we actually get one," he said.

Ida Browder! The tall woman with kind eyes. I had thought she was a prostitute or just a sympathetic ear, but she was holding money for the men and probably holding money for my dad. I thought back to the day I went to see her. She had eyed Cotton—uncomfortably if I remembered right—and had suggested I come back for "girl talk." She wanted me alone. That was it. How could I have not read that? She had something for me. I just knew it. Could it be? I wanted to jump up and run to town right then, but for some reason, I didn't want Ezra to know. I needed to think.

I stood, straightened my skirt, and tried to hide the feeling of hope that suddenly filled my body as we walked toward the Wash to meet Pepper and Moose. But it wasn't the hope that Ezra and I might be together but the possibility that Daddy had found a way to care for me, even in death. It only made sense now. Your choice, he had said. But I had other choices too.

After unloading two of the ten boxes of jars that filled George Goon's car, we all said goodnight, Pepper and Moose making plans for another adventure and Ezra and I with a kiss.

Pepper and I lay on the shore of the river, and he talked about his evening. He ate hamburgers at a side joint outside of Vegas, pretending like he was Moose's son, so no one would think anything different, while they bought the jars and bought a pretty ring, as Pepper described it, for Miss Smitty. And how he had found both of his parents' graves, and Moose had bought him flowers to put on them. "We found your daddy and Grace too. I left a flower for both of them," he said.

I pulled him close and hugged him tightly. My daddy, I thought.

As I curled in my blanket, wrapped in the sounds and the darkness of the canyon, I knew exactly what I needed to do tomorrow: Find Ida Browder, just as my daddy had told me to do over a year ago.

Then, maybe, I could think about my choices.

THREE HUNDRED EIGHTY dollars. The roll of bills was wrapped in a brown bag and tucked safely in the bib of my overalls, but I couldn't help but touch the spot with my hand to make sure it was real. According to Ms. Browder, Daddy had been tucking away five dollars every payday, sometimes more, and she'd been holding it ever since.

"The paper he signed said you were the only person I could give it to other than him. I'm sorry about last year. That man you were with... Things just didn't sit well with me. I figured you got my hint to come back alone, but when you didn't... I'm so sorry," she said.

"Thank you," I said. "I can't believe it. I really had no idea. And that man I was with? You were right. He'd have found a way to get this money, so thank you for that too."

I didn't know much about her, if she was married to one of the men at the dam, or if she somehow lived in Boulder City on her own, but I knew that she kept money for some of the men—apparently a lot of money. If Daddy had almost four hundred dollars, there was no telling how much Ms. Browder had in her house.

She smiled and rested her hands in her lap. "That should be enough to get you out of here," she said. She must have noticed the look of confusion on my face, since she continued, "I hear things around town. I know Bud Bodell was looking for a young woman with long red hair. And if he's looking, you best get out of here."

I opened my mouth to speak, but she raised a hand to stop me. "I don't care why, or what the circumstances are. I didn't see you."

I smiled then patted my chest again. "Thank you, again," I said. "I don't know if... Clive Allen... He died last year too. His son—"

She shook her head. "I remember Clive. He had a few dollars. His wife collected it last year."

I hadn't exactly expected that Clive had money stashed that Betsy didn't know about, but I had told Pepper that I would ask. I was glad he had chosen to stay and look for Gatsby instead of joining me. It was easier to hide in plain sight if I was alone.

As she showed me to the door, she reached for my hand and squeezed it gently. "Be careful, Helen. This world can be a dangerous place for a young woman on her own."

I thanked her again and made my way back through Boulder City, past the park in front of the administration offices, past the movie theatre, the candy shop, the company store, past all the people moving around the small city, living the fairy tale that I once believed in.

I kept my head low, my hair tucked under my ballcap, and slowly moved back toward the highway, back toward Hemenway Wash. I had added it in my head at least a dozen times since I left Ms. Browder: with what I currently had at the cave and Daddy's savings, I could get my divorce from Cotton and pay Tony Badamo for my car and still have over one hundred dollars. I had a brief thought of just hitching out to my car, right then, and driving off with everything and never looking back. But it was brief. I had to take care of things, and those things included Pepper and Ezra. With the salve I would be making in the next few weeks, I would have plenty after I got the divorce and paid Badamo, and I was fully prepared to leave town without even addressing the assault charge. Pepper was the only witness, and the least I could do for him was protect him from having to testify at some trial. It was silly anyway, and when I left, I had no intention of coming back. Maybe, one day, I'd have my picture on a handbill like Queho. Fine.

With the turning of the river planned in a few weeks, I had a lot of work to get done in a short period of time: Gather enough brittlebush and creosote for almost three hundred fifty jars of salve, mix it while switching out empty jars for full ones, and pack it all in George Goon's car, say goodbye to my desert friends, and take care of Queho once and for all. Then I would spend the night at Mae's and go to Vegas the following day, pay Badamo and get my divorce taken care of, and be back a day or two before the first phase of the dam project would be complete. After selling the jars of salve, I would have the money and the means to go anywhere.

I found myself almost running back to Hemenway Wash. I needed to get started but had promised Pepper a few hours at Lookout Point this afternoon and wanted to take some pictures with my new camera anyway.

And amidst all of this, most importantly, I had to make a plan. A plan that would be best for all of us: me, Pepper, and Ezra. Whether they liked it or not.

AUTHOR NOTE: *I'VE SAID before, Ida Browder was a remarkable woman. Holding money for dam workers (she hid the money under her mattress) so they wouldn't blow their wages was just one of the many things she did for the emerging city of Boulder City.*

Ida Browder's Café was opened in 1931 (I took some liberty with the timing of its opening by a few months for fictional purposes), and she is considered Boulder City's first businesswoman. She was also a key figure in convincing the Library of Congress to supply the three thousand books that made up the city's first library.

In 1932, for a young woman in Helen's position, three hundred eighty dollars was a small fortune. It would be the equivalent of about six thousand five hundred dollars today. While it may seem unlikely that her father would have or could have saved this much money, it really isn't. Ben had big plans for his and Helen's future, and saving twenty percent of his weekly wages would not have been uncommon at all. Additionally, with a distrust of banks in general during the Great Depression, having someone like Ms. Browder hold the money made sense to a lot of the men working at the dam.

Chapter 62: Damn You, Beau Dandy!

Ezra

AFTER THREE HOURS OF working in tunnel number three, Frenchie asked for volunteers to go help at Hi-Mix. The equipment from Lo-Mix was being transferred to the larger plant, built at a higher elevation, in preparation for making the massive amounts of concrete that would be necessary for the building of the dam itself. Moose and I quickly volunteered. We'd been in the tunnels for well over a year, and any chance to be outside we took.

Chief caught up with us just as we started up the dirt road that led to the top of the canyon. We could have caught a ride with one of the trucks that passed us, but we weren't in much of a hurry. Moose talked nonstop about his trip to Vegas with Pepper and, most importantly, about what he found out about Pepper's mother.

"When we got there, the night watchman had to help us find Clive's grave. He had a small marker, and it was dark, so we were happy to have the help. He had a map, and he took us to Ben's grave and to Grace's."

I flinched but managed a smile. "Thank you," I said.

He continued. "But Pepper's momma was a little harder to find. Betsy Cromwell. The man checked his list three times. We tried coming up with different spellings. Nothing. Then I asked him to check Betsy Allen. There she was. Nothing but a small wooden cross, not even a name scratched on it."

"So she never changed her name?" Chief said.

"Pepper said she never had a wedding of any kind. They just moved to the ranch and from then on said they were married."

"Well, I'm not sure what that—"

"What that means is, most likely, this Cromwell doesn't have any right to Pepper. Sure, the state would say he's the closest he has to a guardian, and they don't want any more kids than they have clogging up the system. Unless there was someone willing to file the papers."

"But if he just runs away, it's pretty unlikely they'd ever find him. And to be honest, Helen is about to be divorced, and I doubt they'd look kindly on an eighteen-year-old divorcée seeking custody of a thirteen-year-old boy." It didn't make much sense why this was important.

Moose cleared his throat. "I'm not thinking about Helen. Smitty and I have been talking."

"Oh," Chief said.

"You just bought her a ring," I said.

He smiled and held his hands out. "We're just talking. He's a good kid."

Closer to the rim of the canyon, we saw Nig going up a small trail and decided to join him to avoid the dust and dirt stirred up by the trucks. The small dog that had been adopted by the site walked with us for a few minutes before taking off at a dead run toward the concrete plant. The path ran hazardously close to the edge at times, so Chief walked far to the inside, while Moose and I walked closer to the edge, taking time to look down and out across the canyon at the scurrying men on the sheer walls.

Since we were talking, I figured I should tell them about my conversation with Helen last night as well. If I left after the turning,

I didn't owe anyone an explanation, but they had become more than just friends; they were my brothers.

I stopped at a large boulder, needing to rest my leg for a minute, and waved Chief and Moose over to join me. "I may not stick around for the next phase of this," I said.

Their eyes were on me, waiting for me to continue.

"I told Helen last night I would leave with her. I can't see her taking off alone with Pepper and anything good happening to them. I can take care of them."

Moose lifted his chin. "What did she say?"

I took a deep breath and let it out very slowly. "She's thinking about it. But she knows I care about her, and I'm sure she cares about me, too, so I expect she'll be glad to have me. I hope so, at least."

"I thought you wanted to stick around then join the army," Chief said.

I held my hands out, palms up. "Things change. I've got a little money saved. I'll find a job somewhere, and we'll be fine."

Chief shook his head. "Did you forget the reason you are here is because there ain't no jobs to be found? This sounds like a half-cocked plan to me, Ezra. But you're a grown man."

"I gotta agree with Chief. You're a grown man. But she's a grown woman too," Moose said. He shook his head. "Now Pepper, that boy needs some stability. He's got some real issues."

I nodded. "I guess we'll figure it out."

I pushed off the boulder and started walking up the path again. "I want to wait until after the diversion. I'd like to make sure these tunnels hold. We've worked too hard, and I need to know that my time here has been worth something."

"Have you told Pete yet?" Moose asked. "I'd sure like to hear how that conversation—"

A large explosion interrupted, shaking the mountain. Chief scurried ten feet away, climbing on the rocks and falling to his knees. "Damn you, Beau Dandy!"

Moose and I, standing on a narrow part of the path near the edge, looked back at Chief and laughed.

Suddenly, I quit laughing. It felt as if I was being sucked into the ground. I tried to move, but the pull of the earth was too powerful, and it held me. Moose had crawled a few feet higher on the ridge and reached his hand toward me. His eyes were as big as pie tins, and our fingertips brushed as the unstable ledge I was on gave way. I dropped with the dirt and rocks that once formed the rim and became part of the landslide heading toward the beach, six hundred feet below.

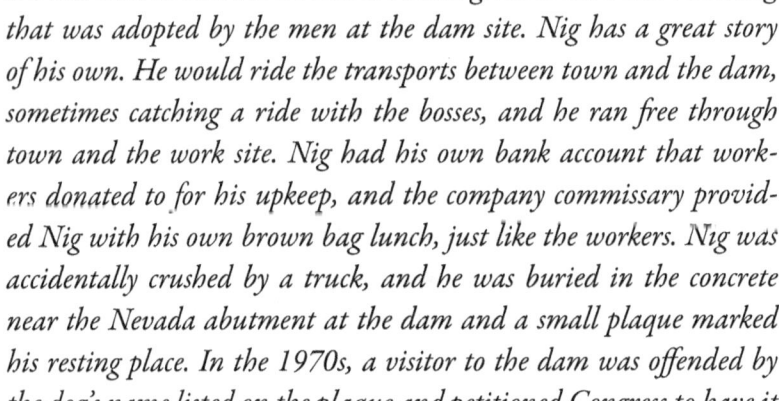

AUTHOR NOTE: NIG WAS the name given to the small black dog that was adopted by the men at the dam site. Nig has a great story of his own. He would ride the transports between town and the dam, sometimes catching a ride with the bosses, and he ran free through town and the work site. Nig had his own bank account that workers donated to for his upkeep, and the company commissary provided Nig with his own brown bag lunch, just like the workers. Nig was accidentally crushed by a truck, and he was buried in the concrete near the Nevada abutment at the dam and a small plaque marked his resting place. In the 1970s, a visitor to the dam was offended by the dog's name listed on the plaque and petitioned Congress to have it removed. The plaque that currently marks his grave does not list his name. However, someone scratched his name in the rock next to it.

Chapter 63: The Luckiest Man on Earth

Ezra

I WOKE UP FACEDOWN on steel. When I rolled over, the sun blinded me for a moment, and I lay on my back, trying to remember where I was and what had happened. My entire body hurt, but I jumped to my feet and stumbled in the small enclosure hanging at a precarious angle. Looking in every direction, I realized I was in the widow-maker. I worked my way to the side and looked over. A circle of men was on the beach below, looking up toward me.

"Moose!" I screamed and punched the hard sides of the steel car with my fists. I remembered the ground falling and reaching out for Moose before everything went dark.

A voice above forced me to look up. "Hey, down there! Quit shaking the damn thing. It's about to fall as it is."

I looked up to see that the widow-maker was being held by one twisted cable line, instead of the four that usually supported it. One of the high-scalers was above me, lowering himself on a bosun seat. Chief was on the ledge fifteen feet up, looking down.

"Be still, Ezra," Chief said. "We're trying to get you out of there."

I didn't move. The high-scaler landed in the car with me and stood close. "This is what we are gonna do," he said. But he didn't finish the sentence. The widow-maker groaned in protest against the extra weight. As the line above snapped, the high-scaler swung his legs between mine, forcing me to sit on his lap, facing him, and wrapped his arms around my upper body in a bear hug. The widow-maker fell, leaving us hanging fifteen feet down from the ledge.

The high-scaler ignored the falling box and yelled to the men above. "You are gonna have to pull us up. There's no way I can climb for two."

As we reached the edge, Chief grabbed me from behind, pulling me off the other man's lap, carried me a few feet to the rocks, and set me down. "Be still," he said. "I'm gonna get you down to Doc's."

"Where's Moose?" I said.

"I'm right here," Moose said from behind me. He sat on the ground while some guy tried to stop the bleeding from a huge gash on his right arm. "Looks like I get to go flirt with the nurses at the hospital again, and all you get is Doc Jensen."

AFTER DOC CHECKED ME out at the clinic and gave me a couple of aspirin, there were still thirty minutes left on my shift, but I went to the parking area to wait for Pete and Chief. In a few days, I might not be checking in at all, and they weren't going to fire me now with only a few days left until we turned the river. Besides, I was still shaking from damn near dying and didn't want to have to retell the story to Frenchie and the rest of the crew. I saw Helen standing by the train platform, dressed in her dungarees and an oversized shirt, her hair tucked under a porkpie hat. I wanted to run to her, take her in my arms, and thank God I didn't die, but I couldn't run, and she was supposed to be a boy. She headed toward me, and as she got closer, I couldn't help but smile. She raised her camera and snapped a picture of me.

"Did you see that commotion with the explosion? I was watching from Lookout Point, and I swear, whoever that guy was is the luckiest man on—"

"It was me," I said. I shook my head and took in a deep breath. A few weeks ago, it was a black widow that almost killed me, and today this. I sure didn't feel lucky.

She started to reach for me but pulled back, remembering her charade. "I'm sorry. What about the other guy?"

"It was Moose. He went to the hospital. But he'll be fine."

She lowered her head toward the ground and whispered, "It's amazing either of you survived."

I rubbed my scalp, trying to get the thought of dying out of my head.

Pete slapped me on the back and almost knocked me over. "Hell of a show today, Easy. I heard Moose is already screaming at the nurses in town." He turned to Helen. "Please tell me you got a picture or two of that?"

She smiled at him. "Of course. I didn't know it was Ezra, though. I—"

He waved a hand in the air. "It's going to be a classic. Let's get going before the train decides we aren't important enough to wait for, and we end up walking to the Pass." He leaned down and whispered to her, "Your boyfriend will be along shortly."

"Oh, I'm not going," she said.

"What? I thought the plan was to—"

"Moose got ten cases of jars last night. Pepper and I are planning to have them all full of salve before Tuesday," she said.

"That sounds like a lot of work in a short period of time," I said. It was still nine days before we turned the river.

She squared her shoulders and lifted her chin confidently. "Right, but I have some other things to take care of too. Can I get you to bring me four more boxes tomorrow night?" She was beaming, but something was wrong. Or maybe not wrong, just different.

Then she turned to Pete. "Tell Mae and Marguerite we'll be there by Tuesday night. Wednesday, I need to go to Vegas and get my divorce started."

Pete and I looked at each other then back at Helen, but she had already turned and was headed back toward the mountain. Something was definitely different.

AUTHOR NOTE: WHILE this particular scene is completely fictional, the high-scalers did perform some amazing rescues at the dam. One story is of a man who fell off a ledge while looking over the top of the canyon. The story goes that one high-scaler caught him by the leg, and another swung over to trap his body against the rock and held him there until others could tie a harness around him and haul him back up to the top. I can't verify the validity of this story, but it sure would make a great scene!

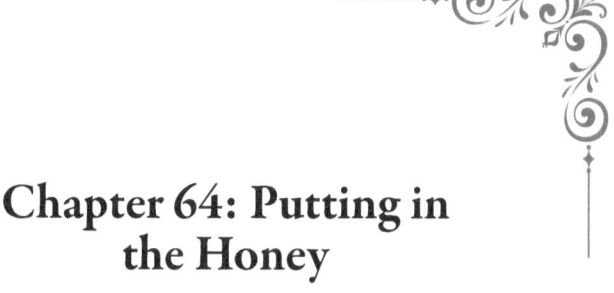

Chapter 64: Putting in the Honey

Helen

I HAD LEFT PEPPER AT Lookout Point while I went to tell Ezra and Pete the new plan, at least as much as I was willing to say at that point. I left before Ezra had a chance to ask me how I was going to start my divorce next week without the money from selling salve. If he asked when he brought the four cases I'd asked for, I'd come up with something. But Pepper and I had a lot of work to do between now and then.

On the walk back from Lookout Point, we gathered as much brittlebush and creosote as we could hold and intended to forage either closer to the dam site or in other areas farther from our cave. I didn't want to strip our area of the mountain dry. While we gathered, I explained my salve recipe and the process to Pepper. He was going to be helping a lot, and he needed to know how to do it and why it had to be done in a certain way.

"I thought you just threw it all together and put it in a jar," he said.

"No, that's exactly not what you do. First we must chop all this creosote and brittlebush as fine as we can and mix it all together. We can use a few of the boxes the jars are in for that. And we also have to put the lard out in the sun and let it melt, then pour it in the jars, about a quarter of the way full, then fill it with the dry mixture of plants, leaving about this much"—I held my thumb and forefinger about a half inch apart—"at the top."

He shrugged. "Okay, that's easy enough."

"Then, we put the jars out in the sun and let the plant mixture cook in the lard. In the middle of summer, I leave it about an hour. It isn't as hot right now, so we probably should leave it longer."

He rubbed his chin. "When do we put the honey in?"

"This is where it gets a little tricky," I said. "After the lard and plants have cooked for a while, we'll need to bring them back to the cave and let them cool off, but we don't want the lard to be completely cool, because it will be too hard, and the salve will be lumpy. After it's cooled down some, then we fill the jar the rest of the way with the honey and stir it very carefully. Then we can let it cool all the way, and the salve will be smooth and almost creamy."

He seemed to be listening intently. "So we can only cook in the afternoon," he said.

"Exactly! Then we have to be ready to stir the honey in at the right time. I did fifty jars by myself at Mae's camp last week, and it wasn't easy. Some of the lard was a little too cool, and I had to hurry through. I don't want to do that. I want them to be perfect."

"There's two of us now. We can do this."

I smiled. "We have to. We have almost three hundred jars to do in just a few days."

After we got back to our cave, we decided to eat something and then go farther north in the desert to collect more plants. We got back to our cave just as it was starting to get dark. We were both exhausted, and the smell from the large amount of creosote we had collected was almost unbearable. We decided to sleep at the river's edge again and get started working in the morning.

BY THE TIME EZRA AND Moose arrived on Saturday to bring the rest of our jars, lard, and honey, Pepper and I had two cases packed. Forty-eight jars. We still had a case that Ezra had brought earlier in the week and eight more that Moose and Pepper loaded on our north shore for Pepper and me to haul to our cave.

"I can help take it up," Moose said.

"No. We got it," Pepper replied.

"Helen—"

"Ezra, I can't sit tonight. We have to keep working," I said. I hadn't answered him about leaving with him. A part of me wanted to, and I had been thinking about it, but something had made me uneasy, and working during the day, I realized what it was.

Pepper.

When he had mentioned leaving with me, he hadn't even mentioned Pepper. It was just me, me, me, and I didn't know what to think about that. Sure, he may have assumed that Pepper being with me was a given and didn't need mention, but I wasn't sure. And I was too tired to think about it right then.

He exaggeratedly waved his hand in front of his face. "You smell horrible," he said.

I laughed. I knew I was covered in creosote, lard, and sweat, so I wrapped my arms around him and made him kiss me.

"Okay, let's take these boxes before anyone sees us dilly-dallying out here. Tomorrow night?" Moose said.

I nodded. "Thank you."

Moose winked at Pepper and turned to go back to the car, carrying the two boxes. Ezra looked at me for a long few seconds then reluctantly followed.

"He didn't look happy," Pepper said after they left.

I shook my head and looked at the eight boxes of jars and packages of lard and honey that sat on our shore. "Well, right now, all I'm worried about is making us happy."

After three trips up the mountain and back down to the river's edge for more supplies, we took a break and ate dinner in the cave before making one last run. We had decided we would move our creosote to an area away from the cave so we could sleep in it at night, and our plan was to get up early, find more plants while the lard had time to melt in the morning sun, and crush all the plants before noon. From the day before, I determined that it took an hour and a half for the first half of the mixture to cook in the sun, and if we managed our time right, we should be able to do three sets of thirty, which would be almost four cases of salve.

"What's wrong?" Pepper said as he speared Vienna sausages from a can with one of Queho's forks.

I shook my head. "I was just thinking. I don't think we'll be able to get all of this made by Tuesday, and I need to be in Las Vegas by Wednesday."

"Why? We have a whole week. Then you can go to Vegas after. When we have all the money."

I hadn't told Pepper how much money I had gotten from Ida Browder, but I had told him that it was enough to get my divorce started. I still hadn't decided exactly what the plan was after that, the fact being I hadn't decided about Ezra. I knew I should tell him; it was his freedom, too, but I was afraid he would withdraw again, and I didn't want to see that happen. All I knew was that I needed to get my divorce done, I needed to get my daddy's car back, and I needed to get out of town soon. I'd been running on nothing but luck, with friends to help, but I was smart enough to know that luck only ran so long. The assault charge could only be resolved if Pepper told what happened in that alley. And if he did, he would be fair game for Mr. Cromwell to take him back. I couldn't do that to him.

"Pepper, I just need to get it done. We need to be ready to leave town right after they turn the river. I need you to trust me."

He cocked his head and looked at me with eyes like a loving pup. "I'll always trust you, Helen."

He finished his can of sausages, stood up and held a hand down to me, and I took it. Then we went to the river and got the rest of our supplies, ready to begin again in the morning.

Sunday went exactly as we had planned. It was very hot, unusual for early November, which decreased our bake time and allowed us to start a little earlier in the day. By the time Ezra and Moose arrived Sunday evening, we had managed to get four cases completely done and had another twenty-four jars cooling in the cave, which we could pack up after they left. We didn't talk much. We were too tired and just wanted to get back to the cave, and they understood.

Monday was a different story. We started early, just as we had the day before, but as I was laying out a second batch for its cooking time, I heard voices in the distance. I couldn't tell what they were saying—they were too far away—but I could tell it was more than one person, and they were so loud I doubted they were looking for Queho. I covered the jars I had laid out with brittlebush so they would be partially hidden and ran back to the cave, where Pepper was adding honey to the previous batch.

"Pepper, someone is out there. We need to go," I whispered.

"Go? This is the best hiding spot there is," he said.

I knew he was right. "Okay, but we have to be really quiet," I said.

He put a finger to his lips and then continued mixing the salve. I sat next to the wall that covered the entrance to the cave and listened. I doubted they would come up this far and even further doubted they would leave the trail if they did, but I had an uneasy feeling. Then I heard a familiar voice yelling my name.

"Helen! If you're up here, you need to come out now!"

I froze. Cotton.

AUTHOR NOTE: I CAME up with Helen's recipe by researching some of the plants and ingredients she would have had access to and putting them together. Brittlebush is a member of the sunflower family, and if you are ever in the desert, you can recognize it by its yellow blooms. Several Native American tribes and Spanish settlers used it in poultices and teas to alleviate pain. Creosote was used for a variety of medicinal purposes, including as an anti-fungal agent and an anti-inflammatory. When making a recipe for Helen, I thought those two plants, which are in abundance in the desert, would be perfect. Adding the honey, which is a great wound healing agent, would not only be beneficial for her salve but might help with the odor from the creosote that many people, including myself, find unpleasant.

ALTHOUGH HELEN DID have a nice stash of cash by this point, she needed to buy her car back from a gangster, pay for a divorce, and have enough money left to leave. She was putting a lot of faith in her friends' abilities to sell her rub. However, during the building of the dam, a lot of children sold bat guano to tourists who came to watch the work being done, and therefore, the idea that she could sell her salve was not too out of line.

Chapter 65: Ragtown Remedy

Helen

HE WAS STILL FAR ENOUGH away, but he had found the right trail.

Pepper had quit stirring the salve and scooted next to me. On his way, he had grabbed my gun, handed it to me, and pointed toward one of the holes in the wall in front of the cave. I shook my head. But I did unholster the weapon.

I thought about the jars I had left out. Even though I had covered them, if Cotton found them, he would know what they were, and he would know I was nearby. I sat silently, holding my uncle Dwayne's gun, and listened.

They were getting closer, close enough I could hear the person with Cotton complaining. "This is ridiculous. There ain't no way a girl is hiding up here," he said.

"Helen!" Cotton screamed my name again, and I shuddered.

"What's that?" the other man said, and my heart sank.

Pepper scooted away from me, and when he came back, he had one of Queho's rifles in his hand.

"No," I whispered. I felt defeated. I was already in trouble. I wasn't going to add shooting someone to it, and I certainly wasn't going to let Pepper do it. I stood up and took a deep breath, ready to give myself up, when I heard Cotton say, "That's one of them crazy lizards. Damn, I hate this place."

I let out a slow breath and sat back down.

"Lizards and snakes and spiders. I'm leaving," the other man said. "I don't know why you dragged me up here anyway. Tony's got the car back, and he don't give two hoots about that damn woman."

"I care! She made a damn fool out of me!" I could hear the anger in Cotton's voice. Just leave, Cotton, I thought. Just leave.

"She'll show up," the other man said. "But I'm gettin' back to Vegas. You can either come with me or hang your hat out here. Your choice."

They were heading back down the trail—I could tell by the way their voices were becoming more distant—and I sat back and waited. Did he say Tony had the car back? How? And how many times had Cotton been out here looking for me, and Pepper and I had been just going about our business like nothing could touch us here?

I waited until I couldn't hear them talking anymore then silently made my way out of the cave and snuck up the mountain until I could see the Wash below. Pepper was by my side, still carrying the rifle. We lay on the ground and watched as they got in a car and left. I let out a long breath.

"Now what?" Pepper said.

"We finish up. At least we know they went back to Vegas, and tomorrow, we'll be gone from here," I said.

"But when you go to Vegas, he's going to be there," he said.

"I'll deal with that when I get there," I said. I didn't know how, but I had two days to figure it out.

By that evening, when Ezra and Moose arrived, Pepper and I were bathing in the river, and the remaining five cases of salve sat on the beach, waiting to be loaded in George Goon's car.

We had done it, despite Cotton and his friend. I didn't say anything about Cotton to Ezra and Moose, since it wouldn't have done any good. He was gone, back to Vegas, and we wouldn't be here much longer anyway. I didn't need Ezra going off half-cocked looking for him, adding more trouble to the mix.

The four of us sat on the beach and ate a turkey dinner, complete with mashed potatoes, gravy, stuffing, and rolls from the company cafeteria. Pepper and I ate like we'd never seen food.

"Slow down," Moose said.

"It's so good," Pepper said. "I can't believe you get to eat like this every day."

I ate silently. I was thinking about Cotton and what I would have to do to get him to not contest the divorce. He was so angry. I knew it had a lot to do with the alcohol that had pickled his body, but that wasn't my problem. He was my problem.

I knew Ezra wanted to talk about his offer to go with us, but I didn't want to discuss it with Moose and Pepper around. And besides, I hadn't really decided yet whether I liked that idea or not. The previous night, when I lay on my pallet, I had tried to envision various scenarios—Pepper and I in California, Kansas, even Gatsby's Long Island—and in each of those dreams, I couldn't see Ezra with us. The only dream I could see him in was if I stayed in Boulder City. Married. Setting up house. Just as I had dreamed of doing not so long ago.

Ezra did not push. He sat next to me, and we listened to Moose and Pepper. With my stomach full, the exhaustion from the day caught up with me, and I laid my head on Ezra's shoulder. He put an arm around me and pulled me close. It was... comfortable. I closed my eyes and smiled to myself as I pictured us sitting on a beach, the ocean laid out before us, the sound of the river rushing past becoming waves crashing against the sand.

It must have been close to an hour before Ezra gently shook me awake. I breathed in deeply, his woodsy scent making me wish I could go right back to my resting place in his arms. "You need to get back up the mountain, Helen. Tomorrow is going to be a big day," he whispered.

I yawned and stretched, willing myself to wake.

"Is it okay with you, Helen?" Pepper said. His eyes were wide and bright, and he wore a childishly wide smile.

"What?"

"I told Pepper he should come stay with Ms. Smitty for a few days tomorrow while you go handle your business. He'll be safe. I'll see to it," Moose said.

I didn't own Pepper—he could do what he wanted—but he still felt as if he needed my permission. I'd gotten to know Moose a lot better over the past few weeks, and he was good for Pepper.

"Of course. That's a great idea."

Pepper almost squealed, which made me smile. "And what about the name?"

"Huh?"

He laughed. "You were really asleep, weren't you? Miss Smitty is putting little labels on the jars and tying a ribbon around them. She wants to know a name to write on the labels. I said Helen and Pepper's Magic Lotion, but Moose thinks that's too long."

"How about Ragtown Salve? After all, that's where you both came from and where you started making it," Ezra said.

"Short enough but doesn't have much of a ring to it," Moose said.

I thought for a minute. "Ragtown Remedy," I said with finality.

They all nodded. Perfect.

On our way back up the mountain, we were surprised to find Gatsby, spread across the trail as if he wasn't going to let us pass if we didn't notice him. Pepper picked him up and let him curl around his arm, gently scolding him for running off.

I ran a finger over his scaly skin. "Hello, friend."

He flicked his tongue at me.

That night, Pepper and I lay in the cave, our arms and legs covered in scratches from handling all the brittlebush but our stomachs full of food and our heads full of possibilities.

"Pepper, what do you want to be when you grow up?" I asked.

He shrugged. "I guess whatever's there for me."

I leaned up on an elbow and looked at him. He was so small, and I knew the kids in Ragtown had made fun of him for his naivety, but I saw something in him they didn't. I guessed, at that time, the only measure of a man was his ability to work hard and labor to provide, and to them, Pepper would never be that kind of man. But I had seen him work hard with me over the past few weeks, never complaining and truly relishing in the simple joys of watching the men work or spending time by the river.

I shook my head at him. "No. Not whatever is there for you. Just because we came from poor stock, our fathers wanted more for us. That's why they brought us here in the first place, to give us a better chance at not just opportunity but at happiness."

He looked at me as if I were speaking a foreign language.

I smiled. "We are allowed to dream, Pepper. And even more so, we are allowed to go after those dreams. That's why I want to leave so badly. I used to be scared, but I'm not anymore."

"So what do you want to be when you grow up?" he asked.

"I am grown, Pepper. I used to want to be a wife, but I tried that, and maybe someday, I'll try it again. But first..." I thought about what Ezra had told me about selling pictures. "I think I want to take pictures and sell them." I shrugged. "And if that doesn't work out, I'll try something else."

"I just want to be smart," Pepper said. "I want people to look at me and say, 'That Pepper Allen, he knows about everything!'"

I lay back down, exhausted. "Then that's what you need to do, Pepper. Learn about everything."

I felt Gatsby curl up next to me, and I fell asleep listening to Pepper talk to Queho, asking him what he had wanted to be when he grew up and telling him goodbye. It felt very natural and almost comforting.

We decided to spend the morning at Lookout Point before meeting at the train after Ezra's shift ended. Then I would ride the train back with Pete, and he would go into town with Moose and George. As I packed, I decided to take the small music box with me and told Pepper to choose something of Queho's to take for himself as a remembrance of our time in the cave. He didn't have to think twice about his choice as he carefully untied the leather pouch that Queho had worn around his waist.

We ate a breakfast of beans and then packed canned meat, a box of crackers, and a jar of peanut butter for a day at Lookout Point. I fully planned to have my Vegas problems resolved in the next few days and didn't expect we'd ever see this cave again. With the rest of our supplies packed in the blanket we had brought, the three of us—Pepper, Gatsby, and I—said goodbye to Queho. He had given us a safe place when we needed it most, and in return, we would keep his secret.

AUTHOR NOTE: I MENTION riding the train several times in this story. The train tracks that ran from the Boulder City depot down to the dam site were cut through the mountain and at times ran precariously close to the edge. The original tracks are gone, but the tunnels that were cut through the mountain for them still remain and are part of a walking trail at the Lake Mead Recreational Area. This

walking trail also overlooks the original site that was Ragtown. While most tourists to the area go to the dam, many don't know about this area and are truly missing a great walk through history. I highly recommend a visit to the Railroad Tunnel Trail, which can be accessed behind the Hoover Dam Lodge.

Chapter 66: A Woman Can Take a Hell of a Beating

Helen

MAE WAS STANDING OUTSIDE the mansion when Pete and I walked up, wringing her hands, her face etched with worry.

"What's wrong?" Pete asked as he put my pack on the picnic table. "Where's Marguerite?"

"She's fine," Mae said as she waved him to the table and wrapped me in a motherly hug. She was warm and smelled like roses, and I took a deep breath, taking in her scent. She pulled back and smiled at me. "We have a visitor." She looked at Pete. "I hope you don't mind. She had no place to go and—"

Pete stopped her mid-sentence. "Lost puppy?" he asked.

Mae let out a slow breath and then looked at me. "Her name is Sally."

"What? Sally is here?" I turned toward the tent, but Mae caught my arm.

"She's sleeping. But Helen... she's been beat up pretty bad." I could see the tension in Mae's jaw when she said this, and my stomach flipped at her words.

"It wasn't because of me, was it?" I couldn't bear the thought that Sally might have been hurt trying to protect me. I thought of the gun in my pack and wished it were that easy.

"No. A guy that didn't feel like paying, and it got out of hand. The bouncer took care of him, but she got fired," Mae said.

"Fired? For what?"

Pete spoke up. "For not keeping the customer happy. Not being able to work with a broken face. Causing a commotion. Take your pick." He looked at Mae. "Is she going to be okay?"

Mae nodded. "Just needs healing time. Thanks, Pete."

"Don't worry about it. I'm going to run down to the Pass and get us some dinner. I'll leave you in charge of our home for wayward women," Pete said.

Mae patted his hand as he stood and headed away from the mansion.

"Where's Pepper?" she asked.

"He's staying in town with Miss Smitty, Moose's girl. He and Moose get along very well," I said.

She motioned for me to follow her in the tent, so I grabbed my pack off the picnic table and followed.

Sally sat on Mae's bed, her back to me, her long blond hair hanging loosely down her back over a white cotton gown.

"You looking for me?" She spoke slowly, and her words were slurred.

When I walked in front of her, my hand flew to my mouth. I was unprepared for seeing my friend in such a state. The left side of her face was dark purple, the eye swollen shut. Her lips were like a small bunch of grapes.

I kneeled in front of her and took her hands in mine. "Oh, Sally," I whispered.

Sally shrugged. "I sure could use some of that stinky cream of yours if you got any."

The right side of her face, save for a few scratches, remained as white as milk, giving an even stranger image of two girls sharing a common face. I could tell she'd been crying.

"I'll make you a gallon if you need it. There are so many people in the Arizona Club. How—"

Sally sniffed and lit a cigarette. "A girl can take a helluva beating in the time it takes someone to hear her scream."

"Where's Ezra?" Mae asked.

I couldn't take my eyes off Sally's face. "He said he'd be out later."

"Good. We need to talk. Remember I said you'd owe me a big favor? Well, I know what that favor is." She looked at Sally, who lowered her head, her hair falling around her face. "I want you to take Sally with you when you go. She's got money, and I've got more."

"I've got money," I said. I sat on the worn rug that covered the dirt floor in front of Mae's bed, crossed my legs, and told them about Ida Browder.

Mae clapped her hands together. "That's it, then. You can get your divorce and pay for your car, then with the money you'll get from selling your rub and what you already have—"

"And my money," Sally added.

"Yes, and Sally's money. You girls can go anywhere you want after you take care of your business in Vegas. What do you say?"

I put my hands on Sally's knees. "Yes. Yes! I would love to have you come with us." My hands fell into my lap. "Ezra wants to go too."

Mae sat on the bed next to Sally and looked at me. "What do you want?"

I'd thought about that for several days and hadn't said a word to anyone. I spoke slowly. "I want to go back a year, wait in the Wash for Ezra, marry him instead of Cotton, and live in Boulder

City with the grass and the trees and the movie theatre. But I know I can't." I paused and cleared my throat. "I want... everything to be right. I can't be running from a mobster and a husband who got their feelings hurt, and I can't marry another man just because he wants to take care of me."

"Does he know how you feel?" Sally slurred so badly that she sounded drunk, and the hurt and the anger I felt about someone hurting her swelled inside me.

"Just the first part," I said.

Mae reached for my hand and pulled me up on the bed between her and Sally. I felt safe in between them, a connection to two other women that I hadn't ever felt. I had Daddy for many years, but I never knew my mother, and I could imagine that if I had, being close to her would have felt something like this.

"God has put a lot on you, Helen, but like my mother used to say, he always puts the most on those with the strongest shoulders. You've got to do what's right for you first, others second."

"Yes, I know." I reached for Sally's hand. "And we'll be fine. Together."

She leaned her forehead against mine and squeezed my hand.

"And you need to consider what's best for Pepper too," Mae said.

I straightened, as if her words had somehow questioned my intentions, then let out a long sigh. As much as I wanted to do what was right for Pepper, I didn't exactly know what that was. I knew going back to Cromwell's ranch wasn't the answer. And although I loved him like a little brother, he would need to go to school, and he would need to find a way to deal with the loss and abuse he had suffered in the previous year. That would require a stability that I didn't possess and wasn't sure when I would. "I know."

"As for Ezra, you'll have to tell him," Mae said.

"I know. But I need to wait, and..."

"And make up your mind for sure. I understand," Sally said.

Mae raised a brow and continued. "We need to figure out what to do about Tony Badamo."

"How well do you know him?" I asked.

Sally snickered. "I know him pretty well, or at least used to. He's not a horrible guy—well, as long as you're straight with him and don't try to mess him over."

Which he thought I'd done. I shook that thought away. If he'd just listen..."You both say he is true to his word, right? And money is the only thing he really cares about?"

"Yes, if he said he'll do something, he'll do it. And getting him to say he will do something usually involves money," Sally said.

I told them about Cotton searching for me in the mountains the day before and how I had overheard that Tony had found the car and wasn't interested in finding me. "But I want the car," I said.

Mae sighed. "You could buy another car and—"

"No, I want that car. My car." My daddy's car.

"All you can do is ask. And be ready to pay him. But there's no guarantee he'll sell it to you," Mae said.

"I know. But I have to try," I said.

I took off my hat and let my braid fall down my back. Mae immediately touched my hair, running her hand down the long braid. "Oh, my," she said. "Enough talk for now. Let's take care of this nest. When you leave here, you're going to look like a woman, not some teenage boy."

AUTHOR NOTE: MY GRANDMOTHER used to tell me God puts the most on those with the strongest shoulders, and I thought her advice was what Helen needed at this point. I think Grandma would have loved that I had a prostitute give her this advice.

Chapter 67: Helen Can Take Care of Herself

Ezra

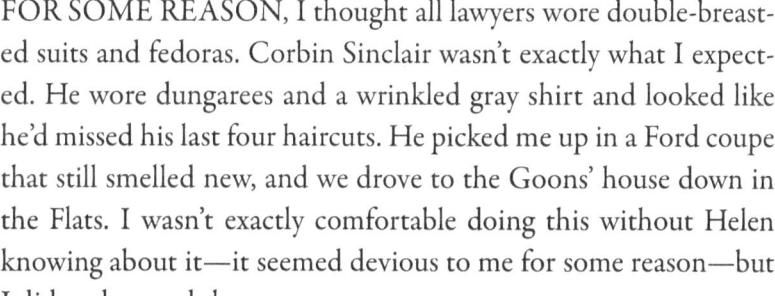

FOR SOME REASON, I thought all lawyers wore double-breasted suits and fedoras. Corbin Sinclair wasn't exactly what I expected. He wore dungarees and a wrinkled gray shirt and looked like he'd missed his last four haircuts. He picked me up in a Ford coupe that still smelled new, and we drove to the Goons' house down in the Flats. I wasn't exactly comfortable doing this without Helen knowing about it—it seemed devious to me for some reason—but I did understand the urgency.

Pepper sat on the porch with George, Smitty, and Moose. When I walked up, he was all smiles. He'd been very withdrawn around me for the past few weeks, maybe even leery of my intentions, but that day, he seemed like the Pepper I remembered from Ragtown.

Moose shook Sinclair's hand, and Smitty went in the house to get two more tea glasses for us. Sinclair did a double take when he saw Gatsby in the corner and outwardly gasped when Pepper picked him up.

"He's friendly," Pepper said.

Sinclair cleared his throat and pulled several papers from his case. "Pepper Allen? I want to make sure you understand what we are doing here."

Pepper sat up straight, still holding Gatsby. "Mr. Moose told me."

Sinclair cleared his throat again. "Right. Since your mother never married Alexander Cromwell, he would have had to petition the court to be considered your legal guardian, which he never did. That doesn't mean he can't do so now, and if he did, you would be returned to him immediately."

Pepper shook his head. "No. I'm not ever going back. I'm going with Helen," he said.

"Helen?" Sinclair looked at Moose, who shook his head and motioned for him to continue.

"Anyway, Mr. Martin wants to file papers on your behalf to become your legal guardian. This would make him responsible for you until you are eighteen. Do you understand?" he said.

Pepper bobbed his head excitedly. "And it keeps Mr. Dumbbell from getting me back, right?"

"Um, yes," he says.

"Okay," Pepper said.

It was that simple. When Moose had asked Charlie Shea for advice, he had called his friend, Mr. Sinclair, who met with Moose on Monday, and one day later, we were on Smitty's porch, signing papers. George and I were to sign as witnesses and references to Moose's character. And within a few minutes, long enough for half a glass of Smitty's sweet tea, Pepper was, on paper, Moose's responsibility.

After Sinclair left, I let out a long breath. Helen was not going to be happy. Not that this wasn't a great idea—at least it saved Pepper from going back to the ranch and would also make it very simple for her to deny kidnapping—but we hadn't told her first.

"Helen will be happy," Pepper said. "She's been worried when we leave that Mr. Dumbbell would find us and take me back, but now, he can't."

"Pepper," Smitty said. "It's your choice if you want to go with Helen. But I think she would be very understanding if you wanted to stay. You could go to school and live with Moose and me, once we're married, of course. You could go to the movies and the park and do all the things your mom and dad had intended for you to do when they first came here."

Pepper scrunched his face together. "But what about Helen?" he said.

Moose smiled. "Helen can take care of herself, Pepper. She has options too." He looked at me.

Pepper pulled Gatsby close.

"But think about it," Smitty said. "In the meantime, let's go downtown and get some ice cream."

"Ice cream!" Pepper's eyes lit up, and it was as if he'd forgotten about Helen.

George was ready to go to the Pass for a night of drinking and dancing, and I was going to catch a ride with him.

Moose walked me to the car. "You don't have to tell her. I'll explain it to her when I see her next. It really is in his best interests."

I nodded. "You don't intend to let him go anywhere, do you, Moose?"

He looked off toward the desert for a minute and then looked back at me. "I know Helen's intentions are good. But he is a thirteen-year-old boy. He needs the next few years to grow into a man. She needs to do her own growing. It's what I can do to help. You help her, I'll help him, and everybody's happy."

That didn't answer my question, but I knew it was the best I was going to get.

AUTHOR NOTE: AS I'VE said before, Pepper is a tragic character and one that was hard for me to write. I felt he really needed his own hero. In considering a second book, I can't help but think of all the ways Pepper can grow into a young man over the next four years it would take to complete the dam. In fact, it may be Pepper that makes me write that next book.

Chapter 68: Ready to Strike

Ezra

WHEN I WALKED UP TO Pete's tent, the smell of ammonia about knocked me out. Mae was sitting at the picnic table facing me, and two other women had their backs to me. Mae motioned toward me, and the two women turned at once. I didn't know which face shocked me more.

"Helen?" I didn't know who the other woman was, but she looked like she'd met the wrong end of a banjo shovel.

Helen ran her fingers through her short hair. "Do you like it?" she said. "We couldn't get all the red out, but I like the lighter color."

I reached out and touched her hair. "I... I'm glad you didn't choose bald," I said. I liked it long, but the shorter, lighter hair made her eyes even brighter green, which I hadn't thought possible. I reluctantly turned my eyes from Helen to the other woman.

"I'm Sally," the woman slurred, "and I've seen better days." She tried to smile, but only the right side of her mouth moved up in a twisted smile.

"Ezra," I said. I sat at the table next to Mae and couldn't keep from staring at Helen. I wanted to wrap my arms around her and lift that dress off her again, like I did a few days ago, but I doubted that would be welcome with others around.

Pete came out of the tent with a bag and handed it to me. "We already ate. I kicked them out of the tent because it already smells like a damn bleach factory in there."

My stomach growled at the mention of food, and I opened the bag, took out a sandwich, and took a bite without even looking to see what it was.

"What's the verdict?" Pete said as he sat on the other side of Mae.

I glanced briefly at Helen and then gave Pete a quick shake of my head. "Oh, everything's fine."

Sally laughed. "Well, that wasn't subtle at all."

"No, it wasn't. What's 'fine'?" Helen asked.

Pete held both hands out, palms up. "Sorry. I thought she knew," he said.

Helen crossed her arms over her chest and stared at me. Damn.

"Well, Moose really wanted to tell you, but he filed papers for guardianship of Pepper today." There. I said it.

"What?" Mae and Helen said at the same time.

"It's just a way for him to make sure that Cromwell has no claim to him. It is in Pepper's best interests. It doesn't mean anything more than that," I said.

"Are you serious? How could he do that? Legally, I mean?" Helen asked.

"And I think it means a lot more than that," Mae added.

Pete held up a hand. "Whoa, let's not attack the messenger. You're right. It means Moose will be his legal guardian. But now that guy in Vegas can't come near him, or Moose will file charges against him, which is better than beating him to a bloody pulp like he wants to. And Pepper has options now. He can stay with Moose if he wants or he can go with you, without worrying about that Cromwell guy."

"Oh, he can go with me, and then Moose can file kidnapping charges against me," Helen said. She turned to me. "And you, or Moose, didn't think to tell me this?"

"It just happened," I said. "And Pepper seemed happy about it."

Mae laughed, and Sally snickered. This wasn't going well at all.

"When did Pepper learn about all this?" Helen said, her words clipped as if she were trying to control her tone.

"Today. Moose explained it to him. He said fine, so Moose had a lawyer come over and signed the papers."

Helen pursed her lips. "Well, at least Pepper didn't lie to me."

"Lie to you? No, it's not like that. You just have so much going on, we didn't want to add to it, and it's not that big a deal—"

Pete kicked me under the table, telling me to shut up. He was right. The more I said, the angrier Helen got.

"Oh, of course it's no big deal. And poor little Helen can't handle all that information? Right."

I wanted to say "I'm sorry" but thought better about saying anything at all. And to be honest, I didn't understand why she was so mad. If Pepper wanted to leave with us, he would, but if he stayed in Boulder City, that would be best for all of us. I definitely didn't want to say that. I took another bite of my sandwich and let Pete try to change the subject.

"So, you are going to talk to Sally's lawyer friend tomorrow about your divorce?" Pete said.

Helen let out an exasperated sigh. "Yes, and I'm going to talk to Tony Badamo tomorrow, and I'm going to get my car back for good."

I about choked on my sandwich. "Whoa. You aren't going to talk to him without me. He's a criminal and—"

"I'm going with her, and I know Tony. We'll be fine," Sally said.

Pete kicked me again under the table. "Besides, the last thing she needs is for you to go in there poking your cane around, looking for a fight."

"I'm not looking for a fight. But if Cotton is there—"

Sally laughed and waved a hand. "For ten dollars, Tony Badamo would bury Cotton in the desert, and if he starts anything, I'll give him the ten dollars."

"I don't like this," I said. And I really didn't like it. Helen was smart, but she was a woman, and women had a habit of being led by their emotions and not their reason. In the hands of some fancy mobster, she could be in big trouble.

"They'll be fine. Tony's only concerned about his reputation and money. Hurting women is not good for his reputation. And this one is going to be giving him money," Mae said.

I dug in my pants pocket, pulled out a hundred dollars, and laid it on the table. "Here. This should buy your car back."

Helen didn't take it at first, but out of the corner of my eye, I saw Mae nod at her, and she picked it up. "Thank you. I'll use it wisely," she said.

"I've got some more money for you from the guys at work," Pete said and got up and headed toward the tent. Once inside, he screamed. "Damn, Helen, you didn't tell me you brought your snake! I thought Pepper had it! Scared the red off my head!"

Helen's and my eyes locked for a second. "Pete, don't move!" I yelled.

Helen was already off the picnic table and through the canvas slit as I slowly maneuvered around and grabbed my cane. Pete was standing by the canvas slit that led to his bedroom, and a large rattler was coiled up before him. I moved closer to Pete, and my cane landed a little too close to the snake, causing it to respond with a slight shake of its tail. "Definitely not Helen's snake," I said as I slowly lifted my cane and moved back two steps.

"Quit moving, Ezra. You're gonna get me killed. Helen, go tell Mae to get the shovel," Pete said, but Helen didn't answer, and I turned to see that she wasn't behind us anymore. "Great, even the snake expert was smart enough to run," Pete said.

I pulled out my pocketknife and took another step toward the snake. "Step on his head, and I'll cut it off. Surely he can't bite through your boot."

"No, but he can bite through my leg if I miss!" Pete backed up, waving at me behind his back, but I was focused on the snake and didn't move fast enough out of his way. We collided just as the snake began to shake his tail, sounding like the sizzle of bacon.

Three large blasts sounded beside my left ear, and I ducked and moved at the same time. The smell of gunshot had filled the tent, and when the smoke cleared, I looked down and saw the rattlesnake, what was left of him, in an exploded mess not far from my boots. I turned to see Helen in a shooter's pose, holding her Smith & Wesson.

Mae and Sally came through the slit of the tent, Mae holding a shovel.

"Ah," Pete said, "there's my shovel."

"What in the—"

"He was about to strike. 'Thank you' is what I think you are trying to say." Helen walked back behind the curtain to Mae's room and came back seconds later without the gun in her hand. She took the shovel from Mae and started scooping up snake guts as well as a good portion of the dirt. I was still staring at her, and she stopped and cocked her head. "Do you think you could find me a bag to put this in, or do you want all his friends to come investigate when they smell him?"

Pete lifted the canvas that led to his room and examined the bottom that was splattered with remnants of the snake. "Mae, find me something to cut this off with. She's right. We'll have a whole herd here by morning if we don't clean this up."

"I thought you said they were hibernating right now," I said.

Helen shrugged. "Supposed to be, but not all are. All that creosote I brought in here last week must have attracted him." She finished filling the bag with snake. "I'll take it up the mountain and bury it."

"I'll go with you," I said. It wasn't exactly my idea of time alone with her, but I needed to talk, and there were too many people around.

As we all walked out of the tent, there was a circle of people standing around waiting.

"Go on," Pete said. "It was just a car backfire."

"You have a car in your tent?" a short, scruffy man standing near the front of the crowd asked.

"None of your damn business," Pete said. "And if you try to find out, it might backfire on you."

Helen and I worked our way up the mountain, and she stopped at a large rocky area well out of distance from any campers. The ground was so hard, my first strike with the shovel barely penetrated.

"It was getting ready to strike," she said.

"But using that gun... you could have shot one of us. And now Pete may have to answer for it if someone decides to tell the law. There aren't supposed to be guns out here. He could lose his job."

She placed one hand on her hip. "Did you hear me? It was getting ready to strike! Some things are a little more important than the damned job."

I swore I'd never heard Helen say a curse word, and I stopped hitting the ground and laid down the shovel. I pulled her close. "What's on your mind?"

She pulled back from me and sat on the ground, placing the bag a distance from her. "I'm going tomorrow, and regardless of what happens, I know what I'm doing is the right thing."

I sat beside her, my legs bent, and rested my elbows on my knees. "I'm sorry about Pepper. It's not—"

"I can't believe you didn't tell me. Moose, fine, he doesn't know me, but you should have told me. You knew what our plan was."

I shook my head. "No, Helen, I don't know what your plan is. I told you I want to go with you, and you haven't said yes or no. I told you I'd marry you, and you could live in Boulder City, and we could be happy, and you haven't said yes or no. I'm starting to wonder if you want me around at all." There, I'd said it.

She looked off toward the setting sun, not looking at me. "Of course I want you around. I just want to do what's right for everyone," she said. She leaned her head on my shoulder, and I put an arm around her and pulled her close. "What Moose did for Pepper was good. But I don't like that you didn't trust me enough to tell me."

"I'm sorry," I said.

"And I don't want you to feel you are responsible for me. You made the right decision last year, taking care of yourself. We need to make sure we do that again."

I swallowed the lump in my throat. "I like this life. I like my job, my friends, even the desert. But I'd like it a lot better if you were here. And I'm willing to start over again for you."

She was warm and soft in my arms, and I knew under all that ammonia smell, she tasted like vanilla. I tilted her chin up and kissed her, and she climbed on my lap, facing me. She held my face in her hands, forcing me to look into those deep pools of green. "It's going to be all right," she said.

I put my hands on her hips and positioned her so she could feel what she did to me and kissed her again, deep. She wrapped her arms around my neck and pulled me closer, and all I wanted to do was lift her dress off her and make love to her in the open again.

But she pushed back and whispered, "We have a snake to bury."

I couldn't help but grin at what she said, and she slapped me teasingly on the shoulder. "Wrong kind of snake. I swear, men only think one way." But I could tell she was thinking about it too.

The ground was too hard, and it was starting to get dark, so we opted to bury the bag under several rocks and let the desert do with him as she wished.

When we got back to Pete's camp, Mae and Sally were sitting at the picnic table, laughing while Pete told one of his stories. Pete hooked a thumb toward me. "And then this one pushed his chest out like a bullfrog and said 'Here, I'll just saw him in half with my pocketknife.'"

Figured he'd have the rattlesnake ten feet long by the time he told the story tomorrow. He winked in Helen's direction. "And then Annie Oakley shows up..."

"I'm sorry if I get you in trouble. I was just trying to—"

Pete cut her off. "Don't worry about it. The look on Easy's face was worth any trouble it brings. And besides, I'm trying to get through this dam-building thing without getting bit by one of those rascals."

"So, what's the plan?" Mae said, looking at Helen.

She took a deep breath and looked around the table. "Well, tomorrow, Sally and I go to Vegas. If all goes well, we'll plan our exit then."

"After we turn the river," I said.

Helen looked down at her hands. "Yes, I don't want to miss that."

Mae and Sally glanced quickly at each other, like they knew something I didn't, and it made me a little uneasy. I was worried about Helen, and I felt they were keeping something from me. But

I also knew with women, if you pushed, it made them lock up even more. I couldn't talk Helen out of what she was doing tomorrow, so all I could do was pull her close to me, hold on for tonight, and pray that she knew what she was doing.

AUTHOR NOTE: RATTLESNAKES, like most snakes, are just as afraid of humans as we are of them. If you encounter one, slowly move away. They won't strike unless they feel threatened, but, if they do strike, it takes them about half a second to do so. I didn't really want Helen to kill a rattlesnake, since she was the one character most likely to understand and respect the snake, but it needed to happen. She needed an opportunity to show that she would do whatever she needed to and also needed to show that she was a bit reactive.

Chapter 69: A Sweet Girl from Kansas

Helen

"WATCHING YOU TWO LAST night... I think you might be in love with each other." Sally and I hitched a ride in the back of a pickup right after Ezra and Pete left for work. The morning wind was cool, and we snuggled together against the weather.

I shrugged. Sometimes love wasn't enough. "I hope I'm doing the right thing," I said.

She pulled me close. "You're doing what you have to do. He'll see that in time." She paused and then asked, "Did you tell him?"

I shook my head. "I couldn't. But I will."

When we got to Vegas, the pickup dropped us at Second and Fremont. Sally pointed me down Second Street, and we headed that way. "We're stopping at a little shop I go to a lot. You can't go see Tony looking like a ragamuffin," she said.

I looked down at my worn cotton dress and boots and didn't see anything wrong with the way I looked.

We stopped in front of a used clothing store, and I looked in the window. Racks of clothes and shoes covered the space, and the floor was littered with children's toys. In the window, a mannequin displayed a mint-green dress with a scooped neckline and a full skirt. Except for the color, it reminded me of the dress my daddy bought for me before he died. "I like that one," I said.

"It'd look pretty on you," she said. "Come on, let's see if it's your size."

I hold back. "Sally, I hate spending my money on a silly dress. I don't—"

She took my arm. "Nonsense. I'm tired of seeing you look like an old woman or a boy all the time. And it's a used clothing store. You can spare a dollar. If not, I'll buy it for you."

Thirty minutes and two dollars later, I stood in front of the drugstore on Second Street and looked at my reflection in the glass. The dress fit as if it were made for me, and we even found a pair of short, boxy heels in cream and green that complemented it perfectly. Against my protests, Sally bought me a royal-blue beaded necklace and matching clip-on earrings as well as a square purse with a short handle. Together, they set the outfit off. I couldn't quit looking at myself. I looked like a real woman.

Sally smiled next to me. "It feels great, doesn't it?"

"I had no idea. I feel so—"

"Open your mouth like this," she said and opened her lips slightly. I did as she told me, and she pulled a lipstick from her bag and carefully painted my lips. Then she tried to rub hers together and smack them, and I mimicked her. "There," she said. "You look like a hundred dollars."

I hoped it was enough.

THE BRIGHT LIGHTS, loud music, constant ringing of slot machines, and yells of satisfied gamblers inside the Apache Hotel didn't help calm the churning in my stomach. Tony Badamo's office was on the third floor, and I wanted to walk right up and knock, but Sally said we would have to wait in the bar until one of his men approached us. I didn't realize there was a code, or a procedure to visit a mobster, but I was sure glad Sally was with me, because she seemed to know much more about the workings of Tony Badamo and his like than I did.

Sally held a cigarette loosely between her fingers. I watched as the blue smoke rose to the ceiling and then spread out through the casino as it encountered the rush of air from a nearby vent. She took a long drag off her cigarette and slowly released the smoke, forming tiny circles that enlarged as they rose.

"How much longer?" I asked. I knew this was one of Cotton's hangouts, and the last thing I wanted to do was run into him before I had a chance to meet with his boss. My eyes darted around the place. I watched an older man with slicked-down hair and high pants, hungrily sizing up a scantily dressed cocktail waitress. He licked his lips, and I turned away quickly.

Sally nudged me as a large bald man approached us from behind the bar. "You don't look too good," he said to Sally. He then turned to me and eyed me up and down, but his face remained neutral.

"I still look better than you," she said.

The large man paused for a few seconds then started laughing. "I think you're on the wrong block, lady. You ain't gonna find any... paying customers in here," he said.

Sally took another drag off her cigarette and blew a long line of smoke into his face. "We're looking to spend money, not make it. As long as Tony Badamo is around to bargain with," she said. She laid a dollar on the bar and pushed it slowly toward him with one finger. He slid it into his pocket without losing eye contact with her.

"Who should I say is calling?" he said.

She snubbed her cigarette out in an ashtray and rested her elbows on the bar. "Helen Vaughn," she said.

The man looked at me and smiled this time, but it was the kind of smile that made cold chills run through a body. He picked up a phone behind the bar and started talking into it without taking his eyes off me. When he came back to us, he motioned over our shoulders. "Romeo will take you up."

When I turned on my barstool, another large bald man that could be the other guy's twin stood behind Sally and me. He looked at me first, his face emotionless, then at Sally, and he smiled.

"Good to see you, Sally, but what the hell happened?" He reached out a hand tenderly and held her chin, turning her face so he could see the damage.

"Hazards of the profession," she said. "Not all men are as sweet as you, Romy."

He turned to me and shook a finger. "And you, young lady, have a lot to answer for."

"Lighten up, Romy. She's not a kid, and she's here to make good," Sally said. She stood and linked her arm in mine, and I grabbed my purse off the bar and stood with her. My knees were weak, and walking on the unfamiliar heels didn't make it any easier, so I was glad Sally was with me to help hold me up.

As we rode the elevator to the fourth floor, where Tony Badamo held court, Sally and Romy chatted about the happenings of the local bars and brothels as if they were old friends. I leaned back on the mirrored wall of the elevator and tried not to throw up. We were led down a hallway to where another man stood in front of the entrance to a suite, which I assumed was where Badamo maintained his office. He knocked twice on the door and then waved us through.

I'd never met Tony Badamo, and I'd only seen him from a distance a few times. He was much shorter than I remembered, only a few inches taller than me, and I could tell that most of what I thought was bulk was from the oversized shirt and trousers he wore. He was a handsome man, dark hair and dark eyes, and a wide smile of straight white teeth. Not what I expected.

He went straight to Sally, and his smile turned into a look of concern. "This looks bad, Sally. It wasn't one of my guys, was it?"

"No. I think most of them know better," she said with a smile.

He waved us to a gold couch, and we sat. "Romeo, gets these ladies a drink."

"Just soda for me," Sally said.

I swallowed hard. "Me, too, please."

He sat in a straight-back chair across from us with a heavy coffee table in between. He leaned forward and clasped his hands in front of him between his open legs. "So, Helen—do you mind if I call you Helen?"

"No, Mr. Badamo," I said. My voice came out low, almost a whisper.

"Please call me Tony. You're Cotton's wife, so we're all family here. Right, Romy?"

Romy set two glasses of soda on the coffee table in front of us, and I immediately reached for mine and took a long drink. The cold liquid soothed my throat.

"Mr.—Tony," I said. "I'm here about my car."

He raised a hand. "You mean my car. Your husband owed me money, and he paid with the car. By the way, nice hiding spot. Not many folks go out to that deadly desert, but one of my guys found it a few days ago. It's now safe in the parking lot out back."

I shook my head. "It wasn't his to give. I want it back."

"Helen, what's yours is his, so it was his to give. And to be honest, even if I gave it back to you, he'd have to sell it to pay me."

"No, I'll pay you for it. A hundred dollars, right?" I reached for my purse, and Sally put her hand on top of mine before I could open it.

Tony leaned back in his chair and took in a deep breath. "Does your husband know you have that kind of money?" he said.

My shoulders slumped. "No, and I don't want him to," I said.

He let out a short laugh and put both hands up, palms out. "I don't want to get in the middle of family business, Helen. It's not my style."

"Cotton beat on her and tried to sell her to Johnny Sparks," Sally said. "Johnny tried to rape her."

Tony's face changed immediately. His brow knitted together, and his jaw tensed. "That's not the story they tell." He looked at me, his eyes searching mine. "Is that true?"

I tried to look away but couldn't. His eyes held mine. "Yes," I whispered. "And the man in the alley, I didn't assault him."

His eyes turned cold, and he stared at me with such intensity that I swore my eyeballs might burst. "I know you didn't." Then he smiled and relaxed again. "And as soon as he found out the little 'girl' in the alley was actually a thirteen-year-old boy, he dropped the charge immediately. It's one thing to mess with little girls, but little boys…"

A man that wanted sexual favors from either was lower than pond scum in my opinion, but I couldn't say anything. I was considering in my head: the charges had been dropped, the kidnapping, thanks to Moose, was null, so there was only my car. And Cotton. Both things relied on Tony Badamo to make them happen. My insides twisted, and my head hurt. I was afraid if I talked, I might start crying, and this was not the time to cry. I needed to be strong.

I tried to keep my voice steady. "I would like to buy the car, Mr. Badamo. So I can leave town. Leave Cotton. I—"

He held his hand up again, telling me to stop. "I told you, I don't like to get into family matters."

"He's hurting her, Tony. And she's a good girl. You've got a sister, don't you?" Sally said.

Tony shot her an icy stare and then, a second later, was smiling again.

"How did you get here, Helen?"

"I came with my daddy, from Kansas. He worked at the dam, but he got sick..." I looked at my lap, fighting the tears again. "And then I was alone," I whispered.

A silence fell over the room for what seemed like an eternity. Then Tony slapped his thighs with both hands. "Well, I'll be honest with you, Helen. One thing I hate is men hurting women. That's not what they were put on this earth for. If what you say is true, and I believe you, then I say go for it. Get away from him and start over."

I lifted my eyes up to him, my mouth half-open. Could it be this easy?

"However," he said, "one thing I love more than women is money. A hundred dollars for the car, and another fifty for the trouble you caused me."

"Deal," Sally said. She nudged me, and I hesitated before opening my purse. My brain was telling me to take his offer and disappear, but my heart was saying something different. I didn't want to push my luck, but he seemed so willing to help. And if it was just about money...

"And can I ask a favor too? I'm willing to pay for it," I said.

Tony rubbed his temples. "Don't push me, Helen."

I cleared my throat. "I filed for divorce this morning. But if Cotton contests it, I won't be able to leave, and I have to get out of here. I can't live like this," I said.

Tony shook his head. "Cotton will be out of town this Friday for me, so tell your lawyer to schedule the court hearing for then. No contest," he said.

Sally shook her head. "She's using Wesley Cole, discount deal. He said it will be at least two weeks before he can get a court date."

He looked at us both for a few seconds. "You got two hundred dollars in that little purse of yours?"

"I... uh..."

"Yes," Sally said, shooting me a look telling me to agree. I nodded.

Tony picked up the phone next to his chair. "Operator, get me Stacey Roberts at the courthouse, please... Hello, Stacey, it's Tony... Who's on the bench tomorrow?... How about Friday?... Great, any openings for a quick divorce... no contest, just stamp it... Wesley Cole... Perfect, tell Judge Brewster I'll be in touch." He hung up the phone and turned back to us. "Tell your lawyer to call Beth Porter at the courthouse. Two o'clock this Friday, no Cotton, no contest. And no more favors."

"But he has to be served, and—"

Sally put a hand on my leg.

"She sure talks a lot, doesn't she?" Tony said to Sally.

"Yes, she does." Sally grabbed my purse, thumbed out two hundred dollars, and handed it to Tony then turned to me. "Say thank you, and let's get out of here," she said.

"Thank you." I guessed if I'd have thought, it shouldn't have surprised me that if he had a judge in his pocket, he would have a way to make it look like Cotton had been served.

"You're welcome. Now get out of here, and don't come back," he said. He gave Sally a quick squeeze of her hand and said, "Good luck."

I guessed for a gangster, Tony Badamo wasn't all bad.

AUTHOR NOTE: ALTHOUGH Bugsy Siegel is the gangster most think of in connection with early Vegas, the Flamingo wasn't opened until the mid-'40s. There was plenty of organized crime activity in Vegas prior to that. However, I can't imagine that someone like my fictional Tony Badamo would waste much time on a domestic issue, and the idea of this being resolved quickly seemed plausible to me. Like most things, the anticipation caused more fear than the actual meeting.

Chapter 70: San Francisco

Helen

THE CAR SMELLED LIKE stale cigarettes and aftershave, but I sat in the driver's seat with my hands on the wheel and smiled. I'd done it.

"Are we going to go or just sit here?" Sally asked. The sun shone through the windshield and hit her face at the right angle to light up the purple and black bruises and make her face shine like a fresh plum.

I started the engine and pulled slowly out of the parking lot. "Can we stop at the secondhand store one more time?" I said. I didn't want to spend much of my money, but the clothes there were cheap, and I wouldn't be dressing like a boy anymore.

"Sure," she said. "But remember, those boys in the bar will talk, and once Cotton finds out you were there, he's going to be looking for you. He won't be happy."

I headed down to Second Street and turned left. "It won't take long. Just a few things. I need to go into Boulder City tomorrow and see Pepper. And I'll need traveling clothes," I said.

We both squealed when I said "traveling clothes."

"Do you really think he'll do as he said?" I was still not completely sure I should have trusted everything to Tony Badamo, but I did trust Sally, and she believed in him.

She laughed. "You know, you had him. When we told him about Cotton and Johnny, he turned as red as fire. And that sweet-little-girl-from-Kansas act finished him off."

"That wasn't an act. I am a sweet girl from Kansas. Or used to be. And he could have just shot me and took my money too."

She shook her head. "Like I told you, not his style. He's a good guy. For a bad guy."

We both laughed.

"Speaking of guys..." Sally said. I knew what she was asking.

"I don't know, Sally," I said.

I parked the car in front of the same store Sally and I visited that morning and turned off the engine. "Even though they all kept it from me, I do think Pepper is better off with Moose and Smitty. They can give him a real home. But only if that's what he wants. And Ezra..." I couldn't explain it. I loved him, just as Sally had mentioned that morning. But sitting in the car with Sally, buying clothes and talking about traveling toward an unknown future, gave me a sense of freedom that I'd never felt. And I wanted more. I knew with Ezra, whether I was in Boulder City or California, or Mexico, I wouldn't have the same kind of freedom. I wanted to be with him, but I also wanted to take a chance on me.

She reached over and took my hand in hers. "You still have a few days. I'm happy to be leaving either way. Now let's shop."

Two hours later and twenty dollars lighter, we headed back to the Pass. I had bought seven outfits, the most clothes I had ever owned, and two pairs of shoes. I thought of buying some for Pepper but decided to wait and see if he was going with us or not. If he chose to stay, I would leave him a share of the money we made from selling the salve so he could buy what he wanted. After all, he did half the work.

When we got back to Pete's mansion, Pete, Marguerite, and Ezra were waiting for us. Ezra took me in his arms as if claiming me. "I can tell by the smile on your face that things went well."

"By Friday, I should be divorced. And my car is parked at Railroad Pass. I'm broke, but the police aren't looking for me, and neither are any gangsters."

"Except maybe Cotton," Sally reminded. "He's not going to be happy when he finds out you went to see Tony."

"He won't find you here," Pete said. "And if he does, he'll have hell to pay."

"I'm staying," Ezra said.

"No... I... No, it's not necessary. I just want to rest, and tomorrow I have salve to make for Mae. And then Friday, all things going well, I go back to Vegas for the divorce. I'll come to Boulder City after that." I couldn't explain it, but I wanted to be alone.

He hesitated for a moment. "Okay," he said, releasing me from his arms. "I've got a lot to do to prepare for leaving anyway."

I glanced briefly over his shoulder at Sally, who stood with her eyebrows raised, then looked back into his eyes and said nothing.

We had dinner, Pete pulled out a bottle of Four Roses, and we drank in celebration. Then Ezra went to the casino to meet George Goon for a ride back to Boulder City. I watched him walk away, feeling sorrow and liberation at the same time.

I SPENT THURSDAY MORNING trying on all my new clothes for Mae and Marguerite, who gave me bits of jewelry to go with certain ensembles. I loved being in the company of these women; they made me feel as if I could do anything. Thursday afternoon I finished the jars of salve, and Mae prepaid me for them, saying she would sell them after we were gone. With that money, after my shopping spree in Vegas and what I had paid the lawyer and Tony Badamo, I was left with one hundred sixty-three dollars, one hundred of which was Ezra's.

"We'll be fine," Sally said. "I have a little over three hundred saved. We can go pretty much anywhere."

"San Francisco," I said. It was the place Sally had talked about many times, and from reading about it and listening to her talk, it sounded like a great place to start over.

She was thrilled. "San Francisco it is!"

I was nervous on Friday, and Mae joined Sally and me for our trip to Las Vegas and my court date with Judge Brewster. He was a kindly man, tall and handsome for his mid-fifties, and when my lawyer said I was divorcing because of excessive gambling and abuse, he took one look at Sally, as if she were a foreshadow to my fate if I stayed, and smacked his gavel. He stamped my papers, and after filing with the court clerk, it was over. We were out of the courthouse within the hour.

I made one stop at Woodlawn Cemetery to say goodbye to my dad before leaving town. I hated leaving him, but I knew he would understand. I promised him I would do something special with my life, just as he always said I should do. As I left, I felt him with me, and I knew everything would be okay.

I had told Ezra I would meet him at his dorm at six p.m., but traffic was heavy going back, and I was afraid that after I changed clothes and got ready, I would be late. Sally and Mae laughed at my concern. "You're allowed to be late. You are single now; you can be whatever you want," Sally said.

I smiled. I was, for once in my life, allowed to do whatever I wanted.

AUTHOR NOTE: SAN FRANCISCO seemed like a great place for Helen to want to be. Also, with the construction of the Golden Gate Bridge to begin in 1933, the connection between that and her life in Nevada with the initial phase of the building of the dam shouldn't be missed. After all, she has dreams of being a photographer, and she is used to construction sites. Another book in the works? Possibly.

Chapter 71: A Woman Like Her

Ezra

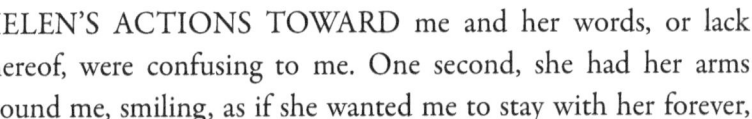

HELEN'S ACTIONS TOWARD me and her words, or lack thereof, were confusing to me. One second, she had her arms around me, smiling, as if she wanted me to stay with her forever, and the next, she would push away. I almost felt as if I had been dismissed.

Thursday morning at work, I didn't talk much. By lunchtime, my mind was full of questions and no one to answer them. But I asked anyway.

"Pete, did Helen act strange to you last night?" I asked. I took a bite of my sandwich and chewed slowly.

He shrugged. "Just acted like a woman, I guess."

"No. I can't quite figure it out. It's like she wants me there, and then she doesn't have time for me. I was just wondering if she said anything."

"Yep, that sounds like a woman," Chief said with a laugh.

"No, it's... different."

"Well, hell, I don't know. It's not like we sit and file our nails together and talk about boys. Women are hard to figure out, even harder when they've got all the baggage she has right now. She made a date with you for tomorrow night, so that says something," Pete said.

Moose shook his head. "See, this is another reason Pepper is better off here. A woman like her doesn't have any business trying to take care of a kid."

I turned to him with a glare. "What the hell is that supposed to mean? 'A woman like her'?"

He held his hands up defensively. "She's got a lot going on, and she's indecisive. I know you think she's got everything all figured out, but she's really just a kid herself. And a girl at that."

"Never mind," I said.

"If you want me to listen to the women gossip and report back, I will," Pete said.

I waved a hand. "No. Never mind. I'll talk to her tomorrow night."

And it was in that mood—broody, irritable, and a little on edge—that I walked into the company mess hall that evening and saw, from across the food line, a face worthy of all my ire. Billy Greene.

He was ragged, looking like he hadn't showered in a few days, which was unusual now that we were all living in town with access to showers. His clothes hung on his gaunt frame, and he kept his head down as he went through the line, grabbing everything and stuffing two boxes full of food. I wanted to jump across the meatloaf and strangle him right there. But I didn't. A fight in the mess hall would get me in some serious trouble, and I wasn't going to risk it.

I sat at a table, ate my dinner, and kept my eye on him, letting my anger build. He ate quickly, barely chewing, and when he'd finished one box, he left with the other. I followed him. I hadn't seen him but once since Grace died, and I'd missed my chance then. I wouldn't miss it now.

He cut across the park and behind the movie theatre, down a darkened alley. It was perfect. I caught him by the arm just as he passed the emergency exit for the theatre, turned him around fiercely, and was finally standing face-to-face with the little ass that had been, in my mind, the reason for my sister's death.

My sudden movements caused him to drop his dinner box, and he looked at me with hate in his eyes, until he recognized me and saw what was lurking behind mine. "Ezra," he said.

"Well, you remember my name. Do you remember hers?" I said. I tightened the grip on his arm, and he started to squirm.

"Ezra, it was all just a mistake. I didn't know she was pregnant, and besides, I'm sure she's better off without me. Now let go of me," he said, trying to twist his arm away from me.

"Better off? She's dead! You mean in all this time, you've been right here, and you've never even inquired as to what happened to her or your baby?" I squeezed his arm so hard I thought it would snap. My face was hot, and I was starting to shake.

"I told you already it probably wasn't my damn baby anyway," he said and lifted his chin in defiance.

And that was when my rage overtook my better sense. I hit him. Then again and again. He tried to fight back, but he was no match for all the emotion inside of me: the loss, the anger, the pain. If he'd stayed down when he fell, that might have been enough to stop me, but he didn't. He got back up and swung at me, and I beat him until he couldn't stand anymore. He lay on the ground, moaning, and I kicked him with my heavy boot so hard he rolled against the side of the building and didn't move again.

I waited for him to get up again, but he didn't. As my head started to clear, I realized what I'd done. I looked around, and it was silent except for the sounds of the construction going on around us. Instead of checking to see if he was dead or alive, I wiped my hands, covered in Billy's blood, on my shirt and made my way through the darkness back to the dormitory.

I knew I was in trouble. I'd beat him bad, and if he went to Bodell, I'd be in jail. If he was dead, well, maybe no one had seen me, but if they did, I'd be in jail for that too.

Although I should have felt good about getting revenge on him for Grace, I slept fitfully. In the morning, I went to breakfast as usual and listened for the gossip. A guy had been found behind the theatre, and he was taken to the hospital, not talking.

I went to work as usual, and right after lunch, Bud Bodell caught me leaving the beach. My stomach ached. All I could think of was Helen showing up that night and me being in jail.

"Deal, got a minute?" he said.

I took in a slow breath and tried to steel my nerves as I turned to face him.

"One of the guys said you was in the mess hall last night when that vagrant was stealing food. Did you see him?"

Vagrant? "You mean the guy that got beat up?" I said. I didn't know why I didn't just spill it right then, other than he didn't seem to know it was me.

"Yeah. Snuck into town and was pretending to be a worker so he could get food. Probably sleeping in that alley they found him in. A real piece of work." He wrinkled his nose and curled his lip, as if he'd never seen a starving man before.

"Did he say anything?" I hoped I didn't sound suspicious, but Billy knew who beat him.

Bodell smiled. Damn. "You know, I heard about your girlfriend. Seems she sweet-talked Tony Badamo and got herself clear." He shook his head. "I'm real disappointed you didn't tell me you knew where she was. You did owe me one," he said.

I was so close to being with Helen, leaving this all behind, and in a moment of rage, I'd blown it all. "He had it coming. My sister—"

He raised a hand to stop me. "I'd say you owe me fifty now," he said.

"What?" Surely I'd heard him wrong.

"He screamed your name all the way out to the gate. I say he tried to steal your wallet, and you fought back like anyone would. Wouldn't you say that's what happened?"

I slowly nodded. "But why are you doing this?"

"There's too much going on in the next few days to worry about a beggar that wasn't supposed to be here anyway. And besides, he didn't have fifty bucks to give me, and I figure you do." That smile again.

"I've got it in my dorm," I said.

He slapped me on the back, a little too hard. "Fine, fine. I'll stop by and see how you're doing after work. And Deal? I don't want to hear your name again. Causing trouble gets real expensive."

AUTHOR NOTE: IT HAD to happen. Ezra has held on to a lot of anger over his sister's death, and with all of the confusing emotions he's experiencing, it had to come out. But, like everything else, it will come back to haunt him.

Chapter 72: A Few More Days, and She'll Be Mine

Ezra

AS PROMISED, BODELL was waiting for me when I got back to the dorm. I paid him his money, and it was over. He tipped his hat and smiled, but as he turned to leave, I asked, "How did you know about Helen?"

He shot me an icy stare. "Don't worry about it. You worry about not lying to me anymore, and we'll get along just fine."

After he left, I showered, changed clothes, and counted the money I had left from cashing in my savings with Ida Browder earlier in the week. Three hundred fifty, plus it was payday, so I could sell my scrip and have another twenty-eight dollars. That was more than enough for Helen and me to leave.

After we turned the river, we would move on. The thought was bittersweet but a little sweeter knowing Helen would be with me this time. When I'd moved into the dormitories last year, I enjoyed my freedom, but after being with Helen for the past few weeks, I realized how very alone I was. I had been responsible for someone my entire life: my mother then Grace, and I missed that responsibility. What would come next, I didn't know, but with Helen, I felt anything was possible.

But I still wished things could be different. The excitement at work the past few days was something I'd never experienced. Two years, we'd gone through tunnels that choked us, heat that damn near burned us alive, and battled a mountain and a river that seemed set on letting us know that they were stronger than man. And we'd done it. Almost. In two days, we'd show the river that it could be tamed, that it could be changed. Maybe I could convince her to stay.

It was almost six o'clock, and I was standing outside the dorm, waiting for Helen.

"Got a date?" Moose said as he and Smitty walked up to where I was standing.

"Actually, I do." I couldn't help but smile. "How's the arm?" I said.

He flexed his right arm and showed off the large white bandage that covered the area of his wound from yesterday. "Just a scratch. I needed another scar anyway."

Smitty put a hand on my shoulder. "Moose told me you might be leaving; I hope you don't mind. I really wish you didn't have to go. You are part of our family now, and I'm going to miss you."

Her words stung in all the wrong places. My experience with having a family was not always pleasant. Other than my mother, then she died. Other than Grace, then she died. I always thought I wanted to join the military, but I now thought the only reason I ever wanted to do that was so I could be part of something—have brothers, others that I could count on and that counted on me. But the men I worked with had become my family.

"Thanks, Smitty. Maybe someday I'll be back with a family of my own." Or maybe I could convince Helen not to leave.

Over Smitty's shoulder, I saw the familiar Model T slowly moving toward us, and I let out a sigh of relief. Helen parked the car and was out and moving quickly toward Smitty, both women with their arms out. In a pretty green dress and heels, she looked like any other woman getting ready for a casual night in town. But she wasn't any other woman.

"Oh, Helen, you look lovely!" Smitty held her at arm's length and looked her up and down. I couldn't wipe the grin off my face because she was a beautiful woman. "I've been wanting to come to the mountain to see you, but I thought too much traffic would attract attention. I am so glad to see you. And I'm so sorry about everything, Helen. I came back for you, but you were gone. I heard later that you went to Vegas with Cotton, and I just figured everything was fine."

Helen waved a hand in the air. "It is fine, Miss Smitty. Now. And thank you for your help. Pete said you've been labeling and dressing up the salve for our big sale day." She glanced at me and smiled, and my entire body felt weak. I wanted to wrap myself around her and take her right there on the sidewalk, but instead, I put my arm across her shoulder and was surprised when she put her arm around my waist. "Where's Pepper?"

Smitty smiled. "He went with Chief's oldest, Danny, to the rec center. They seem to be getting along well."

Helen let out a slow breath. "I need to talk to him."

Moose and I exchanged a serious look. Helen rolled her eyes. "Did you two do something else without telling me? I swear, men and their—"

"Ezra told me you were upset, but—" Moose said.

She removed her arm from around me and stood with her legs apart, squaring with Moose. "No. Not upset. Downright angry. Disappointed. You went behind my back for no good reason, and I won't forget that. I need to talk to Pepper and find out what he really wants."

Moose nodded. "He'll be back to Smitty's in a few hours. We can—"

Helen laughed. "I'll talk to him tomorrow while all the men are at work. Tonight, I'm going to see if this town lives up to its hype."

"We're going to the movies. Wanna double-date?" Smitty said.

Helen turned to me, and I could tell by the look on her face that that was exactly what she'd like to do. I wanted her alone so bad I couldn't stand it, but just a few more days, and she'd be all mine. Until then, I could share.

AFTER FILLING OURSELVES with too much popcorn and soda pop, we walked alongside the building, cutting through the active construction site behind the theatre to take a shortcut back to Helen's car in the dorm parking area. Although Sims Ely, the city manager, had halted construction around the houses during sleeping hours, it was still full bore in this area of town.

Helen was excited and laughing, talking nonstop about the movie. "I can't believe it's air-conditioned! And twenty-four hours. No wonder it was packed. And Marlene Dietrich is even more beautiful than her pictures," she said.

"You're prettier," I said.

She lowered her head then looked off in the distance. We couldn't see the black mountains in the night, but we both knew they were there. "You love the mountains, don't you?" I said.

She shrugged. "Yes. They make me feel... free." She fidgeted a little then gave me a nervous smile. "You like it here too. I can tell how much Moose and Smitty care about you, and there's Pete and—"

I pulled her closer to me. "Then stay. I know you want to go away, but right now, this place is really great. But nothing lasts forever. The job won't be here in a few years, and I expect Pete and Moose will move on. Then we can go wherever you want."

She shook her head. "You are wrong. Some things do last forever." She looked at the clear night sky, searching, and then pointed. "There. The Big Dipper. It's been there forever, and I suspect it will be there forevermore."

"The what?" I tried to follow her finger but saw nothing but a sky full of stars.

"The Big Dipper. See those seven stars?" She traced the outline in the air with her finger.

I followed where she was pointing. "Oh, I see it. It looks like a big saucepan. How do you know about that?"

"From school," Helen said. "And there's more up there too. A fishhook, a butterfly, a kite. I haven't found them yet, but I will."

I looked at her in the moonlight—the sparkle of her eyes, the determination in her face—and I realized she was right. I also realized that if we were going to make it, we had to be honest with each other. And that started right now.

"Helen, I did something yesterday that I'm not proud of, but I did it."

She looked at me, concern etched on her face, or was it panic? "What did you do?"

I told her about Billy and about Bodell and about how it felt good while I was doing it but how scared I was afterward. "I honestly thought I'd have to leave today, before we finished this phase, and I knew you wanted to watch. But it all worked out," I said.

She didn't say anything, just turned back to her stars, and I didn't know whether that was good or bad.

"Spend the night with me," I said.

She laughed. "I can't spend the night in the dorms. I borrowed the pass to get in here from Pete, and he'll want it back."

"I can sneak you in. And I can give Pete his pass in the morning." Her lips were twisted up like she was thinking, so I added, "Please."

Finally, she shook her head. "Not tonight. I need to pack up all my things. Once I come back tomorrow, I'll need to stay here until it's over. Traffic is already bad, and I don't want to risk not getting back in. But I promise, tomorrow."

I lit up like the desert sun. Tomorrow. As I walked her to her car, I had a thought. Maybe the reason she hadn't mentioned us leaving was that she was having second thoughts. I needed to reinforce the option of staying right here, setting up housekeeping, and putting all our money away for something better someday.

Tomorrow, I'd give her that option. Tonight, I'd have to say goodbye.

AUTHOR NOTE: IT'S HARD to imagine that in just a little over a year, the town of Boulder City went from a few administrative buildings to a fully functioning small town, complete with cafes, a candy store, tennis courts, a rec center, an air-conditioned movie theatre, a hospital, and houses for the workers at the dam. But Boulder City was meant to be a model American city, a bright spot in the middle of the Great Depression, if you will, and the powers that be took that challenge seriously. For those living in the small town, it was an oasis of sorts in the desert. Today, with its small-town feel, historic and eclectic downtown area, and of course access to Lake Mead and the dam, it is still a unique city and one of my favorites to visit.

Even though Grand Hotel *won the Academy Award for Best Picture in 1932,* Shanghai Express, *starring Marlene Dietrich, was the top-grossing film of that year. Other interesting trivia about 1932: I mentioned earlier the Bonus Army, a group of over 40,000 protestors, who gathered in Washington to demand an early cash-out of World War I veterans' service bonus certificates. The US Attorney General ordered them removed from government property, they resisted, shots were fired, and two veterans were killed. President Hoover then used the US Army to evict them. Infantry, cavalry, and six tanks were sent to kick the protestors—veterans, wives, and children—out of their makeshift camp, and their camp and belongings were burned. This army effort was led by Douglas McArthur. Sounds like a great setting for a book!*

Chapter 73: Not My Story to Tell

Helen

I WANTED TO STAY. THE evening had been perfect, almost too perfect, up until the point that Ezra told me about Billy Greene. I knew his intention was to be open and honest with me, as if he were trying to establish that early in a relationship, and while the honesty was appreciated, the thought of a relationship scared me. The story itself appalled me.

I had loved Grace too. And I understood that Billy Greene had done her wrong—very wrong. And maybe a year ago, he deserved a punch or two from the overprotective older brother that Ezra was. But nothing good could come from beating a man almost to death. He was angry about Grace, probably somewhat about me, and I knew he was anxious about leaving Boulder City, and he had taken all of that out on a man and left him for dead in an alley. It made me ill.

He didn't want to leave Boulder City. He had endured Ragtown for the promise that the small town had offered and, for the past year, had been living it. It was a wonderful place, and I could appreciate it, but he didn't really want to leave. He had dropped small hints throughout the night, talking about the dances, the women's clubs, and the Thanksgiving spread that the mess hall had been advertising for all families coming in a few weeks. He didn't want to leave, but he would if I said I wanted it. And he would, I feared, become that overprotective man that might again, one day, let his inner rage dictate his actions.

I sat at the picnic table in front of Pete's camp and listened to the sounds around me. I remembered in Ragtown, there were some peaceful nights, the camp made up mostly of families, and many having a modicum of respect for that. Here, in Little Oklahoma, there was constant activity, as if the color of the sky meant nothing.

"I figured you would stay in town," Pete said as he came from behind the canvas and sat with me at the table. Mae was at work, and Sally and Marguerite were sleeping. Although I should have been sleeping as well, my mind wouldn't shut down.

I shrugged. "I came back to pack up my things. Tomorrow when I go in, I probably won't leave until after the river is turned."

He nodded. "I don't blame you for that. So what's on your mind?"

I liked Pete. He was smart, funny, and easygoing, and so far, had been open to all the "stray puppies," as he called us, that wandered to his door. If he was a friend, he was a good friend, without ever letting you think that he didn't come first. I admired that. But he was, ultimately, Ezra's friend, one of his best friends, and I knew better than to talk to him too much about Ezra.

"Did you see Ezra today?" I asked.

"Yeah, he ate lunch with us as usual. He seemed a little anxious, but he's been that way for about a week now. I figure you've got something to do with that."

I tilted my head and raised one brow. "Did he tell you about Billy Greene?"

Pete scrunched his face up as if thinking. "I've heard the name, but can't recall... No, he didn't say anything about it today. What about Billy Greene?"

I waved a hand. "Not my story to tell. I'm sure Ezra will say something to you and the guys. I was just wondering."

"You know, Helen, you can talk to me. I'm you friend too," he said.

I chuckled. "I suppose I'm already one of the big conversation points at lunch. I really don't need to give you any fodder for that."

He put a hand on his chest and faked offense. "Me? Sure, we talk about women, but we don't gossip like they do."

I outright laughed. "No, I suppose you don't. I suppose when you talk about women, it's about how you'd like to bed them, maybe marry them, possess them."

"Or protect them," he said.

"Exactly. Protect us. Have you ever considered what exactly you protect us from? What women's biggest threat is? Other men."

"A blessing and a curse. We are all imperfect beings trying to do what we think is necessary, sometimes right, in a world that right now isn't always just."

"I know," I said, looking down at my hands in my lap.

"Have you told him yet?" he said.

I looked up and searched his face. "Told him what?"

This time, he chuckled. "I've been around four women for the past few days and no less than two for a lot longer than that. You ladies may not tell me everything, but I hear a lot in passing, and believe it or not, I don't go to work and tell the guys everything."

He waited for me to answer, but I didn't say anything, so he continued. "Okay, here's the thing. If Ezra leaves with you, which is what he is planning to do at this point, you two imperfect souls can wander around and find yourselves and have someone you can depend on to protect and care for each other. Notice I said 'each other,' not just him taking care of you. Second, you could stay in Boulder City and get married, and it would be the same, only he'd have a job, and you'd both be around friends. Honestly, I think that is the option Ezra would like to see."

"And then there is option three," I said.

"Yes. Option three. And I would never think poorly of someone who wants to put themselves first. It's kind of my thing. He'll be heartbroken, for a while, but he'll get over it. He'll be fine."

I looked down and said nothing.

Pete stood and stretched. "You need to get some sleep. It's going to be a wild couple of days, and I know you don't want to miss it."

"No, I don't. I've got my camera loaded and extra film and a lot of salve to sell so that whatever I choose, I'll at least have money to do it." I stood and suddenly did feel ready for sleep. "Thank you, Pete. I really haven't made a decision yet, but I will."

He gave me a knowing smile. "Yes, you have." Then he made a zipping motion across his lips. "But, like you say, it isn't my story to tell."

I turned back toward the canvas and the waiting couch that welcomed me. He was correct. I had made a choice, and of all the people that I might disappoint or hurt, the one person I wouldn't let down was myself.

AUTHOR NOTE: LITTLE Oklahoma was the name of a real camp established by the Railroad Pass. Some of the others in the area were Little Texas, Picher (which is a small town in Oklahoma), and Dee's Camp. After the government evicted the homeless from Ragtown, McKeeversville, and anywhere else around Boulder City, these camps at the Pass, outside the gate, grew to be very large. While inside the gate, Boulder City was thriving, outside, the effects of the Great Depression were evident.

Chapter 74: Another Dead Indian

Helen

I HAD PLANNED TO BE at Miss Smitty's house by nine, but with the turning of the river scheduled for the next day, traffic was already thick with those wanting to watch. I didn't know if they planned on sleeping in the desert, or maybe in their cars, but by nine thirty, when I reached Boulder City, the town was alive with activity. I parked at the dormitories, again using Pete's pass to gain access, and decided to walk. I had something I needed to do before going to see Pepper and Smitty, and it was best if no one knew about it.

After my talk with Pete last night, it had all become clear to me. Thinking back over the previous few weeks, I realized a couple of things. I had never invited Ezra to leave with me. He was the one that proposed it, and although I never answered, he assumed I would agree. In fact, he assumed quite a bit. The biggest thing was that whether he left with me or we stayed in Boulder City, we would be together.

I guessed part of that was my fault. I did love Ezra. In a way, I always had. And when I was with him, I was sure my feelings toward him were apparent. I was sure he interpreted that as me wanting to be with him forever, regardless of the cost. And there was a cost. My freedom. My independence.

And what Ezra didn't realize and what I could never tell him was that when I wasn't with him, I dreamed of being far away. I thought of him at times, but it wasn't a longing to be with him. It was more of a fondness. Love, no doubt, but not the kind of love that would last a lifetime.

I stood in front of the Boulder City Police Department for a long time, considering my choice. Once I walked through those doors, there would be no turning back. Ezra would hate me. But as Pete had said, he'd get over it. Eventually.

I thought long and hard about what my father would say if he were there to guide me. I wanted to believe that he would say, "Do what is going to make you happy." And I didn't know exactly what that was. I was rolling the dice, making a bet, but in the end, I knew I had to bet on myself.

A little over a year ago, my father had told me to stay away from Bud Bodell, and from what I'd heard from others, that was sound advice. A year ago, I might have taken that advice. But I was not that fearful girl anymore. I knew what men like Tony Badamo, Cotton, and Bud Bodell wanted: power. Control. Money. I could give them money, and I could make them believe they were in control.

I watched women with their children playing in the city park across from the police station, others going in the candy shop, the movie theatre, the company store. It was ideal. But to me, it wasn't real. I took a deep breath, rolled the die, and walked into the police station to make a deal with Bud Bodell.

I WALKED THROUGH THE dirt streets of the residential area, looking for the address Smitty had given me the night before, and found myself surrounded by identical two-room houses lined in neat rows. Each structure was built in a large square, with a covered porch that extended off the front and around one side. Although the planners of the town had taken great pains to plant grass and meticulously landscape the common areas with a variety of plant life and flowers, they had obviously left the yards to the residents. Scraggly gardens of begonias, posies, and daffodils wilted from the desert heat, plants that were never meant to flourish in the desert. A few yards had planted native cacti and purple sage, which I thought were so much prettier than the ragged flowers that seemed out of place and were almost an affront to the natural beauty of the land.

I saw Smitty sitting on the porch, and when I approached, Pepper came running from the house and wrapped his arms around me. "Wait until you see what we've been doing," he said. He pulled me by the arm toward the house.

The air was filled with the lingering smell of cooked food, and my stomach growled in protest. I hadn't eaten since having popcorn at the theatre the night before, but food hadn't exactly been the top thing on my mind.

The inside of Smitty and George's house was sparse. A small wooden dining table with four non-matching chairs separated the small living area from the kitchen. In the living area, a worn red couch, with a tan blanket covering the back, occupied the center. The radio that sat on a wooden crate in the corner looked brand-new and out of place against the stark wall free from any pictures or additional paint. A bedroom led off from the main room, forming a large box shape.

Along one wall, twelve cases were neatly stacked. Pepper opened one and pulled out a jar of salve that had three thin ribbons, red, white, and blue, tied around the neck, the ends curled. A white label had been gummed in place on the top with the words "Ragtown Remedy, 1932" written neatly with a fountain pen.

"It was Miss Smitty's idea to add 1932," Pepper said. "I picked the ribbons."

I turned it in my hand, examining the simple yet pretty packaging on my homemade salve. "These are beautiful," I said.

"Donna Sue did all the writing. She has a much prettier script than I do," Smitty said.

"I can't begin to thank everyone. How much do I owe you for the ribbon, labels, and ink?" I said.

She waved a hand. "Ezra paid for it."

I sucked in a small breath. "Of course he did," I said.

"I'll be right back. Gatsby is outside, and I know he wants to see you too," Pepper said as he turned and ran out the door.

"I like your house," I said to Smitty as I placed the jar back in its case.

"Normally," she explained, "this big a house is reserved for families, but George was able to get it because he's a high-scaler and claimed that he had me to take care of."

"The high-scalers are kind of the stars of the show, aren't they?" I said.

She shook her head as she pulled a large flour sack from her pantry. "I think they are all crazy, George included."

"What about teaching? Aren't they opening the schools soon?"

She lowered her head for a moment then looked straight ahead. "The grade school is open. I've been offered a job at the high school, which is due to open next fall. I haven't taken it yet."

"Why not? That's wonderful!"

She shrugged. "Moose. That's why not. They won't hire me unless I'm single, and Moose hasn't officially proposed, but we talk about a future together frequently, and with Pepper..." She paused, looking at me for some response, which I did not give. "I love Moose, but I also love teaching. I hate that I'll have to make that choice," she said.

"Men don't have to make that choice. It makes me so mad," I said.

"It won't always be like that," she said without much conviction.

"I want to take Pepper for ice cream so we can talk," I said.

"Of course. Helen, know that we, Moose, George, and I, want to take care of him. We can give him a home. I don't want you to think—"

"He's not mine, Miss Smitty. He's my friend. I want what is best for him too," I said.

After getting reacquainted with Gatsby by stroking his cool skin, Pepper and I ventured off. We stopped by the dormitories first so I could retrieve my camera from the car and then went to the company store to purchase film. In the next two days, I intended to take a lot of pictures: of my friends, the dam project, the town, Ezra. Just thinking about him made my stomach hurt. I had to remind myself that I was doing what was in both of our interests, whether he understood or not.

"I see you're wearing Queho's pouch," I said.

His hands grazed the worn leather that hung at his side. "I can't take it off. It was one of his secrets, and I promised him I wouldn't tell."

Pepper seemed more like the child I had known in Ragtown, even if he was still claiming he had talked to Queho. He did at times go into himself, but for the most part, he was excited and generally happy. He pointed out all the places he had been in the previous days—the park, the stores, the rec center—and added, "Me and Danny wanted to go to the movies, but right now they are playing some kissy love-story thing."

I laughed. "You really seem to like it here, Pepper," I said.

He nodded several times. "I do! It's just what we always talked about. And they keep building things, and it's getting better every day." He stopped and looked at the ground.

"What's wrong?"

"We could stay, you know. Mr. Moose said he could get a house soon, and you and Ezra could, you know, get a house too." He looked at me hopefully, and when I didn't say anything, he said, less enthusiastically, "But, I'm sure when we leave, we'll find someplace to have fun too."

We stopped at the park, and I sat Pepper on a bench to take his picture. Green grass surrounding a bed of roses in red, yellow, and pink rose up the slope behind the bench, providing a beautiful, if not unnatural, background. "Smile," I said.

He stuck out his chin, straightened his back, and gave me his widest grin. "Perfect," I said as I sat down next to him on the bench.

I wanted Pepper to stay. I knew everyone else was subtly trying to tell me it would be best for him, and I was glad they didn't just come out and say it, because I knew myself, and I probably would have rejected their advice on principle alone. Deep in my heart, I knew what was best for him. But I would not make that decision for him.

I took a deep breath and chose my words carefully. "I can't stay here. It's lovely, and it's everything we always talked about, but I can't stay here on my own, on my terms. I know that sounds selfish of me, and maybe it is, but our first responsibility has to be to ourselves."

He looked at me, a sadness shadowing his face. "Okay. Where are we going?"

I squeezed his shoulder. "I am choosing to leave for me and me alone. I want you to do the same, Pepper. If you want to stay, and I think you do, I want you to stay. Moose and Smitty can give you so much that I never will be able to."

I saw his eyes moisten. "But we promised to take care of each other."

A hard knot formed in my stomach, but I continued. "Yes, we did. But sometimes, the best way to take care of someone is to let them take care of themselves."

His brow furrowed. I knew he didn't quite understand that, but I also knew, someday, he would.

We got up and walked toward the ice cream parlor as I had promised, stopping to take a few pictures along the way, wanting to get back to Miss Smitty's before the men came home from work. Smitty was making a big dinner and inviting several people, a party of sorts, before the show began the next day. The town was electrified, and there were activities planned everywhere, but I think Smitty had the right idea: spend the evening with family and friends. Those who had suffered to complete this phase, those who understood what it took to get to this point. It would be my going-away party, although most, including Ezra, would not know that.

As we walked back toward the houses, Pepper stopped me with a hand. He cleared his throat. "Will you write to me? If I stay?"

"Of course I will. And when I find my place, and you are older, you can come and visit, and bring Gatsby, and tell me all about school and Boulder City, and watching Moose and Ezra build the dam, and—"

"I thought Ezra was going with you?"

I let out a long sigh. "Can I tell you a secret?"

He smiled. "It's not another dead Indian, is it?"

AUTHOR NOTE: MARRIAGE *bars, the policies held by many states that banned married women from working to some extent, became even more prevalent during the Great Depression. Women were degraded for working, called selfish for wanting their "pin money." In*

1932, the US government even joined in the bars. Section 213 of the Economy Act of 1932 required that one member of a married couple who worked for the government be fired from their position. Although this was repealed five years later, it wasn't until the 1940s, when the country needed women to fill key positions to support the war efforts, that this trend began to change.

Chapter 75: We Could Stay Here Forever

Ezra

THE ACTIVITY AND EXCITEMENT around the work site had reached a level that could be called nervous anticipation. The tunnels were complete, and many of us spent the entire day checking a tunnel, inch by inch, for possible weak areas or fractures that could risk the integrity of the tunnel itself. Then we checked it again. Four tunnels, almost a mile long each, would soon be holding the entirety of the flow of the Colorado River, and they had to hold. Diverting the river would leave a dry riverbed, and on that, we would build a dam.

Well, they would build a dam—my friends, my brothers. I would be off to some unknown destination with Helen. Damn. As I peered out the end of tunnel number four and watched the high-scalers, whose job, it seemed, would never be done, I thought about how poor this plan was. Lack of a plan was more like it. I wanted to go with Helen, or at least I wanted to be with Helen, but it was my life too. I had basically left it all up to her, as if I were a puppy that was willing to follow wherever she chose to go.

I could imagine that my father would call me weak, allowing a woman to make all the decisions, but maybe it was my desire to avoid being the overcontrolling ass that he was that made it easy for me to simply follow. Or maybe I was weak. Either way, I felt somewhat helpless, and I didn't like it. I had to know where we were going and what she—what we—planned to do once we got there. Otherwise...

Otherwise, what?

Otherwise, we could stay here until we had a good plan, a solid plan. I shook my head. Originally, there was some urgency to leave, but now, since Helen had taken care of her marriage and her legal problems, there wasn't. In fact, we could stay here forever if we wanted to. I looked out across the site and tried to imagine the massive slab of concrete we—they—would wedge into this canyon and found myself smiling.

I turned to walk back through the dark tunnel to the opening, nearly a mile away. My shift was almost over, and I would shower and change in the dorm before Smitty's get-together. Then tonight, Helen and I would talk. Maybe I could convince her to stay here. At the very least, she had to tell me where we were going.

A hard slap on the back brought me out of my thoughts. My flashlight had been trained on the wall of the tunnel, and I hadn't even noticed Chief coming from behind me. "Just think, this will be our last walk in one of these tunnels. They'll soon be full of water instead of men."

"Yeah," I said, unable to mimic his excitement.

"You haven't been very talkative today," he said.

I shrugged. "Got a lot on my mind."

"I'm listenin'," he said.

"You know, when I came out here, I didn't have any reason to stay in New Hampshire. Grace was all I had, and when she said, 'Let's go,' I didn't even think twice. We were running toward something, even if it was a little crazy. But now, it seems I'm running away from something good, and running toward... I don't know."

"You're having second thoughts about leaving. What does Helen have to say about that?"

"Nothing. We haven't talked about any of this. We haven't really talked at all," I said.

"Well, I'm not one to give advice, but I'll say this. Everything you get, you have to give something up for it. It's up to you to decide if what you're giving up is worth it," he said.

"She's worth it," I said automatically.

"That's what I keep hearing. I can't wait to meet her tonight. And as much as I hate to see you go, I'll wish you the best and try to build this dam without ya." He turned his flashlight toward the entrance. "Let's get out of here. We've done all we can do. Tomorrow is a new day."

To my surprise, Helen was waiting for me in the lobby of the dorm as I was leaving to walk to Smitty and George's house for the party. She was sitting on the bench, wearing a summery dress covered with flowers. Her hair was pulled back with two clips, and her lips were shiny with a pinkish gloss. She stood and smiled when she saw me, and the entire lobby lit up. I took her in my arms, and she seemed to melt into me. "What are you doing here?" I asked.

"I was getting a little stir-crazy sitting around the Goons' and thought you might like a walking companion," she said.

I let her go, held her hand, and led her out the door. "I will never turn down your company," I said.

She was in such a good mood, commenting on all the people that had filled the small town and telling me about her day. I hated to break the magic and get serious, but this was as good a time as any and might be the only time we were alone until later that evening.

"Helen, I need to know—"

"San Francisco. I've got everything I own packed in the trunk, and Sally will have her things ready as soon as the diversion is over."

"Sally?"

"You met her the other night. Tall, blond?"

I frowned. "Yes, I remember, but I didn't know she was going too."

"Oh. Uh, yes. She has to get out of here. If she stays, well, I hate saying this, but as much as we love Mae, she doesn't want to end up like her. San Francisco is a fresh start for both of us. I want to look into going to college. It's what my dad would have wanted."

"It's a fresh start for all of us," I corrected.

"Yes," she said quickly and squeezed my hand.

Sally was going with us. That changed things. I understood her circumstances. It was difficult for a woman to get a job of any kind, but the Sallys of the world had it even harder. Sure, she could try to get a café job like Helen had had, or even a cocktail waitress job like Marguerite, but as soon as her employer found out she had been a prostitute, which wouldn't take long considering the chances of a past customer seeing her at work, she would be gone. There were too many "good" girls out there to keep the Sallys around. And marriage was even harder. Who wanted to marry a whore? Their only options, save for a lucky few, were to stay in the field, as Mae had done, or leave town and leave their past behind. I sucked in a deep breath.

"What's wrong?" she said.

"Nothing. My leg is just getting tired," I said as we approached the Goons'.

George, Chief, and Moose sat on the porch, while Pepper, Chief's four kids, and a few others from the neighborhood played tag in the yard. Helen released my hand and went in to help Smitty and Donna Sue, and I sat on the stoop and joined in the talk about work. Within minutes, the women joined us. Smitty called for the kids to gather around, and Moose stood and cleared his throat.

"Now that everyone is here, we have a few things to tell everyone." He waited until the kids were settled then wrapped an arm around Smitty's waist. I knew what was coming and wanted to see Helen's reaction, but she had her camera in front of her face, wanting to capture the moment.

"Smitty said she'd take care of me, so I bought her a ring," Moose said. Smitty elbowed him in the side playfully and stuck out her hand for all to see. Everyone clapped and cheered, and when Helen lowered her camera, she was smiling. I liked that. I could picture her on the porch of our own house, showing a ring to our friends.

"And"—Moose motioned for Pepper, who had grabbed Gatsby and let him wrap around his arm—"if we're going to get married, we thought we might need a kid too. So we found a good one. Pepper's decided to stay with us, and we couldn't be happier." Another round of cheers and claps followed, and this time, I noticed Helen watching me for my reaction. Sally may need to leave town, but surely Helen didn't want to leave Pepper. He'd been her friend and runaway buddy, and they had a bond. Maybe I could still convince her that staying right here was our best option.

Pepper tugged on Smitty's arm, and she nodded. "Also," she said, and she glanced at Helen. I felt my face warm. "Pepper and Little Dan went uptown this afternoon with a case of Ragtown Remedy, and I have to say, these two have a real future in sales."

Helen cocked her head and looked at Pepper, who just shrugged. "We want to go back after dinner and take Gatsby," Pepper said.

Moose laughed and rubbed his head. "Seeing as you got two dollars a jar without him, I expect letting those city folks pet a snake will get you even more."

"Two dollars?" Helen gasped. "You got two dollars a jar?"

Little Dan spoke up. "Pepper told them it was made by two kids who lost their daddies working at the dam. He said they hid out in the mountains, fought off rattlesnakes and Indians to make it." Everyone laughed, except Helen and Pepper, who shared a knowing glance.

It was George who finally stood up and said, "Okay, let's eat. We all need to get to bed early. Tomorrow is going to be one hell of a day."

AUTHOR NOTE: I CAN'T help but feel an amazing amount of sympathy for the prostitutes during this time, as you can probably tell by my treatment of them in this book. That is why, in this book, I needed to "save" one, or at least give her a chance at something better.

Chapter 76: Let's Not Talk About Tomorrow

Ezra

DINNER WAS FESTIVE, and afterward, the kids—all five of them, with a snake in tow—took three cases of Helen's salve and headed to town. It was starting to get dark, and she worried they would be out too late and offered to go with them and walk them back.

"They're fine," Donna Sue, Chief's wife, said. "This place is safe, even at night."

Helen shot me a glance. Well, not safe if you were a vagabond named Billy Greene, I thought, and I hoped she wasn't thinking the same.

After the dishes were all cleaned up, Chief stood and stretched. "Let's get out of here. I want to be wide-eyed in the morning," he said to Donna Sue.

Helen stood, too, and reached for my hand. She had said last night she would stay with me tonight, and I was glad she hadn't forgotten. I had been wanting to wrap myself around her all evening, and now, I'd be able to do just that and, at the same time, make my case for staying here.

We stopped at her car to get a few things she needed out of her trunk, and I distracted the front desk clerk while she made her way to the stairwell. By the time we got to my room, we were both laughing like two kids that stole a penny licorice from the general store.

She pulled a small music box out of her pack and opened it. The tinny sound was a Christmas song that I recognized but didn't know the words to. "Where did you get that?" I asked.

"From a friend. I like the sound of it. It reminds me of home," she said.

"Kansas?"

She smiled. "I don't know. I guess home in general. Kansas, the desert, my daddy... all the things I love. Home."

"This could be home," I said. "We have friends here, and Pepper is here, and we could have a life. Right here," I said.

She looked at me without saying anything. I couldn't read the expression on her face.

She dug in her pack again and said, "I have something for you."

I took the piece of paper she held out to me. It was a picture she had taken in the desert, a close-up of a large turtle making its way across the desert floor. With round legs shaped like an elephant's, it seemed to struggle to lift its high dome off the ground. Its small, snakelike head was raised high.

I looked at the photo in the moon's light that shone through my window. "Is it a male or a female?"

"Definitely a male," Helen said. She pointed at a spot on his lower front shell, under his neck. "See that part of the shell that comes out from underneath? If it was female, it would be short and flat. His is longer and angled up. That's how he flips his opponents over in a fight."

I looked at her as she spoke and then back to the photo.

"He reminds me of you," she said.

I smiled. "I know I'm slow with this bad leg, but a turtle?"

"It's a tortoise, actually, which is a specific kind of turtle, and it has nothing to do with your leg," she said. She took the picture from me, sat on my cot, and motioned for me to sit next to her. "He likes to be in his space—he's comfortable there. He burrows in and makes it his home. He's kind of shy. And he's very special," she said.

I took the picture from her and put it on my bedside table. "Thank you," I said.

I put my arm around her and pulled her close. "Tomorrow, after the river is turned, I'll come back here and pack my stuff, and we can go." I looked around my small room. "Or we can stay right here, and I'll go apply for one of the houses right down the street from where Pepper will be."

She pulled back, sat on my lap, put her arms around my neck, and kissed me. "Let's not talk about tomorrow," she said.

That was fine with me.

AUTHOR NOTE: THE DESERT tortoise was put on the endangered species list in 1989, and while you can have one as a pet, Nevada has some very tricky rules about the legality of this. For instance, since they are endangered and are wildlife, technically, they belong to the people of the state of Nevada. So if you have one, you don't actually own it, but you are its custodian. If you would like to be a custodian for a desert tortoise, remember, they can live up to 100 years in captivity, so you will need to make arrangements for a forever home once you are gone.

Chapter 77: Las Vegas Age #273 November 13, 1932

Ezra

NOVEMBER 13-14, 1932
    EXTRA!
    DIVERSION OF COLORADO STARTS TODAY
    RECORD CROWD VISITS DAM PROJECT
    Las Vegas Age #273 November 13, 1932

THE EMPLOYEE PARKING lot was full when Moose, Chief, and I arrived at six thirty a.m. We'd picked up a few other guys along the way, and the sedan was at capacity. After driving around the lot for ten minutes, Chief shot across the desert and started a new line of parking outside the general zoned area.

I saw Pete jump off the train, and I joined him, while Moose and Chief headed for a group of other men who were talking to Frenchie.

"Helen never came back to the mansion last night," Pete said.

"She stayed with me. We're going to meet when this is all over, and from there, I guess San Francisco is the destination." I didn't say that was the extent of the plans we had talked about. What we would do once in San Francisco, I hadn't pushed at the time. We were busy with other things, and I guessed it would all work out. I was still hoping she'd change her mind and decide we should stay.

Pete cocked his head. "So she laid it all out for you like that, huh?"

"Well, no, not exactly. We got a little sidetracked and... Somethin' you ain't telling me, Pete?" I felt a little uneasy. Pete was acting strange, like he was hiding something, and I didn't like it.

He raised both his hands in the air. "Not a thing. I'm just a little on edge today."

"She did tell me Sally was coming with us," I said.

Pete smiled. "She's a good woman. Deserves a chance. What about Pepper?" he asked.

"He's staying with Moose and Smitty, so it looks like things will work out for everyone," I said.

Pete nodded. "I'm sure they will."

Pete snapped his fingers and smiled. "I didn't get a chance to tell you yesterday, but I got a promotion. I'm going to be supervising the colored crew for the next phase. Seems they won't work for anybody but Charlie Rose, and he's going to Denver for a bit."

"Think they'll work for you?" I said.

He smiled. "Of course. All you got to do is respect a man, and he'll work. Doesn't matter what color his skin is."

"So you're definitely staying," I said more as a statement than a question.

"I figure once this thing is done, they're still going to need people to man it. They'll also need bankers in town soon, so I've got options. And I've grown kind of partial to this dry desert living." He stopped before we got to our group of friends talking with Frenchie. "If you go away for a bit and want to come back, there'll be a job for you. I'll pull whatever strings I have to to make that happen."

"It's gonna be a zoo out here," Chief said.

Pete snorted. "Yeah, it's going to be at least that. Where you all at today?"

Chief pointed a thumb at two of the truck drivers that routinely brought cement to the tunnel. "I'm double ugly with these two today."

"Rock pile for me," Pete said. "Loading trucks with my new crew."

"I'm at tunnel four," Moose said. "We've got to clean the debris from the blast after they blow that cofferdam and before the water hits the tunnel."

"You held me in reserve, Frenchie," I said. "Where are you sending me?"

Frenchie looked at his clipboard, shifting it to catch the light of the rising sun. "Go with Moose. I'll mark you off at number four."

"Well, this is it," Pete said. "Gonna be a hell of a day."

AUTHOR NOTE: THE Las Vegas Age *was one of the early newspapers, founded in 1905, before Las Vegas was even a city. It was published until 1947. Thanks to my good friends at the Nevada State Museum, I was able to find edition #273 on microfilm in order to get the headline at the beginning of this chapter.*

Chapter 78: Not Going to Miss It

Helen

I COULDN'T TELL HIM. Last night had been a night to remember, and as I walked out of the dorm, straight past the wide eyes of the desk clerk, I knew that a memory was all I would have. I could have handled this in so many different ways, and I must have been crazy for telling Bud Bodell about Ezra, but hindsight was always better than foresight, and what was done was done. I still had until tomorrow to find Bodell and change my mind. But I had to think about myself.

I hit the wheel of the car several times in frustration. Damn, I felt so selfish. He loved me, he trusted me, and what did I do with that? I trusted Bud Bodell, the man my dad had warned me to stay away from, to hold him back; that was what I did with it. It was deception and betrayal in the worst way, when all I had to do was tell him. It was the coward's way, and Ezra was going to suffer for it.

I tried to hold my head up high. I had to think of myself, no matter the cost. I wasn't that sweet girl from Kansas as Sally had suggested. And I couldn't be if I were going to survive in this world. Ezra would get over it, he'd get over me, and we could both move on with our lives. I blinked back tears that threatened to fall. It still felt as if I'd drilled a hole in my own heart.

But there was also Sally. It wasn't that I was choosing her over Ezra. But she was fine with Ezra, Pepper, even Mae going with us if they wanted to. But Ezra—I saw the disappointment when I told him about Sally, and I saw the joy when he heard Pepper was staying. I also realized he wanted to talk me out of leaving, regardless of Sally. All he really wanted was me, and all I really wanted was to go somewhere and start over.

"I hear the reservation gates have been swinging all morning with visitors coming to see the river turn," Smitty said as I approached her porch. "They've closed Lookout Point and already barred anyone from the work site, except for a few VIPs and news crews."

"I know some better places than Lookout Point, if you don't mind a little hike," I said.

Smitty smiled. "You know as well as I do that the men aren't the only ones who have worked for this. I've spent almost two years in this desert, and I am not going to miss it."

"I figured you'd say that."

Smitty dug in her pocket. "The kids are already out this morning with more salve to sell. All five of them went this time. Here's your money from last night." She smiled as I counted it.

"This can't be right. Two hundred fifty dollars?"

"Two dollars a jar for the four cases total. With the snake and Pepper's sad stories, they got some pretty good tips. They said one man gave them a five-dollar bill and didn't even take the salve."

I shook my head. "That sounds like begging. I appreciate the money, but..."

"Helen, the story is true, basically. And for those that buy the salve, it's worth the money. Just appreciate it. You'll need it," she said.

"I don't want Pepper to miss this, though. We've talked about it nonstop." I wouldn't let him miss it.

"He won't. I told him to be at the train stop by eleven, and I'd meet him there and show him where we were sitting."

"You are going to be a good mom, Miss Smitty. I'm glad Pepper decided to stay."

She smiled but waved a dismissive hand. "It likely won't happen until sometime tomorrow, I hear, but I'd like to see the start of it and watch for a while today. Then we can come back here and sleep and be back before sunup, if that works for you," she said.

One more day. I knew Sally was ready and would be listening for news of the progress at the Pass, and she'd figure out that I'd stayed in town. She knew I was not going to miss this.

Donna Sue knocked on the door and carried blankets and a basket of food. It was nine a.m., and I figured if we left then and parked at Hemenway Wash, we could walk the trail that the men used to take to work and find a good spot to watch from before they began by noon. Smitty had a picnic basket full of food and drinks, enough to feed several people. We didn't know exactly when the river was going to start on a different course, but we intended to be there when it did.

AUTHOR NOTE: I HATE perfect characters, don't you? Helen may be independent, headstrong, and a girl everyone wants to love, but everyone has flaws. Scheming with Bodell at this point can't be good, and she knows it, but she'd rather do that than give up her own dream. Selfish? Maybe. A little cowardly? Absolutely. Even kind of mean, considering she claims to love Ezra. But nobody is perfect.

Chapter 79: Diverting the River

Ezra

AT ELEVEN A.M., THE drivers climbed in their big trucks, ready with their first load of rock and gravel. The upper cofferdam had been built on the Nevada side about halfway across the river, forcing the water to flow along the Arizona side. At the sound of a starter pistol, the trucks would drive in a continuous stream across the trestle bridge two hundred feet downriver from the diversion tunnels and drop their loads then circle back to the rock pile for reloading and get back in the truck line. The goal was to build up a dam of rock faster than the river could wash it away, which would cause the water to go through the lowest Arizona tunnel first, tunnel number three.

Throughout the morning, Moose and I had been taking direction from Charlie Shea. When the dynamiting began, he explained to us first thing that morning, the first charge would be the blowing of the concrete barrier that had been built to prevent overflow of water into the tunnels while they were being bored. The starter pistol would be our signal to begin clearing the massive amounts of debris from in front of the fifty-six-foot-diameter opening of the tunnel. We had one truck—the rest were in use at the bridge—and most of the work would have to be done with no more than shovels and the strength of a hundred men. It would take several hours to clear the debris, working nonstop, and our goal was to get as much cleared as possible before the river turned.

Despite nearly two years of work, there were still some who questioned whether the tunnels would hold the force of the Colorado River. If not, we'd be in danger from the overflow, since the water would try to find an outlet—any outlet. Anxiety was high. As we got closer to the start time, a general breakdown in the work occurred as men began to lose focus on their tasks. Several paced back and forth, while others shut their eyes and raised their heads toward the heavens.

Moose and I were high. We had full faith that the tunnels would hold—hell, we'd broken our backs to make sure they would—and today, we'd get to see the results of our work. We didn't care if we had to stay all night. We were not leaving until the river left its path and flowed the way we wanted it to.

Charlie spat on the ground, a habit I hadn't noticed until today. "They're firing up the trucks. Get ready, men," he yelled to our rag-tag band of workers as we stood outside the massive tunnel.

I looked across the river at the mountains. Lookout Point was all but deserted, but the mountain was dotted with people. It looked as though everyone in the state had made the trip to watch this show. But I was only concerned with one.

At eleven thirty, the entire canyon shook as the barrier to the Arizona tunnels exploded, followed by over three thousand sequenced charges along the Arizona and Nevada walls, throwing every bit of loose rock into the water below for ten full minutes. As the gray cloud from the blasts started to clear, a single shot sounded and echoed through the canyon.

We knew this was our cue to get to work, but we waited a few more minutes, watching, as the army of trucks, one by one, assaulted the trestle bridge.

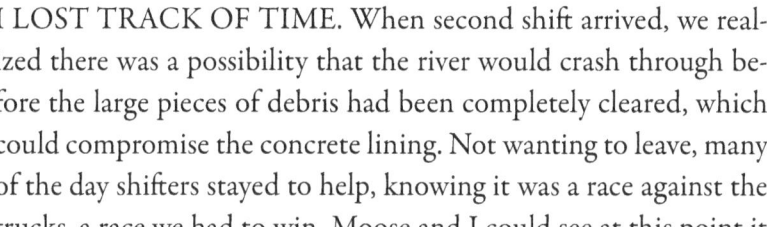

I LOST TRACK OF TIME. When second shift arrived, we realized there was a possibility that the river would crash through before the large pieces of debris had been completely cleared, which could compromise the concrete lining. Not wanting to leave, many of the day shifters stayed to help, knowing it was a race against the trucks, a race we had to win. Moose and I could see at this point it was going to go well through the night, so we took our break then and planned to be back to work by midnight.

We found Chief, his face masked in chalky sediment, and he was happy to give his truck to the next man. The massive amounts of dust that had been expelled from the earlier blasts, combined with the continuous cloud caused by the dumping, had made it very difficult for him to breathe. He planned to go home and sleep it off, but he wanted to watch the work with us for a few hours first. We knew we'd never find the women in the mountains above us, so we found a safe spot high on the Nevada side, under an outcropping that provided shade from the afternoon sun, where we could watch the work ourselves.

For hours, the trucks drove over the bridge, with as many as four at a time dropping their loads simultaneously before crossing and circling back to be reloaded. "They're unloading fifty tons of earth and rock every sixty seconds," Chief said, "and it's hard to see from here, but the cofferdam has been rising underwater hour by hour. And they will keep going all through the night."

From our vantage point, we watched as hundreds of men scrambled to reload trucks at the rock pile. I tried to pick out Pete, the one redhead amongst the colored crew, but with everyone covered in soot and dust, they all looked the same. Across the river, more men furiously cleared debris from the explosion of the cofferdam that had been protecting the tunnels. But the seemingly endless line of trucks, crossing the bridge and dumping their loads, was hard to turn away from. It was as if they were in a continuous tango: a dance with a raging river they intended to lead.

AUTHOR NOTE: I THOROUGHLY enjoyed writing this chapter. While the excitement surrounding the project and the number of people who came to watch is apparent, the general anxiety, anticipation, and emotion of the workers, as well as the technical aspects of how they intended to divert the river through the tunnels, made this a lot of fun to write.

Chapter 80: The Return of Cotton

Helen

WHEN I WAS LITTLE, one of my favorite outings with Daddy was to go to the bank on his payday to watch the skeleton clock they had in their lobby. The walnut-and-glass frame stood taller than Daddy, and a large pendulum swung back and forth in front of three brass chimes of different sizes. The hour, minute, and second hands moved smoothly, continuously, each at a different speed, while the pendulum swung back and forth, back and forth. The clock had glass walls on all four sides, so you could walk around it and see the insides at work. The various wheels and gears turned constantly, at different angles, different speeds, and all were interconnected, somehow related, all dedicated to the effort of making the face, the hands, continue to move, minute by minute, second by second. One large gear moved very slowly, one tick per minute, its tension building until the top of the hour, when it would release and swing wildly, resetting itself as the chimes played their melody. Then it would begin again.

Watching the trucks move across the wooden-framed bridge and dumping their rocks, the men at various sites removing chunks of concrete following the large blasts that had rumbled through the canyon, others loading the trucks with more rock, moving in synchronized motions of nonstop activity, I was reminded of that clock. The dam of rock that was building slowly under the water would eventually cause the river to swing to its left, out of the only path it had known since the beginning of time.

It was the most amazing thing I'd ever seen, and I couldn't imagine that it would ever be equaled in my lifetime.

Smitty, Donna Sue, the kids, and I watched for hours, pointing out various aspects of the site to one another, trying to imagine where Ezra, Moose, Pete, and George were at any time, speculating on how long it would take for the rock that was slowly rising under the surface to begin to force the river in its new direction. I took an entire roll of film, using the long lens to get better shots, and by five o'clock, we were all exhausted from the excitement and made our way back to town. The kids had sold all five boxes of salve before meeting us at the train stop at eleven, and Pepper had handed me another three hundred forty dollars. Almost seven hundred dollars was what I had now, one hundred of which I still owed to Ezra, and still three cases of salve to go.

It took us almost an hour to go the few miles from the Wash to Smitty's house, and when we got there, George was lying on the porch, his boots off and his feet resting on one of the porch chairs. When he saw us, he turned his head and smiled but didn't bother to change position. "I haven't had a chance to tell you, but you sure look all grown up," he said to me.

"It's been good to see you, too, George. And your feet," I said.

"I'm usually sitting on one of those swinging chairs all day, but they had us all running in circles today. My feet aren't used to that kind of wear," he said. "Did you watch?"

"Of course," Smitty said. "It's unbelievable. I can't even describe it."

"That's what is unbelievable. Between the two of you, I'd think you would have all kinds of words for it."

Pepper giggled at his jab and sat on the porch, digging through the lunch basket, looking for more to snack on.

"Monumental," I said.

George winked at me. "There you go. I knew it wouldn't take long."

"We're going to eat and sleep for a few hours before going back. We don't want to miss it," Smitty said.

"It'll be morning," he said. "I'd say if you get there just before the sun comes up, you'll have a show that will make today look like a teaser."

"Did you see Moose or Ezra today?" Smitty asked. I noticed when she talked of Moose, her face turned rosy, and her eyes brightened. I knew Smitty was truly in love, and from the way they acted together, I'd have said it was mutual. I was happy for her, if not a little jealous. Of course, I knew that I loved Ezra, too, but it was different. When I was with him, I couldn't get enough. But I hadn't thought much about him this afternoon, at least not in a romantic way. Maybe it wasn't love at all. It certainly wasn't something I felt we could build a future on.

"They are both at tunnel number three," he said. "The one where the river will be flowing through first. I didn't see them after our shift, but a lot of the guys were sleeping out there and going back in the middle of the night so they could be there when it happens."

"That would be Moose and Ezra," Smitty said. She moved past him and opened their front door, and I followed.

After a few minutes, we heard a commotion on the porch and headed to the door to investigate. George was arguing with someone, but I couldn't hear what he was saying. As Smitty opened the door, she said, "Oh, no." I followed her onto the porch, and there stood Cotton.

My ex-husband.

"I figured you'd be here if you weren't at your boyfriend's," he said with a sneer. It'd been almost a month since I had seen him last, and he looked like he'd aged five years. His hair was uncut, and he hadn't shaved in a while. His clothes were wrinkled, and he'd lost weight. When he moved closer to me, I turned my head to avoid the stench of body odor mixed with whiskey.

"Go away, Cotton. It's over," I said. George was standing, barefoot, and moved by my side.

Smitty grabbed Pepper's hand and whispered for him to go inside. Reluctantly, he did as he was told.

"Get off my porch, Cotton, before I make you get off," he said.

Cotton ignored George and grabbed my arm. "You want to leave? Well, let's go, honey. I hear you got a pack full of money and a tank full of gas in your daddy's car. After you making me look like a fool with Tony, I need to get out of here anyway."

George got between us and pushed Cotton away from me. He stumbled as he fell off the porch and into the yard. "Leave her alone, Cotton. I'm warning you."

Cotton sat on the ground and laughed. "You're warning me?" He reached into his pocket, pulled out a small gun, and pointed it straight at George. "Now I'm warning you. I've come for my wife, and I ain't leaving without her."

George moved so he was standing in front of Smitty and me, and from behind him I yelled, "Cotton, don't do this."

"Don't do what? You mean this?"

A shot rang out and echoed through the small neighborhood, and I felt myself being pulled to the ground. Miss Smitty had both arms around me, and George was now crouched in front of us. We both reached for him at the same time, and he turned to us and nodded. I looked around him, and standing at the front of my car, twenty feet from Cotton, was Bud Bodell, his gun drawn and pointing at Cotton.

"Now, firearms are against the law in this town," he said. "So I figure you've got about two seconds to drop yours before I make this next bullet count." He moved closer to Cotton, his gun still trained on him, and finally, Cotton dropped his gun and put his hands over his head.

Bodell hauled him to his feet and cuffed him then led him to his waiting car and put him in the back seat.

"Oh, my," Smitty said. "Thank goodness you were there!"

George wasn't as happy to see him. "What are you doing here?" he said.

Bodell walked back toward the porch, looking at me. "Mrs. Vaughn told me he might be coming to town, so I've been keeping close. Good thing, wouldn't you say?"

George looked at me, and I stood and straightened my blouse, smoothed my hair, and put my shoulders back.

Bodell motioned with his head for me to move off the porch, away from George and Smitty. I knew I wouldn't be able to explain this to them, and I didn't even look in their direction as I followed him to his car. We moved to the front, away from Cotton and out of earshot of the Goons.

"You haven't come back to see me like you promised," he said.

I looked at my feet. "I know. I was going to this evening. It looks like they won't be done until the morning."

He pointed toward the car. "I can hold him for twenty-four hours. So if you plan to go, you better do it while I've got him occupied too."

I bit my lip. "Okay, two o'clock tomorrow. That should be plenty of time to see the work at the dam and..." And what? I thought. And make up my mind for sure.

"Two o'clock at Browder's Café. See ya there."

"What if I change my mind?" I asked.

He chuckled. "Well, you could always just tell me, but you won't get a refund."

I glanced back at his car, feeling a little sorry for Cotton but not much. "Thank you," I said.

He put his hands on his hips and lifted his chin. "Now, please tell me other than this one and Deal, you haven't got any more boyfriends or ex-husbands to worry about. My jail's going to fill up fast if you do."

I WENT WITH PEPPER and Little Dan that evening into town to sell the last three cases of salve. People were everywhere, already celebrating, and I watched the two boys work the crowd. I couldn't help but smile. Pepper was in a comfortable place, he had made a friend, and it made me happy.

When we got back to Smitty's, I counted all the money that we'd made. I had over eight hundred dollars. I took out one hundred for Ezra and handed Pepper three hundred dollars. His mouth dropped open. "That's your half," I said. It wasn't exactly half, but I knew he'd understand.

"No," Smitty said. "He doesn't need the money."

"He'll need it for college. It will be a good start," I said. "I said I'd take care of you, and this, I can do."

Pepper looked at the money in his hand for a long time then set it on the table. "Helen, when you're gone, do you care if me and Little Dan make more of the stuff? You taught me how, and we can gather all the brush." He stopped and looked at Smitty. "On the weekends, not on school days. And only a few jars at a time." He smiled.

"I think that's a great idea, Pepper. As long as you promise to use the money to save for college one day." Why hadn't I thought to suggest that? "If it's okay with Moose and Miss Smitty," I added.

"Only if Moose or Chief go with you into the mountains. I've never felt right about you two being up there with that Indian running around," Smitty said.

Pepper agreed, trying to sound serious, then turned to me and made a zipper motion across his mouth. Our secret. Forever.

He handed the money in his hand back to me. "Here. You need it more than me, and I'll make ten times that!" I didn't doubt he would.

"You have to do me one big favor after I'm gone," I said. I took one hundred dollars from the pile of bills and handed it to Miss Smitty, who tried to refuse it, but I pressed it in her hand. "There are four graves at Woodlawn Cemetery that need real headstones. I trust you to pick them out and see that they get placed."

AUTHOR NOTE: THE FIRST Sears full general catalog was distributed in 1894 and soon became known as the "Big Book" or the "Consumer's Bible." You could find just about anything in the Sears catalog, including headstones. I found an advertisement from the 1927 Sears catalog for a very nice white-clouded Vermont marble headstone for $15.50. Even assuming inflation from 1927 to 1932, $100 would be plenty for Pepper to get four nice headstones for Helen's dad, Pepper's mother and father, and Grace and the baby.

Chapter 81: She's Taking It, Boys!

Ezra

WHEN THE SUN CAME UP, it covered the entire work site in a blanket of gold. Moose and I worked as a team throughout the night, going beyond simple exhaustion and working from a reserve of strength neither of us knew we had.

George Goon found us in the muck and talked to us while we continued to work. He told us about Cotton and Bud Bodell, and I found myself turning my rage into muscle, slinging more rock and cement as if I had found a hidden reserve of energy. "Helen said she gave Bodell ten dollars to keep him in jail until tomorrow. Figures. That man is crooked as a question mark," he said.

"Did she say anything else?" I asked.

"Yeah, she said to tell you to meet her at Browder's Café at two o'clock. She'll be waiting."

I smiled. I'd be there.

"They've breached the surface!" someone yelled, and we all three together scrambled high above our positions to see the trucks, still dumping. A small rock protrusion stuck out from the water about halfway beyond the Nevada cofferdam. The river continued to rush past, around and over it, fighting for its freedom.

"I'm going to take this front-row seat up here," George said as he continued to climb up the massive wall of rock. Covered in sweat, dirt, and dust, Moose and I got back to work, listening for the call of the lookout thirty feet above the tunnel. At the first sign of the river turning, everyone would have to hustle high above the site to avoid being swept away with the approaching flood.

At seven thirty, we got our warning. "She's tipped the bank. Everybody get out of there!"

The men scrambled up the side of the canyon wall, one after another, to the safety of an area between tunnels three and four. Moose and I hit the rocky wall and began to climb, hand over foot, side by side. When we were twenty feet up, I looked back at the river. It was coming.

Water began to creep onto the shore as the river struggled against the man-made barrier being raised beyond the turn point that led to the tunnel. As the swiftly moving water fought harder to be free, large waves hit the shoreline, determined to remain in their bed, yet more water was forced onto shore. Since the barrier was built higher, the river had no choice but to seek another path and turned into the narrow valley that had been carved from stone.

Rapidly increasing in intensity, the deluge picked up dust, rocks, and bits of blown concrete, throwing them angrily against the canyon walls and into the air, devouring what was left in its path. Roaring in protest, the river surged toward the tunnel that would contain its fury.

The sight of the water mesmerized, and I stopped moving, until I felt a hard punch on my shoulder. The noise from the trucks and the approaching water made it impossible to hear even from such a short distance, but I could tell Moose was yelling as he pointed at the top of the rocks. Ignoring the thunderous sound of the water below, we continued to climb. I focused on a spot high above the entry point of the tunnel. Moose was by my side, and I was thankful for the company.

As we cleared the top of the opening, I felt the rush of wind and the spray of water on my legs as the river raged past us below. I didn't stop or look down, afraid that the power of the water might suck me into its path.

A cry rang out from the men. "She's taking it, boys. She's taking it!"

When we were sure we were clear, we collapsed against the rocks next to George and watched the water rushing through the tunnel, set on its new course.

I STAYED A FEW MORE hours, running on nothing but excitement, and helped the men at number three start clearing debris. Most of the guys that worked through the night had gone back to town for celebrations that would go well into the night, but I needed to be alone for a bit before cleaning up in my dorm and meeting Helen.

The trucks would continue dumping throughout the day and another night; by dawn, the river would be contained, running through the two Arizona tunnels, bypassing the site of the proposed dam by three-quarters of a mile. The high-scalers would be back to work, preparing anchorage for the cofferdam that would replace the rock dike built today. Another set of cofferdams would be started at the exit site of the diversion tunnels, and the six high-capacity pumps would start sucking the water from the space in between, leaving nothing but a mile of muck that was the riverbed.

Tomorrow, the energy and focus of the project would change. Tomorrow, my friends would start preparing to build the largest dam ever to be built. But today, we'd done something spectacular. We'd moved a river.

And tomorrow, I'd be gone.

The rumble of the work site behind me, I walked until I was directly across from Ragtown before I stopped. Murl Emery's ferry was still running across the river, carrying spectators back to Arizona. After Emery unloaded and was preparing to return, I walked onto the ferry.

"Can I catch a ride over?" I asked.

Emery squinted in the light, and then his face broke into a smile.

"Why, anytime, Ezra. I gotta say, I didn't think you would have stuck around here for as long as you did. It's been a rough time for ya, I know."

"I wasn't done here yet," I said.

Emery nodded. "You still aren't done. It's just beginning."

My stomach churned at his words, and I said nothing. I silently cursed whatever power had forced me to run from this place, this place that I once found ugly and dreary and now realized was what I'd been looking for all along. A place where I had brothers, all of us working together toward a common goal. I hated to leave. I didn't want to leave. With Helen, I had a chance at something else, something unknown, which both terrified and excited me. But I still felt like I was losing a part of me that I'd never get back.

As the ferry started across, I leaned over the side and watched the water swirl beneath me, calm, content. Change had done it good. I kneeled, wet my fingertips in the cool water, and lifted my hand to my lips. I inhaled the sweet, musky scent like fresh fallen rain on tilled earth. I stood and watched as the river ran a new course as if it had been doing so for a thousand years. If an ancient river could settle in so easily to a new path, why couldn't a man?

As we reached the Nevada side of the river, I thanked Emery and declined a ride back to town. I'd walk out of Hemenway Wash to the highway and catch a ride in a bit. Right now, I wanted to sit by the river.

Ragtown was gone. Everyone had either moved out or moved on. Nothing was left of the camp Grace and I had shared before she died. Before my only nephew died. I tried to push the image of him, lying still in my arms, down in my heart. I walked along the shore, the faint sounds of the work crews before me, the silence of the desert behind. I heard movement from behind a large boulder and turned in time to see the shadow of a small animal steal toward the mountain. I found the Joshua tree that Helen used to sit under, reading her books, talking about how beautiful she thought this place was. I sat and leaned my back against it and looked out across the water.

With the help of a thousand friends and a little divine intervention, a lot had been accomplished in the past few days. The powerful river before me that had once determined its own path was now controlled by man, and I now knew one thing for certain: nothing was impossible. I smiled. Helen once said miracles happen every day, and today, I believed her.

My hand lightly grazed the rocks beside me, and as I thought of Helen, a tingle began in my fingertips and coursed up my arm. I picked up a pebble the size of a dime and felt the rough edges then placed the rock in my mouth. The gritty outer coating washed away, revealing the hard smoothness underneath. I moved the pebble around with my tongue, settling it in my lip like a plug of tobacco.

Raising an imaginary glass into the air, I looked to the heavens. "Here's to you, Ben." I thought about the promise I once made to him to look after Helen, the promise that I neglected for too long. I searched the sky, settling on a hole in a small white cloud. "I'll do my best," I said.

As I started walking through the emptiness of the Wash to the highway above, I couldn't look back. A part of me knew I was leaving the only place that had ever truly felt like home, and instead of looking back, I needed to look forward. But the farther I moved toward my future, the more I was pulled back toward the river; back toward my friends and brothers; back toward the empty bed waiting for a concrete wall.

The uncertainty of the future scared me, and I could only admit that to myself.

AUTHOR NOTE: FROM RESEARCH records, as the river began running through the tunnels, someone yelled, "She's taking it, boys! She's taking it!" I felt it important to include those exact words in this book. The truth is, they weren't quite sure it was going to work, again, according to some of the oral histories. So imagine thousands of men testing a project they had slaved over for almost two years and seeing the results of their labor.

Chapter 82: Where I Belong

Ezra

HELEN WAS STANDING outside the café in a pair of blue sailor's pants with a blue-and-yellow blouse and open-toed shoes. She smiled when I walked up, and I took her in my arms and kissed her. She was trembling, and I knew she was as scared as I was, but she was also strong—a lot stronger than me, I feared.

"Did you see it?" I said. The sound of the water rushing below me, the way it fought against its containment, the spray against my legs, the cheers of the men—an experience I knew I would run through again and again, over and over in my mind.

"The pictures are going to be amazing," she said. "That camera is the greatest gift I've ever had. Thank you. I just—"

I stopped her with another kiss. She was hungry, as if she were trying to take in all of me, and I let her. When she pulled back, she looked at me, and the usual sheen of her eyes appeared dull. I knew she had to be moving on little sleep from last night, and I held her hand and entered the café. We sat at a booth toward the back. The place was loud; everyone was engaged in lively conversations about the work we did today and were getting ready for the parties that had already started in the streets. We'd done it. I couldn't help but smile when I thought of it, and when I looked at Helen, I was brought back to reality. Tomorrow, it would be nothing but a memory.

The waitress set two glasses of water and two menus in front of us. Helen didn't even look at the menu. She drank her water and kept looking back toward the crowd. "What's wrong?" I said.

Her eyes were damp, and I reached across the table and took her hand.

"Helen. We don't have to go. We can stay and get a house, and I promise, it will be everything you need it to be." Please, Helen, let's stay.

She shook her head. "I want you to stay. But Sally and I are leaving," she said.

"What? I thought... Helen, what are you saying?" I squeezed her hand. "No. No. I will not let you go alone!" I was trying not to raise my voice, but we had plans. Didn't we?

"I have to, Ezra, and you have to stay and live your life. You are so happy here, and I need to find my happiness too."

I shook my head. "No, I won't let you go. You aren't getting in that car without me." I was starting to get angry.

"I thought you'd say that," she whispered.

I felt my face flush. "There is nothing you can say or do to keep me from leaving with you. You understand that? I won't let a woman go off by herself and just..." Just what? I thought.

She looked at our clasped hands. "I thought you'd say that too."

Bud Bodell walked into the café, and when his eyes met mine, he headed straight toward our booth. Helen turned, and when she saw him, she said, "Mr. Bodell, I—" She paused and then turned back to me and pulled her hand away from mine. "I'm sorry, Ezra," she said.

Bodell turned to me and said, "Ezra Deal? We have a witness that says you admitted to the attempted murder of Billy Greene. I have to take you in, son."

I looked at him and then at Helen but said nothing. My stomach knotted up, and I felt like I was going to vomit.

Helen looked at me as a tear ran slowly down her cheek and dropped on the table in front of her. "I knew you wouldn't just let me go."

THE EVENING AIR WAS cool, and as a slow breeze blew over me, I could smell the distant perfumes of a desert night. I quickened my pace as I moved through the crowds gathered in the streets and the families celebrating together. I was numb to their words and glided through like a ghost. My leg hadn't hurt all day, and now it was starting to throb, but I kept moving, toward the dormitory where everything I owned was waiting to be packed so we could leave together.

Bodell and I had left Helen sitting in the diner, and I hadn't looked back. Anger mixed with hurt, and the dread of what was to come filled my body. I couldn't do anything but keep walking, keep following Bodell. When we got to his office, instead of throwing me in his one cell, which was currently occupied by Cotton, he directed me to a chair in front of his desk.

"You are one lucky man, Ezra Deal," he said.

I certainly didn't feel lucky. "You and I had a deal about Billy Greene," I said.

He waved his hand in the air, and I wanted to smack that smile right off his face. "Well, that was until you went and told your girlfriend all about it. She came in here and signed a statement, and there wasn't much I could do after that."

"You could tear it up and let me leave," I said.

"I could. And in fact, that girlfriend of yours—one helluva woman, I might add—struck a deal with me to do just that," he said.

"She's obviously not my girlfriend," I said.

I heard Cotton snicker from his cell, and I shot him a glance filled with daggers.

"Well, here's the deal. You sit here for a few hours and stew while she gets down the road, and I tear it up, and you can keep it for a souvenir."

Cotton outright laughed, and I jumped from my chair. I was only a few cell bars away from breaking him in two.

"Or," Bodell said, "I could throw you in that cell for a little while and walk away. But then I'm sure that weasel would find a way to make your life more miserable."

I spat on the ground at Cotton's feet. "Not worth it," I said.

I stood at the window with my hands behind my back, watching the happy faces of the townsfolk and visitors, until the sun went down. My anger slowly subsided, as I began to understand why Helen had done what she'd done. She was right. I wouldn't have let her go, and there was only one way to stop me. I hated that she didn't want me with her, but I hated even more that she felt she needed Bodell to get away from me.

As I walked in the dormitory, the clerk behind the desk stopped me. "Deal?" he said. He handed me a brown bag. "Some little chick left this for ya," he said.

I took the bag and made my way slowly up the stairs to my room. I sat on my cot with the bag next to me and picked up the picture of the turtle on my bedside table. "He likes to be in his space—he's comfortable there," Helen had said.

I opened the brown bag and pulled out one hundred dollars and the small silver music box. I hadn't noticed it before, but on the top, there was a picture of a man and woman walking through the snow, holding hands. I turned the key on the side, opened the box, and let the tinny sound of the Christmas carol echo in my small room.

Home.

Tomorrow, a dry riverbed would be waiting, and on it, I was going to build a dam. Not just any dam but one that would stand the test of time and would prove the strength of my brothers and me. The Hoover Dam. I closed the music box and set it and the picture on my small table. I couldn't help but smile. *I love you. And I'll miss you.*

But this was where I belonged.

AUTHOR NOTE: I CONSIDERED titling this chapter "What's Love Got to Do With It" because Helen does love Ezra, but she is willing to sacrifice him for her own dreams. Sure, she could have done things differently, but she is young and imperfect. She really wants to do what is best for everyone, but in the end, she puts herself first. As I was writing this, I began to realize Helen wanted to be the heroine of her own story, and I wanted that for her as well. But keep reading. She isn't totally ruthless.

Over the next several years, thousands would work on the dam, but the original men who started in the diversion tunnels in 1931 and their families will always be remembered as the "31ers," those who came to the Nevada desert in 1931 to take a chance on the project.

Now that the river has been turned, the work of building two cofferdams and a rock barrier would begin. These were necessary to create a dry bed for the building of the actual dam. It would be three more years until the dam was finished, and at the time of its completion, it was the tallest dam in the world at 726 feet. Today, it is listed as a National Historic Landmark and hosts a million visitors each year. It really is a marvel to see.

Chapter 83: Changing Course

Helen

MIRACLES HAPPENED EVERY day, but sometimes, you had to look for them. That was what my daddy used to tell me, and I looked at the purple and pink hues of the evening sky and smiled. *You were right, Daddy.* And sometimes, you had to take a few chances.

"I think that's everything," Sally said as she loaded the last of her things in my car. Mae and Marguerite stood with us in the parking lot of the Railroad Pass, Marguerite loading us down with food from the casino for our trip, Mae wringing her hands and asking at least every minute if we were sure we had everything. It was easy to pack when you didn't have much.

"Now don't forget, you tell Suzette that I sent ya, and she'll put you up for a month in San Fran. She owes me one. And when you get there, send Marguerite a postcard to the casino so we know you made it safe. Are you sure you got everything?" Mae said.

I smiled and gave her a big hug. "The only thing missing is you."

She dismissed me with a wave. "You two go and make a life for yourselves. I've got my own plans. And don't you worry about old Mae." She wiped her face with the back of her hand and pulled me in for a second hug.

Pete was behind Marguerite. He put a finger to his lips so I wouldn't tell, then he snuck up and grabbed her from behind, causing her to shriek. She slapped at him playfully, and my stomach ached for Ezra. "Did you see him?" I asked Pete.

"He'll be fine," he said. "You get your life straightened out, and maybe in a year or so, you'll come back." He lifted an eyebrow at my noncommittal nod. "Or maybe not." He shook his head and laughed. "He'll be fine once the shock and hurt wears off."

I hoped so. For me, I just wasn't willing to give up myself. It wasn't about Sally, or Pepper, or Cotton, or even Ezra. It was about taking a chance on myself. I had to. I could feel it in my heart. But I also knew Ezra was already home.

I grabbed my camera and told everyone to get together for a picture. Sally protested, and I told her to look toward Mae so only her good side showed.

Pete took the camera from me. "You get over there. It's not often I get four gorgeous women to smile at me at once."

We stood together, Marguerite, Mae, Sally, and I, with our arms linked around one another's waists, and smiled for Pete. I knew it was a picture I would cherish: four women, determined to beat whatever the world threw at us, no matter the cost. "Survivors," Mae said, as if she'd read my mind.

After one more round of hugs, Sally and I settled in my daddy's car—my car—and pulled onto the highway heading toward Los Angeles and then to San Francisco. It would be a long journey, but we wanted to drive up the coast with the ocean beside us. We had time. "I know you're worried about him," she said, "but Pete's right. He'll be fine. Wounds heal."

"I do love him," I said, choking back the tears I refused to let fall.

"I know," she said.

The mountains loomed on either side of us, the shanties and tents of the forgotten lining their bases. I was going to miss the mountains. But there would be other mountains to climb.

I thought about Queho, and I knew his secret would be safe with Pepper. His cave was well hidden and wouldn't be found for many years, if ever. Maybe I'd come back some day when Pepper was a man, and together, we'd go up that mountain and claim the reward for ourselves. Or maybe we'd let him be at peace in a place he'd felt safe.

After driving throughout the evening and into the night, we finally reached the California coast and decided to sleep on the sandy beach. The crash of the waves and the salty air were so foreign that instead of sleeping, I sat and looked out across the blackness of the sea. I'd found a new kind of beauty, and I couldn't wait to see what morning would bring. Stars dotted the clear night sky, and I looked up and found the Big Dipper. I knew the others were out there—the fishhook, the butterfly, the kite—and I intended to find them someday. In fact, there were a lot of things I intended to find, and I'd keep searching until I did.

But love was not one of them. I didn't think it was something you found as much as it was something that found you. One day you happened upon it through no intent of your own, and you knew from then on, you'd hold a piece of it deep in your soul, and your life would always be better for it. It was the serenity I felt when I was in the mountains, the security I found with a dead Indian, and the passion and desire I had for Ezra. And I would always love him.

But sometimes, love wasn't enough. There was also life. Although I'd always thought I'd one day marry a man I loved and raise a family, my life took a different path, and I wanted more. I wanted to live, to experience, to explore—to be free. And that was what I intended to do, no matter what it took.

If a river that had raged for thousands of years could be calmed by changing its course, then I could surely find peace by changing mine.

THE END

AUTHOR NOTE: WHY SAN Francisco? Earlier, I mentioned this and basically said, "Why not?" But the truth is, a lot of Midwesterners migrated to California during the Great Depression, hoping for agricultural jobs, which they thought were aplenty. Helen going to San Francisco is a nod to Dorothea Lange, who famously photographed Depression-era rural America, and who I imagine Helen to be as an adult. At the age of 23, Lange and a female friend had made the decision to travel the world, but their journey was cut short when she was robbed. She did make it from New York to San Francisco, however, and this was where she made her home and became one of the most important photographers of the twentieth century.

EPILOGUE

Queho, the Renegade Indian Part II

IN FEBRUARY 1942, SIX years after the completion of the Hoover Dam, Queho's cave was discovered by three men prospecting in the mountains, and Queho's body was finally removed. Although his death was ruled as "natural causes," his mummified remains still held a handkerchief tied above the ankle, possibly indicative of a rattlesnake bite. Various supplies and instruments littered the cave—utensils, dynamite, and several weapons, including a shotgun, a rifle, and a bow with steel-tipped arrows. Also among the items was special deputy badge #896, formerly belonging to "Doc" Gilbert of the Gold Bug Mine. The prospectors did not receive the advertised reward.

But it would be another twenty years before Queho was finally laid to rest. When no reward was offered, one of the prospectors demanded that the body be turned over to him so he could sell it to the Elks Club, who had, for some reason, shown an interest in purchasing the remains. After three years of lying in a Las Vegas funeral home while possession of his body was argued, Queho became the "property" of the Las Vegas Elks Club.

For several years, his body was used in displays for various events, including a "Queho's Village" at the yearly Helldorado event in Las Vegas. The attraction, where people could view the remains of the infamous Indian, was very popular. In fact, one year, Queho's body was propped up in a convertible, where he rode in the Helldorado parade. Eventually, people lost interest, and Queho quit making public appearances.

In 1962, a call was received by the Las Vegas police that a bag of bones had been found at the city dump. Upon investigation, detectives discovered the bag of bones were what was left of Queho.

A local attorney, appalled and disgusted by Queho's story, bought his remains and finally buried him in the desert around Las Vegas. A simple headstone marks his final resting place and reads:

Quehoe
1889 - 1919
Nevada's Last
Renegade Indian
He Survived Alone

ACKNOWLEDGMENTS

THIS BOOK HAS UNDERGONE a decade-long journey, going through five complete rewrites. The number of times it has been edited, proofread, and read by writers, editors, and friends is too numerous to count, and naming everyone would require several pages. Nevertheless, each individual involved has contributed something special to this book, often while working on their own projects. To all of them, I express my sincerest gratitude for leaving a piece of their heart with me in *Ragtown*. You know who you are.

I am incredibly fortunate to have an exceptional team of editors, proofreaders, cover designers, supporters, and hand holders at my publisher, Red Adept Publishing. My deepest appreciation goes out to every member of the Red Adept team, with a special mention to Rashida Breen, Erica Lucke Dean, and Streetlight Graphics.

Originally conceived as a thesis for my MFA, this novel would not have reached its current form without the invaluable guidance of my mentors and friends: Robert Begiebing, Rick Carey (once on the team, always on the team), Captain Merle Drown, and Craig Childs (my desert daddy). Their unwavering support over the years has been instrumental, and I have no doubt they will be as happy as I am to finally see this book in print.

The dedication required to bring *Ragtown* to life has necessitated time away from my family. To my late husband, Joe; my sons, Dillon and Theron; and my bonus son and daughter, Milam and Brittan, I extend my heartfelt thanks for your constant encouragement, support, and understanding.

The creation of a work like this demanded extensive research, and I am grateful to the Boulder City Museum and Historical Association, the Boulder City Public Library, the University of Nevada Las Vegas Special Collections Library, the Nevada State Museum, the Railroad Pass Casino, the Clark County Heritage Museum, and the United States Bureau of Reclamation for graciously providing the resources I needed.

Dennis McBride, who spent a large portion of his adult life documenting, archiving, and writing about the Hoover Dam, generously shared his knowledge of the dam's technical aspects, described its colorful personalities, and familiarized me with the area's geography during the 1930s. Dennis read at least three of the original versions of *Ragtown*, ensuring historical accuracy and suggesting true dramatic events to include. Thank you, Dennis, for everything.

Apart from me, Beth Garland is the only person who has read every version of *Ragtown* at least once. She has been a constant presence, supporting me through the highs and lows in not only writing this book but also life in general. Thank you, Beth. I love you like a sister.

For Bobby Saugus and all the other pirates: "Arrgh!"

Lastly but certainly not least, I want to acknowledge the men and women who toiled on the dam project, whose oral histories breathed life into the setting for me. Their hard work and resilience during a challenging era in American history should serve as an inspiration to us all.

About the Author

Kelly Stone Gamble was born in a small Midwestern town and has lived all over the US, including 25 years in Las Vegas, before settling in Tulsa, Oklahoma. Currently a faculty member at Southeastern Oklahoma State University, Kelly shares her passion for literature, the humanities, and writing with aspiring minds.

When not working or writing, she immerses herself in travel, building projects, and spending quality time with loved ones. Always on the lookout for her next big adventure, she is determined to leave an indelible mark on the literary landscape and inspire others to embrace their own journeys of exploration and self-discovery.

Read more at www.kstonegamble.com.

About the Publisher

Dear Reader,

We hope you enjoyed this book. Please consider leaving a review on your favorite book site.

Visit https://RedAdeptPublishing.com to see our entire catalogue.

Check out our app for short stories, articles, and interviews. You'll also be notified of future releases and special sales.

www.ingramcontent.com/pod-product-compliance
Lightning Source LLC
LaVergne TN
LVHW040034080526
838202LV00045B/3341